Seasons of Fate

Autmn and Winter

L.C. Berriman

Copyright © 2016 L.C. Berriman

The moral right of the author has been asserted.

Apart from any fair dealing for the purposes of research or private study, or criticism or review, as permitted under the Copyright, Designs and Patents Act 1988, this publication may only be reproduced, stored or transmitted, in any form or by any means, with the prior permission in writing of the publishers, or in the case of reprographic reproduction in accordance with the terms of licences issued by the Copyright Licensing Agency. Enquiries concerning reproduction outside those terms should be sent to the publishers.

Matador
9 Priory Business Park,
Wistow Road, Kibworth Beauchamp,
Leicestershire. LE8 0RX
Tel: 0116 279 2299
Email: books@troubador.co.uk
Web: www.troubador.co.uk/matador
Twitter: @matadorbooks

ISBN 978 1785890 390

British Library Cataloguing in Publication Data.
A catalogue record for this book is available from the British Library.

Printed and bound in the UK by TJ International, Padstow, Cornwall
Typeset in 11pt Aldine401 BT by Troubador Publishing Ltd, Leicester, UK

Matador is an imprint of Troubador Publishing Ltd

Thank you to William and Ian for all their support
and encouragement.

Also thank you to Doncaster Libraries' Literacy Team
Especially, Shirley, Carol and Jill.

Thanks to John Freeman, who kindly gave me
permission to use his painting, Staithes Nocturne,
for the cover of my book. To see more of his work visit
john@johnfreemanstudio.co.uk.

And thank you indeed to everyone at Matador
for their expert advice and support.

Part One

Autumn

Lastly, stood War, in glittering arms yclad,
  With visage grim, stern looks, and blackly hued;
In his right hand a naked sword he had,
  That to the hilt was all blood imbrued;
  And in his left, that kings and kingdoms rued,
Famine and fire he held, and there withal
He razed towns and threw down towers and all.

CHAPTER ONE

Now and Then

Bravado crushed the panic in his small chest. He'd run upon the moors. Faced a hungry wolf. He'd escaped from folk he'd been planted with after being dragged away from his ma and da. He'd find a way out of the maze filled with strangers. Somehow.

Two rainy days and nights went by without any sign of an end to his isolation within the city walls. A stab of fearful panic would suddenly consume him, propelling him into the nearest alley. From its dingy protection, he would scour his surroundings in furtive apprehension, and was always relieved that no one appeared to be showing any interest in him.

Driven by hunger, he snatched an apple. Someone called out and began to chase him, as if he had stolen a precious jewel from the market stall. He clutched the bruised fruit in his small fist. Terrified of being caught, he ran as fast as his young legs would carry him, not knowing where he went. The stallholder was left behind. But ahead he ran into a gang of lads much older than himself. They seized the apple. They would have done much more if the two women had not come around the corner and stopped them from hammering the daylights out of him while laughing at his efforts to swing a fist the way his da had taught him.

Having dispatched the alley gang with boxed ears, clucking over his bloody flesh, the two women took him to a nearby tavern. He was reluctant to go with them, but they were not like the stern-faced matrons who had inhabited that grand house he had been forced to stay in. For the first time since he had been taken from his home and dumped in York, he felt someone cared.

★

There were hoards of them! Red-haired. Muscular. Brandishing all manner of barbaric weapons. Worst of all, Fishergate Bar was beginning to splinter under their determined onslaught. The walls rang with their berserk Highland cries.

One of them seized his shoulder and shook him. What he could not understand was how the Scotsman knew his name?

Martin Wedgwood awoke with the contents of his dream spurring him on to do damage to whoever had their hands on him. The soldier, his newly appointed second-in-command, found himself suddenly on his backside and being pummelled.

Hamish Hamilton quickly overcame his surprise at the younger man's reaction to him waking him. The burly veteran retaliated, albeit with ill-humoured restraint. "What ye about, Sassenach?"

Pain reverberating around Wedgwood's muzzy head did the trick. His dream-induced ferocity faltered. Blurry-eyed, he stared up at Hamilton.

Satisfied, the older man grunted and straightened.

"Sorry," mumbled Wedgwood.

"We've an armed pack at Bar."

Wedgwood stopped running a shaky hand through his unruly brown hair. "The Scots?"

"What? No ye dunder 'ead." Hamilton was a relative newcomer to York, having accompanied the Scottish Lord Eythin from Newcastle when the time had come to make a prudent retreat from their hostile countrymen. "D' ye know of the Master?"

"Everyone knows of him," replied Wedgwood, getting to his feet.

"Aye, but would ye recognise the man?"

It was passed midnight. The Bars of York were firmly closed to all-comers. It was a time when the spectre of the enemy ran riot through the minds of those on sentry duty. And Hamish Hamilton was no exception.

"I saw him a little while ago," said Martin Wedgwood, "here in York. He was entering Isaac's goldsmith's shop in Stonegate."

"Well, if it be the man, he's at the gate," answered Hamilton, warily.

★

"He's back," observed Richard Massone.

Mounted beside him, his leader did not react. Accustomed to the icy reserve, Richard's attention remained on the soldiers above them on Fishergate Bar's castellated rampart. Like the horsemen behind him, he was braced for any hostile action. All of them had been in the saddle for over two days with very little respite, only to be met at journey's end with a nervous refusal to open the east Bar. The garrison's caution was due to the rumours rife in York that the Scottish Army was marching south. The Master's men were too disciplined to show impatience, but their disdain was directed upwards into the torchlight flaming brightly in the night. The delay, they realised, did not bode well for whoever was in charge of the guard judging by their leader's stillness. The mastiff beside the black stallion looked up at its master, giving an hesitant wag of its tail.

Nowadays only the big, shaggy dog was tolerated. No one had any real contact with the Master beyond the affairs of war. Everyone at the Lodge had come to realise to what extent Catherine Verity had chipped away at the dark, sinister ice. During her stay, the ancient half-ruin deep in Stillingfleet Forest had developed an almost family atmosphere. After her departure, the children had gone, too. Their mothers were no longer carefree in their work in the medieval kitchen. Overall, there had been a notable return to the exclusive business of war.

Richard caught sight of the younger man who had appeared in some haste with the heavy-set, auburn-haired guard glimpsed a few minutes ago.

Martin Wedgwood peered over the battlements. He found himself staring down into cold, soulless eyes, black as the midnight beyond the flaring torches. There was no doubting it was Shadiz, the notorious Gypsy. The powerful, influential Master. Nor was it possible to withstand the silent command

5

from the charismatic authority. Wedgwood turned to Hamilton. "Open up, dammit."

★

He remained in the tavern-whorehouse. The first Christmas, he sat in the corner of Maggie's chamber while she gave an errant husband a festive treat; crying silent tears for his lost ma and da. During the second festive season, he was plied with ale. The only thing he remembered about that Christmas was it proved to be the beginning of the nightmare.

Used as a serving lad, he became accustomed to the many comments about his height and the width of his shoulders. But as time went by, he found himself increasingly having to shrug off the arms that found their way around him. Then there was the apparent collisions and the rough hugs by way of apology. Worse were the drunken caresses he was not strong enough to fend off. On those occasions his young fierceness only served to inflame attention. Although Maggie and Marianne tried to shield him, to their own detriment, the sister and brother owners of the Dark Horse quickly came to realise they could make capital out of him. When he tried to object, the beatings were done in such a way they did not mar his attraction.

A year later, Maggie and Marianne were galvanised into action when the landlord of a whorehouse situated in Hull's busy harbour district offered for him at a price the sister and brother partnership could not refuse. Riddled with guilt at the way they had unwittingly condemned him to a life of abusive bondage at such a young age, the two women conspired to set him free. It wasn't the first time they had tried. That unsuccessful bid had resulted in both of them being whipped and him being thrown naked into a dank hole he had been barely able to stand up in. Only when their clientele clamoured to have him reinstated did the joint proprietors realised they had cut off their noses to spite their faces. Made to work harder because of loss revenue, it left him wondering which was the worse punishment.

By now York was no longer a mystery to him. But the rest of the country was. He slipped away from the Dark Horse with only a couple of qualms, carrying a small bundle containing food and a few coins given to him by Maggie and Marianne through floods of tears that of necessity had to be shed in silence. Marianne had taught him to read and write. She had also taught him to speak French, and was proud of his fluency. Maggie had taught him the practical skills needed to survive in a heartless world. Both women had fallen on hard times which, he realised, he had made tolerable by his presence.

Late on a cool spring evening, he slipped through Fishergate Bar shortly before it was closed for the night, believing the world was his oyster. His resilience would ensure he found the pearl.

★

Catherine Verity could no longer stand being cooped up in her chamber even though it was spacious and airy after she had flung open the casement windows. She slipped out into the broad corridor, careful to avoid Keeble, snoring on the truckle bed to one side of her chamber door. On quiet feet, she glided down the staircase, a regal sweep lost in the cool darkness. By now her familiarity with her new home meant she did not require a candle to light her way. It was an easy matter to let herself out of the chateau.

She knew the ever-present guards would be aware of her presence out in the night and that Junno would soon appear. Slightly resentful, she wandered barefoot over the damp grass, listening to the murmur of the Mediterranean as it stirred in the secluded cove at the base of the sheer cliffs upon which Shannlarrey was situated in splendid isolation.

Junno's soundless approach detained her. "Rauni?" There was an anxious note in his deep, rumbling voice.

He had addressed her in such a manner since their first meeting at her father's estate close to Driffield. Some years later, Catherine and her father, Sir Roger Verity, had been made to flee from Nafferton Garth. It had transpired that the orchestrated hostility had been directed at the man who gave his oath to watch over her before Sir Roger died of wounds he had sustained while attempting to prevent her capture by Parliamentary troopers allied to Francois Lynette of Fylingdales Hall.

In an unexpected turn of events a month ago her guardian had become her husband. Immediately afterwards that dark, dangerous, incredible man she had fallen in love with had sent her away to his chateau in France. For her own benefit.

The night glistened with her tears. Catherine was glad of its cloaking darkness. Yet when Junno put an arm around her shoulders it was plain there was no way to hide her misery from her husband's large cousin, who had become her faithful bodyguard.

"Ah, Rauni," he murmured with a regretful sigh.

"I miss him," she said, leaning against his massive chest.

"I knows y' do."

"I punish him," she admitted in a tremulous whisper. She held up her pendant. The jet stone was edged with silver engraved with curious symbols. For a long time, she had believed the pendant to have been a present from her father. Only after his death had she discovered it had been given to her, through her father, by Shadiz. She had also discovered the jet pendant was far more than a simple piece of jewellery. Shadiz wore the counterpart, a moonstone set in the same inscribed silver. The Romany legend had proved to be potent. "I punish him by way of the Stones. Then he tries to concentrate on other matters."

A chill went down Junno's spine.

★

Martin Wedgwood rushed out of the city as soon as he was able to get under the grumbling portcullis. Hamish Hamilton followed at a more prudent pace. He was accompanied by several well-armed soldiers, wary yet eager to witness the arrival to York of Prince Rupert's legendary mercenary in the light of the hissing torches they held aloft.

Shadiz urged the stallion forward ignoring Wedgwood's garbled apology. Riding through the stony darkness of Fishergate Bar no one saw the brief twitch of his hard mouth at a rueful thought, 'Swines come afore pearls.'

He instructed Benjamin Farr to deliver the munitions they had brought from Scarborough to the ordnance depot in Aldwark.

"May I escort you anywhere, sir," asked Wedgwood, hopefully.

"T' King's Manor."

The young captain had difficulty hearing the whispery tone above the receding clatter of hooves. He was acutely conscious of the Master's chilling glance as he tried to control the post horse he had made skittish by his haste to mount. He had thought to take the lead. Instead, he found himself riding alongside the thin, fair-haired man accompanying the Master. He briefly took note of the long bow the obviously well-bred fellow carried on his back and the quiver of arrows at his hip.

Richard would have preferred to accompany Benjamin and the rest of the Master's men to the ordnance depot. But a curt gesture from Shadiz had meant he was not trusted in the city. Although it had been several weeks since Catherine's departure from the Lodge, he was still simmering under a cloud of bitter gloom. When he had learned that Shadiz had bizarrely forced a marriage at Whitby – he would not countenance any other explanation – and then sent her away to France in a corsair ship, he had been incandescent with rage. Not that it had done him much good. Fortunately for Richard, Benjamin had proved himself to be an excellent peacemaker. He had mitigated Shadiz's caustic menace. Thereafter, there had been no communication between the improbable half-brothers save for the pressing duties of war.

Leaving the torchlight around the guarded Bar behind them, the three riders were soon swallowed up by the night. The passing of their mounts disturbed only chained dogs, cats on the prowl and scurrying rats, both four and two feet. Wedgwood fretted that the Master would be defeated by the twists and turns of the sleeping city in the unrelieved darkness. Yet when the Master swung the stallion down a series of alleys, it wasn't long before it was Wedgwood who become hopelessly lost. Richard was, too, despite his familiarity with York due to the visits he had paid to his aunt's grand mansion in Petersgate.

Shadiz drew rein, whistling to the mastiff, who had gone off on its own reconnaissance. While he waited for the return of the dog, he gazed at a derelict tavern on the corner of a dingy alley. Its signboard was hanging by a single, rusty nail. The faded letters became discernable when the moon sailed briefly clear of leaden clouds, making it comparatively easy to read the name Dark Horse.

Shortly afterwards, Richard and Martin Wedgwood found themselves within sight of the King's Manor. At which point,

9

Shadiz briefly halted the big, black horse and addressed Wedgwood, "Can y' get y'rsen back?"

Without waiting for an answer he rode down the tree-lined drive.

Richard gave Martin Wedgwood a sympathetic glance before urging his mare forward.

CHAPTER TWO

Arms, Portraits and Urchins

In the past, when Parliament had been dismissed by royal decree with absolute impunity and discord had been merely an annoying rumble across the land, King Charles had visited the King's Manor at frequent intervals in order to bestow his seal of approval on the weighty business of the Council of the North. At present, the hard-pressed monarch would find it expedient to journey to York with a steel army instead of a velvet retinue to consult with the Marquis of Newcastle, the current President of the Council.

The sentries around the L-shaped, red-brick King's Manor demonstrated the same zealous apprehension that had been evident at Fishergate Bar. Faced with their armed challenges, the Master brooked no delay in a caustic, authoritative manner. When a small head, wearing a woollen nightcap at a jaunty angle, answered his hammering on the intricately carved door he was more oblique.

"When a man dies they who survive him ask what property he has left behind. The angel who bends over the dying man asks what good deeds he has sent before him?"

The brown eyes beneath the nightcap had grown enormous. Uncomprehending Arabic philosophy, the startled fellow attempted to shut the door, at the same time shrieking a warning to all and sundry. Shadiz kicked open the door. Richard thought he was going to walk over the squealing door-keeper who had been catapulted onto the flagstones in the dim hallway. Catlike, Shadiz sidestepped all obstacles. But then was confronted by half-dressed men who materialised in sword-brandishing confusion to investigate the reason for the commotion.

"God dammit. Enough o' the caterwaulin'," bellowed Lord

11

Eythin, having arrived at the bottom of the elegant staircase in disgruntled haste. "Shadiz…" he added, with an air of irate caution.

While Richard offered the bemused door-keeper a helping hand to stand, an uneasy silence descended upon the crowded hallway. Men stood back, giving Shadiz unrestricted passage through their midst. Following Eythin's example, they surveyed with restraint his imposing height and muscular build, the great broadsword slung across his back and the curving scimitar at his hip. Above all, they experienced the intimidating charisma, serrated by feral menace.

Eythin dismissed is officers, curtailing their interest in the disfigurement on the left side of Shadiz's barbarous face. He turned to Richard. "An' who might you be, laddie?"

"Lord Richard of Fylingdales." He introduced himself with a polite bow in a fit of defiance against his half-brother.

Eythin hoisted bushy eyebrows. "An' y' be wi' 'im?"

Richard gave the short, stocky Scot a grim smile. "When needs must the devil drives."

The Scottish Lord chuckled. "Y've that right, laddie."

Richard accompanied Eythin down the hallway, narrowed by the steel uniforms of past ages. Its gloomy walls were lined with portraits of past Presidents of the Council of the North.

It was the second time Richard had encountered the grizzled veteran, and was once again drawn to him, though the older man appeared to have forgotten their first meeting.

Prior to him joining his half-brother's company, Richard had accompanied Prince Rupert when he had escorted Queen Henrietta Maria from Bridlington on the East Coast of Yorkshire upon his aunt's return from a fund raising mission to the Low Countries. While there, she had persuaded James King to return with her to England. The Scot had spent a considerable amount of his life abroad, mostly in the service of the King of Sweden. In response to his loyalty at a time when many of his fellow countrymen were ranging themselves against King Charles, he had been created a peer of the realm and given a high ranking post on Lord Newcastle's staff.

It had been Eythin who had masterminded the defence of

Newcastle. Whereas he would have continued to occupy the strategic city situated on the Tyne, Lord Newcastle had chosen discretion over valour. When spring had brought an improvement in the weather and the spectre of the enemy's release from boggy trenches, he had removed his Royalist Army to York.

Lord Eythin's gruff prediction that they would be pursued by the Scots seemed to be coming true.

Upon discovering into which chamber Shadiz had disappeared, Eythin paused in the doorway and called for food to be brought for the late night visitors. Moving deeper into the chamber, he made no comment about Shadiz's manner of entrance into the King's Manor, or his present conduct.

Lord Newcastle put in a tardy appearance. There was evidence of much-needed sleep being rudely interrupted in his hollow-eyed gaze, sparking with ice-blue annoyance. Although immaculate in a green silk robe, it did appeared his nightcap had been replace in haste by his wig.

Turning round, Richard was caught holding a chicken leg in one hand and a goblet of wine in the other. He immediately got rid of both and bowed. Newcastle's critical attention remained upon Shadiz for a moment longer before he responded to the introduction made by Eythin. He acknowledged Richard with a courtly inclination of his head, followed by a quick impatient adjustment of his wig.

Both Richard and Eythin watched with interest as Newcastle, an expression of supreme displeasure on his long aristocratic face, made a point of approaching his desk. Ensconced behind it, Shadiz ignored Newcastle's haughty, purposeful halt. When he continued unabashed to peruse the various documents on the walnut top, Newcastle, a stickler for protocol, was nonetheless forced to abandon the futile gesture. He made a stiff, brisk retreat and sat down, ill-suited, in a tall-backed chair close to the marble fireplace.

"We ain't had any clear sightings o' trouble," Eythin said into the ponderous silence. "But, it's coming, that's for sure."

"Indeed, sir. From what information we have gathered," responded Richard, glancing in his half-brother's direction, "I'm afraid the Crop-Ears and their Scottish allies would appear to have their sights set firmly on York."

Henceforth the discussion dwelled exclusively on the course of the war. At various times one or other of the three men cast speculative glances in the Master's direction. His detached attitude continued. It was at his own leisure that he concluded his inspection of the paperwork on Newcastle's desk. Standing up, he took an apple from the silver tray a nervous servant had placed at his elbow. The food and wine remained untouched.

"All meets with your approval?"

Shadiz froze Newcastle's sarcasm with the briefest of looks.

Newcastle bristled impotently. Sitting opposite him, Richard gleaned the guarded aspect in his lordship's obvious aversion to Shadiz.

"We'll be ready for any bastard trying to force their way through the gates or over the walls," stated Eythin, his Scottish brogue thick with confidence.

"Y' reckon?" muttered Shadiz in his customary whispery tone.

"To what are you alluding?" snapped Newcastle.

Shadiz bit into the apple and chewed before answering. "Y' ready for when Leven rendezvous with the Fairfaxes, probably near Wetherby? Between the old Scottish laird an' English father an' son they'll be marchin' sixteen or so thousand foot an' about four thousand horse. Y' ready for the batterin' pieces they're draggin' wi' 'em? An' y' be ready for when Manchester joins 'em wi' 'is army?" Shadiz shrugged. "Well, that's alright, then."

Their lordships Newcastle, Eythin and Richard of Fylingdales sat quite still, all staring at the Master. Shock, dismay and the resilience of soldiers flittered in turn across their faces; haughty, grizzled and thinly handsome.

Eythin was the first to react. "Ye Gods, laddie!" he blurted out, erupting out of his chair. "Y' could've said summat afore now."

Newcastle rose with outraged dignity. "Does the mercenary now propose to return to our enemy's camp and divulge what you have learned here?" he accused, gesturing to his desk. "I take it the supplies you conveyed to York were simply a means of entry."

Getting to his feet, Richard responded with indignation. "My

Lord, we came with good intent to deliver those munitions you now pour scorn upon."

Shadiz did not appear to be listening to any of them.

Richard followed the direction of his gaze to a shadowy alcove, but from where he was standing he could not see what had caught his half-brother's attention.

Upon taking up residence at the King's Manor, Newcastle had been at pains to inspect with a connoisseur's eye the many paintings donated by previous residents. At present, the conduct of the despicable Gypsy made him care little about the ruffian's interest in the painting of a fair-haired, young woman sitting in a rose arbour.

> *There is a garden in her face,*
> *Where roses and white lilies grow;*
> *A heavenly paradise is that place,*
> *Wherein all pleasant fruits do flow,*
> *There cherries grow, which none may buy:*
> *Till 'Cherry Ripe' themselves do cry.*

There was an odd pause. Both Newcastle and Eythin glanced at Richard. But he was as bewildered as them by Shadiz's reflective stillness.

It came to an abrupt end. Shadiz walked up to Richard and, seizing his half-brother by the arm, propelled him forwards.

"At least inform us of the Prince's whereabouts," demanded Newcastle.

Ignoring Richard's irate attempt to extract himself from the unrelenting grip, Shadiz halted their precipitous departure. He turned back to the two men standing in the middle of the candlelit chamber. "Between 'ere an' 'ell o' Charles's council chamber."

Further angered, Newcastle gave an exasperated sigh.

"What y' need t' look for is the readiness o' York," said Shadiz, low-pitched. "'Tis all very well y' summarisin' what soldiers an' arms y' can muster. Y' need t' look further than that, into 'eart o' place y' defendin'."

"I will not have you lecture me on such matters, gypsy," retorted Newcastle.

"Some sod should." Shadiz jerked his chin in Eythin's direction. "If y'd listened t' Jamie y' might still be in y'r own city. 'e wanted y' t' rely on folk there. But no. Y' wouldn't trust the very folk y' were supposed t' be defendin'. Or were y' just watchin' out for the bloody architecture? An', o' course, y'rsen."

Richard switched from Newcastle's aristocratic face, mottled with fury, to Shadiz. He had been listening to their discussion, after all.

Shadiz's harsh attention turned to Eythin. "This time trust y'r guts. Trust folk t' back up soldiers. They're ones wi' most t' lose." There was a strange quirk to his cruel mouth as he added, "Even the whores in the taverns."

Left alone in the chamber with Newcastle's simmering ire following Shadiz's and Richard's departure, Eythin picked up a chicken leg from the tray of food Shadiz had ignored. There would be no going back to bed this night, not after what the Gypsy had told them. "Wonder how laddie's face got marked like that?" he mused, idly.

"In the cauldron of Hell," retorted Newcastle.

"Heard tell they're brothers. Well, half-brothers."

"Who?"

"Shadiz and Lord Richard of Fylingdales."

"A ridiculous notion," snapped Newcastle. "That young man has no connection with the devil's spawn other than the dictates of the war. God help him."

★

Richard joined Benjamin Farr and the rest of the Master's men in Aldwark. He had gone first to the big warehouse close to the Merchant Taylors' Hall that had become the main munitions depot in the city. From there he had been directed across the way to a tavern aptly called the Bugle and Musket. Apart from the well-guarded depot, it was the only other building to shed light upon the deserted cobbles. The landlord had seized the opportunity to make a profit by opening his door to the Master's men. His wife, the cook, had been less enthusiastic.

16

"Where is he?" asked Benjamin.

Richard nodded his thanks to the scowling cook as she placed a tankard of ale and a plate of bacon and beans none-too-gently on the table in front of him. "Haven't a clue. One minute he was behind me, the next he'd disappeared."

"To see one of his Romany scouts, probably," commented Benjamin.

"Probably," muttered Richard, picking up a chunk of bread from the communal board. He was sure he had been watched in Aldwark. Indeed, nowadays, the feeling of being under observation wherever he went left him in no doubt his half-brother was responsible. Did the bastard expect him to bolt to France at the first opportunity?

He gulped down the ale too quickly. His bout of coughing drew glances from the men enjoying the respite in the smoky common room.

Benjamin pushed his mug of water across the rough boards towards Richard. "This might help," he murmured, giving his friend a worried appraisal.

Before leaving the Lodge, Catherine had instructed Mary, the girl from Glaisdale who had acted as her maid-cum-companion, in how to prepare the medicinal herbs, particularly for Richard, trusting in Benjamin's assistance. But despite his and Mary's efforts, in the absence of Catherine's expert ministrations, he suspected Richard's chesty cough was growing worse.

★

The entire length of Stonegate was buried in darkness. Likewise, the rearing bulk of the tavern was shrouded in slumberous night. Shadiz tethered the stallion beside the stone water trough. Knowing the Starre well, the mastiff was at the thick, nail-studded door before its master. Man and dog slipped through the unlocked door. Shadiz quietly cursed the lack of security.

The ever present odours of ale and cooked food assailed him. They were mixed with the equally familiar scent of urchin. Light on his feet as he was for a big man, he still had to take care as he made his way to the big, stone hearth. A silent shadow, he knew the order in which they lay. The oldest further away from the fire, the smaller ones, some as young as three, closest to the glowing fire that was never allowed to falter. Small or large, all were tucked up in warm blankets. Accustomed to the sleeping forms, the mastiff was as adept as its master at avoiding them.

Shadiz reached the hearth and the man asleep in a rocking chair grossly inadequate for his burly frame. Each muscular arm cradled a child. A third was sprawled across his powerful chest, rising with each restful breath he took. All three were no more than two years old. Four more, slightly older children were asleep wrapped around his thick, outstretched legs. Shadiz lightly touched his shoulder. He brought reassuring pressure to bear as Skelton woke abruptly. The great, ginger-haired bear of a man managed not to disturb the sleeping limpets about his person. When he saw who was beside him, he gave a toothless grin and an acknowledging grunt. Shadiz pointed to the low, discoloured ceiling and Skelton nodded.

Taking the narrow, unlit stairs two at a time, Shadiz wondered how many urchins, York's cast-offs even before they were fully grown, could be packed into the Starre of a night. There seemed to be more every time he arrived. But where would he have been all those years ago without the guardian angels?

At the head of the steep flight of stairs, he turned into a sloping passageway. At either side were a series of doors, buried in the gloom. One door was open and the light from within the chamber was spilling thinly out into the passageway. A small, plump woman wearing a fringed shawl over voluminous night attire was walking slowly away from him, murmuring to the baby she was rocking in her arms.

Soft-footed, Shadiz approached her. "What the 'ell've y' found now, Maggie?" he asked in a whispery tone.

The woman spun round, causing the baby to whimper. "Bleedin' 'ell!" she exclaimed. "I'll put a flamin' bell on you yet."

Shadiz chuckled. He leant against the rough plastered wall, arms folded across his chest, grinning. "Well?"

"What was I supposed t' do?" Maggie retorted, defensively. "'er

18

poor ma would've given birth in the alley if I ain't got Skelton t' carry poor lass in. An' then she ups an' dies."

"So y'r stuck hoddin' bairn."

She gave him a sheepish grin. "I reckons so. But, there y' go."

Shadiz followed her into the chamber, ducking under the low lintel. "I ain't bought this place for y' an' Mari t' turn it into a bloody orphanage," he said, mildly, closing the door behind him.

Maggie didn't answer until she had settled the baby in the wicker crib close to the bed. Straightening, she looked across the small fire lit bedchamber to where Shadiz was perched on the low windowsill, his long legs stretched out before him. "I recall…"

"Aye, Maggie," he murmured, dismissively.

"Bairns'll be sorry t' o' missed this hairy mutt o' yours," she remarked, stroking the mastiff. It sat down beside her when she lowered herself with a weary sigh onto the stool between the small, flickering hearth and the rumpled bed.

Usually dragged back and fastened up in no particular style her grey hair presently hung loose about her shoulders. There were remnants in her round, fleshy face of the coarse attractiveness that had made her father a good deal when he had sold her, barely fifteen, to the sister and brother proprietors of the Dark Horse. Fortunately, her character had proved strong enough to survive the degradation of a whorehouse. And despite the difficult years her caring nature had flourished. Signs of a burgeoning earth mother had been apparent when her and Marianne had encountered a scared gypsy child trying to hold his own against older and larger odds. Nowadays no one could hold a candle to him. And since Shadiz had purchased the Starre, Maggie had made sure her buxom figure had comforted many a teary-eyed, starving youngster. But she was no push over. Skelton, himself a social reject, had named her right when he had called her 'a harridan with a mighty heart'. It had earned him a swift kick in the shins. Yet everyone knew the well-renowned establishment ran smoothly because of her formidable grasp. It gave Shadiz a handsome profit each month. Not that he took any interest in financial gain.

Nevertheless, she told him, "Business is grand. What wi' all Newcastle's lot descendin' on York."

19

"Y' should keep the bloody door locked," he remonstrated.

"We ain't got above a pot o' stew an' a full ale jug t' steal down there. An' can y' imagine the row that'd go up if some poor sod walked over that lot. There'd be 'owls from 'ere t' Bootham."

The fire shifted. One of the logs burning orange and yellow in the grate fell onto the small flagstone hearth pockmarked with blackened smudges. Getting up, she rearranged the logs with poker and prongs. Satisfied, she straightened and turned back to him, poker in hand. "We're managing well enough. If that's whats botherin' y'."

Shadiz burst out laughing. "Maggie, put that bloody poker down. I don't trust y' wi' it." His expression grew ominously serious. "Especially wi' what I've t' tell y'."

"What up?" she muttered, replacing the long black iron on the hearth.

"I want y' away from York."

Alarmed, she spun round and stared at him across the bedchamber.

"Make no mistake, Maggie. It ain't just Scots that're 'eadin' t' York. I want you an' Mari away from 'ere."

"I ain't leavin' bairns," she retorted, looking shocked.

Shadiz dismissed her objection with a curt gesture. "Tak 'em wi' y'."

She saw the grim determination in his dark, scarred features lit poorly by the firelight. His random visits usually did cause havoc of one kind or another. But this…what he was demanding. She hoisted her hefty shoulders and spread her thick arms wide. "An' go where exactly?"

He sat forward on the window ledge, meeting her questioning gaze. "T' Driffied. T' a manor thereabouts. Nafferton Garth."

"An' whose t' say folks there'll tak us in?" she asked, aware of his ruthless efficiency.

Shadiz appeared to hesitate. Something, Maggie had not seen in a long while. He gave a barely audible sigh. But she caught it.

"It's Kore's home."

Maggie was now truly baffled. "Who's Kore?"

Shadiz put his elbows on his knees and looked down at his outspread hands. "Kore. Catherine. She's me wife."

Maggie sat down abruptly. Unfortunately, she missed the stool and landed heavily on her ample backside on the pitted floorboards beside it.

"Develesko Mush!" growled Shadiz, rising. Beside her in one fluid stride, he picked her up and placed her on the stool. All Maggie could do was stare at him, nonplussed.

Eventually, she found her voice. "Y're wed?"

He was standing over her, gazing into the fire, his expression unreadable. He nodded.

"An' y'r…wife's at this Nafferton Garth?" she asked, unevenly.

"No."

The finality in that single word made her suddenly wary. She straightened herself up on the stool, watching him walk back to the black window with the feline gait he'd possessed from being young. She and Marianne, Skelton and his brother, all enjoyed a rapport of sorts with him few could boast. They were links on a strong chain secured back in a fragile childhood. Nonetheless, they remained cautious. It was rather like having an approachable alpha wolf in their midst occasionally.

"I'll get some o' me men t' escort y' there. Family men who'll give 'and wi' bairns. Skelton an' 'is brother can mind Starre well enough until its safe for y' t' return."

A thought struck Maggie. "What about Isaac? Doubt 'e'll leave York. Besides, 'e ain't well."

Isaac's goldsmith's shop was two doors down Stonegate from the Starre. Maggie and Marianne had known the goldsmith before they had discovered his connection with Shadiz. Maggie had long since taken the old man under her maternal wing. Because he had dealt with the purchase of the tavern and was responsible for Marianne's wealth acquired on her behalf by Shadiz, she had learned of Isaac's other profession as a lawyer.

Shadiz leant against the shadowy wall beside the small, casement window. He grimaced. "I'll wake dead tryin' t' get in to see 'im this time o' night. Even if the Nubian ain't long in openin' up."

Maggie nodded. She knew as well as he did how each night the Nubian, who Shadiz had rescued from lord knows where and now

21

served Isaac, had strict instruction to secure the premises beyond normal measures, so determined was Isaac to protect his valuable assets, including the documentation of the clients he discreetly served.

"Go see 'im. Give 'im option o'...." Shadiz broke off, looking towards the door.

Seconds later, it was flung open. Maggie knew instantly who was bursting in with such gusto even before Marianne appeared. She gave Shadiz a quick glance as she rose to intercept the French woman. She was always slightly ill-at-ease whenever Marianne was around him. And was especially so at present. Although he appeared relaxed, she felt him to be different somehow. A suspicion she couldn't nail down.

Her delight at seeing him again childlike, Marianne skipped gracefully towards Shadiz, her flimsy night robe floating around her. "I knew you to be here!"

It was Maggie's quick, detaining grasp on her arm that caused Marianne to rock back on her heels a short measure away from where he was standing, having straightened at her approach.

"For god's sake, Mari. You'll 'ave Lily awake an' 'ollerin'," chastised Maggie.

Marianne's mouth became a sweet o. Her two hands fluttered like dainty butterflies as she looked towards where the baby was sleeping peacefully.

"Then we'll both be in for it," said Shadiz, soothingly. He smiled at Marianne.

Although only a year younger than Maggie, her refined beauty had aged more gently. The lines of time had been written softly in her pale skin, around her smiling mouth and gentle blue eyes. But the brutal struggle with a life far removed from the one she had been born into had left its mark in other ways. She had not survived the years of enforced prostitution as well as Maggie, even though Maggie had tried to shelter her from the harsh regime at the Dark Horse. Unlike the girl who had become like a sister to her, Marianne was neither low-born nor of a strong disposition.

It was through Maggie that Shadiz had learned how Marianne's father, a French nobleman, had responded when his sixteen-year-old daughter had become *enceinte* by one of his contemporaries. To avoid any social disgrace, he had taken the extreme measure of having her shipped off to England and sold as a whore. Although the joints owners of the Dark Horse had soon discovered they had been duped, because of Marianne's beauty and foreign allure, they had taken measures to keep her and get rid of her unborn child. Only Maggie's devoted nursing had saved Marianne's life.

Shadiz had paid his debt. It had been no hardship to discover Maggie's da had died too drunk to escape his family's burning hovel. As for the Count. Shadiz made sure when he had fleeced the Frenchman at the gaming tables and consequently acquired his chateau and estate near Lyon that he understood the funds from the sale of the ancestral property would be used on behalf of the daughter he had so cruelly spurned. It was the only reason he had allowed the Count to live, in dire poverty.

Although he could have bought the Starre ten times over, he had used the Frenchman's money to purchase the tavern. Only Maggie and his lawyer Isaac knew. And both knew the remaining substantial sum was there to be used for Marianne's benefit. And Maggie's, though she refused anything for herself.

"Oh, my sweet! Your poor face. What befell you?" Marianne exclaimed. As she spoke she reached out to him, gazing with concern at the disfigurement the flames had cause to the left side of his face when he had saved Rose Van Helter from the fire in the Dutch port of Ijuimden.

Before Maggie could intervene, Shadiz gently took hold of her hand and kissed her knuckles. "It were fire, Mari. Y' recall."

She giggled at his gallant gesture. "Ah, oui. Of course." She half-turned in Maggie's direction. "It was terrible the fire. Did you know about what happened?"

Maggie smiled and murmured, "Terrible." She was not surprised when Shadiz disentangled himself not unkindly, never unkindly, from Marianne and reached the door without apparent haste.

"Oh! You are going!" cried Marianne, looking crestfallen.

Maggie tucked her robust arm in the other woman's thin one.

23

"Lord know's 'ow 'e finds time t' keep comin'," she commented, brightly.

"You must have a care. They're coming. When they do, they'll seal York."

Shadiz and Maggie regarded Marianne. They were both aware of her uncanny ability to 'know' things.

Shadiz switched his attention to Maggie. And this time Maggie was truly chilled. "Four days. No longer."

She cast a quick look at Marianne and was relieved to see she was arranging the lacy folds of her night attire. She looked back at Shadiz and nodded.

He waited only a moment longer to reinforce his command. And then after a quick smile for Marianne's benefit, he and the reluctant mastiff left the chamber.

CHAPTER THREE

Hide and Seek

Upon Shadiz's eventual arrival at the tavern in Aldwark, having been conspicuous by his absence while his men had enjoyed an early breakfast, he spoke at length to several of the older ones. They then left the Bugle and Musket. Curious about their comrades' mission, the rest of the Master's men followed their leader out of York.

Standing on the Roman battlements, Martin Wedgwood watched them go. His attention remained on the Master until he was lost in the misty grey light of dawn.

As the sun rose and endowed the earth with sparkling warmth, the Master led his men through fertile country to the north-east of the city. Village folk viewed their swift passing with apprehension. Of late, those who went to market in York had returned with unsettling rumours of the approach of armies. Even one from over the Border with Scotland.

It was late morning when the Master called a halt in a secluded meadow filled with nodding buttercups. Dismounting, the men allowed their lathered mounts to crop the grass and drink from the gurgling stream ambling through the meadow, at the same time slaking their own thirsts from the crystal water. Some stretched out in the long grass. Yet all remained on guard against whatever the verdant landscape might conceal. When their leader rode off on the stallion, the mastiff in hot pursuit, experience had taught them that his Romany scouts were not far away. And sure enough as he drew rein at the northern end of the meadow, one emerged from the tall hedgerow.

"Looks like we might be going hunting," Benjamin commented, squinting against the sunshine.

Richard snorted, invariably cynical about his half-brother's motives.

Shortly afterwards, Shadiz returned. He drew rein beside the two men. While the tempestuous stallion trampled buttercups, it was with cold indifference he surveyed Richard when his half-brother turned away, trying to disguise a bout of coughing by retrieving his longbow from where it lay in the grass.

"We ride, sir?" asked Benjamin.

"We ride," confirmed the Master, low-pitched.

★

Catherine dashed around the corner of the elegant chateau, desperately seeking a hiding place. She was about to dive into the shrubbery bordering the well-tended gardens when a voice emanated from within her intended refuge.

"Go away," hissed Lucinda.

"He's right behind me," Catherine retorted. Balancing on the balls of her feet, she scanned the immediate vicinity for ideal cover.

"There!" directed Lucinda. A graceful hand and arm, tinkling with gold and silver bracelets, shot out from her place of concealment.

Catherine ran across the flagstone path in the direction indicted by the young Romany woman. Moments before Peter came into view seeking her and his mother, she managed a rushed disappearance behind the tall bushes growing in a thick clump against the wall dividing the formal gardens from the kitchen garden.

After what seemed like an abnormally long time, Catherine was still waiting to be discovered.

Peter had found his mother by a comical fluke. Having lost his balance while searching, he had pitched headlong into the very bushes in which she had been hiding. Catherine had seen it happen from her hideout and expected to be discovered by the sturdy youngster shortly afterwards, only he had gone off in completely the wrong direction. His mother had tossed a conspiratorial grin over her shoulder as she had been dragged away.

Hoping Lucinda would guide Peter to her if the extensive grounds threatened to defeat his young endeavour, Catherine wrapped her arms around her bent knees and leant back against the flaky brick of the wall. Listening idly, she could hear the bees buzzing around the ripening fruit, the sweet musicality of birds and the murmur of conversations from several different places. The morning sunlight flittered through the camouflaging bushes and the feathery fronds of a nearby willow tree. Her gaze roamed over the emerald lawns to the azure Mediterranean beyond the sharply defined boundary of the tall cliffs. A distant ship appeared to be gliding over the glittering surface of the sea. Its puffed out sails were a painful reminder of where she had come from. Sighing, she switched her attention back inland to the white chateau. The simplicity of its tall windows and columned entrance gave the square frontage an air of classic nobility. Indeed, she had discovered the chateau had once belonged to a member of the nobility. Upon being informed that the Countess De La Tours had bequeathed the chateau to Shadiz, Catherine had been dismayed, especially after inspecting the portrait of a beautiful young woman, until she had also learned that the lady in question had been over forty when she had succumbed to a long illness.

In her mind's eye, she viewed the Lodge, ugly in comparison to Shannlarrey's sun-bleached stones and yet hauntingly familiar. Whatever happened in the future, she would always possess a great fondness for the ancient edifice buried deep within Stillingfleet Forest. Despite her initial misgivings, she had spent several happy months at Shadiz's dilapidated headquarters.

Movement on the broad pathway closest to her place of concealment caught her eye. She recognised Philippe's awkward gait. Accompanying him was a man she had never seen before.

Philippe was Shadiz's custodian of Shannlarrey. Although he had been forewarned of their arrival, en masse, it was clear he was accustomed to having the place to himself for long periods with only a few servants to maintain the chateau and its grounds several miles along the coast from Marseille. At times, his reserved politeness did not quite conceal his struggle to come to terms with the sudden influx of company.

Catherine remembered him from her previous visit when she had been recovering from an illness Mamma Petra, Shadiz's grandmother, had cured. Nowadays, she was more discerning. He was much younger than she had previously thought from the standpoint of a twelve-year-old. Upon her second visit it had soon become apparent that his gaunt features were the result of his physical condition. He walked with a pronounced limp. Though he masked it well he seemed to have difficulty using his left arm. When she had tentatively probed his condition, he had blocked her concern with firm courtesy that had left her no wiser. Only when she had encountered him one evening in severe pain in the library had he reluctantly agreed to her administering an infusion of bogbean and elder. From then on, his sober approach to all of them, except for Junno whom he had met several time before, had become less apparent.

Abreast of the spot where she remained hidden from Peter, Philippe called her name.

In an attempt not to seem like an emerging wood nymph, Catherine waited until the two men had walked further down the path before trying to make an innocent appearance behind them. What she had not anticipated was Peter catching sight of her furtive escape from the shrubbery.

"The best laid plans of hidden lasses," she muttered, as the two men turned back in her direction.

She was almost out in the open, smiling brightly in spite of the spiky bushes snagging her gown and long fair-white hair, when Peter, in his glee at his eventual success, barrelled into her despite his mother's sharp call to heel. The youngster's enthusiastic momentum caused both he and Catherine to bounce against the trunk of the willow tree and then tumble in a clumsy tangle into the bushes from which she had just emerged. At which point everyone hurried to give her the aid she could very well have done without.

In an attempt to hide her embarrassment, Catherine defended Peter against his mother's scolding before the crestfallen youngster was marched away. While discreetly dusting herself down, Philippe introduced her to the man beside him. "Madam, may I present, Monsieur Louis Fordor. Your husband's lawyer."

28

Two words resonated within his usual quiet manner. The first gave her a poignant thrill. The second caused an icy qualm to assail her. Her courteous gaze upon Fordor, she tried to keep her smile in place. He was an extraordinary sight. A vague glint in Philippe's serious green eyes gave her cause to surmise he was of the same opinion.

Although Philippe was in no way tall, being slightly shorter than herself, he towered over the rotund lawyer. Yet it was not the fellow's physical dimensions that were unusual, it was the outlandish garb in which he clearly took delight in hanging upon them. In comparison to Philippe's habitual dark, almost monkish attire, Fordor's pink doublet and silk breeches positively glowed in the bright sunshine. Catherine had never seen such an elaborate wig as the one he had planted on his head. The mass of horsehair curls were soaking up some of the sweat on his brow. It was unfortunate that rogue rivulets were making their way through the powder that he had deem fit to plaster on his large, heavy-jowled face. His painted lips appeared startlingly red against the artificial whiteness.

That his shoes, decorated with large white bows, had two inch square heels went some way to boosting his height but did nothing for his balance as they moved off down the path towards the chateau. Catherine could quite understand why he needed the gold-topped cane, and the shoulder of the young Negro boy who walked sedately beside him. Dressed in red velvet, he carried his master's paperwork. Because she had caught sight of the sly smirk on his mahogany face when he had been considering Lucinda and Peter, Catherine was inclined to dislike the boy.

What she could not understand was how such a popinjay as Fordor had become Shadiz's lawyer. She was interested to find out. Nevertheless, while accompanying him and Philippe into the coolness of the chateau her apprehension grew as to the reason for his visit.

CHAPTER FOUR

White Stones

While his men made haste to remount, the Master walked the stallion out of the meadow and into a narrow lane, followed by the mastiff. A brief survey of the tall hedgerow showed him the patrina, the Romany sign left for him by his mulesko dud. By such seemingly innocuous arrangements of nature, constantly overlooked by Gorgios, he would be led to his prey.

His attention was drawn to a cottage further down the lane just before a meandering bend. Its rough white stones beneath the overhanging thatched roof glowed in the strong sunlight.

*

His finely honed instincts alerted him to her presence. Standing on the cliff edge, he half-turned. A small shadow moved slowly across the stucco-white chateau, lit by the silvery glow of the full moon. Frowning, he turned back to gaze across the Mediterranean reflecting the ethereal light upon its peaceful surface.

Without turning a second time, he was aware of her hesitation a few feet behind him. "Y' ain't supposed t' be out 'ere."

"I awoke and found you missing," she said, moving forward to stand beside him. Her soft, cultured voice held an involuntary trace of the distress she had experienced at his absence. She pulled her silk robe tightly about her thin body.

Stepping behind her, he wrapped his arms around her. His muscular height and warm nakedness sheltered her from the cool midnight air. The silence of the night was broken only by the constant murmur of the waves lapping on the shore in the isolated cove at the base of the cliffs. As time went by he was having to gently support her frailness. Eventually, he said, "We'd better get y' back in."

Weak as she was, she resisted him. "I do not understand, Cheri?"

"What?"

She turned in his arms, looking up at him. "I do not understand why you bestow your attention upon an old, ill woman?"

Enigmatic, he shrugged away her bewildered probe.

"When you were our horse master at such a ridiculous age your interest lay more in the library and the music room. As I recall, Philippe was your tutor."

"Are y' malignin' Philippe?"

"You know very well I would not do such a thing."

He laughed softly. "Y' were jealous o' Plato an' the lute?"

"I was insulted," she retorted, her illness ravished beauty smiling nonetheless. She sighed and laid her head against his chest.

"I were keepin' y' safe," he murmured against her grey, wispy hair. Without another word, he took her up in his arms and carried her back into the chateau.

"I want to show you something," she said.

They were in the cool darkness of the marble entrance hall. Whereas he radiated virile warmth, she was shivering.

"Louise ... "

"Please, Cheri," she pleaded, making a feeble attempt to leave his strong arms.

With a disapproving sigh, he lowered her down onto her feet. While leading the way through indistinct chambers and corridors, she leaned heavily upon his supportive arm. Upon entering the spacious library, she headed for a particular section of the shelves that lined the chamber on three sides from the parquet floor to the ornate plaster ceiling.

"I'd got whatever book y' were after, dammit," he chastised, making her sit down in one of the tapestry-backed chairs arranged around the polished oak reading table.

Though moonlight was spilling through the series of tall windows down one wall of the library it was not sufficiently reliable for him to see to follow her slightly breathless, persuasive instructions. He lit the beeswax candles in a silver candelabra on the reading table. Following her guidance, he took down Dante's Inferno from the third shelf and then pressed on the space left clear. He felt through the broad walnut shelf rather than heard the sluggish release of a hidden mechanism not employed regularly. He needed no prompting from her to establish a grip in the slight gap that had opened up in the shelves. Thereafter, it took little effort for him to swing a section of the bookshelf outwards into the chamber.

While he gazed into the black void his sponsored actions had revealed, she got slowly to her feet. After he had picked up the candelabra, they went together through the opening. Once again she relied upon his support as they descended the narrow flight of stone steps. The musty coldness of ages assailed their progress, making Louise cough. She shivered and murmured, " You should be clothed, Cheri."

Taking in his gloomy surroundings, he did not answer. The light of the candles revealed two tall-back chairs close to the bottom of the steps. He sat her down on one after brushing away the thick layer of dust upon what turned out to be an embroidered seat. She watched him as he strode around the large, stone chamber. "Philippe and I stumbled upon it a few years ago. During our marriage, Maurice never mentioned its presence below the chateau, which leads me to believe he was unaware of what one of his ancestors must have created. No doubt had he been aware of its existence, he would have used it as my cell whenever he sought to punish me."

Shadiz looked at her over his shoulder. His bleak expression made it plain what he thought of her late husband, the Count De La Tours.

She met his gaze with a humble poignancy. "I thank you constantly."

He inclined his head before turning back to the extraordinary chamber.

Wielding the candelabra to highlight his scrutiny, the flickering glow revealed how it had been carved out of the cliff upon which the chateau was situated with an artistic dexterity. Where the chisel had found it impossible to smooth out the rugged stone in the low ceiling, barely two feet above his head, the resulting ridges had been made to resemble engraved beams. The sloping floor had clearly proved more malleable. Here the grizzled stone had been worked upon until its smoothness gave a polished appearance. A low bench and large chest, both smothered in cobwebs, stood against one wall. A huge oak desk was centralised where the floor had less of an incline. Its thick sturdy legs were embellished with snakes climbing intricately carved branches. Several documents and ledgers, yellowed with age and dust-infested, ink pots long since dried up and discoloured quills were strewn over the studded leather top.

Frowning, he turned back to her. "Why y' shown me this?"

"That door leads down to the cove," she told him, indicting the iron-studded hulk behind him.

He walked over to it. There was initial resistance when he tried the large discoloured key. He exerted a little more force and it grudgingly turned in the equally rusty lock. The thick heavy door gave groaning access to his curiosity. The freshness of the breeze flowing up from the small cove dispelled some of the musty atmosphere in the chamber and caused the candlelight to shed giddy light down a steep narrow slope until its strength was defeated by thick darkness. As far as he could make out, the tunnel to the shore had also been painstakingly chiselled out of the cliffs.

"As you are aware, the cove is considered inaccessible from the cliffs. I thought this might be of use to you. "

The rustling murmur of the sea retreated when he closed and locked the old door. His black eyes speculative, he walked across the chamber to her and, placing the candelabra close by on the floor, crouched down before her. "Why should that be?"

As the moonlight had emphasised the state of her health out in the night, so too did the candlelight within the stone chamber. With a trembling hand, she brushed his long black hair away from his dark, unforgettable face and traced the faint scar in his left cheek. That he was accepting of her touch remained, as ever, precious to her. "It won't be long now. When I'm gone, Shannlarrey will be yours, Cheri."

Few things surprised him these days. "What about Philippe? Surely ..."

"He is in full agreement," she was quick to point out.

His sigh was more of an exasperated growl. "I ain't wantin' Shannlarrey as some kind o' reward."

Her hand slipped down his broad shoulder. Her long fingers wove through the thick mat of hair upon his chest, still warm despite their cold surroundings. There were unshed tears in her eyes. "I never expected to see you again after ... what happened."

"Y' were wed t' a drunken bully."

"Who for no reason was jealous of his own brother. He maimed Philippe. And would have inflicted far worse upon both him and I if you had not happened along when you did."

"I'd 'ad enough' o' 'im. I ain't daft. I'd seen the bruises. The only other thing the bastard gave y' was an empty title. 'e only wanted y'r wealth an' y'r beauty t' puff 'issen up." He grimaced. "Y' weren't the first I made a widow."

"You set me free," she said, earnestly. Her smile faded. Softly, she added, "And then you were gone."

He straightened. "Come on, y' freezin'. Let's get y' back upstairs. No more talk o' death. Shannlarrey's under my protection."

Rising, she looked around her. "This can be your sanctuary," she murmured.

★

"I said, where do we ride?"

The Master glanced around the mounted men waiting in quiet formation around him in the narrow lane. They all felt the chill of his black eyes, especially Richard, who had spoken for the second time.

Without answering his half-brother turned the stallion, heading down the country lane, passed the white stone cottage

CHAPTER FIVE

Hill-Top Vantage

The range of hills folded in on themselves, resembling untidy creases in God's topography. At their base, forming natural moats were deep valleys in which sheep and cattle grazed, and predators lurked.

At a signal from their leader, with practised ease, the horsemen formed a line at either side of him. When the next authoritative signal came, they responded as one. It was with immaculate, inescapable precision that they surmounted all obstacles which previously had given verdant cover to the covert band of Romany who had preceded them up the steepest of the overlapping hills. The sudden absence of birdsong caused by the horsemen not the tribal mulesko dud should have warned the group gathered on the breezy hill-top of their imminent encounter. However, they were too engrossed in their perusal of the sweeping carpet of spangled greenery and the distant grandeur of York minister.

When the net was tightened decisively, all at once the hearts of the ensnared hammered hard in their chests and hands went instinctively to the hilts of swords.

"Hold!"

Those with a keen Scottish gleam among the trapped company were reluctant to heed the command. Theirs was a near-suicidal defiance.

"Hold, I say!" commanded Sir Thomas Fairfax. In one swift glance he had taken in the situation. He understood the alarm of the men who had accompanied him on the morning reconnaissance. He was also acutely aware of the Master's ferocious unpredictability.

"I came wi' Sun o' Midas an' wi' Morn o' Minerva t' catch a sigh from Thistle Titans," murmured Shadiz, walking the elegantly nodding,

high stepping stallion into the midst of the circle consisting of mounted Gorgio interspersed with soft-footed Romany. He halted his mount a few feet away from where the startled horsemen had formed a tight, grim pack. The mastiff sat on its haunches a prudent distance from where the stallion pawed the tough grass. "An' look what me mulesko dud found when I sent 'em mushgayin."

"A poor example of Vigilance. And a deplorable dose of Conceit." In contrast to his rigid companions, both English and Scottish, Sir Thomas appeared at ease astride his fine white horse. Momentarily switching his attention, he added, "Hello again, Benjamin."

"Hello, sir," responded the younger man.

It had been Benjamin who had undertaken the dangerous mission to the Parliamentarian held city of Hull in order to assure the dignified, slender Parliamentarian Commander he had known since childhood that his wife and daughter were safe within the Master's protection after they had become separated from him after the battle of Adwalton Moor. Benjamin had then escorted Fairfax to the rendezvous with the Master to be reunited with his family.

Fairfax's brown-eyed gaze was unflinching upon returning to Shadiz's scarred, barbarous countenance. A rueful smile twitched his neat beard. "Come to share the view?"

The sunlight sprang upon his single gold earring as Shadiz shrugged. "Seemed like a good notion."

The closest, kilted man to Fairfax spoke boldly. "Your games'll come t' nowt before our armies, gypsy." The last was a drawling insult. He would have said more even in the face of chilling dismissal if it had not been for Fairfax placing a restraining hand on his arm. The short, thickset Scotsman jerked free, a thunderous expression suffusing his already ruddy features. Nevertheless, he held his peace, albeit with clear aversion.

"I arrived t' introduce me kin t' Angel o' the Mornin'," said Shadiz, unexpectedly. "Little brother."

Labouring flushed under the unwanted attention that had swung his way, Richard reluctantly urged his chestnut mare forward until he was abreast of Shadiz.

"This be Lord Richard o' Fylingdales. Me ...."

"Half-brother," muttered Richard through gritted teeth, forestalling Shadiz.

"Ah, the archer. Moll was most impressed," Sir Thomas commented, glancing at the longbow slung across Richard's back and the quiver of arrows secured on the pommel of his saddle. Returning his attention to Shadiz, he raised a quizzical eyebrow. "That makes you .... "

"A bastard," came the flippant response.

"You never cease to surprise me."

Richard detected an air of familiarity between the two men, despite them being on opposing sides of the Civil War, and felt no particular surprised when his half-brother introduced Sir Thomas Fairfax. He suspected there had been previous encounters, apart from the one he had missed through ill-health when Shadiz had handed over the Parliamentarian's wife and daughter. But he was taken aback when David Leslie was made known to him. Shadiz's sardonic courtesy gave the Scottish commander further reason to bristle with impotent rage.

Ever the noble diplomat, smiling, Sir Thomas addressed Richard, "I'm thankful for the opportunity to offer my gratitude for your thoughtful care of my wife and daughter."

Richard had been the one to take charge of the women and shield them from Shadiz's less hospitable traits." I hope they are both in good health, sir?"

"Indeed. And out of harms way."

"Catherine was also a great comfort to your family, sir," added Richard, deliberately.

"Ah, yes. My wife informed me of her consideration. How fares .... "

"So," said Shadiz, with softly spoken harshness aimed more at his half-brother than the Parliamentarian. "The 'oards're gatherin' around Troy."

Considering himself to be silent overlong, David Leslie was eager to declare. "Our armies are closing in on York. The place will not withstand our combined onslaught."

The strange black eyes were viciously mischievous. "Y' ain't t' forget Manchester. It won't be long afore 'im an' 'is merry band joins the party."

Leslie looked shocked. "How the devil …? "

"Your information is impeccable as always," put in Sir Thomas, prudently. He ignored Leslie's scowl. "Do you intend to lead the devastation of all before us to thwart our requirements?" he added, indicating with a sweep of his hand the rural landscape, visible in beautiful clarity for miles in the morning sunlight.

Shadiz surveyed the Vale of York in silence from the breezy vantage point. Eventually looking back at Fairfax, his habitual forbidding expression changed to one of mild amusement. "Y' measurin' me for a coffin or a bible-thumper's smock?"

"I was merely wondering …."

"Don't we all, at one inconvenient time or another, Sweet Tom. Anyway, we've been through that mill afore."

"I would much prefer to have you as a friend by my side than an enemy, goodness knows where," admitted Sir Thomas with an honest grimace. "The offer remains."

"So's Rupert's," pointed out Shadiz, irritatingly.

Fairfax continued to ignore David Leslie's glowering remonstration. He filled the brief pause with a regretful sigh. "David believes we'll enter York before June."

"T' be sure, gypsy," put in Leslie with malicious satisfaction.

"Shouldn't y' deal wi' trouble on y'r own doorstep first off."

"What trouble? There is no trouble?" retorted Leslie.

"Really?"

The Scottish contingent in the ambushed horsemen looked at their commander and then centred the glare of their resentful speculation on the Master.

Soft-voiced, he informed them, "Huntly, so a wee birdie told me, 'as ousted all Covenanters, 'aloes an' all, an' is presently occupyin' Aberdeen for the king."

"You're a liar!" exclaimed David Leslie above disbelieving mutters.

Shadiz's dark brows shot up. "Not this time, I ain't. There be a dispatch 'ot-footin' its way t' Milord Argyll right now."

Did the Master's network of Romany spies reach as far as Scotland?

Richard realised how mundane a band of Romany travelling the highways would appear even in the present troubled times. Certainly, Leslie looked to have had the wind taken out of his sails. "You are a lair," he reiterated, trying hard not to sound dubious.

Shadiz dismissed the Scotsman with cold contempt. Turning back to Fairfax, he challenged, "What if Rupert was t' march from Shrewsbury?"

"That is one likelihood we are not foolish enough to dismiss," answered Sir Thomas, thoughtfully. "However, the Prince would have to defeat two, possibly three armies to relieve York."

"Out-manoeuvre?"

"He would require you, I believe, for such a task," commented Sir Thomas, quietly.

"Develesko Mush," responded Shadiz, "Me, the bleedin' Moses o' the North."

"More like two fiends in league to wreak havoc," put in David Leslie, fiercely, "Upstart prince an' gutter gypsy. You'll both burn in Hell afore year's out."

"Is that a promise?" The whispery tone held a sinister element.

The Scottish commander seemed briefly unnerved. His tartan-clad clansmen by whom he was surrounded, staunch Presbyterians, appeared to be fighting the desire to cross themselves.

"Sweet Tom. Now that I've seen what y're up t' wi y'r thistle playmates, what am I goin' t' d' wi' y'?"

"The problem is entirely yours," responded the older man.

Richard suspected for the first time since the beginning of the curious hill-top encounter Sir Thomas's admirable composure held fissures of wariness..

Even the Master's men wondered about their leader's intentions. The light breeze stirred the heightened tension. Both sides exercised greater vigilance.

Shadiz turned the stallion. He walked the restive black beast to the perimeter of the circle he had instigated. Drawing rein, he gave a curt order.

He swung the stallion around, and looked back at Sir Thomas. "A trapdoor to Hell or a doorway to freedom?"

Ignoring Leslie's hissed warning, Sir Thomas touched up his

horse. The ride was short. Yet the dark creature who awaited him was a many-headed hydra whose silent observation was a soul-piercing challenge.

Arriving at the breach in the ring of steel, Sir Thomas did not put spur to his white horse. Instead he drew rein, so that white and black mounts stood neck to neck. And such a man was he, his consideration was for his unpredictable foe who had created the deadly tension upon the crowded, breezy hilltop. *"The Seasons do not touch you?"*

> *"To everything there is a seasons,*
> *An a time to every purpose under the heaven;*
> *A time to be born, and a time to die."*

Giving a cynical shrug, Shadiz added, "A lament as old as the seasons." It was with an elaborate show of chivalry that he indicted freedom.

The older man inclined his head, accepting the deep bow of goodwill with a regretful smile. But he was not anxious to be gone. Unlike the others in his party, English and Scottish alike. With a mixture of suppressed eagerness and caution, they followed Sir Thomas's lead to safety. Accept David Leslie.

He hung back holding himself tensely and was one of the last to escape detainment. Coming abreast of Shadiz on the stallion beside the break in the circle, he acted abruptly with deadly purpose.

Shadiz reacted with lightning speed.

Instead of moving backward or sideward to avoid the reckless lunge of the long-bladed dirk Leslie had whipped from out of his stocking, Shadiz unexpectedly bent forward in aggressive defence. He grabbed the blade aimed at his heart and, despite the damage inflicted to the palm of his hand by such an action, rammed the jewelled hilt of the weapon into the Scotsman's face. The powerful forward momentum of the blow broke Leslie's already crooked nose and split his thin lips. Blood spurted profusely as he screamed in a mixture of painful surprise and irate frustration. Turning back to see what had happened, his countrymen would have avenged him had not Sir Thomas blocked their return with his startled horse, long enough for the Master's men to reform into an impregnable knot.

The bloody dirk lay on the ground between Shadiz and Leslie.

"'e that diggeth a pit shall fall into it," stated the Master in a whispery tone, "Or, put another way. Y' ain't 'cock o' the midden' on this side o' Border."

His men sniggered.

Wild-eyed, David Leslie's outrage was swimming in the blood on his smashed face. His pain-filled threat was muffled. The sentiment was plain to all.

The sneering black gaze altered as it settled on Sir Thomas's tense features, several feet away. "Go, sweet child o' y'r God."

"I implore you. Mock not our Lord." And he gently quoted. "I shall light a candle of understanding in thine heart, which shall not be put out."

"Not in mine y' won't," snapped Shadiz. He indicated freedom with a bloody hand.

With a last, searching look at him, Sir Thomas turned his horse. The others in his party, having seen that attack was not an option, were already riding down the steep hillside, crashing through bushes and hastily skirting soughing trees. Leslie followed more slowly, riding one handed, his other clutching his face.

The motionless horsemen still occupying the hill-top watched their departure.

"Fairfax."

Riding beside Leslie, Sir Thomas checked his nervous mount.

"Nice meetin' y' again," called Shadiz, grinning.

Sir Thomas gave a short laugh and an amused shake of his head. "I look forward to our next."

CHAPTER SIX

Hidden Ways

Catherine sat in silence, staring at Fordor. The Negro child was kneeling beside the large winged chair accommodating the Frenchman's fancy bulk. He was holding open a portfolio that allowed his master to consult the documents he had been commanded to bring to her attention. Upon first sight of Fordor, she had wondered why on earth Shadiz had chosen the garish fellow to be his lawyer, but after Philippe, Junno and herself had become ensconced in the leather-bound study adjacent to the impressive library, she had quickly learned how appearances were liable to be deceptive. Despite his flamboyant garb and quirky mannerisms, Fordor clearly possessed an extraordinary flair for legal and financial matters.

But then, she had been guilty on one other notable occasion of a grave misjudgement of character.

The thought brought her to her feet. She walked across the chamber to the open French windows. Deaf to the relentless drone of Fordor's stunning information behind her and blind to the sunny vista of the gardens stretched before her, she recalled her first impression of Shadiz.

It had taken place in the combat tent of Colonel Page in the Parliamentarian stronghold where she was being held, close to Fylingdales Hall. Within minutes of encountering Shadiz, he had cut the throat of a soldier with chilling ease, and threatened to do the same to the colonel. The vibrant shock of their meeting had been confused with the universal impression of the cruel, dangerous Gypsy. Shadiz's lethal actions had reinforced the tales that circulated about him in Driffield, the market town close to her home, Nafferton Garth. Only her father, Sir Roger Verity had held a contrasting opinion. When dire circumstances had forced him to reveal his friendship with Shadiz, he had spoken of an extraordinary man within the notorious legend.

When Sir Roger had fled with her from Nafferton Garth in search of Shadiz's protection, they and their accompanying neighbours had been ruthlessly pursued by Parliamentarian troopers loyal to Francois Lynette of Fylingdales. In the skirmish that had followed, Catherine had been captured despite her determined struggle. Sir Roger had been mortally wounded. Before dying in a tavern in the coastal hamlet of Mercy Cove, he had given his beloved, sixteen-year-old daughter into Shadiz's safekeeping.

Catherine's world had turned inexorably since then. She had found her improbable guardian harder to read than most people. Within her time at the dilapidated Lodge deep within Stillingfleet Forest, she had developed the unique ability to peal away the hard-bitten layers of a ruthless mercenary, brilliant covert commander and charismatic leader. Before long she had found herself standing precariously on the threshold of a man with whom she could fallen in love, despite the twelve years difference in their ages, and the worldly experiences that had made the years far longer for him. She abhorred his feral violence, she had witnessed on occasions. Yet in mitigation she blamed his turbulent past. When he was just five-years-old, his father, Lord Richard of Fylingdales, had ordered the removal of his bastard son from his foster home with Tom and Janet Wright on the Estate because his French wife, Lady Hellena, had been carrying his legitimate heir. Shortly afterwards, Shadiz had disappeared from the restrictive home of Lord Richard's sister at York. And so had begun a tumultuous life.

Catherine found herself holding the jet pendant. It had become far more than a piece of jewellery. Given to her through her father by Shadiz, the polished jet with its silver mounting inscribed with strange symbols had become a mystical link to its moonstone counterpart worn by him. Jet and moonstone had spun a remarkable, gossamer thread between the two of them.

Shadiz had also marked her in a more public manner by making her his wife. Not that she had taken much persuading. Yet she had found only a heart-rending barrenness in being his wife in name only. The feeling was made worse by the certainty it was not simply the Civil War in England or the threat his enemies at Fylingdales Hall posed to her safety that had made him send her away directly after their marriage. She had learned from his grandmother, Mamma Petra, the strange matriarch of the Romany tribe, he had obsessed about her since she had been quite young. And from her new husband had come an admission prior to her departure from Whitby. Since her father's death he had charged Junno to protect her from himself. She had been told how he had raped and murdered his half-sister, and raped and almost killed Lucinda. However, Catherine had never felt threatened by him.

She was astounded by the way Shadiz had commanded Fordor to give her complete access to his financial affairs, she would much rather have complete access to him, be he a beggar or the wealthy man she had been informed he was.

Emerging from the difficult reverie to discover she was still being bombarded by the seemingly endless revenues of shipping companies and an abundance of vineyards and estates throughout France, Spain and Portugal, Catherine took solace in the balmy air wafting through the open French windows. Her attention focused on the ship she had seen earlier whilst in the grounds of the chateau. Like those she regularly watched plying between unknown ports and Marseilles, several miles further along the coast, its sea-borne trading route had brought it closer to shore. She could now distinguish the full-blown sails upon its three tall masts and the bow wave glistening like frothy white petticoats.

Dismissing the wistful hope, she realised that Fordor had finally fallen silent. Feeling the attention of the chamber resting upon her, she slowly turned round to face the men. "How did my... husband acquire such wealth?" The question had raised its ugly head shortly after Fordor had started

Philippe's thin features remained noncommittal. Junno fidgeted. Fordor cleared his throat before speaking. "That you would have to ask your husband, Madam."

"Chance would be a fine thing," Catherine muttered.

With a whisper of pink silk, she returned to her seat beside the elaborate hearth strewn with rose petals. She caught Junno's concerned eye and gave him a resigned smile. He had entered the chamber in haste after being informed of Fordor's visit while in the extensive stables. The lawyer's initial reaction to the presence of the bald-headed Romany had been tempered by Junno's prodigious size, which overshadowed even Shadiz's commanding height. Also, Philippe's respectful introduction of Shadiz's cousin.

Following an elaborate nod from his master, the Negro boy in the velvet doublet and breeches closed the comprehensive portfolio and, with tongue protruding concentration, tied the leather laces. After executing a perfect bow, he then presented the proof of her husband's comprehensive interests to Catherine. Without responding to her smile, he shuffled back to again kneel at his master's feet. Pricked by disquiet, she looked up from the child-servant to Fordor.

"Well, Madam. You now possess all the details of your husband's wealth."

Fordor sought to conceal his disbelief. That the Gypsy had seen fit not only to marry the child, comely to the eye though she was, but also to reveal his vast wealth to her, was beyond belief. Never in a million years had he considered the unique, bewitching brute to possess a heart capable of harbouring finer feelings.

Exchanging a glance with Philippe, it was clear the reclusive fellow had read his mind. Fordor gave an imperceptive shrug. And turned his attention to the fine, golden wine from Malaga. The lecture on the status of his powerful client had made him quite thirsty.

A hail of musket fire disturbed the peace of the late afternoon.

Junno shot to his feet, one large hand gripping the hilt of his sword. He took an instinctive stride toward the chair in which Catherine was now sitting bolt upright. Already on his feet, Philippe froze in the process of refilling Fordor's silver goblet.

There was another burst of musket fire. It sounded alarmingly close at hand.

Junno and Philippe shared an understanding glance. Catching sight of their wordless exchange, the quickening of apprehension caused Catherine to rise.

When the clash of steel came hard on the heels of the third blast of musket fire, thoroughly alarmed, Fordor clambered upwards, wobbling on his lofty heels. His young page clung to his thick, satin-encased leg.

Bill Todd and two Romany youths burst through the open French windows. Lucinda and Peter were in their midst. Gripping her frightened son in her arms, she quickly established Catherine's presence, and then turned her fearful gaze upon her husband. At sight of his family, Junno relaxed fractionally, shooting Bill a grateful look. The other man reciprocated with a slight nod.

Breathing a sigh of relief, Catherine went to stand beside Lucinda. She absently stroked Peter's tense arm wrapped around his mother's neck.

"Lynette's lot?" demanded Junno, closing in on the women.

"Who else," replied Bill. "Bastards reckoned they could tak' us by surprise."

"We are under attack!" wailed Fordor.

Junno ignored the Frenchman's near-hysterical demands for protection. Taking both Catherine and his wife by the arm, he began to steer them from the study. "Right, y' know what t' do."

"'Tis already bein' dun'," Bill replied, grimly. Sword in hand, he headed back outdoors in the direction of the armed struggle that was getting louder by the minute.

While Catherine, Lucinda and Peter had been settling into their new home, Junno and Bill Todd had gone around the chateau and its grounds with Philippe putting defensive measures in place and formulating a plan should Shannlarrey come under attack.

Understanding it would become known where he had sent his new wife, and well aware of Francois Lynette's determination to thwart him, Shadiz had ensured that Catherine and Junno's family were protected by a formidable combination of his Gorgio and Romany men. For the usurper of Fylingdales knew only too well if he got his hands on Catherine there would be every chance Shadiz would capitulate. Indeed, it appeared he and his sister, the embittered Dowager of Fylingdales, had long been in possession of the knowledge that could bring down the Master. Only his fierce cleverness had kept Catherine and himself safe from their desire for revenge for the deaths of his father, Sir Richard and Elizabeth his half-sister. Nowadays, Lynette was also seeking revenge because of Shadiz's brutal slaughter of Gerald Carey, his young, foppish lieutenant and constant companion.

The two, well-armed Romany who had appeared with Bill Todd positioned themselves at either side of the French windows. Despite their youthfulness, both appeared quite capable of combating any violent incursion. They prevented Fordor from dashing out into the strife torn gardens. Having abandoned his fancy heeled shoes in his panic, he did a clumsy about-face in his socking feet and together with his equally terrified child-servant rushed to the same door Junno was leading Catherine and Lucinda towards.

Grimly absorbed in getting his precious charges into the hallway and up the grand staircase to the comparative safety of the upper chambers, at first the big man gave little heed to Philippe until the other man reiterated his detaining call. Philippe's uncharacteristic sharpness caused him to slackened his pace. "What is it?" the big man snapped over his shoulder.

Philippe appeared to shake off a momentary hesitation. "There is a more suitable place of safety until the attack can be defeated," he said, walking to the study's other door and pausing on the threshold of the library. He gave Junno a significant look. "He would want Catherine in that place. Your family, too."

Scowling, Junno ground to a dubious halted. He saw within the Frenchman's steady gaze an apology for his insight into Peter's true parentage and the resignation of someone taking what they believed to be the correct course of action whatever the consequences. Harbouring a generous heart made Junno give the other man the benefit of the doubt. With a slight, understanding nod, he turned Catherine and his wife with Peter and ushered them in the wake of Philippe's ungainly lead.

Hurrying down the library's considerable length, the series of tall windows lining one entire wall to their right gave all of them worrying glimpses of the assault on Shannlarrey. The grounds of the chateau seemed to be heaving with the violent onslaught. The attackers, though they had probably thought to encounter some form of resistance, had swiftly been engaged by an insurmountable ring of steel which had stalled their progress to their inevitable target. Each individual battle, four or five strong, were being fought with fierce determination on both sides. Bloody gore glistened on the churned up emerald expanses. Blood was smeared on broken statues. A body floated in the largest fountain.

Several of the windows in the library were open allowing the clamour of swordplay to assail those within. Worse than the thunder and lightning of fighting men were the harrowing screams of the wounded. Lucinda held her son even closer. Trembling, Peter hid his face in her long black hair. Cringing inwardly, Catherine caught sight of a man fall to the ground clutching his chest. God forgive her, she was relieved to see it was not one of the Master's men. Another staggered upright and was promptly flung down without quarter being given. Again it was one of the attackers.

She was reminded of the battle in Longdrop Hollow within a stone's throw of Fylingdales Hall when the Master's men had charged Lynette's retinue to retrieve her.

A thought struck her with horrifying impact. "Ye Gods and little fishes. Keeble!" she exclaimed, resisting Junno's anxious pace. "He was feeling unwell while we were playing with Peter. He fell asleep on a bench near the Artemis fountain."

"Don't fret, Rauni. 'e can tak' care o' 'issen. 'e'll know t' go t' ground."

Fearing for her small friend despite Junno's confident words, she dashed over to the nearest window and frantically scrutinised the deadly conflict.

"Please, Catherine," called Lucinda, "we must hurry."

Giving timely emphasis to her words, there was a loud crash alarmingly close to the chateau. Without further ado, Junno collected Catherine and led her to where his wife and son were waiting in silent consternation.

Mystified, he regarded Philippe's action. "What y' about?" he demanded.

"I'm looking for…." began Philippe, running his hand along a shoulder-high shelf.

"We ain't time for…."

"Reading," Philippe finished for him ironically. "Ah!" he exclaimed, pulling out Dante's Inferno. "But this one will see Catherine, Lucinda and Peter safe." He tossed the book onto the polished oak reading table and pressed against the gap it had left.

Upon the hidden mechanism giving grudging release, fearing Philippe's strength to be insufficient, Junno lent powerful assistance. Whereupon a section of the bookshelves swung outward, enough to reveal a slice of thick darkness. The musty odour of an ancient crevice wafted into the library. A thousand dust motes drifted free in shafts of warm sunlight upon Junno widening the intriguing gap.

Startling everyone with his awkward impetus, Keeble rushed into the library as if all the hounds in Hell were on his heels. Sweat was pouring down his large, ugly face. His clothes were covered in the clinging detritus of concealment. Skidding to a halt beside Junno, he could barely speak so out of breath was he. "There...."

"Aye. We know," said Junno, quickly but not unkindly. "Y' be all right?"

The little man nodded, still fighting for breath.

Immensely relieved to have him join them, Catherine gripped Keeble's crooked shoulder. He returned her glad smile with a wry, rosy grin.

Philippe struck tinder. The candles flared as he gave Catherine the silver candelabra he had picked up from the reading table. "Go. The stairs are narrow and steep. Have a care," he told her. He then turned to Junno. "They will be safe within his domain."

Catherine was aware Junno desperately wanted to be elsewhere, dealing with the attack on Shannlarrey, but that his need to keep her and his family out of harm's way was just as demanding. He cast an uncertain look at Philippe. It was plain the unassuming Frenchman was seeking a further measure of trust. He remained steadfast beneath Junno's scrutiny.

A silent acknowledgement passed between the two men. An understanding that their bond was loyalty to Shadiz, and neither would falter in their mutual allegiance.

"Go, Rauni," the big man commanded, eventually, glancing reassuringly at Catherine and then his wife while stroking his frightened son's back. Switching his attention back to Philippe, he said, "Let Keeble go wi' 'em. 'e can warn us if owt goes amiss."

"It won't," stated Philippe.

"As a back up, that's all," persisted Junno.

After briefly regarding the little man who the Master had allowed to become Catherine's merry page, who previously had served for several years as a member of his crew on board the Sea Witch, Philippe gave his sober agreement.

"Keep safe," Catherine murmured to the two men before Lucinda, Peter, Keeble and herself were shut away from a dangerous world.

There was a moment of collective disorientation as the cool, eerie darkness closed about their pool of flickering candlelight.

Keeble gently removed the candelabra from Catherine's tense grasp and, holding the pale light aloft, slowly led the way down the steep descent into the unknown. At one side was smooth stone, at the other was a cold void that seemed to threaten every footstep hesitantly taken. Arriving at the bottom of the uneven stone steps, they stood together in a wary group, viewing their shadowy surroundings edged by unnerving darkness.

Wielding the candelabra, Keeble discovered sconces set at regular intervals in the grey rock. He used the flames of the waning candles to ignite the torches set within them. The stronger light revealed a cavern honed out of solid rock. The ridges in the low ceiling had obviously proved hard to negate. They had been disguised as engraved beams by dexterous chisels. The sloping floor was a lighter shade of grey and appeared polished between the large rugs, splashes of exotic colour.

Though sparse, the furniture had been expertly made from beech, oak or willow. The desk was huge. Its sturdy legs were embellished with snakes wound around intricate branches. An amazing seat that appeared to have been carved from the trunk of a beech tree evoked for Catherine memories of Garan, the Druid, who lived within Stillingfleet Forest. Shelves of polished oak had been set into a tall, deep niche in one wall. It held a large collection of books, their titles in a variety of languages. Nearby stood a large chest striped with broad lengths of iron. An array of weapons were hung on one wall, some of which appeared wholly foreign.

"Look, that you!" cried Peter. His fascination with their remarkable surroundings had served to mitigated his fear of their need to take refuge in the stone chamber below the chateau.

The two young women swung round together. Lucinda gasped. Catherine's breath left her abruptly. She raised a trembling hand to her suddenly dry mouth.

The portrait given pride of place on the smoothest stone wall was indeed of herself. It must have been painted when she was about fourteen years old. It was stunningly obvious to her who the artist was. After all, Shadiz had admitted to painting the portrait of her father hung in her bedchamber at Shannlarrey, as it had done at the Lodge after he had included it in her possessions he had transported from Nafferton Garth. Whereas her father's portrait had features of camaraderie, hers possessed attributes from a tenderly wielded brush. Staring at her past likeness, tears sprang into her eyes.

Peter was regarding her with the black eyes of his father. "Cat?" he whispered.

Catherine took a ragged breath, seeking to remain calm. She was aware of Lucinda's horrified expression. Although it irked her, she gave a little, embarrassed laugh, attempting to make light of the obvious. "It would indeed seem to be me."

"It is," stated Lucinda. Her opposing reaction to the portrait was entrenched in the look she gave Catherine. She turned away and sat down in one of the two ancient chairs, their embroidered seats faded, at the bottom of the flight of steps. The array of gold bangles on both her wrists jangled in the stony silence as she wrapped her arms around herself. Her troubled gaze followed Peter's curious wanderings around the chamber.

Despite appearances to the contrary, Catherine had not entirely succeeded in either forgetting or forgiving Lucinda's poisoning of Shadiz at Whitby, even though she suspected Lucinda's action could quite possibly have been at the behest of Mamma Petra, Shadiz's grandmother. Catherine had realised Lucinda might very well have been persuaded into such drastic behaviour by the old

Romany woman because she believed she had been safeguarding her. Catherine was painfully aware that Peter's conception had been a traumatic experience for Lucinda. She remained terrified of her husband's cousin. And intimidated by their present, unexpected surroundings.

Life at the chateau had affected all of them in different ways.

Catherine's second visit to Shannlarrey was under very different circumstances. When she had stayed with her father at the age of twelve, she had been unaware of Shadiz's ownership. Upon her return several years later, she had felt the full impact of his influence. In a rare moment, Philippe had confided in her how, some years earlier, his sister's young horse master had thought nothing of visiting the library and the chamber dedicated to music. With shy pride, he had explained how he had attempted to quench a thirst for knowledge of the classics and anything else the comprehensive library boasted, and how he had coaxed the flair for melody. Listening to the mild-mannered Frenchman, she sensed that whenever Shadiz had visited Shannlarrey, he had found an ease of spirit.

Being within the stone chamber, Catherine experienced a strong sense of Shadiz's presence. The very air made her believe it had become his inner sanctum, into which he had placed the portrait of herself.

She tried to keep concealed beneath normality the terrible, aching hurt cause by his rejection of her due to his dark past. At times, like the present, it spiked painfully. She sometimes wondered whether he had never really come to terms with his own harsh rejection at a very early age. It seemed to have laid the foundation of his brutal existence.

She walked over to the desk. It reminded her of the nautical one strewn with charts she had seen in the captain's cabin of the Sea Witch, Shadiz's flag ship she had sailed in to what she considered her exile in France.

There were quills in a tall, ivory container and a large ink pot upon the desk's leather, studded top. Opening at random one of the neatly stacked ledgers, she scanned the comprehensive shipping records describing an assortment of cargoes destined for ports throughout the Mediterranean and the Levant, even as far afield as Persia. All were in a neat script she recognised as belonging to Shadiz. Upon opening another ledger and browsing through its pages, she found clear evidence of every kind of armament being supplied to both Christian and Moslems countries alike.

"I've fought against Christians. An' I've fought against Moslems. They all bleed the same way."

Recalling his word, Catherine sighed regretfully.

Her attention was drawn to a map laid out at the other side of the desk. To her surprise she found it to be of North-East Yorkshire. Outlined upon it was the far-reaching boundaries of Fylingdales Estate. When she skimmed through several ledgers, again in Shadiz's hand, it became plain he had acquired an amazing amount of detailed knowledge regarding Fylingdales Hall and Estate. Its yearly accounts going back to when Sir Richard, his father, was alive. Every arable hectare, every seasonal herd of cattle and flock of sheep, every horse, every cart, wagon and carriage, every worker's job, wages and home, and every piece of furniture, silver and gold in the Hall.

It was disturbingly plain that there was nothing Shadiz did not know about Fylingdales, including the origins of the men Francois Lynette had gathered together to protect the Hall and Estate. Mainly from himself, disguised as active allegiance to the Parliamentarian Cause.

An icy shiver rippled down her spine. There was a cold sensation in the pit of her stomach.

She looked up from all the documented evidence.

Meeting Catherine's tortured gaze, afraid, Lucinda got to her feet.

"He is going to seize Fylingdales Hall. That's why he's in England!" muttered Catherine. She looked towards her portrait, adding, "Ye Gods and little fishes!"

CHAPTER SEVEN

Moon Fire

It was not only the oppressive atmosphere of an unusually warm day that consumed the air in the large upper chamber of Scarborough Castle. A silence not of nature's making stretched from one grey, gritty wall to another. Richard and Benjamin exchanged sidelong glances. Neither man wished to attract the bleak attention of the Master. Even Richard had become accustomed to treading cautiously around his half-brother since Catherine's departure. Blasted by their leader's cold, authoritative decree, the rotund Governor of the Castle had withered before their sympathetic gazes.

"If y' get a whiff o' Scots or Crop-Ears sniffin' around, y' let me know. Understand?" The last word was a whiplash.

Sir Hugh Cholmley nodded obediently.

Since the Master had entered the chamber, Cholmley had been at pains to keep his large desk between himself and the Gypsy. He detested the arrogant delivery of his orders in front of the two fair-haired, well-bred young men, especially Lord Richard, who he had known since childhood. War did, indeed, breed strange bedfellows.

A year ago, Cholmley had held Scarborough Castle for Parliament. Though not possessing a military background, he had been zealous in his commitment. He had also relished the prestige of his friendship with Lady Hellena and her brother, Francois Lynette, the present controller of Fylingdales Hall and the sprawling Estate. Unfortunately, the association had come to an unhappy end for Cholmley when the Gypsy had entered the castle's lofty domain under a flag of truce, armed only with his charismatic darkness. Consequently the garrison had turned against Cholmley. Now as then the Governor could not override the demands of his garrison to serve the Master, or withstand the domineering influence.

"D' I mak' mesen clear?"

Cholmley once again nodded. Beads of sweat glistened on his creased forehead.

Shadiz strode away, leaving the older man to swelter nervously in his finery.

Cholmley willed the Gypsy through the door, unable to crack his rigid stance until the savage was gone from the chamber. So absorbed was his hopeful gaze on the long, midnight-black hair, draped untidily over the great sword slung across the broad back, he barely acknowledge the polite departure of the two young men accompanying Shadiz.

If it had not been for the worrying fact that the Gypsy halted abruptly halfway through the door, Cholmley would have been amused by the comical sight of Richard colliding with him and Benjamin in turn walking into Richard.

Motionless, seemingly oblivious to the collision he had caused, Shadiz raised his right arm in an odd jerky manner. While Cholmley remained mystified, Richard and Benjamin shared a suspicion. At one time or another, both men had glimpsed what lay beneath their leader's rough shirt.

Gripping the moonstone pendant in his fist, Shadiz slowly turned back into the chamber. He seemed distracted and uneasy for several moments. And then his manner became fraught with purpose.

He almost walked through Richard and Benjamin, causing them to move hastily aside. Continuing to grip the pendant, he crossed the sunny chamber. Halting at a high, narrow window, he shaded his keen, questing gaze against the inconvenient glare of the late afternoon sun.

The three men behind him were united in a motionless, puzzled silence.

Residing in formidable, ancient splendour on its rocky plinth, the castle's lofty position ensured a panoramic view of Scarborough. The north and south bays were sculptured arcs, glistening marine-blue and surf laced on golden shores. Gathered around them, shrunk by distance into toy-like existence, was the neighbourly jumble of cottages, taverns, stores and the dark ribbons of narrow, steep alleyways. Suspended on verdant slopes above all lowly life were the grand homes of captains and merchants. Then all was abandoned to vertical cliffs, the ideal defence for the castle. Similar to Whitby, there was a clear divide in the sprawling harbour between fishing and commerce. Although the merchant ships were easily distinguished from the fishing smacks and the bigger cobles, individually they were difficult to identify from the castle without the benefit of an eye-piece.

"What ships're in port?" demanded Shadiz, without turning.

Responding shakily, Cholmley fumbled with a ledger.

"Well?"

"The *Swan* has just discharged."

"She'll 'ave t' do," muttered Shadiz. He swung away from the window and strode out of the chamber with fluid urgency..

Halfway down the dismal, stone passageway, Richard and Benjamin caught up with their leader.

"What do you mean, the *Swan* will do?" demanded Richard, stifling a cough "Where are you going?"

Richard was still trying to obtain an answer from his ominously silent half-brother when they reached the large stone trough where their horses were being watered close to the anvil-pounding smithy in the castle's grassy precincts. The Master's men were lounging around their mounts, weary after delivering munitions to York and then having trapped the combined Scottish and English reconnoitring party on a hilltop overlooking the verdant landscape a few miles from the city. But as one they straightened upon their leader's arrival and looked at him expectantly.

Ignoring Richard, agitated beside him, Shadiz ordered, "All o' y' get back t' Lodge." To Danny Murphy, he said, "Tak' 'im back wi' y'. An' make damn sure bastard stays there."

"You're going to France, aren't you?" demanded Richard, ignoring Benjamin's warning look and Murphy's advance. "You are, aren't you?" He had no idea how his half-brother knew, but the suddenness and urgency of Shadiz's decision to take ship could mean only one thing. Catherine was in danger.

"I'm coming with you. I know you're sailing to France. You are not…."

Shadiz struck fast and hard.

The blow felled Richard. Concealing their surprise, several of the Master's men, unbidden by either their leader or Danny Murphy, picked up his senseless form and hoisted him over the saddle of his mare, securing him there.

Benjamin took a deep, bracing breath, and said, "Sir, if there is a difficulty in France, would it not be wise for a few of us to accompany you?"

His preoccupied leader showed no sign of having heard him. Instead, the Master rode away with the mastiff following the stallion's flying heels.

Benjamin watched him go, uncertain what to do. Murphy walked up to him. The two men stood for a couple of moments, watching their leader's rapid departure beneath the raised, well-guarded portcullis.

"Well," said Murphy, grimly, "I doubt 'e'd knife you if y' were t' follow."

Released from his indecision, Benjamin took heart that it would simply be a matter of keeping his leader in view. However, it proved easier said than done.

During the journey up to the castle he had been part of the Master's formidable troop whose strength and purpose had demanded respect. Now he was a lone rider obliged to negotiate fellow riders, people on foot, wagons and carts. Nor did the twists and turns in the cliff side highway down to the harbour make his task any easier. He fretted around each lopsided dwelling or canting tavern, catching sight of his leader for a moment before he disappeared around the next occupied corner up ahead. Then, suddenly, his leader was no longer in sight at all. Curtailing his mare's rapid momentum down the steep incline, for the first time Benjamin surveyed his surroundings. The fresh, salt air and the cry of the gulls made him aware he was approaching the harbour. At either side of him were humble dwellings interspersed at regular intervals by the yawning gloom of narrow alleyways.

Two old men were blowing hard on their pipes while glowering at him.

It was with an unsettling qualm that he fleetingly marvelled at how in his haste he had missed the children darting about the busy thoroughfare or playing in the rutted dirt haphazardly around its brink. His worst fears were realised when he caught sight of a group of women and children. They were gathered round a girl of about eight or nine. Slowing his mare still further, he was relieved to see the youngster was sitting up and, though crying, appeared unhurt. Surrounded by the constant flow of two way traffic, a pang of guilt prised Benjamin out of the saddle. He was subjected to motherly scowls and waspish comments as he walked his mare past the small crowd.

Despondent, he turned the last corner and came in sight of the harbour, but not the Master. He was about to remount and set off to scour the waterfront when he was dragged into a nearby alley.

His first reaction was to retaliate, while at the same time trying to hang onto his startled horse. Belatedly, he realised it was the Master who had roughly detained him. Hard on the heels of the discovery, Danny's words came back to haunt him. He stiffened. But Shadiz had already switched his attention back to the waterfront.

Benjamin quickly tethered his mare next to where the stallion was tied. Returning to stand quietly beside his leader, he gazed out from the dismal alleyway at the two ships secured alongside one of the wooden wharves. He could see their names clearly. The Swan's lettering was neat and unassuming. The *Enterprise* was announced with a bold golden flourish. The merchantman was the ship Shadiz had deemed suitable while up at the castle to sail to, presumably, France. The *Enterprise*, Benjamin knew, was Francois Lynette's high seas hunter. It dwarfed the Swan which appeared work-a-day ugly while rocking in the rising harbour water beside the Enterprise's sleekness.

Suspicion dawning, Benjamin surveyed his leader. Although Shadiz's barbarous face was set in stone, he glimpsed resolve in those unique dark features. And a hint of something else not normally associated with the Master.

"Get back t' men. Tell 'em I want them who 'elped wi' rescue o' *Eagle* when she run aground in Mercy Cove. Them who knows 'ow t' sail. Go."

Benjamin was loathed to make a hasty return up the cliff's twisting highway in order to waylay the Master's men before they left the castle. He began his ascent at a prudent canter, only giving the brown mare its head in the intermittent gaps between various obstacles. And all the while his pressing hope vied with his caution.

CHAPTER EIGHT

Reinforcements Of A Dubious Kind

"What was that?"

The fearful note in Lucinda's query penetrated Catherine's preoccupation with the disturbing details of Fylingdales collected by Shadiz. "What?" she muttered, looking up from the paperwork.

"It's comin' from 'ere," said Peter, excitedly, pointing at an ancient door.

Sudden anxiety manifested itself as irritation. "What is?" Catherine snapped, aware she did not possess Romany instincts, developed over generations of travelling in a world more often than not hostile to them.

"Voices!" exclaimed mother and son in fearful chorus.

"Y' right," muttered Keeble. Not much taller than Peter, the little man pulled the boy away from the furthest end of the chamber where it sloped down to the half-moon door. Peter met his mother in mid-chamber, and clung to her brightly patterned skirt.

Swallowing convulsively, Catherine went to stand next to Keeble. They both remained motionless, staring at the door. Behind them, Peter whimpered fretfully. Catherine half-turned. But her mute warning was not needed. Lucinda had already picked up her son and muffled his distress.

During a tense couple of minutes, the voices grew louder; definitely approaching the other side of the door. Keeble pushed Catherine behind him. In the midst of danger, she was warmed by the little man's courageous protection.

There was a sturdy piece of driftwood nearby on the smooth, stone floor. She picked it up, weighing its potential as a weapon. Keeble, having drawn his long bladed dagger, gave her a pained look. Hoping she had not insulted him, she gave him an apologetic grin. But his attention had whipped back around to the door. He held himself even more tensely than before, listening hard, scrutinising the iron-studded wood.

Catherine had no idea how Lynette's attackers had managed to find their way to the other side of the door. Philippe had told her it was impossible to descend the sheer cliffs upon which the chateau stood to the small, sandy cove below. It could only be reached by the sea.

Judging by the heavy footfalls and the mutterings at the other side of the locked door, there was a frightening number. All Catherine and the others in the stone chamber could do was put their trust in a rusty lock and the thickness of the medieval oak, and hope the invaders had not been resourceful enough to bring with them a battering ram. With that thought in mind, she gripped the stout driftwood even more tightly.

One voice could be heard above the rest, issuing orders with a distinct Irish lilt.

"Nick?" muttered Keeble under his breath.

Frowning, he took a couple of steps closer to their side of the door. And, if possible, listened even more intensely. After a couple of moments, he repeated the name with much more conviction.

Catherine started to question his response. But he motioned for her to be quiet.

"Nick be that you?"

"Well, it ain't any soddin' leprechaun trying to walk through wood. Open the damn door!"

United in surprise mixed with stark misgivings, Catherine and Lucinda switched from the door to Keeble in time to witness tension be replaced by elation. He grinned up at Catherine. "It's Nick!" he exclaimed, merrily.

"I rather got that," she responded, without enthusiasm.

Keeble rushed forward, saying over his shoulder, "Nick Condor. An' lads."

"Oh, good," she murmured, exchanging a sceptical glance with Lucinda.

According to what she had been told by both Junno and Tom,

Nick Condor worked for or worked with the Master. Their base was situated on the island of Formentera, the smallest of the Balearic Islands, located in the central part of the western Mediterranean off the east coast of the Spanish mainland. And now, all of a sudden, he was here at the same time as the onslaught on Shannlarrey by Lynette's men.

Believing Condor's appearance to be disturbingly convenient, Catherine scooted up to Keeble. She grasped his arm as he struggled to turn the large key in the reluctant lock. "Are you sure, he's here to help?" she hissed in his ear.

The little man looked at her as if she had gone quite mad. "O' course."

The Irish voice came again, demanding to know what was the hold up.

Keeble managed at last to turn the key, saying to her, "I'd trust 'im wi' me life, an' yours. For Master's sake."

In the next moment the door was flung open and heavily armed men of all sizes and races poured into the stone chamber.

Catherine retreated out of their way, still brandishing the trusty driftwood.

"'ang onto that thought, sweet darlin'," said the Irishman, striding past her.

Her wary attention remained squarely on him. He issued rapid commands while men sped in foreign array through the chamber and up the stone steps. They soon disappeared into the library, careful to push the false panel which had given them access to the violent world above the stone chamber back in place behind them. Even so, two burly Negroes remained on guard at the head of the flight of steps.

The Irishman remained in the chamber, too. Of medium height, thick-set and muscular, he was festooned with weapons. His curly, sandy hair shot through with streaks of auburn was tied back from his square rugged features by a thin strip of leather. He possessed an air of authority they had seen demonstrated. But, having deployed his men, upon turning back to the chamber's silent, watchful occupants, his manner was one of affability. Strolling past Keeble, he gave him a hearty slap on the back.

"This be Nick Condor," introduced the little man, grinning from ear to ear.

"Well, Nicolas O'Reilly, truth t' tell." With an impish gleam in his green eyes, he added, "Condor does a better job." He looked at the driftwood Catherine was still holding in a determined manner. "Ah, sweet darlin', y' makin' me awful nervous wi' that jetsam."

"'e's 'ere t' 'elp," pointed out Keeble, persuasively.

"How convenient," pointed out Catherine, still holding to her defensive pose. "How is it you are here?" she asked, defiantly meeting Condor's interested gaze.

He squirmed in elaborate embarrassment. "Ah, well. If it'll make y' see I'm no threat, I'd best come clean t' bein' nosy."

"About?" Yet Catherine already knew the answer.

"Why, about you, sweet darlin'," Condor responded, with a courtly bow. "T'aint every day I gets t' meet a bride. Especially the Beast's."

She was immediately reminded of how Shadiz had made it plain he did not want anyone in the Mediterranean believing she was his whore. It had been just before they had entered St Mary's Church to be married.

Catherine slowly lowered the driftwood. In spite of Condor's timely appearance at Shannlarrey, she had to admit she sensed no underlying threat from him. Only a real desire to help. And immense curiosity.

"When *Sea Witch* an' *San Juan* berthed at Formentera after sailing y' 'ere, folks were fallin' over theirsens t' tell me 'e'd married you."

"Yes, he did," murmured Catherine, stiffly. "To protect my reputation."

Condor snorted. "Never 'eard tell o' the Beast givin' a flying fart, if you'll pardon language, for anyone's reputation." Giving her a frank, admiring look, he smiled. "Until now." And again he bowed to her.

Faced with his acceptance of Shadiz's uncharacteristic gallantry, Catherine was hard pressed to mask the pain of rejection caused by Shadiz sending her away to France. Added to which was the terrible doubts due to her discovery of the information he had gathered about the Fylingdales Estate. With studied nonchalance, she walked across the chamber to Lucinda and Peter, smiling reassuringly at both mother and son. Peter was far more easy to convince than the young Romany woman. Her slender back remained apprehensively rigid and her hold on her squirming son had not slacken.

Condor followed her. "An' this must be big fella's wife," he said, pleasantly. Coming to a leisurely halt, gazing at Peter, he hesitated before adding, "An' 'is son." He acknowledge both with another of his courtly bows. "I'm also pleased to be at your service." He straightened, winking at the boy.

"So what now?" asked Catherine.

"We wait," answered Condor, strolling around the chamber.

"Shouldn't you be up there, helping," she challenged.

He halted before her portrait. "They can manage. Besides, I'm 'ere to guard you, sweet darlin'." He half-turned her way, indicating her image. "This is you?"

"Apparently." She moved unobtrusively to block his view of the paperwork on the high, nautical-type desk. "It was your ship I saw early this afternoon, wasn't it?"

He was still looking up at the painting. "It was that," he answered. "You're younger there?"

Catherine regarded herself with mixed emotions. "I would be about twelve."

He gave her a sidelong look. "You'd no idea 'e'd done it of y'? I know 'e's nifty with a brush."

"'e painted my father."

Condor nodded. "Sir Roger, 'e spoke o' 'im. Seemed like a good man." His considering gaze remained on her. "I was sorry t' 'ere o' 'is passin'."

Catherine nodded. She needed a different subject. "How is it you know of this place?" she asked, indicating their unusual, torch lit surroundings.

He gave a mischievous grin. "Ah, well," he began, bending towards her conspiratorially. "A couple o' times, I've seen the Beast disappear into a cave on the beach. I just thought it were a way up t' grounds of the chateau. I didn't expect this. Did you?"

64

She was about to answer him when his expression altered. She sensed the sudden stillness in him, and watched the warrior emerge from beneath the geniality. He was looking up at the two men at the head of the steps. Following his gaze, she realised the Negroes had raised their weapons, apparently hearing something she could not as yet discern.

Condor reacted to their heightened vigilance. He stepped in front of her, a lithe move that had a protective prowess. At the same time, he drew one of the three swords hung about his person. Keeble jumped to obey his commanding gesture. The little man grabbed hold of Lucinda and Peter and shepherded them closer to Condor.

They all stood in silence for several moments, listening.

"Belay!"

The word was muffled but distinguishable. Condor, Keeble and the two Negroes visibly relaxed. None of the four men reacted aggressively when the sound of the false panel being moved echoed in the stone chamber.

Condor was sheathing his sword when Junno appeared at the head of the steps. For a moment, the Irishman appeared to regret his action. The torchlight wavered in the rush of fresh air that accompanied the big man's arrival. Nodding in acknowledgement to the two burly Negroes, his anxious attention quickly slide past them as he began to descend the narrow steps. Peter escaped from his mother and ran to his father. Junno swept him up in his arms. He quickly reached his wife and put an arm around her waist. Lucinda leant against him. Over her head bent upon his chest, he looked across at Catherine. Shaky with relief, she smiled in answer to his questioning gaze.

Having assured himself of their safety, his wary attention settled on Nick Condor.

"Nice t' see y' again, big fella."

"Y' lads were a good 'elp."

Condor's greeting seemed overly bright as opposed to Junno's unusual coolness.

If the two men had issues, they both seemed loathe to air them in the wake of Lynette's defeated assault on Shannlarrey.

Saying nothing, Condor looked on as Junno scanned his cousin's private chamber with something akin to reluctance. When he saw the portrait of Catherine, shades of awkwardness became more pronounced in his large, round face. His gaze leapt to her. Whereas Lucinda's reaction to the portrait had been to recoil in horror, Junno appeared embarrassed for having inadvertently stumbled upon evidence of his strange cousin's secret obsession. His gaze accusing, his attention returned to Condor

The Irishman raised his arms in supplication. "I ain't touched a thing, big fella. I've only stared in awe at his lovely bride. The Beast's a lucky fella."

Catherine made an unladylike noise. She was fast coming to the conclusion that Nick Condor was a charmer; a dangerous one at that, she had no doubt. Preparing to quit the stone chamber, she glimpsed the brief look the two men exchanged.

Once they were all in the library, she turned to Junno. "Are there many who need attention? You included," she asked, studying the nasty gash in his arm and the deep scratch in his right cheek just below his eye. Blood oozed upon his sweaty features.

"There were a goodly number o' 'em," he admitted, glancing at Condor. "We reckon some were mercenaries recruited in France t' bolstered their numbers. The majority were from Fylingdales though, I reckon."

"But you sent 'em away with their tails between their legs," put in Condor, leading the way out of the library. "Good on y'."

Junno did not appear amused. "'ow come y' be 'ere?"

Condor gave an exaggerated cough. He glanced sideward at Catherine. "I just wanted t' make sure, y' were all settled."

"Right," muttered Junno, grimly.

CHAPTER NINE

Coming Ways

Her footsteps dragging, her shoulders wearily slumped, Catherine walked to the door of the chamber. Opening it, she looked out into the long corridor, and blinked at the honey glow of evening sunshine pouring through the series of narrow, tall windows. With a mixture of relief and guilt, she saw the corridor was empty apart from Nick Condor, Keeble and Peter occupying the polished parquet floor. Condor was leaning against the immaculate white wall beneath a window. Keeble and Peter were sitting cross-legged nearby. Peter was fascinated by how regularly the ball of wax slipped like magic from first one to the other of the three silver goblets Condor had appropriated from an elaborate cabinet further down the corridor. Keeble kept urging the tousle-haired, dark-eyed youngster to make the correct choice, but try as he may, Peter could only find the ball when Condor gave him a helpful wink in the right direction.

The Irishman looked up at Catherine and, inclining his head, gave her a smile of gratitude for what she had done for his men.

She acknowledged the gesture, and then turned back into the chamber that had been transformed into a makeshift infirmary. It was far grander than the closest-like chamber she had used at the Lodge. Yet whether it be in England or France the injuries were disquietingly similar.

For the past three hours, she had attended to a series of them. The most serious of necessity first. They had included retrieving musket shot from arms and legs and in one sadly fatal instance the chest. Then there had been the sword wounds and the broken bones. Last of all the damage inflicted by wild, slashing cuts and pathway grazes. Her tireless ministrations had used up most of her stock of herbs she had brought with her from the Lodge.

The haunting guilt remained. She was acutely aware that the men of differing nationalities had suffered because of her. Added to the burden she laboured under was the knowledge that Lucinda and Peter were now in danger. All because, if not protected, she was apparently the harbinger of doom for Shadiz.

Yet, now that the hours of healing had come to an end, she was once again prey to a harrowing suspicion. Were all of them being duped? Her most of all.

All along, it seemed, Shadiz had been planning to strike at Fylingdales. To reclaim what he considered to be his birthright? The information gleaned from the exhaustive paperwork she had stumbled upon in the stone chamber below the chateau gave every indication as to why he had returned to England and become Prince Rupert's mercenary commander in the North-East of Yorkshire during the Civil War. Plagued by doubts, she failed to realise she was standing in mid-chamber and staring into space until Lucinda spoke.

"Yes, indeed. All done," she replied, giving Lucinda and Junno a tired smile.

Throughout, Lucinda had been invaluable, mixing the herbs and administering them and applying poultices. Junno had been an immense support when the wounded had found it hard to cope with the treatment to relieve their suffering.

Lucinda removed her bloodstained apron. Immediately a servant took it from her and the one Catherine had worn. The male servants and a few of the females ones had been a constant, helpful presence clearing up after each patient, supplying water and cloths. Catherine was at pains to thank all of them.

"Y' both look done in," Junno commented, putting his arms around the two young women. "Both o' y' go an' get some rest."

"Yes," murmured Catherine. "That would be nice."

"Peter?"

"I'll see t' 'im," he assured his wife as he ushered them out into the corridor. "'e seems t' be well teken care o', anyways."

Condor got to his feet in one fluid movement, remarkably unhampered by his weapons, as they approached. Peter jumped up beside him. "Da y' tr!."

"Go," ordered Junno, smiling.

Lucinda and Catherine walked slowly up the elegant, sweeping staircase. They paused at the door of Catherine's chamber. She swayed.

"You look drained," announced Lucinda, taking her by the arm and leading her through the door. "Why don't y' lay down."

Catherine shook her head. Stupid tears were too close to be hidden from Lucinda's keen gaze. "I need a bit of fresh air," she muttered.

"I don't reckon 'tis wise venturing out wi' all them men around," responded Lucinda, still holding Catherine's arm. She glanced at the open window. "Why don't we pull up a couple o' chairs."

Moving the tapestry-backed seats proved harder than they had expected. They were large enough to curl up in but incredibly heavy. Working together, they succeeded in dragging them across the chamber, and even managed a few cheery complaints in the process. Eventually, they were able to sink thankfully down into the velvet cushions. They sat in silence for a few minutes, appreciating the cool, evening breeze wafting through the open windows. The after affects of the day's events stole ponderously between them.

Lucinda looked across at Catherine. "Y' can 'eal 'em, can't y'?" she asked, softly. "Just like Mamma. I mean not just wi' 'erbs. But like she does."

The renegade tears crept down Catherine's pale cheeks. She shook her head in mute denial, making her untidy fair-white hair ripple in the dipping glow of sunset.

Moving with quiet grace, Lucinda slipped out of her chair and knelt beside Catherine's, taking gentle hold of both her hands. Her long black hair spilt down her slender back as she looked up. Her attractive, dusky face filled with compassion, she said, "It ain't nawt t' get upset about."

Catherine did not want to be anything like Mamma Petra, the White Witch and matriarch of the tribe of Romany her father had allowed to pass the winters at Nafferton Garth.

Possessing extraordinary gifts of healing and prophesy, she had taught Catherine how to heal the sick and wounded with medicinal herbs, beginning with the injured animals the young Catherine had cared for. Over time the motive for the old, Romany woman tutoring a Gorgio had become clear. On a fateful voyage from the Low Countries, Catherine had been forced to use all the skills of healing after the White Witch's grandson had gone into a burning building to save a Dutchwoman, because Catherine had begged him to.

She had gone much further than simply healing Shadiz with potions. On a cold, night-time deck in the middle of a wintry North Sea, she had used a fledgling power, assisted by the twin stones of Romany legend. Her jet pendant and the moonstone he wore.

She did appreciate her flair for healing, and was grateful to Mamma Petra for recognising her ability to do so. Nevertheless, the fact remained, over time she had developed from an enthusiastic child to a young woman increasingly wary of her strange, blind mentor. Her heightened sensitivity had detected a malevolence completely at odds with the old, Romany woman's incredible capability to heal. Nor had she been comfortable witnessing the manner in which Mamma Petra manipulated people. God help her, she had discovered such a chilling attribute ran in the family.

"Those men risked their lives for us. I did nothing other than ease their pain as best I could," she commented, wearily.

"Y' do much more," insisted Lucinda, carefully. "Aye, those men did risk their lives t' protect us. But they'll 'eal much faster because I saw each one o' 'em receive a part o' y'r special magic. Just like I've seen Mamma give t' folk."

Again Catherine shook her head. "I do not wish to be like her."

"No," murmured Lucinda, despite her confident assessment. "Y' don't."

It was because she had cared for the tribe's matriarch, even before her and Junno had been married, that she had been able to give Catherine such efficient help during the long afternoon. Like her, Lucinda had toiled under Mamma Petra's strict guidance. Both of them were well acquainted with the old woman's acid tongue.

"Not even Mamma could bring 'im back at Whitby," Lucinda

said, so softly her awkward words were barely audible. Her pained gaze slipped downwards.

It had been the beginning of the end of Catherine's time at the old Lodge deep within Stillingfleet Forest. The evening they had all celebrated Tom Wright's life after burying him next to his wife, Shadiz had held her; certainly not like the guardian he was supposed to be. Instead, there had been a release of hitherto repressed emotions which had flared between them. And, afterwards, he had disappeared from the Lodge. Only to be found by Lucinda at Whitby, and to be poisoned by her. Mamma Petra had cured him physically. But it had been Catherine who had brought him back from the brink, once more with the aid of the jet and moon stones.

A sudden thought hit home hard, making her heart thud painfully in her chest. She sat bolt upright. The dying rays of sunset glistened in the frozen tears on her startled face. Her trembling hand rose to the jet pendant.

"He knows," she whispered.

★

Junno glanced up at the open window of Catherine's chamber as he and Condor strolled around the shattered grounds, taking in the damage to their surroundings.

The extensive gardens bore the evidence of just how fierce the fighting had been that afternoon. Ornamental bushes had been trampled down, flowerbeds crushed underfoot and statues overturned or damaged beyond repair. The lawns had been torn up in several places. There were traces of blood everywhere, on the flag-stone paths, the rustic benches and in the fountain. There was even blood splattered on the white walls of the chateau. Several of its windows had been shattered by musket shot. Nevertheless, no hostile intent had managed to penetrate its interior.

Having seen off the enemy, the men from both England and Formentera stood or sat in companionable groups amongst the damage, talking among themselves in the peaceful evening. Although he was miles away, the Master was their solidarity. A fascinating mixture of races and attire, with a well-armed toughness in common, many were nursing their wounds, some worse than others. They were presently being served a meal by flitting servants, some of whom also bore the marks of the afternoon's hostilities.

Junno and Condor were being accompanied by Peter. When he grew tired his father scooped him up into his powerful arms. Philippe made his way over to them. The thin, reserved Frenchman's limp appeared much worse, caused by an attacker who had thought to benefit from his disability. There was a ragged gash in his chin. His raw knuckles were covered in one of Catherine's soothing salves.

Keeble hobbled up to them, informing Junno that Catherine and Lucinda had been served a meal and were both resting in Catherine's chamber.

Reassured, the big Romany nodded.

Condor said, "They both deserve to take their ease. If y' pardon me sayin', big fella. Catherine certainly got a sweet way o' makin' a body feel better."

Junno looked sharply at the Irish man.

Laughing, Condor held up his hands in a defensive manner. "'ave no fear. I'd not tread in that direction. Reckon the Beast'd toss me in Old Nick's handcart in a second."

After Junno's noncommittal grunt, the three men walked on in silence for awhile in the balmy evening.

Eventually, frowning, Nick Condor mused, "Keeble explained t' me why this Lynette's after Catherine. A dear sweet sprat t' catch a mighty mackerel. But 'ow the devil did bastard get t' know about 'er in first place?"

"Good question," growled Junno.

Condor regarded the other man through narrow eyes, his geniality having vanished. "Well, don't look my way," he said, coldly, coming to a halt. "I knew nothing about lass 'til 'e sent Keeble for Sea Witch."

Junno had also stopped abruptly.

Philippe retraced several limping footsteps. "I am quite certain we all seek to give the women protection," he said, quietly, looking to first one and then the other of the tense men. "Oui?"

After a further moment of belligerently studying one another,

Junno gave a curt nod. Condor appeared mollified despite an irritable twitch of his mouth as the big man turned away.

They wandered to the cliff edge where the sound of the sea became more pronounced. The riding lights upon the tall masts of Condor's ship, anchored a mile or so offshore, were beginning to glow in the gathering dusk.

"They'll 'ave another go," he remarked. "Y' know that."

"I'll get a message t' 'im," responded Junno, thoughtfully.

"Shadiz'll come," said Peter, sleepily.

Surprised, the men looked at the boy, cradled against his large father.

He opened his eyes. "Shadiz loves Catherine," he continued, surprising the men further. "'e looks at 'er like da looks at ma." His expression became a childish caricature of an adult's adoring gaze.

Junno, Condor and Keeble burst out laughing. Even Philippe's serious countenance broke into an unrestrained smile.

"Shadiz scowls when anyone gets close t' 'er," Peter added, warming to the limelight. Only this time the expression in his black eyes and on his dark features drew a different response.

There was a slight pause. Junno suppressed his reaction to the knowing silence of the other men. He spoke gently to his confused son, "Come on, y' little imp. 'Tis about y'r bedtime."

"Oh, da!" Peter objected.

"I'll give y' a lift," volunteered Keeble.

Wriggling away from his father, Peter let out a whoop of joy. Keeble's piggy-backs had become legendary among the children of the women from Glaisdale who served the Master's men at the Lodge.

Condor continued to watch Peter, his gaze speculative, as the boy rode away towards the well-lit chateau on Keeble's lumpy back. Upon turning back to the other two men, the big Romany ignored him. After suffering a stern glance from Philippe, Condor kept his own counsel. The three of them stood without speaking on the grassy cliff edge, looking out to sea.

Nick Condor broke the reflective silence. "Y' know, big fella. I reckon 'e was pretty desperate to send the sweet lass 'ere to Shannlarrey."

Junno said nothing. He continued to gaze out across the calm, darkening waters of the Mediterranean.

Condor sighed. "Toil with me 'ere, big fella," he urged.

Looking down at the Irishman, Junno drew a resigned breath.

A slight, scholarly figure, Philippe had unobtrusively put himself between the two battle-hardened men.

"He knew you'd guard Catherine, and Lucinda and Peter, wi' y'r life. An' so would the men he sent across water wi' y'. But look at this place." Condor flung out an arm which encompassed the luminous chateau and occupied grounds. "It's hardly a fortress, is it?"

Junno's unwavering gaze remained bent on him. "What be y'r point?"

Condor went on, "Hell, I'm not sayin' you didn't do y'r best against them bastards. But, y' must admit, our arrival just might o' tipped balance. If it ain't been for the fact I got tidings o' some damned odd movements toward 'ere, we might o' come too late t' cook nuts." He shrugged regretfully. "But me an' lot can't stay 'ere indefinitely. And, like as not, bastards'll come again, more'n likely in greater numbers. And when they do, because o' today's strike, they'll know y'r weaknesses."

"So what d' y' suggest?" snapped Junno. There was a hint of desperation in his rumbling tones.

Condor's brown eyes travelled over the men a little way off. "He must've been desperate," he murmured.

"Aye, t' get Rauni t' safety," growled Junno. "If y' weren't so wrapped up in prowlin' seas 'untin' for booty y'd realise there's a war goin' on over in England." He drew a long, aggravated breath. "An' ov'er there, even 'ere, I ain't sure, there's some drabaneysapa's informin' that barripoari Lynette."

"Jesus wept blood. You're like 'im, spouting off in y'r mother tongue," commented Condor. Nevertheless, he grasped the significance of Junno's bitter words. "More reason we've t' work this out between us, big fella. We can't wait for direction from the Beast. Besides," he added, studying the big Romany, "Peter believes 'e'll come."

"Me son...."

"'is son," interrupted Condor softly. He held up a hand to halt Philippe's conciliatory shift. "You must o' saved Lucinda, or her an' Peter'd not be here now."

Junno's expression altered. His rigid stillness was telling.

"My wife wasn't so lucky," admitted Condor, in the same calm, quiet manner. He gave a rueful shrug. "Well, I'd intended makin' an' honest woman out o' 'ere." His green eyes grew misty. "She was the dusky, almond-eyed beauty of every man's dream." Then his gaze sharpened on Junno. "Y' can make a good guess what happened."

Junno grunted as if he had suffered a physical blow. There was sympathy mixed with understanding in his gaze.

Condor returned the sentiment with a regretful smile. "'e is...."

"Flawed," put in Philippe. When the other two men looked at him, he continued, "My sister was beautiful. All men adored her. Except him. At least not until she was older. Dying." He indicated the isolated cove below them. "He carried her down there. We watched over her until she passed. Afterwards, he told me how he had kept her safe."

"Ah, my friend," said Nick Condor, resting a gentle hand on the Frenchman's thin shoulder. "All kings are flawed in some way. Their courtiers mask it with their loyalty."

The three men were silent for several pensive minutes.

"So," began Condor, at length, "We need t' keep 'em all safe. Agreed?"

Junno stirred. "An' 'ow d' y' reckon we do that?"

Condor visibly braced himself in an almost comical manner. But there was a definite seriousness in his unflinching regard. "We sail everyone to Formentera."

"Absolutely not," responded Junno, forcefully.

"They stay at the Casa with Marie an' the twins. Peter'd love company o' 'is own age," continued Condor, persuasively. "They'll be at the other side o' island."

Junno glared at him, knowing at first hand what the island boasted. Slave markets. Hostages held for ransom. Lawless men only kept in check by Shadiz's unrivalled, corsair-master authority, and, for all his apparent easy-going manner, Nick Condor's presence. The dangerous chameleon.

"There is some merit in Nick's suggestion," put in Philippe, after a few moments of thought. "No one, however deep their purse, would risk an assault on Formentera. It would be a suicidal act."

Looking grimly stubborn, Junno said nothing.

Condor appealed to him. "By sending Catherine here. By marrying her. The Beast was giving me a clear message. He knew I'd come." He gave a self-deprecatory shrug. "He knew I wouldn't be able t' resist. An' 'e knew it'd more'n likely be about the time Lynette'd make a move against Shannlarrey. Because he knew I'd pick up information o' what clouds were gatherin' around the place. Y' know as well as me he's a past master at second guessing folk. Y' really must toil wi' me 'ere, big fella."

Junno responded by striding away a few paces from the two men..

Condor looked towards Philippe, raising his eyebrows in a mixture of irritation and resignation. Philippe remained outwardly impassive.

Junno stared out across the whispering sea, being overlaid with darkness. Experiencing the debilitating feeling of being all at sea, he simply did not know what to do for the best. Shadiz would condemn him for taking Rauni and his family to Formentera, with all its brutality. But he also knew it would be the absolute undoing of his cousin if anything happened to Rauni. All he had to do was weigh the pros and cons. If only... He swung back around to face the other two men.

His hopes raised, indicating his ship riding at anchor, Condor stated. "*Sea Pearl* will get 'em there safe."

"Aye," retorted Junno, "An' what's t' stop y' sailin' t' England an' sellin' us to Lynette."

"I'm deeply hurt," Condor remonstrated, hand on heart. His expression altered into one of unmistakable sincerity. "I'm a courtier, big fella. Just like you."

CHAPTER TEN

Knotty Matters

"He has done what!" exclaimed Francois Lynette.

For once, the urbane Frenchman was utterly astounded.

Standing before him, the captain of his sea-going hunter, *Endeavour*, squirmed in apprehensive embarrassment. The large, red-haired fellow had lost his renowned jollity. His usually ruddy, weathered face was ashen and bathed in nervous sweat. "They came at us like a storm from 'ell," he explained, defensively. "Most o' lads were on...um...shore leave." He shrugged his powerful shoulders. "We weren't given a cat in 'ell's chance. I'm sorry, sir." he finished, mortified by his own spectacular failure.

During the frosty pause, in which normality could be wistfully heard, Lynette regarded the other man with lip-curling condemnation. His narrowed eyes, slivers of sapphire-blue ice, impaled Alf Logan. Although the shame-faced captain was taller by a head than his leader, the impact of Lynette's lordly, authoritative bearing caused him to drop his gaze down to his muddy boots.

It was with a measure of relief Logan viewed Lady Hellena's entrance into the elegant, sunlit chamber overlooking the Quadrangle at Fylingdales Hall. A straight-laced, diminutive figure resplendent in hissing black silk, she walked briskly towards her younger brother. "What is amiss?" she demanded, her critical gaze raking over the unfortunate captain.

Francois Lynette threw up his hands in disgust. "This cretin has lost the *Endeavour* to that infernal gypsy."

"It were so sudden," mumbled Captain Logan.

"When?" snapped Lady Hellena, ignoring him.

"Yesterday," Lynette replied, glaring at the other man.

"At Scarborough?"

"Yes," affirmed Lynette and Logan together in different tones of voice.

Although she was less than half his size, Captain Logan shrank from Lady Hellena's accusing blast. Any hope of feminine sympathy he had entertained vanished, leaving him floundering in the mud of deeper torment.

Her fair-haired brother, immaculate in purple velvet, took an irate turn around the French furniture in the stately chamber, his handsome features flushed with rage, his jewelled fists balled behind his rigid back.

"Why did you not put in to Hull?" Lady Hellena demanded.

"'Twould o' been safer, to be sure, milady," admitted Logan, miserably. "Even wi' Royalists' siege o' port. But the rudder were actin' up again. So I thought it wiser to put into Scarborough an'...." His voice trailed away into a difficult silence.

Lynette came to an agitated halt beside his coldly condemning sister. "That is a damned lame excuse. The rudder was working perfectly after its recent overhaul. Then to compound your incompetence, you allowed the crew shore-leave beneath the castle, for god sake. No, better still, you allowed the bastard gypsy to sail away on the *Endeavour!*"

Unable to tolerate Logan's cringing presence a moment longer, Lynette dismissed him with a sharp gesture that promised further reprisals. While the captain shut the door of the chamber with overly quiet deference, Lynette turned to Lady Hellena. "The bastard's gone to France," he rasped. "It is the only possible answer."

"Well, of course," she retorted.

Disgruntled by her censure, Lynette flung himself down into a damask covered chair. "Damn the wretched fellow."

Lady Hellena seated herself with more decorum on the settle. "One thing this sorry business has shown up," she murmured, reflectively, her French accent more pronounced than her brother's.

He gave her a moody glance. "Yes. Logan wants stringing up?"

"The gypsy is acting spontaneously."

"And look where it has got him," snapped Lynette, with a frustrated gesture. "Half way to France in our ship!"

"Someone must have alerted him to our undertaking," she pointed out, with a degree of frosty patience.

"I shall personally dispose of them when I find out who," promised Lynette. He took a repressive breath. "We deliberately kept the Endeavour in England and instead hired other vessels to take the men across to France so that he would not suspect our intention. And looked what has happened!"

"You are missing the point."

Annoyed at her superior tone, his answer dripped sarcasm, "Well, do enlighten me, soeur."

There was a vicious gleam in her gaze as it focused beyond him, out of the chamber's window. "Whatever has occurred over the past few months, it has to be said, the gypsy has combated with feral cunning. Yet, once he heard of our mission to France, what did he do? Methinks he simply boarded the nearest available ship, which happened to be the *Endeavour*. What is more, there is little doubt he sailed away without first considering how to respond to the force we have dispatched, and our ability to procure reinforcement from Normandy to overcome the men he sent to guard Catherine Verity." Her severe, aristocratic beauty grew scornful. "If it were anyone else, I would say panic set in."

"You are forgetting the brute has walked into Satan's lair already for Catherine Verity, on more than one occasion," pointed out Lynette, sourly. "Possibly emerging unscathed due to his acquaintance with the Devil. Moreover, you are overlooking Nick Condor. If the Irishman were to come to his aid."

"I doubt very much the gypsy would contemplate taking her to the Balearic Island. That is why he chose the chateau of Shannlarrey, even with its disadvantages."

When his sister was called away to deal with a domestic matter, alone in the chamber, Francois Lynette rose and sauntered across to the window. It gave an unrestricted view of the sunlit fountain splashing in the Quadrangle. His thoughts elsewhere, he leant a slender hip against the deep window seat.

Above all, he had to spare Hellena from more dire misfortunes. For beneath the stern, noble demeanour, beyond the obsessive desire to defeat the gypsy, deep sadness reigned supreme within her battered heart.

He recalled his older sister as an extraordinarily beautiful, fun-loving young woman. He had already been living on Malta for several years when she had written to him about the wonderful, handsome Englishman she had met at the French court. It had been clear she had adored him at first sight; enough to leave her beloved family and country to live in the wilds of North-East England. And, despite its drawbacks for someone accustomed to far grander places, she would have been happy in her new husband's environment, the letters she had sent him provided the evidence. But then, slowly a terrible wistfulness had crept into her writing. Only when she had requested his presence some years later to assist in the running of the estate had he fully understood the true measure of the unhappiness she had endured.

She had married Sir Richard of Fylingdales for love, but soon discovered the feeling was one sided. Shortly after becoming pregnant with her first child, she had learned about Gianca, her husband's gypsy mistress who had lived with him at the Hall. Gianca had died in childbirth. Her son lived on the estate with Tom Wright and his wife Janet, who had been present at the premature birth. When Hellena's demands to see the child removed from the estate had begun to threaten his unborn, legitimate heir, Sir Richard had sent the five-year-old away to York. Although he had not said another word to her about the boy, she became convinced of his resentment, especially when the child disappeared from his sister's establishment in the city.

Much to her dismay and lasting sadness, Hellena's first encounter with her husband's bastard son was when he had entered the Hall one stormy night and placed his dead father at her feet. She had poured scorn on whatever Tom Wright had tried to tell her, blaming the gypsy for the death of Sir Richard. Thereafter, she had striven with every resource available to her to bring the notorious murderer to justice.

Yet worse was to come, which would reinforce her craving for revenge.

Three years after Richard had been born, Hellena had given birth to a girl, Elizabeth.

At the time, he, Francois, had been paying a fleeting visit to England on business for the Knights of St John, and managed a rare visit to Fylingdales Hall before returning to Malta. Elizabeth's christening had been brought forward in order for him to become her godfather. During that brief sojourn to the wilds of Yorkshire, he had been struck by the change in his sister. Whether it had been the influence of the bleak moors upon which Hellena lived or the dour attitude of her husband, he had been unsure. What had been certain, the sweet baby Elizabeth had lightened his sister's spirit far more than the presence of her sickly son.

That beautiful young light had been cruelly extinguished at twelve-year-old. What had made Elizabeth's violation and murder the more harder to bear was that it had been perpetrated by the same foul brute who was responsible for the death of Hellena's husband.

Elizabeth's death had touch him far more than anyone else's, even Gerald Carey's, who had been recently dispatched by the same vicious hand.

Lynette straightened, simmering with renewed rage.

The gypsy had come back to England at the start of the Civil War. To make matters worse, he had made his base upon the isolated boundary of Fylingdales Estate in Stillingfleet Forest. His arrogant proximity was a horrendous reminder of tragedy, along with a deadly threat.

He had to admit the gypsy was undeniably clever. The man had dragged himself out of the gutter and, by all accounts, the sewers of Islam to become a charismatic leader with a large, cosmopolitan following. A corsair warlord who straggled the West and the East.

Lynette grimaced, recalling his own reaction to Shadiz's strangely compelling darkness.

He wondered if, despite his passionate protestations, Richard had been affected by his improbable half-brother's black magic? The boy had set out on his clandestine quest determined to find a way to bring down the gypsy from within his own substantial company. Yet, of late, he seemed to have deviated. The reports he and Hellena had received from their deep placed Judas kept them informed of events, making them aware Richard was likely to become a loose cannon. There was little doubt that Catherine Verity's presence at the old hunting Lodge had some bearing on his present conduct. It certainly appeared to have created increased friction between Richard and the gypsy. Conversely, also putting him at loggerheads with his mother and himself. Ruefully, Lynette had to admit that the boy, who seemed to have matured during his time in his half-brother's company, had not had the smoothest of rides in life.

Whatever Richard's motive for acquiring an irritating waywardness, Lynette was convince his nephew understood better than most his half-brother was a sadistic killer and rapist, from whom no one was safe.

A thought dawn on him "Mon Dieu!" he muttered, startled. "That's why he sent the girl away. Why he did not keep her in Stillingfleet Forest."

★

Two days out of Scarborough, and Benjamin had just about got his sea-legs. In mitigation, he had realised when stepping, or rather making an aggressive leap, onto the deck of Francois Lynette's ship the *Endeavour*, as she had gently rocked beside the quay in the East Coast port, that it was the first time he had experienced the rhythmic sensation of a ship.

It would not have been if only he had been allowed to accompany his father and two older brothers to Malta several years previously. At the time, he had been highly resentful at having been left at home to complete his studies while they had gone to the island to collect his young cousins after both their parents had died in a boating accident in the Grand Harbour. Yet had he voyaged with his family, he, too, would have probably become fodder for the swords of murderous corsairs.

Prior to the start of the Civil War, Benjamin and Richard Massone had been determined to bring Nick Condor and the Master to justice. Both men were renown for their crimes throughout the

Mediterranean, and in England, as far as Richard was concerned. But before they could embark on such an ambitious venture, they had been obliged to demonstrate their loyalty to their endangered king by volunteering to serve on Prince Rupert's staff. As a result, both men came into contact with the Master when he became the Prince's mercenary commander in Yorkshire.

The unexpected association had differing outcomes for Richard and Benjamin. Taking the decision to join his half-brother's force for reasons that were not only of his own, had hardened Richard's unforgiving animosity, whereas Benjamin's unlooked-for preoccupation with the man Shadiz and not the notorious legend had resulted in him also serving the Master. While doing so, by irrepressible degrees he had found himself laying the blame for the tragedy that had befallen his family solely on Nick Condor. His attachment, which had driven a wedge between Richard and himself, meant he had readily jumped into the unknown by becoming a member of the boarding party at Scarborough.

Two strenuous days later, and he had become absorbed in learning the ropes, literally. His ongoing tuition was being conducted in a companionable manner. A latecomer to their tightly-knit company, Benjamin had established his place among the Master's men by his quiet, genial character. This allowed for good-humoured jesting at his amateurism and brusque praise for his seafaring efforts while the *Endeavour*, sleek as any corsair ship, ploughed through the North Sea on a southerly heading.

All of the Master's men had been willingly to join the voyage. But after Lynette's skeleton-crew had been ejected in a brief attack bearing all the hallmarks of the Master's corsair expertise, only those among his men whose seamanship had contributed to the rescue of the *Eagle* when the merchantman had floundered in Mercy Cove were recruited by him, with the notable exception of Benjamin. Their leader's demanding presence gave the voyage a sense of urgency, obliging every man aboard to ensure each energising breath of wind was captured by the taut canvas.

The rumour inadvertently began by Benjamin when he had failed to deny their probes had developed into real concern among the hastily assembled crew for the safety of the well-bred sixteen-year-old girl who had lived among them at the Lodge. They had found her approachable and engaging. At one time or another, she had ministered to their hurts with an astonishing maturity. They were all aware she had made an impact on their enigmatic leader.

The knowledge heightened the speculation already rife among them that his reaction was not due simply to his anger at being thwarted. Though how he knew Catherine was in danger baffled them.

During crystal blue days and star bright nights, Shadiz remained topside, more often than not a phantom-like presence at the helm, the loyal mastiff at his heels.

CHAPTER ELEVEN

Flight to Self

Richard Massone raced through Stillingfleet Forest. Desperation nipped at his heels.

His chest hurt abominably. Each breath he struggled to take came in a wheezing spurt and felt as if it was being dragged over jagged rocks. His pounding heart matched the rhythm of his urgent pace. Yet he would not surrender to either the hunters or his overtaxed body while his quest to locate his bastard half-brother was paramount.

The narrow track he had followed after managing to slip away from the Lodge had soon disappeared into the maddening confusion of thick undergrowth and close-knit trees. Cursing his misfortune at not being able to follow the more reliable track to Glasidale due to its exposed nature, he had no option but to beat his way through the forest maze. In revenge low-hanging branches battered his sweat-bathed face and tore at his clothes. Undeterred, he continued to weave an erratic path around oak, beech and ash and stumble through their discarded detritus that more often than not concealed thick, twisted roots. Distorted by his frantic bid for freedom, it appeared to him the trees formed barriers in a rooted effort to thwart his escape.

Disturbed by his reckless intrusion, the feathered and furry inhabitants of the forest had abandoned their perches and secret pathways. In the wake of their own quick flights, the forest had become eerily quiet, save for the rasping of human presence loud in Richard's ears. Even the evening sunlight, when it succeeded in pouring a honey glow through the thick canopy of leaves, hindered his search for a viable route.

Suddenly his way was block by the weed-infested carcass of a tree brought down by the vengeance of a past storm. He skidded to a halt, fighting for breath. In no mood to suffer a reversal, he sought an alternative route, only to be confronted by another, more formidable barrier.

Romany loomed up around him without stirring the heavy air.

Startled, Richard nonetheless reacted with the practise ease he had acquired as a member of his half-brother's mercenary force. He swung the longbow off his back and notched an arrow. Thus armed, he slowly made a threatening turn within the detaining circle, aiming at the ominously silent, dark-skinned men. They made no hostile move in response. Yet in the months he had been with his half-blood leader, Richard had come to appreciate the impressive capabilities of the elusive nomads.

In the end it was not the Romany who ended the challenging pause.

Led by Danny Murphy, men from the Lodge were heard before they appeared through the trees. They made their way to where the Romany held Richard in check. Clearly, they were not in the best of humours after ploughing through Stillingfleet after him.

"Disarm the bastard, then!"

The whiplash of Murphy's impatient voice ended the heavy breathing interval in a manner not anticipated by him.

Keeping to their united silence, after an imperceptible signal missed by the Gorgio, the Romany reformed into a line between Richard and the men from the Lodge.

Murphy's scowl deepened at their unexpected action.

Richard was puzzled by it.

Dismayed, he felt a coughing fit well up within him despite his best efforts to stifle the familiar urge. It burst forth, shaking his thin frame with its potency. His breathing, already greatly depleted by the exertions of his flight from the Lodge, became excruciating. The notched longbow slipped out of his hands. As if night had suddenly descended, the surrounding forest grew dim. The last thing he was aware of before collapsing in strong arms was Imre Panin informing Danny Murphy that the Master's half-brother was wanted.

Richard regained consciousness slowly. He instinctively braced himself against the chronic discomfit which had resulted in him pitching into senselessness, but discovered through a muzzy haze that his body, though feeling heavy with weakness, possessed none of its usual painful complaints.

The realisation that he was laid on the ground, softened by bracken, alerted him to his whereabouts. A light breeze had sprung up and was rustling the leaves of the forest. The dancing hues of a fire penetrated his flickering eyelids. Surreptitiously testing his limbs, made him aware they were covered.

"Open thine eyes. Ye be not fooling a soul." The woman's voice crackled with irritation.

Richard's wary gaze settled on the old Romany woman sitting on a blanket to his right. He had heard enough about her from Tom Wright and others to recognise the intriguing presence of his half-brother's grandmother, Mamma Petra. She looked old enough to be Methuselah's wife. Her sharp, deeply lined features were dominated by dead eyes, held fast upon some distant object. Long plaits, a speckled mixture of grey and silver, reached down to her waist. Snug to her small, thin frame, her black garb reminded him of his mother's persistent mourning noir.

Upon sitting upright he discovered his body had played him false. His head began to throb. He slumped back down again, swallowing the nausea and closing his eyes against the dizziness. As the pretty stars receded, he was vaguely conscious of Mamma Petra's testy gesture. The young woman kneeling behind her moved forward. She handed him a mug and shyly urged him to drink. The contents smelt similar to those Catherine had administered on occasions. He drank with only the slightest hesitation. And afterwards grimaced at the familiar bitter taste.

Sitting up again, gingerly this time, there was no repeat of his previous afflictions. Fully conscious of his altered situation, he surveyed the tough-looking Romany who had earlier sprung up around him. He was acquainted with most of them. They were his half-brother's shadowy scouts, the other half of his warrior company. He had a vague recollection of them preventing Danny Murphy and the other men from marching him back to the Lodge. There was a feral silence about them. Their movements were soundless, animalistic. Even though they showed no real sign of menace, he got the impression the men of her tribe were vigilant while he remained close to Mamma Petra.

"Why am I here?" he asked, huskily.

Imre Panin, one of the older Romany who Richard knew was regarded as leader when Junno was not around, walked over to him and squatted down on his haunches.

"It was you who told Murphy I was…wanted?"

The stocky, muscular Romany, nodded and then glanced across at Mamma Petra.

"How many did thee send?" she demanded, turning eyes that although were sightless seemed to bore into Richard.

"Send?" he replied, at a lost to know what she meant.

"Across to France," put in Panin

"I do not understand," answered Richard.

Mamma Petra spoke in her own tongue.

Appearing uncomfortable, Imre Panin seemed to hesitate. Mamma Petra spoke curtly. His expression changed to one of grim resignation. He seized hold of Richard. When Richard began to struggle, fearing what was to come, two Romany came forward to assist Panin.

Mamma Petra dismissed with an irritable gesture the help to rise from the forest floor the young woman would have given. For a woman of advanced years, she moved with noble ease.

Held securely by the three Romany, consumed by impotent fury, Richard watched her approach. He squirmed when she bent down to him and placed her small, wrinkled hands on either side of his face. The three men clamped down harder on him.

Fear swept through him. His eyes darted to right and left but failed to make contact with any of his captors. Even in his agitated state, he was conscious of how disconcerting their participation was to them. Yet the iron will of their Puro Daia prevailed.

Her hands grew strangely warm on either side of his face. An odd, lethargic sensation crept over him. When he tried to move his head in a desperate attempt to shake off the light-headed affect, he found he could no longer move. Not because of the grip the men had upon him. It had far more to do with the way the old

Romany's fingers seemed to have turned into claws, sinking into his trapped features.

Upon her releasing him, Richard felt curiously drained. He continued to stare up at her as she straightened, pulling her fringed shawl about her thin shoulders. For a few moments, he failed to realise the men were no longer restraining him.

"The Whelp hath no knowledge," Mamma Petra muttered in disgust. "He be of no account to them. They play him false."

"Mayhaps you do not seek the correct answers."

At first Richard thought one of the Romany had spoken. When they reacted as one with agile purpose, he realise the owner of the quiet voice had managed to thoroughly startle the nomads by his hitherto undetected presence.

Glancing her way, it seemed to Richard that the sightless old woman appeared not to need the fearful girl who had taken Lucinda's place to inform her who was walking calmly into their midst. She greeted the newcomer's approach with a contemptuous curl of her thin lips.

It was one more complication to a bewildering evening for Richard.

He scrutinised the tall, incredibly thin man. White like his long hair, his beard rested like a fluffy cloud upon his narrow chest, almost down to his waist. His robe was a mixture of light and dark shades of green which appeared to blend together with each of his silent, unhurried movements. Even his eyes reflected a fern hue. His lean face was brown as a weathered branch. Age was dignified yet elusive. In the absence of a cloak, he seemed attired in a fascinating mantle of inner peace that gave a strong impression of an affinity with his surroundings, as if he too was a part of the forest. He held a white staff. Its top consisted of definable features, crafted by nature alone.

He was accompanied by brown boar. Dog-like, it kept pace with him at his bare heels. Though bulky, the watchful creature moved with light-footed grace, its curved tusks glowing in the flickering light of the Romany campfire.

Richard felt the man's brief touch on his shoulder as he passed the place where he remained sitting on the forest floor. Curiously, the lingering affects of Mamma Petra's eerie, seeking influence seemed to dissipate. He stood upright with ease.

"Well, Garan, what answers wouldst thee claim?" she demanded.

Halting close to where she stood, her lined countenance defiant, Garan smiled. "Not the ones of self," he murmured.

"Bah," she muttered, huffishly. "Thy mind be addled by bark. Ye fail to see wood for trees."

She dismissed his presence without another word. While the Romany prepared to leave, they kept Garan in nervous view. Indeed, after they had recovered from their initial shock at his ability to come upon them unawares, they had considered his presence with unbridled superstition.

When Mamma Petra was mounted on her piebald pony, the young woman took hold of its reins and began to lead it from the clearing.

"What does thy heart fear?" asked Garan. He had not raised his voice yet it was carried easily on the light wind, an inescapable messenger.

For one brief second, the old Romany woman turned her head and looked directly at him with her blind gaze.

Her expression made no impression on Garan. It caused Richard to experience an icy shiver down his stiff spine.

After Mamma Petra and her escort had disappeared into the trees, he breathed a sigh of relief, but left alone with the strange old man, he felt awkward. With false nonchalance, he walked over to where his longbow, full quiver and sword lay on the ground. Although he picked them up with little effort, he remained shaken by his bid to escape his half-brother's men. The surrounding trees gave no clues as to where Murphy and the others from the Lodge might be. He swung the longbow and the quiver over his shoulder, but kept his sword in his hand. Only then did he meet Garan's steady gaze.

"You are safe from capture," the old man said, as if he had read his thoughts. "Come," he added, smiling. He turned and made his way across the clearing, heading in the opposite direction taken by the Romany.

Richard stood irresolute. That was until he felt a sharp jab in the back of his left leg. Startled, he half-turned to find the boar close beside him. He had forgotten about Garan's unlikely companion. He could have sworn there was a gleam of amusement in its beady black eyes. Its wicked-looking tusks hovered close to his legs.

"She's good at herding. So, methinks, you should follow and avoid another prod. That was just a warning." Garan's mild voice drifted through the trees.

Richard began to follow the old man's lead.

His long boot had taken much of the sting out of the boar's sharp persuasion, nevertheless his leg felt sore. Mindful that the brute was keeping pace close behind him, he was careful to show no sign of deviating from the invisible path Garan appeared to be following. Up ahead, the old man seemed to float through the forest, whereas Richard found the going difficult. By the time Garan's wordless guidance had led him into a much larger clearing than the one he had found himself in with the Romany, he was sweating and coughing. He blamed his condition on the after-affects of his mad dash from the Lodge.

"Be seated," invited Garan, indicating a rickety, three-legged stool.

His breathing slightly ragged, instead Richard lower himself down onto a pile of bracken. Garan leant over and placed a gentle hand on his chest. "Breath easy, my boy." Within a few moments, Richard found he was able to do so. He gave the green-robed, old man a searching look.

Placing his weapons beside him on the ground, at the same time aware the boar was keeping a watchful eye on him, he looked around the clearing, bounded by beech and ash. Their interwoven branches swayed in the mild, evening breeze. The only break in what appeared to be a protective ring was a narrow path leading out of the clearing into another. Richard glimpsed mighty oaks and the crystal surface of a pool.

Garan busied himself at the fire over which hung a cauldron of hissing water. He picked up a couple of the small earthenware pots in a large wicker basket. Close by larger pots and pans hung in neat rows on a cleverly constructed structure made up of interwoven branches. Several minutes later he approached Richard, mug in hand.

"Oh, don't mind Myr," he said, glancing at the boar. He half-turned in its direction, adding, "Well, if you did not appear so fierce, I wouldn't have to say anything, would I." Shaking his white head, he turned back to Richard. "She really does like to play mother hen, and then wonders why I get so annoyed with her when its clear folk mean no harm. You don't mean harm, do you, my boy?"

"No," answered Richard, glancing at the boar, feeling slightly dazed.

"There you are, then!" exclaimed Garan, once again addressing the creature, reclining on its thick haunches a few feet away. He thrust the mug at Richard. "Here, my boy, drink this."

Suspicious of the brew, Richard sniffed the mug's contents.

"Camomile to calm the spirit and honey to soothe the throat," assured Garan. "Drink, my boy."

Richard felt obliged to obey beneath the old man's compelling gaze. He was reassured by the taste of the infusion. It was reminiscent of the ones Catherine had made for him at the Lodge.

Thoughts of her induced the agonising return of wanting to pursue his half-brother. He was convinced Shadiz's undisguised desperation to get to his chateau in France meant that by hidden means he knew something had gone terribly awry. Bad enough if that was so. But what continued to plague him was the fact that Shadiz had married Catherine. Whatever might have occurred in France, he wanted his half-brother nowhere near her. For he had seen how Shadiz's manner towards Catherine had softened during the time she had spent at the old Lodge. If he was to make her his wife in the biblical sense, the outcome would be unthinkable. And Richard was determined to prevent any such thing from happening.

He had not realised his frustration at being detained by one means or another had caused him to groan out loud until Garan placed a thin, wrinkled hand on his slumped shoulder.

"I must go," Richard announced, starting to rise. He looked around to see if any of the Master's men where lurking in the ancient trees.

In the next moment, he found he had badly underestimated the old man's strength. The hand on his shoulder kept him seated on the forest floor, apparently with little effort. "You have not yet finished your drink," Garan said, quietly.

"To hell with the damn drink!" exclaimed Richard, trying a second time to get to his feet. The power of the man overlooking him was undeniable. It felt not only to be physical. And yet, Garan's peaceful expression had not altered.

"Yes, I understand the rudeness," commented Garan, as the boar approached him. "But the boy is upset, so we will forgive him." Brief amusement flittered over his lean features. "After all, he has encountered a difficult relation."

"What relation?" demanded Richard.

"Your half-brother's grandmother, of course."

"She is no relation of mine. And neither is he."

"It is oft said, we can choose our friends, but that we are basically stuck with our relations," declared Garan, his white head cocked to one side. "All to do with the decree of birth." He let go of Richard's shoulder. Glancing sideward at the boar, he said, "I'm quite certain he will remain." He switched back to Richard. "You will, won't you, my boy?"

Scowling, Richard switched from Garan to the boar, once again seated on its haunches a little closer now. It was plainly ridiculous, yet he got the impression the old man was communicating with the ugly, brown beast.

Garan shrugged as if Richard's lack of affirmation was of little consequence. He sat down cross-legged with a nimble grace that belied his medieval appearance. He prodded the fire. The sudden flare up of flames banished the encroaching darkness. "What made you of her?" he asked.

"Who?"

"Your newly encountered relation."

Richard grimaced. "I was informed Mamma Petra was an old witch."

"By Tom Wright." Garan stated.

Surprised, Richard considered him.

"And you believe him to have been correct."

"Yes."

Garan gazed into the fire. "He will see the deep tracks of her influence from where he now views," he murmured.

"There's not a good one among them." Richard shrugged. "With the exception of Junno, I suppose."

"You trust him?"

"He does what Shadiz tells him to do."

"So do you."

Richard jumped to his feet. "I most certainly do not," he exclaimed.

Neither Garan nor the boar reacted.

Some of the indignant tension left Richard beneath their collective gaze. "Well, all right," he continued, grudgingly. "Have it your own way. When we are involved in one of the Master's missions, I do, for the sake of all who blindly follow him." He roamed the clearing, declaring, "I hate him. I detest him."

"They do say, hate is the morbid slice of love," observed Garan, quietly.

"Don't be absurd, old man," growled Richard, rounding on him, his boots grinding down bracken. "He is the devil's spawn."

"Well, if you think about it," pointed out Garan, undeterred, "You are addressing your father as the Devil."

Exasperated, Richard swore roundly. Flinging out his arms, he bitterly complained, "I cannot win, whichever way I turn. It has been so all my life."

"You pour blame on your half-brother."

Richard responded vehemently. "A thousand time so. If it were not for him I would have a father and a sister still alive. There would be no Francois trying his utmost to keep me from my inheritance. I think I've every reason to blame the murderer." Through gritted teeth, he added, "The rapist." He met Garan's steady gaze. "Elizabeth wasn't the first. Nor the last. Won't anyone believe me when I say Catherine is in very, real danger."

The crackle of the fire, the sea-swishing murmur of the leaves in the surrounding forest fanned the fumes of Richard's desperation. He chafed to be away from the strange old man, from Stillingfleet and from England.

Garan rose, with his ageless grace. He walked over to Richard. "You are hurting. But that is only because you will not accept you are upon the correct path."

"Leave me alone, old man," Richard said, surprised that his words sounded like a cry from the heart.

"I think not," refused Garan. Before Richard could evade his touch, he gripped his shoulder. The cough that was about to erupt died away. "If you would simply be loyal to yourself and not others, then the true reason would prevail."

Richard found it impossible to look away from the forest-green eyes. His shoulder gradually sagged beneath Garan's comforting touch. "I just want to keep her safe," he muttered, wretchedly.

"Trust your half-brother. He will come to understand the she-devil that rides him."

Richard shook his head in renewed frustration. "You make no sense, old man."

"Sense is for Lord Time to unravel. We must treasure the feathers on his wings."

With an air of finality, Garan dropped his hand and stepped away from Richard. "Take up your bow and be ready for his calling. But, first, the cup of life must be drained."

"'e's comin' round. What the 'ell did the bastards do t' 'im?"

The rough voice, filled with annoyance, came to Richard from a long distance. His eyelids would not obey his groggy command.

Someone shook him.

He tried again to peer out into the world. This time he managed to squint through his lashes. Only to have his vision play tricks on him. At first he thought countless men surrounded him. Slowly the wavering figures condensed into three. Hands raised him up into a sitting position. Trees bent crazily. Leaves fluttered up to the night sky. He closed his eyes against the giddy movement of the world.

"'e gonna be alright?"

"Aye," said Danny Murphy, curtly, his expression showing no sympathy. "Get 'im back t' Lodge. An' this time mak' sure y' lock bleedin' door."

Richard was pulled to his feet. Bewildered, he muttered, "Garan?"

"Who?" snapped Murphy.

"The old man," answered Richard, weakly.

"What old man? There were no old man wi' Romany."

CHAPTER TWELVE

Track The Moon

Philippe limped into the long, sunny, book-lined library. Skirting round the large, oak reading table, he surveyed the two broken windows, relieved the chamber had suffered only minor damage. Upon removing several books from a particular shelf and locating the well-oiled mechanism, the heavy false panel caused him a little difficulty, especially after the recent injuries he had sustained when Francois Lynette's men had stormed Shannlarrey. The wounds had aggravated his disabilities. Yet, whatever their condition, he would not allow his ruined leg or arm to make of him a cripple.

The unease he was presently experiencing was tethered beneath his habitual calm reserve. Having slipped through the gap in the shelves, the descent into the subterranean chamber by way of the steep stone steps proved something of a challenge. He missed the last step and staggered in the cold darkness. Seconds after his shaky efforts to light a torch thrust in a sconce on the smooth wall, there came a hammering on the old, nail-studded door. Bracing himself, he hurried as best he could across the dimly lit chamber to where it sloped down to the door. Immediately upon him turning the key, the heavy door was flung open.

The torchlight flared in the sudden inrush of salt-tinged air. Philippe limped a few paces backwards.

It had been a while since he had last encountered the owner of the chateau of which he was custodian. The dark, raw presence of the tall man accosted him. A sinister, jet-black glare swept over him, lingering on the bandage on his arm, visible beneath his shirt, and taking in the large purple bruise on his forehead.

Shadiz strode further into the stone chamber with long-legged menace "Where is she?" he demanded, swivelling on grinding heels.

Having none of Shadiz's animalistic fluidity, Philippe's more moderate pace was accomplished with ungainly restraint. He had no idea how Shadiz knew about the onslaught on Shannlarrey, but had long since given up wondering how the extraordinary creature to whom his sister had willed her chateau gleaned his information. What exercised him at present was the information he had to impart, which might not be either anticipated or welcomed.

Philippe took a deep breath and spoke in his usual quiet manner. "By chance, Nick arrived shortly after we came under attack from Lynette's men. With his help and that of his crew, Junno and the men you sent from England were able between them to defeat the attack. The large number we were confronted by made us believe Lynette had recruit men-at-arms from his family's estate in Normandy. There was a fear there could be a second attack, especially when Nick and his ship's company returned to Formentera." He was conscious all the time he spoke of Shadiz's glacial scrutiny upon him and his utter stillness. Philippe doubted he was even breathing. Only the flickering light of the torchlight reflecting in his one gold earring showed any sign of life. Philippe finished on a cautious, persuasive note. "In the end, it was decided to take Catherine, Lucinda and Peter to the island."

For a long while, or at least it seemed that way to the Frenchman, Shadiz said nothing. Eventually, his glacial attitude thawed. He glanced around the chamber. Still without speaking, he walked across to his nautical-type desk and looked down at the paperwork strewn in disarray upon it.

"Who decided?"

"Nick put forth the suggestion. Junno reluctantly agreed it would be the safest option. To make it clear to all, Nick sailed to Marseille. After journeying by land to the port, Catherine, Junno and his family, their escort, they all boarded the *Sea Pearl*. The consensus of opinion was it would be suicidal for anyone to attempt to abduct Catherine from Formentera. She and Junno's family would be safe on the island."

Philippe remained where he was, supporting himself against

the bench carved from a beech log. He had known Shadiz for a number of years. Firstly as a dangerous youth with a rare gift for dealing with horses who had become his sister's horse master. Then, intermittently, as a man of extraordinary attributes and highly dubious accomplishments. Although he had always been aware of the nature of the beast, whenever Shadiz had been at Shannlarrey, either as an infrequent visitor or the chateau's owner, he had never shown claws or fangs. Indeed, down the years, the two of them had spent entertaining hours together either in the music chamber or the library.

The present meeting was very different.

Though Junno had warned him about the disfigurement, seeing the ruined side of Shadiz's barbarous countenance for the first time, Philippe found himself staring as the other man continued to shift through the paperwork on the desk. While his cautious attention rested on Shadiz, he noted the dark hollows shadowing the compelling black eyes. He was accustomed to Shadiz's rough appearance, which was only smoothed out to some degree during those times he spent at the chateau. Beneath all that was familiar and that which was disconcerting, Philippe glimpsed torment barely kept in check.

Philippe had never personally encountered love. But he had existed on its periphery more than once. The duplicity of love had had devastating consequences for his mother. Louise's marriage had floundered because of the heartless cruelty of her husband. After his deserved demise, her freed heart had known the pain of loving cautiously from a distance. He had learned after his sister's death that the man who could only be a considerate lover towards the end of her life, easing her physical pain, had done the unthinkable. Whatever dark cavern had trapped his soul had been emptied by a young, unknowing girl. Why else would he offer a place for her to recuperate after a serious illness, only to gaze upon her from the shadows, as Philippe had caught him doing on more than one occasion?

"Where was she when they came at y'?"

The curt inquiry, coming at the end of the thoughtful pause, made Philippe jump slightly. "I thought down here would be the safest place for her. And Lucinda and Peter." After a slight hesitation, he added, "Junno agreed."

Shadiz inclined his head.

Philippe breathed a quiet sigh of relief.

Shadiz scooped up several of the papers he had been sifting through and headed towards the half-opened door. Philippe followed him. When Shadiz stopped abruptly, he was caught off balance. He could not help grimacing at the pain that shot down his damaged leg. Shadiz steadied him.

"Y' be all right?"

"Oui." Philippe smiled self-consciously. "Merci."

"Thank you for 'elpin' t' keep 'er safe."

"She is worth protecting," Philippe replied, aware of the pressure on his arm.

A muscle flexed in Shadiz's scarred cheek. "Y' ain't t' come any further."

Philippe had not set foot in the cove since Louise had died there in Shadiz's arms.

Benjamin caught sight of his leader emerging from the cave's dank entrance. Once again, like the two oarsmen with him, his curiosity was spiked. He straightened as Shadiz approached the skiff. It had been pulled up onto the sandy beach in the small, secluded cove below the chateau. Riding at anchor in the glittering Mediterranean, the *Endeavour* awaited the return of the Master.

Striding into the placid waves lapping the shore, Shadiz indicated that the skiff should be launched. Swinging himself aboard the same time as Benjamin, he murmured, "An' thus the whirligig o' time brings in 'is revenges."

Benjamin's shocked stare collided with the icy, knowing glint in his leader's black eyes. Whereupon, he experienced a chilling sensation in the pit of his stomach.

.

CHAPTER THIRTEEN

Another Place of Safety

It was late evening when the *Sea Pearl* arrived at Formentera. Excitement had ensured Peter remained awake. He was forced to curb his eagerness to go topside. Much to the chagrin not only of Peter but also Catherine and his mother, the three of them were politely detained in the spacious cabin they had shared on the voyage from Marseille.

Catherine and Lucinda got the impression their late arrival was no random occurrence and that their wait below decks was a calculated development. Only when they were told a coach had arrived to take them to their final destination were they escorted topside by Junno and Keeble.

Once allowed out into the balmy night, they found the ship secured to a stone quay and the sails stowed. There was very little else for them to witness. Apart from the stars above them in a cloudless night sky and lights shimmering in the distant the harbour was lost in concealing darkness. Only the creaking of marine wood made them aware of the presence of other vessels.

Peter and the young women were handed into the sumptuous interior of the coach by a huge Negro almost as tall as Junno. He had a polite, easy-going manner, and a smile that kept flashing white in the flickering light of a torch held by a curious, bony youth.

Once they were settled inside, they heard the sound of horses gathering around the coach, and then the crack of a whip. As the coach jerked into motion, Peter tried to see out of the windows but failed, even with Catherine's help to raise the stubborn leather shutters. By the time wheels were rumbling over paving stones, he had drifted off to sleep, lulled by the rhythmic motion of the well-sprung coach.

Although a small lamp hanging from the ceiling of the coach had been lit for their benefit, when the ever-smiling Negro helped Catherine and Lucinda, with Peter in her arms, to descend from the semi-darkness they were briefly blinded by the rosy glow of several ornate lanterns hung at regular intervals beneath a covered portico. They shed light on wrought-iron benches interspersed by large, flower-filled terracotta pots.

Only the coach and the mounts of Keeble, Junno and Nick Condor had entered the courtyard. The unseen escort had melted away into the night. Despite the lateness of the hour, servants quickly appeared to deal with the horses. The big Negro touched his forehead in a salute to Condor as he drove the coach away.

Murmuring to the sleek, brown dogs that fussed around him, Nick Condor led the way beneath the portico, smothered in sweet-smelling roses, to the double doors of the white villa. Inscribed with dolphins, mermaids and smiling suns, they were suddenly thrust open by a small, plump woman.

She bustled forward, sniffing in disgusted upon passing Condor. In contrast, she gave Keeble and Junno an effusive welcome, causing Peter to stir in his mother's arms. The big man took the boy and rocked him back to sleep at the same time warmly reciprocating the greeting of someone who was clearly a friend not seen for a while.

"This be me wife, Lucinda," he said, half-turning, "An' me son, Peter."

The black-haired woman smiled broadly at Lucinda and then, standing on her tiptoes cooed over Peter.

Nick Condor walked up behind her. Bending towards her, he said, "And this, Rosa, is *his* wife."

It was clear the little Spanish woman had been warned who to expect. Yet, sobering as she turned her full attention to Catherine, she seemed uncertain, as if she didn't really believe what she had been told. Her smile was hesitant. "I am most honoured to meet you, senorita."

"Please, Catherine."

Although her dark eyes remained unsure, Rosa nodded eagerly, her warm, motherly smile returning.

"Where's my greeting?" complained Nick Condor, feigning hurt.

Rosa rounded on him with a finger-pointing tirade in rapid Spanish.

Laughing Condor, advised her, "Berate me in English so all the world knows."

Her plump cheeks puffed out condemningly, she told him, "You deserve not greeting. Making wait for late hour bring them."

"I beg you, refrain from huffing at me," he replied, grinning, hand on heart, "The tides decree."

"I thought the Mediterranean was a tideless sea?" queried Catherine.

Suddenly, a shriek from within the villa, caused everyone to look towards the open doors.

A young woman of exceptional, sultry beauty glided through them and flung herself at Condor. Laughing, he caught hold of her as she wrapped her long legs around his waist.

"I wait and wait. You not come. You are near but you not come."

"Ah," sighed Condor, grinning down into her dusky, almond eyes. "The wait makes seenin' you all the sweeter, me darlin' Bianca." As she pouted with smug triumph, he reminded her. "We've company."

She slid down his muscular length in a provocative manner. In doing so, the gauze robe she wore road up to her thighs. When she turned and leant her back against his accommodating chest, the soft folds of her white robe fell to her bare feet, in the light of the lanterns leaving little to the imagination.

Nick Condor interlaced his fingers with hers and held her around the waist while he conducted the introductions.

She gave smiling welcome to both Keeble and Junno, with whom it was clear she was already acquainted. Ignoring Lucinda, she focussed her attention on Catherine.

Rosa's furtive curiosity had made Catherine feel awkward. The blatant scrutiny of the houri made her feel too tall, too thin and labouring under the bizarre impression she was letting down her absent husband.

Bianca's exquisite face grew spiteful. "What he see in her?"

Catherine stiffened. What normally she would have made light of, because she was feeling displaced and exhausted through lack of sleep, not to mention a ponderous sense of rejection, she retaliated with a caustic observation of her own.

"The reason of the strongest is always the best," she remarked in Latin.

"What she say?" demanded Bianca scowling.

Condor grinned. "I ain't a clue, me darlin'," he admitted, regarding Catherine approvingly. "But I'd be nice if I were you. I reckons Fair Princess has a sting in her tongue t' match yours."

"Huh," she muttered, flinging her long silky black hair over her shoulder. "Too dull English. I not," she snapped, glaring at Catherine.

Leaving him to stand alone, she floated with evocative grace to Junno's side and tucked her arm in his, seemingly oblivious to the fact he was holding his son. Chatting excitedly, she urged him forward into the villa. The big man gave his frowning wife an apologetic look over his shoulder. Rosa and Keeble followed. Stepping between Lucinda and Catherine, Condor gallantly ushered them over the tiled threshold.

"Welcome to the Casa."

Catherine awoke from yet another haunted sleep. Ever since Shadiz had taken her to the mysterious Crystal Pool deep in Stillingfleet Forest, she had been prone to such nightly torment. Yet upon escaping Morpheus's clutches in an inevitably abrupt manner, her dreams remained disturbingly elusive. The muzzy sensation was presently made worse by the strangeness of her surroundings. It took several moments before she recalled she was no longer at the Lodge or Shannlarrey. That the island of Formentera was now to be her home for the foreseeable future.

She got out of bed, weary but shunning sleep. Stumbling in the dark into the elegant furnishings in the spacious, unfamiliar chamber, she eventually reached the French windows. Stepping out onto the balcony, she heard the distant murmur of the sea, smelt the heady perfume of flowers and was glad of the cooling night breeze after the hot discomfort of her dreams. Between the pine trees, standing tall beyond the high wall surrounding the courtyard, she glimpsed the silvery reflection of the sickle moon on the tranquil Mediterranean.

She heard voices. Intrigued, she cocked her head to listen. Words were indistinguishable. But she caught feminine tones, followed by a soft masculine laugh.

Catherine experienced a painful jolt of longing.

Gripping the balcony's wrought iron rail, she closed her eyes, but could not stop the tears from springing into them. They escaped her damp lashes and slid down her cheeks. Overtaken by a sudden surge of anger, she opened her eyes and dashed away the tears.

Shadiz had used her. Worse. He had used her father. And that cruel manipulation had led to his death.

And for what?

She now understood only too well after discovering the papers in his secret lair beneath Shannlarrey. It wasn't her he wanted, it was Fylingdales Hall and Estate. All he had ever wanted was to acquire what he considered to be his birthright. It was the real reason why he had returned to a land torn by civil unrest. Such a dangerous predator as he was quite capable of defeating a faction standing against the monarchy and then hold their possessions in a legitimate manner.

It made her feel sick to think she had been used to disguise his true objective.

Yet, even now, a crippled hope crawled beneath the hurt and resentment of betrayal. Had he set out to use her and discovered… what? Did the man have finer feeling? Or was he too accustomed to the ice of hatred or the burning fury of vengeance? Or worse still. Did he relish the wilful destruction of innocence?

She could not bear to contemplate what he had done to Elizabeth. His half-sister. To Lucinda, or would have done had not Junno prevented him. How many others had become victims of his grotesque brutality. Would he, given the chance, do the same to her? And, if she was given the chance, would she ever trust him again?

The bewildering, painful mixture of emotions threatened to crush her.

"Ye Gods and Little Fishes!"

She swung away from the turmoil of night and sort the dubious refuge of her chamber. She uttered an unladylike oath as she connected in the absence of candlelight with a ponderous shape. Her anger reinforced, she wanted to lash out. Her hand shot up to clutch her jet pendant. Until recently she had believed the unusual piece of jewellery was a present from her father, but discovered it had in fact come from Shadiz.

The unexpected, overwhelming rush of frustration, regret, self-loathing and anguish stayed Catherine's hand from ripping the silver chain from around her neck. Instead, her trembling fingers stroked the symbolic silver surrounding the jet stone while it seared her entire being with second hand emotions.

CHAPTER FOURTEEN

The Locals

Someone was calling her name.

Waking up sluggishly, Catherine blinked at the bright sunlight flooding her chamber. Shading her eyes, she found Peter standing beside her.

"Why y' in chair?" he asked, his young dark-skinned face crinkled in bewilderment.

"Oh, hullo," she mumbled, struggling into a sitting position.

"I told y' not to disturb Catherine," scolded Lucinda, hurrying into the bedchamber.

"Sorry, daia," muttered Peter.

Lucinda switched from the chair to the crumbled bed. Looking back at Catherine, taking in her night attire, she grimaced sympathetically.

During the voyages, first to France and then to Formentera, Catherine had shared a cabin with Lucinda and Peter, and in doing so had been unable to conceal the reason for the regular dark smudges beneath her blue eyes.

"I want tell Cat about Jack an' Katy."

"Y' can later," Lucinda told her son, starting to shepherd him away.

"But!" said Catherine and Peter in unison.

At the same moment two children peered through the half-opened door. Peter escaped from his mother and dashed to them. With great enthusiasm he propelled the hesitant pair towards where Catherine was sitting in the chair near the French windows.

Rising, she greeted them with a smile. Although she had been told of their presence at the villa, she feigned ignorance. "Well, who do we have here?"

"Jack," introduced Peter, pushing forward the brown-haired boy smaller than himself and much leaner. "Katy," he continued, dragging the dainty girl beside her brother. Her curly auburn hair and small creamy features gave her an ethereal appearance.

Both smiled shyly. The boy said, "You missed breakfast."

"Oh, dear," replied Catherine, "It would seem I have overslept."

Rosa could be heard bustling down the corridor. Her Spanish mutterings were cut short as she entered the bedchamber. She threw up her plump arms at sight of the children. "There you scamps are!" She wagged a thick finger at Jack and Katy. "I hope you minded manners."

The two children looked crestfallen. Rosa was immediately contrite. She placed a loving arm around both of them.

"I forgot to bow," said Jack.

"I forgot to curtsy, " whispered Katy.

"Cat ain't mind," Peter told them, confidently.

Aware of Lucinda's concern, disguising her own, Catherine knelt before the children. "I think if we are going to be friends, we should start by not standing on ceremony. I much prefer hugs, don't you?"

The boy gave an uncertain shrug. The girl nodded timidly.

Catherine gathered them to her. Standing stiffly at first, as she spoke quietly to them gradually they relaxed within her embrace.

After they had accompanied Rosa from the bedchamber, with Peter happy to be included in her motherly clucking in order to be with his new friends, his mother remarked, "Did y' see 'ow quick she was t' comfort bairns? "

"Their reaction to her mild scolding was certainly odd," commented Catherine. She sighed. "Don't you think we are living in a very odd world at the moment? My fault."

Lucinda was quick to disagree. "Tis not y'r fault were 'ere." Ending the implied pause, studying Catherine, she asked, "Be y' feelin' well? Ever since we went into that underground place at Shannlarrey, you've been sort o'... different?"

Catherine tried to dismiss the hesitant probe with a cheery rebuff. For how on earth could she tell the young Romany woman who had become a firm friend that all of them had been ruthlessly duped? "I'll admit not all is quite right with my world. But I'm cantering along."

A compassionate expression on her attractive face, Lucinda stepped closer to her and put an arm around her shoulder. "Things'll right theirsens."

"I hate him," exclaimed Catherine, fiercely.

Although absorbed in her emotional outburst, which had taken her by surprise, she registered Lucinda's startled reaction, and her fleeting apprehension.

Not for the first time, Catherine wonder about the true reason for Lucinda's out-of-character action at Whitby, when she had poisoned Shadiz's ale. At the time, Lucinda's apparent motive had been to have Junno back with her and Peter instead of obeying his cousin's command to guard Catherine at the Lodge. Yet Catherine had always suspected Lucinda's confession was false, and that Junno knew the real reason for his wife's murderous attempt. Unbidden, thoughts of Mamma Petra sprang to mind.

There was one thing of which Catherine was quite certain. "He is coming," she stated, folding her arms around herself.

Beside her, Lucinda stiffened, her apprehension deepening.

After their late arrival the night before, the day was spent settling into their second home in as many months. There was a host of servants, all of whom were happy to guided them around the sprawling villa. They soon learned that the fascinating assortment of ages, races and disabilities all came under the command of Rosa.

The pretty Spanish girl who had become Catherine's maid was unable to speak. If she had been that way inclined, Catherine would have entertained the cynical thought the choice was deliberate.

Peter beamed with delight when Jack and Katy persuaded a crinkly old mariner to whirl a tray full of crockery on the stumpy remnant of his left arm. While he obliged, Junno laughed at Catherine and his wife as they both held their breath in doubt over the feat. Grinning, Junno excused himself and left Keeble to be dragged along by the children as they sought out the legless Egyptian who could perform summersaults and land with finesse on his two robust sticks.

Finding their way down one of the villa's cool, white-washed corridors, Catherine and Lucinda were both astounded by the African woman they met in passing. She was almost as tall as Junno in her bare feet. What amazed them the most was how her neck was elongated to an amazing degree by the many colourful rings she wore.

They were just getting over the sight of her when the two young women encountered a bare-chested Negro. The youth's entire upper body was covered by a fascinating array of tribal markings. He greeted them with a low bow and a broad grin that stretched his bright, facial tattoos.

By the time they had brought their meeting with a long-nosed Greek in an ancient robe to an end, their insides were heaving. For they had tried most admirably to keep the bubbling hysterics within while the short, stocky fellow had attempted to practice his indecipherable English upon them.

The two young women learned two facts during their morning exploration. Life it seemed was cosmopolitan on Formentera. A world away from Nafferton Garth, the Lodge, even Shannlarrey. It also became clear, whatever was beyond the high walls surrounding the villa and the life within them, there was only one master.

Catherine grasped the significance of being Shadiz's wife. Wherever their wanderings took her and Lucinda, she was confronted with a mixture of curiosity, apprehension and elaborate respect. In an attempt to mitigate such behaviour, she sought to put those she met at ease by making it plain she possessed none of the Master's harsh reserve. It worked to a certain extent, but it was plain everyone she met was scared stiff of upsetting not particularly her, but the Master.

Catherine found the gardens surrounding the rambling villa enchanting. She and Lucinda could hear the children playing elsewhere while they meandered along the paved walkways in the warm sunshine. The heady scent of lavender, jasmine and roses drifted on the cooling sea breeze. Delicate ferns and tall palm trees offered shade to the many lazy cats. Catherine bent to them in passing, stroking the more gregarious amongst their variegated number, coaxing the timid ones who crept up to her and sniffed her hand before allowing a gentle touch. The smooth-coated dogs that had greeted their arrival the previous night had attached themselves to the two young women. They watched with disdain each time Catherine greeted a feline.

"You've a way wi' creatures, y' know," observed Lucinda.

"My father maintained I would make a good shepherd. I would make the wolf lay down with the lamb."

Lucinda laughed. Then, unseen by Catherine, frowned over a sudden thought.

Catherine crouched down to stroke a playful kitten. Like the rest they had come across in the garden, it was slimmer and had a more sharper face than English felines. "It's said the Egyptians were the first to domesticate the cat once they discovered their usefulness in guarding their grain stores," she remarked.

"We're supposed t' be descended from an Egyptian tribe."

"Really," said Catherine, straightening. "Ow...you little rotter!" she exclaimed as the kitten made a needle-sharp lunge at her ankle.

"We're also supposed t' come from Romania," added Lucinda, "an' Russia."

"H'm. I get the idea."

"We ain't fond o' cats."

"Each to his or her own, I suppose," commented Catherine, mildly. "As for myself, I have to admit, I do have a preference for animals over some humans." A moment later, she added, "Speaking of which...."

They both looked to where Bianca was lounging on a divan beside one of the fountains. They exchanged a glance of mutual understanding. Changing direction, they rounded a palm tree and bumped into Bill Todd.

"Me apologises, ladies," he said, with a quick, clumsy bow. Straightening, his usual bright grin encompassed both Catherine and Lucinda. Wath, the oldest of the Romanies to have accompanied the Master's men, was with Todd. Far more reserved, he inclined his head to both of the young women.

"Where are you?" asked Catherine.

"Here," answered Bill, mischievously. The Romany gave him a sidelong glance.

Catherine pulled a face, accustomed to his humour.

"We've set up shop in buildings around walls," he explained.

Despite Bill's joviality, Catherine sensed the reticence of the two men. Clearly, the Master men and the Romany who had accompanied her and Junno's family to France and then to Formentera were guarding the villa. After the attack on Shannlarrey, the men had been convinced she would be safe from Lynette on the island. Yet their conduct and the way Nick Condor had awaited nightfall before allowing them to disembark upon their arrival at the smallest Balearic Island made her wonder just what the Master's corsair stronghold held beyond the enclosed opulence of the villa.

"Y' ain't seen Junno?" asked Bill, scanning the lush garden, "This lots like a maze."

"'e's around 'ere somewhere," pointed out Lucinda, looking around for her unusually tall husband.

"We'll use Wath's trackin' skills," said Bill, moving away with a cheerful wink. After another polite incline of his dark head, the Romany started walking in the opposite direction taken by the Gorgio.

Catherine and Lucinda laughed together as Bill Todd performed a comical u-turn and followed the dark-skinned man's decisive lead.

Strolling down a paved path bordered by magnolia and hibiscus they came across the chant and sparkle of yet another fountain. Sitting beside it, beneath a colourful awning, was a slight, robed figure. As they approached the man, he looked up from the book he was reading. His bronzed, lined features, dominated by an aquiline nose, creased into smiling greeting. The youth sitting at his feet jumped up to assist him to stand. In spite of his senior years, he possessed an aura of regal authority. He salaamed to them with great dignity. Catherine and Lucinda reciprocated with polite curtsies. His scarlet robe shimmered with each of his unhurried movements. The ruby in his silk turban glinted in the strong sunlight. As did the matching ruby on the hand that held the gold handle of his ivory cane.

When he spoke his mellow voice held a strong accent. "I am blessed to meet two serene ladies."

"Forgive us if we have interrupted your reading," said Catherine.

The man looked down at the book in his left hand. He held it out to the youth, who hastened to take it from him. "The company of words have been surpassed."

"I have found great delight in their company," she remarked, taking a liking to their new acquaintance. Lucinda appeared less sure.

He regarded Catherine with wise, steadfast eyes. "A scholarly mind is a gift from Allah."

"Or, in my case, my father."

"You are then an excellent daughter."

Regret clouded her young features. "I was."

He put a hand on his thin chest. "Your loss is recognised and understood," he offered with sincerity.

Wanting a change of subject, Catherine asked, "Are you visiting?" Clearly, he wasn't a native of Formentera and certainly no corsair.

Behind her, a light, mocking voice said, "Cretin. Hostage he is."

Catherine and Lucinda turned together to find Bianca behind them. Responding to her startling disclosure, they looked back at the richly attired, elderly gentleman.

He gave a delicate sigh. "The truth will out. I wait while my ransom flies on the back of an eagle from far off lands."

Bianca floated around the two women. Her scornful gaze rested on Catherine. Coming to a halt, she infused her introduction with sarcastic courtesy. "You speak with Prince Ardashir, Grand Vizier of Persia."

Astounded, Catherine and Lucinda stared at him. Little wonder he appeared regal.

"You are abundantly considerate to make the introduction, highness," countered the Persian, giving delicate emphasis to the title.

Slowly recovering from one shock, Catherine and Lucinda

received another. They switched from the Persian prince to Bianca.

"Allow me, in turn, to introduce her most serene highness, Princess Tamrist," he continued, his calm expression stoic.

Yet Catherine sensed his distaste. She was unsure whether it was due to Bianca's presence on the island, which suddenly seemed bizarre, or the way she flaunted herself.

She was wearing a satin top that barely covered her ample breasts, with sleeves of transparent silk. It left her slender waist bare. Her baggy, gold-braided silk pants hung low on her hips. There were thin gold chains around her slender ankles, her wrists and her swan-like neck.

Standing between the Persian princess and Lucinda, who looked striking in her embroidered red and white linen gown and colourful bracelets, Catherine felt quite dowdy.

"We tire, uncle, for my eminent brother to offer payment," stated Bianca with venom. "Perhaps your place been usurped beside boy Shah, and now little worth."

"Now, sweet darlin'," said Nick Condor, strolling up behind her. "Play nice." He bent and, as if he had read her thoughts, whispered to Catherine, "You are an English rose."

Junno was with him. The big man scowled at his proximity to her. Condor feigned ignorance of his obvious displeasure.

Bianca made it clear she was annoyed by his admonishment, however mild, and the attention he showed Catherine. She gave him a withering look. Tossing her long black hair over her shoulder in a tempestuous manner, she flounced away.

"Never fear," Condor told Catherine, "Bianca, or should I say Princess Tamrist, is more yap than nip."

"She'd better be," snapped Junno.

For a brief moment there was discernable tension between the two men.

"Gentlemen," said Prince Ardashir, diplomatically, "My niece has long been given to a petulance best ignored."

"You are indeed related?" asked Catherine, taking her lead from him to defuse the tense atmosphere.

The Persian smiled. "I serve her ten-year-old brother, Shah

Abbas 11, my late brother's son. I was voyaging to Spain at the invitation of the king to discuss trade between our two countries when I was, how shall I say, intercepted." He gave Condor a polite yet meaningful look.

The expression on Condor's rugged face was one of complete innocence. "Don't pile blame on me. She suggested it. He endorsed it."

"Bianca? Shadiz?" Catherine and Junno said in chorus.

Grinning like a fool who only does other peoples' bidding, Nick Condor nodded.

The dark foreboding that the fragrant garden had largely dispelled returned, engulfing Catherine.

CHAPTER FIFTEEN

Learning Curve

"Do you grow tired of this?" asked Catherine.

"Aye," replied Lucinda. "Definitely."

They were both unaccustomed to inactivity. At an early age, because of her mother's death and with her father's encouragement, Catherine had become immersed in the day-to-day running of Nafferton Garth, her home close to Driffield. Even during her stay at the Lodge, she had managed to keep busy, frequently to Shadiz's annoyance. As for Lucinda, she had been expected to perform tasks for her Romany tribe from an even earlier age than Catherine before becoming the handmaiden to their demanding Puro Daia, Mamma Petra.

Therefore, in complete agreement that they needed to stave off boredom, the two young women turned their attention to the children. They decided to curb any tendency to run wild. Although it was kindly done, Jack and Katy had no boundaries. Similarly, without the discipline of their tribe, Lucinda feared Peter would grow wayward. Catherine had come to recognise the element already existing to a certain extent in the boy's nature had not been inherited from either Lucinda or Junno.

They resolved to use the extensive grounds of the villa as both a schoolroom and a playground, hoping to make learning fun. With Rosa's enthusiastic help, Catherine gathered together quills and paper and embarked upon teaching the children, and even the Greek youth who watched over them along with Keeble, to draw, write and read, using attractive features of the garden. As the days went by in pleasant, constructive harmony, the children gained a fascinating insight from Catherine's and Lucinda's combined knowledge of the plants and aromatic herbs that filled the balmy air with their abundant scents. Whenever they rested in the shade of palm and fig trees, Lucinda would recount tribal legends or Catherine would speak of mythical tales which invariably led to the children acting out fantastic deeds

Catherine hated the hours of siesta at the hottest time of the day for she invariably found the rest period plagued by disquieting thoughts. In an effort to ward off gruelling reflection, each day she took it upon herself to clear away after the children as Lucinda led them into the villa. And afterwards she would enjoy the stillness of the shady terrace when everyone had gone to their rest.

"Well, me sweet darlin', if you weren't bride o' richest devil around, I'd say you'd make an excellent governess."

Catherine straightened, her arms full of the clothes she and Lucinda had dressed the children in for the latest fable. She gave a wry grimace. "Better than feeling rather akin to a canary in a gilded cage."

Nick Condor's bright smile did not falter but his green eyes grew serious. "Ah, sweet darlin', 'twould be death o' me, t' be sure, if I allowed anything to befall you."

She had seen very little of him. Only on an evening did he reappear for the banquet-like dinners served in one of the villa's airy chambers, its French windows open to the mellow beauty of the garden.

"Where did they come from?" she asked, "Katy and Jack?"

Before he could answer, Bianca appeared. Glowering at Catherine, she put a possessive arm around Condor's waist and leant against him. He rubbed his chin over the top of her head and then looked down at her as she spoke.

"Soft fool rescued them."

Feigning hurt, he responded. "What was I supposed to do? Let 'em burn?"

Catherine frowned. "What do you mean?" she asked, looking from one to the other of the couple. As she spoke she sensed Junno's approach. He halted a few paces behind her.

"We board merchantman out Malta," explained Bianca.

"We?" queried Catherine. "You accompany them?"

"Of course," snapped Bianca, giving her a smug look. "After bombardment and gathering, we leave when he come topside through fire with a brat in arms." She sighed heavily in disgust. "Why cretin bother. Nuisance, pair them."

"The Beast wasn't too fussed, either," put in Condor, with a defensive shrug.

Bianca gave a short unpleasant laugh. "He rolled his flames out. He curse him for being...."

Catherine did not hear the rest of her tirade. She suddenly felt dizzy. Without realising what she was doing, she put a hand out to Junno. He seized it, and then placed a comforting arm around her, fully aware of what memory the explanation of the rescue of the children had resonated with her.

Standing in the warm peace of the garden, her thoughts had flown of their own accord to the hot trauma of a wintry lane in a Dutch port. A man in flames staggering towards her, in his arms the woman she had begged him to save.

"English child hates hearing...."

"Shut up, bitch," growled Junno.

Turning his massive back on Condor and Bianca, he led Catherine into the cool privacy of the villa's marble hallway.

She could not stem the tremors. Or the painful hope within the thought that surely paying such a high penalty to uphold a ruse made her entirely wrong about Shadiz. Because of his action that day on her behalf, he had almost died. Only her wielding of their jet and moonstone pendants, which seem inexplicably linked, had brought him back from the brink. Yet, conversely, the existence of the paperwork she had come across in his private chamber below Shannlarrey could not be denied.

"'Y' be all right, Rauni?"

She nodded. And then shook her head.

CHAPTER SIXTEEN

Signature Salute

The Master had returned to the *Endeavour* looking like the Devil ready for The Day of Reckoning. Benjamin hadn't looked too rosy, either.

Ever since his leader's ominous reference to his desire for revenge, he had been cast into a maelstrom of conflicting emotions. One of them being shame. For how he had allowed his fascination with Shadiz to erode his determination to seek justice for the slaughter of his father and older brothers.

When the florin had eventually dropped even the most hardy of the Master's men experienced a few qualms about their destination being the infamous island of Formentera. Unlike them, Benjamin could not take comfort in the knowledge they were sailing there with the Master. What none of them could fathom was why he appear to be smouldering with dangerous fury.

When the smallest of the Balearic Islands came in sight, a tiny hazy dot in the azure waters of the Mediterranean, shading his eyes against the glare of the hot sun, Benjamin experienced an apprehensive tightening in his guts. Turning inboard, his insides grew cold when his leader's black-eyed glare rested briefly upon him. He was at a lost to understand how Shadiz had become aware of his harrowing link with Formentera. It seemed they both had issues regarding their arrival through the tranquil sea

"You would make a good pirate, my warm-hearted brother. Take from the wealthy merchants and give to the poor. A Robin Hood of the sea. "

"And you, my little sister, make an excellent dreamer."

Four years younger than him, Sofia pulled a face at Benjamin.

119

"All I was trying to point out. Perhaps some who embark upon such a role have been driven to it by dire circumstances. Take the crews of the ships that defeated the Armada in so-called Good Queen Bess's time. Did you know more men died of their wounds and starvation than those who took part in the battle?"

Sofia rolled her sparkling blue eyes. "Yes, brother. You have told us, *ad nauseam!*"

"Well," retorted Benjamin, playfully, "Master Cutler would be pleased with your Latin."

"Ha!" She jumped down from the high drystone wall upon which she had been perched, her fine, curling fair hair bouncing about her shoulders. "I please him not."

"If you use that kind of grammar, I can quite understand why." He began to follow her skipping steps along the sloping garden path. He frowned. "What is wrong with mother? She looks as if she is...weeping?"

Benjamin came to himself, and realised he was being given an order. The Master wanted the topgallants furled.

Thoughts of that fateful day two years ago when his life had changed forever dogged him as he climbed the rigging. His mother had indeed been weeping. She had gathered him and Sofia into her arms and informed them that their father and two older brothers had been killed by corsairs during their homeward voyage from Malta. What was more, it seemed their two young cousins had also perished. They had been orphaned after their parents had drowned in a boating accident in the Grand Harbour at Malta. Benjamin's father and brothers had gone to the island of the Knights of St John in order to bring the children home to the Yorkshire Dales.

Over the following two years he had grown up quickly, become the man of the house. Having painstakingly pierced together what exactly had befallen his family on their homeward voyage and who was responsible, he along with his friend Richard Massone had been ready to bring the Master and Nick Condor to justice. There were several courts in as many lands that would gladly accommodate the two men. Only, fate had intervened. Benjamin and Richard had been obliged to put their duty to their king before vengeance for the wickedly slain. Fate appeared to have played her part once more when, in Scarborough, his leader had boarded the *Endeavour*. Benjamin had never imagined his inclusion in the ship's company would lead to him sailing to the isle of corsairs.

He had no illusion. It was highly unlikely he would leave Formentera alive.

Wanting to be isolated for a time with his grim thoughts, Benjamin did not follow the other men down the rigging after they had stowed the sails. Instead, he remained perched upon the lofty vantage point above the main deck.

The smudge on the horizon gradually developed into an island less than twelve miles in length, Benjamin calculated. Foremost among the features becoming discernible was a tall, stone watchtower situated on a rock promontory. As they sailed closer, he glimpsed another further along the coast. Similar to the first one he had spotted, cannons were positioned at its base, giving the impression of shiny, black guard dogs staring out to sea.

In marked contrast to the baleful outposts, inland there were signs of peaceful habitation that belied the evil nature with which Benjamin had embellished the island. Clusters of white houses nestled upon pine covered slopes above ripening crops. Two windmills stood several miles apart. Their wooden, lattice sails turned lazily through a summery haze. A couple of fishing hamlets, separated by a long stretch of golden beach, overlooked the sparkling shoreline. Gaily painted fishing boats rocked idly in the clear, blue sea.

Benjamin caught sight of the Master's purposeful move away from the helm far below him. Curious, he descended the rigging with an ease he had acquired during the voyage from England. He dropped easily down to the deck in the midst of men rushing to obey their leader's commands, and tagged onto the group who were following the Master below decks.

Once in the gloom of the *Endeavour's* gun deck, at Shadiz's terse bidding two of the cannons that had once threatened the Eagle in the wintry waters of the North Sea were run out. Those men who had gunnery experience assisted him in the loading of shot and powder from the conveniently placed stockpile Francois Lynette had seen fit to equip his ship. Quick to obey the new captain of the *Endeavour*, one of the men lowered a lighted taper.

Like the rest of the men present, Benjamin quickly turned away and cover his ears. Even so, the thunderous boom of the cannon in such a confined area assault his senses. The lower deck beneath his feet shuddered as the gun rebounded against its thick restraining chains. Seconds later, tasting the acrid smoke all of them had become engulfed in, he heard the whoosh of water when the cannon ball having run its course landed in the sea. Peering through the open gun port, it was plain no harm was intended.

Upon the second cannon being readied, the Master held up his hand. He seemed to be waiting. After a tense few seconds, he gestured for the hissing taper to be lowered once more. The discharge followed the same pattern as before. Only now the accumulation of trap smoke made men cough and their stinging eyes to water while they sought to reload the first cannon.

Once again the Master held up his hand. Hard-faced, only he seemed immune to the bitter atmosphere. He made them wait longer than before. Nerves were crumbling in much the same way as the glowing taper before he indicted the third shot should be made.

The distant clamour of the busy kitchen, from where aromatic smells emanated, had ceased. It seemed as if the entire villa had suddenly fallen silent.

Alarmed, Catherine got to her feet. Lucinda followed suit beside her. She glanced at her husband. Junno stepped away from one of the fluted columns supporting the covered portico he had been leaning against and moved closer to them. Bianca rose, giving an exclamation of delight. Only Nick Condor remained outwardly impassive. Until the third distinct cannon boom rolled over the island

"Bianca!"

She ignored him. Sighing, he made no further effort to prevent her fleet of foot dash to the stables. "It's a signature signal," he said, tonelessly. The two sleek brown hounds resumed their places at his feet. He smiled with his lips only. "Nought to be worried about." His casual dismissal sounded hollow.

The villa came alive again. The activities in the kitchen resumed their industrious pitch.

After Junno had given her a reassuring nod and made a show of resuming his whittling, Lucinda slowly retook her place on the wrought iron bench.

"Catherine?" she murmured, anxiously.

"H'm," Catherine responded, gazing through the soft evening light enveloping the perfumed gardens. Absolute conviction had initiated the wild beating of her heart. Adding to her disquiet was the tidal wave of jealous washing over her upon hearing the sound of a horse galloping away from the villa. Taking a deep, calming breath, she attempted to dismiss Bianca's wilfulness. She needed a subject to take her blood-pounding attention from the one closest to her heart, that was in danger of shredding it. "How did you become acquainted?" she asked, sitting back down next to Lucinda. She gave a tight-lipped smile as the young Romany woman placed a hand on her arm in a comforting gesture.

"Bianca? I acquired her during an…expedition."

Catherine met his look, aware he was being evasive. "With Shadiz?"

Condor hesitated before answering. His relaxed manner was not entirely convincing. "Well, sweet darlin', him and me, we were acquainted afore Formentera sailed into our sights."

"They used t' try an' outrun each other t' booty," put in Junno, without looking up from the wooden horse he was expertly carving.

"We'd compete," said Condor, grinning, "by crowding on sail after bein' blessed with a favourable wind and…. "

"Compete t' plunder a merchantman," interrupted Junno. "Or any poor sod."

"The outcome being?" prompted Catherine.

"Finally blew each other out watter," commented Junno, flatly.

Condor grimaced beneath the astonished gazes of the young women. "Look, ye 'eathen Romany," he complained, scowling at Junno. "'ow the hell was I to know all o' a sudden wind'd freshen." Looking for sympathy, he turned his attention to the women. "I

123

ordered a warning shot across trading ship's bows afore boarding. Damn thing hit his instead." Quickly, he added, "I tried to make reassuring signals. But the reprisal came with a vengeance. So I saw red." He shrugged. "There weren't any manoeuvrability, so.... "

"The tupids blew each other out watter," reiterated Junno.

"Well, yes," conceded Condor, reluctantly. He held up a defensive hand. "But. Ah but! We saved most of our crews."

"Aye," retorted Junno. "Y' all bobbed about on wreckage for 'ow long three...four days."

"The big fella doesn't come often," Condor told the women.

"And?" prompted Catherine, smiling in spite of herself.

"And," Condor replied, giving Junno a pained glance. "Well after glaring at each other for one or two days, forget which. We came to conclusion. 'If y' can't beat 'em, join 'em'."

"So you were rescued altogether?" asked Lucinda.

Condor squirmed. "In a manner o' speakin'."

"All o' 'em ended up as galley slaves," pointed out Junno.

"I'm really glad big fella doesn't come often," remarked Condor, emphatically.

Catherine and Lucinda were both shocked. Catherine asked, "For how long?"

"Seemed like years," Condor replied, turning over his hands and staring at his palms as if the calluses were still visible. "Sweet Jesus, for weeks after bein' freed, I'd be rowing in me sleep." He spread his hands on his knees. "We were on the benches until the Bey got wind his sweetheart was chained to an oar."

Catherine frowned. "I don't understand."

Junno stopped whittling. Giving Condor a meaningful look, he said, "Shadiz is known to the Bey of Algeria. He paid his ransom. Shadiz paid for the rest to be set free."

"We're all in his debt," said Condor, airily.

"Keeps y' 'ere in style," commented Junno, solemn-faced.

Condor gave a short laugh. "True enough, big fella."

"An' then y' came t' Formentera?" asked Lucinda, switching from her husband to Condor.

"We needed a base after deciding to pool our resources. The island of Formentera was suggested to us by an envoy from Spain.

Quietly, like. The king allowed Shadiz to purchase a slice of the island. In return, he agreed to protect its people from Barbary pirates. Being the smallest and most vulnerable, Formentera more than any other of the Balearic Islands was prone to raids. One time, they seized a goodly half o' population. Needless to say, nothing's happened since we arrived. The island's flourished."

"So," said Catherine after a length pause, "You and him are partners?"

Condor looked from her inquisitive face to Junno. "Well, big fella. What d' you think?"

"Y' serve 'im, like rest o' us."

"Ah, but," answered Nick Condor, brightly, "Him an' me, we made a pact while chained to those damned benches. Whatever happened in future. We'd not strangle each other."

★

Benjamin followed Shadiz topside. He inhaled the fresh sea air in an effort to dispel the lingering affects of the smoky gun deck. Curious about what response the staggered cannon fire had elicited, he surveyed the long golden shoreline. It was now crowded with the inhabitants of two substantial fishing villages, a mile or so apart. Taken by surprise, he scanned the moderate heights, one to the east and the other south-west of the *Endeavour's* present position. Even there distant figures were rapidly multiplying on pine covered slopes between fields of rippling wheat. He was sure he heard the faint ringing of church bells. Above all, it was the sight of two sloops rounding the promontory that ultimately held his attention and those of his shipmates. Both sleek vessels were flying a fiesta style array of pennants.

Half-turning, Shadiz handed Benjamin a black bundle. "Run 'em up foremast," he commanded.

Benjamin wasn't sure whether it was the shrewd glacial look from his leader while accepting the two flags or the thought of entering the dragon's den accompanied by the dominant dragon that caused his hands to shake as he completed what had to be the final part of a procedure for recognition.

When the distant between the Endeavour and the two fast sloops had diminished significantly, the Englishman was hailed. Neither Benjamin nor any of the other men understood what passed between their leader and the flamboyantly-dressed, grinning man on the vessel off their starboard bow. Whatever it was seemed at once to satisfy and irritate Shadiz.

Having altered their heading in a mirrored, expert manoeuvre, the two sloops followed in the wake of the Endeavour as she sailed around the promontory where eager spectators had gathered around the base of the tall watchtower.

Shadiz was once again at the helm. He navigated the Endeavour through the array of vessels anchored in the unusual clarity of the water in the horseshoe bay.

The unease her crew had experienced upon proximity to Formentera was significantly increased as they viewed in silent passing fast sloops similar to the ones at their stern, formidable Spanish galleons and impressive bertones. One knowledgeable crewman among the Master's men explained that such vessels were of medium tonnage with a solid hull and depth of keel which enabled them to ride any kind of sea. Ideal for the lucrative business of piracy.

Upon encountering such an extraordinary sight he suspected would rival the naval strength of most countries, Benjamin's resolve was strengthened. His first impression of Formentera had been misleading. Basking like sharks in the natural harbour was a corsair fleet bristling with the means of death and destruction.

Approaching the shore, Shadiz sailed the *Endeavour* through the inconvenient maze of smaller service boats with practise ease. Issuing precise commands to his temporary English crew, he brought the *Endeavour* alongside the sweeping arc of the stone quay with an expertise that made it plain to everyone aboard how accustomed he was at docking any vessel at the island's thriving port.

Standing at the ship's rail, Benjamin's guts knotted upon scrutinising the many buildings crowded around the quayside. There were barn-like warehouses, their black mouths ajar, gaudily painted taverns, some with what looked like ships' figure-heads nailed to their rambling upper stories, and an assortment of stores that would not have looked out of place in any large port in England. The bewildering array of white brick and bleached wooden buildings were dissected in several places by narrow shady lanes fanning out from the harbour. Benjamin's attention was caught by the inhabitants of the white-washed houses pouring down the sandy lanes. In no time at all they were rushing on a tidal wave of expectation into the boisterous crowd rapidly gathering on the quayside. The jovial mass appeared to represent every race under the glorious sinking sun.

Caught off guard, Benjamin staggered sideward upon being push towards the gangway. Recovering his balance, at the same time attempting to conceal his apprehension, he followed Shadiz down to the crowded quayside.

Any other man stepping into such a joyous welcome would have been engulfed and subjected to cheerful jostling. In contrast, the Master walked a deferential corridor filled only with effusive hails.

Hard on his leader's light, animalistic heels, it was Benjamin who was accosted by the raucous throng. Gritting his teeth against the rough shoves and merry, none-too-gentle slaps, he felt like a whipping boy. He stumbled after an exceptionally hard whack on the back, and was in danger of pitching headlong under the many eager feet. Without missing a stride, Shadiz half-turned, seized Benjamin's arm and thrust him in front of himself. Thereafter, Benjamin was careful to keep one step ahead of his leader's charismatic protection, in much the same way the mastiff had done from the start of their progress along the length of the horseshoe quayside.

Brown, black, bronzed and white, weathered and youthfully smooth, coarse and pretty, the gallery of faces, all split by broad smiles, marked their passing while bodies, worn and strong, slovenly fat and temptingly slender jostled one another. This was not simply an enthusiastic homecoming for a leader. It was the island's embrace of an undisputed admiral of the fleet.

Benjamin's curiosity got the better of him. A quick glance over his shoulder revealed Shadiz's reaction to the clamorous homage. The enigmatic expression upon his tribal dark, scarred features appeared not to have altered and yet the striking persona of a powerful renegade with a genius for command was being effortlessly projected. Right or wrong. Bewildered or bewitched. Benjamin had to admit the man was compelling and unique.

He swallowed his confusion. The esteem he had developed for the extraordinary Gypsy was in direct conflict with the manner of Shadiz's arrival on Formentera. Such an enthusiastic, loyal homage he was witnessing made it impossible for him to go on considering the possibility that it was Nick Condor who had been solely responsible for the deaths of his father, brothers and young niece and nephew.

Eventually they came to a group of men who stood apart from the roaring euphoria. Although they too clearly shared great pleasure at seeing the Master, their welcome was more in keeping with their collective air of authority. Benjamin saw each man take surreptitious notice of the disfigurement on the left side of Shadiz's face. It came as no surprise to him to learn they were the Master commanders. Paying their respects to him, their various accents made plain their different origins. Together they formed a dubious melting pot of Spanish, French, Italian, Arabic and English. What Shadiz said to them was lost on Benjamin. While considering them, his attention was captured by the most exotic beauty he had ever seen. The fact she was wearing male attire in an enticing manner made him stare even harder.

She sidled up to him in such a provocative manner his cheeks grew hot. "Who do we have here?" Her soft foreign accent added to her sensuous allure.

"Leave 'im be, Bianca," Shadiz commanded.

Her almond eyes remained upon Benjamin for a couple of moments longer while she pouted with extravagant innocence. When her disconcerting attention slipped away from him, he witnessed the devouring look she gave Shadiz as he mounted one of the restive horses tethered nearby. He indicted that Benjamin should do the same. Unbidden, Bianca also mounted.

Before leaving the tumultuous harbour scene, Shadiz turned his mount to face the rippling sea of people. He said nothing. His commanding survey of the numerous, upturned faces ensured an obedient hush in less than a minute. When he addressed his attentive audience, Benjamin could not understand a word he said.

Noting his confusion, Bianca walked her horse alongside his, and explained, "He talks Common Tongue."

"What is he saying?" asked Benjamin.

Bianca gave a delicate shrug. "Usual nonsense."

When Shadiz singled out a priest at the forefront of the throng and apologised, in French, for some blasphemous utterance and then laughed at the stout Father's feigned dismay, Benjamin was struck by how much younger he suddenly appeared.

Benjamin heard a name. And watched as the people looked around at their jolly neighbours until a tall, blond, blue-eyed man was hustled forward.

"The ship I sailed 'ere in be yours. Pick y'r own crew," said Shadiz in English, "Take care o' men they'll replace on the *Endeavour*. Make 'em welcome while they're 'ere."

The young man's suntanned features beamed with pride and pleasure. He bowed. "I thank you greatly, sir," he said, in Nordic English.

Shadiz inclined his head.

Before Benjamin could ask, Bianca translated his parting words to the crowd. "He stand's their revelry this night."

The Master turned his mount away from the deafening roars of approval. He glanced across at Benjamin. "Let's go see y'r other Nemesis."

At their backs, the taverns were being illuminated in anticipation of a good night's trade. Benjamin caught a fleeting glance of a large warehouse, its doors standing open, full of people either standing or sitting in the cavernous gloom. And then they too disappeared behind him while the dipping sun infused the Mediterranean Sea in a rosy glow.

Before him lay revenge.

CHAPTER SEVENTEEN

Swords and Quills

The first indication they were being watched was when Peter looked up from his plate and spluttered in childish astonishment. The assembled company sitting around the large dining table pursued Peter's wide-eyed gaze to where Shadiz was standing in the open French windows. A silent, shadowy manifestation of their expectations ever since they had listened to the precise cannon fire.

A pause of heavy magnitude descended upon the candlelit chamber.

Despite having sensed his approach before anyone else, Catherine was unable to escape the paralysing force bearing down on her neck.

Escaping the moment's pressure, she slowly raise her head. In making the deliberate contact, the raw intensity of Shadiz's jet-black gaze upon her robbed her of breath, and resolve to greet his arrival with nothing other than contempt because of what she had discovered in the stone chamber below Shannlarrey. Worse, a fleeting dizziness clouded her vision while her face drained of what little colour remained. Swallowing convulsively, she blinked away the image that had continually stalked her days and nights. Only to have her gaze sharpen upon the tall, powerful, incredible reality.

"Look what I find," declared Bianca, a smug expression on her beautiful, dusky face.

Her familiar manner beside Shadiz, albeit at a prudent distance, caused Catherine to experience a surge of inner fury. She became aware of Benjamin standing slightly behind Shadiz and Bianca. It was the odd expression on his bronzed face, a mixture of heartbreak and bloodlust, that captured her full attention.

Sudden chaos replaced the muted blend of emotions prevalent in the chamber.

The two hounds close to Nick Condor's chair took exception to the mastiff's presence. Barking aggressively, they attacked in unison from each side of the dining table. The large grey dog retaliated with a battled-hardened defence. Whereupon frightened screams erupted from Jack and Kate. Just for good measure, Peter joined in the shrill chorus. In her fearful haste to avoid the canine argument, Rosa dropped the large silver tray from which she had been serving honey glazed chicken. The loud metallic clatter rivalled the grind of steel being unsheathed.

"You murdering bastard!" Benjamin roared. Rushing past Shadiz, he charged the head of the table where Nick Condor was sitting.

Evidently taking into consideration the earlier waterborne herald, the brawny Irishman had prudently sat down to the lavish evening meal with his sword at his side. Judging by his expression as he shot to his feet, tipping over his chair, he had anticipated threats from an entirely different quarter. At once, he was forced to defend himself against Benjamin's earnest attack.

By now, Rosa was screaming, too. The terrified children were becoming hysterical. Distressed, though not quite so vocal, Lucinda and Keeble both had the presence of mind to appease the clamour of alarm by rounding up the terrified Spanish woman and the children and shepherding them away from the battleground. Their hasty efforts were hampered at the door by a knot of aghast servants.

Junno broke up the dog fight by seizing the two hounds by the scruff of their necks and bundling them into a small antechamber. At the same time Catherine risked a deluge of rare porcelain as the human duellists crashed against the table in order to grab hold of the mastiff to prevent it from responding to the fierce indignant barking set up by the hounds from the other side of the slammed door. While she hung onto the large, shaggy-grey dog, the snarl of battle faded and was replaced by an effusive greeting.

Responding to the clash of arms, Bill Todd raced through the

French windows, only just avoiding Shadiz at the last minute. Several of the Master's men and a few Romany who had been close on Todd's heels immediately backed off upon discovering their leader's presence at the villa. For a couple of moments, upon seeing the reason for the clash of steel, Bill stood transfixed. Coming to his senses, he shouted at Benjamin to cease what he viewed as his irrational aggression.

Knowing better than Bill what a lethal opponent Benjamin had engaged, Junno added his own loud remonstrations to both of the active protagonists. To no avail. For it was clear Benjamin was determined to fight to the bitter end. And Condor, by dint of self-preservation, was ready to oblige him.

Bianca had stepped behind Shadiz without coming into contact with him. She called out to her uncle, still seated at the dining table, while her glittering eyes remained upon the duellists. His terrified servant was only too glad to escort his elderly master to the safety of a corner seat. The youth cowered beside the chair while the Persian regarded Shadiz. He wasn't the only one to ignored the sword fight.

Shadiz's lack of interest in the conflict earned him Catherine's disgust. Rising from pacifying the mastiff, she exclaimed, "Do something!" The paleness that had stolen into her face at first sight of him was now being infused with angry hues.

He appeared unmoved by her urgency. His black scrutiny remained centred upon her. "Walk wi' me?"

Catherine had difficulty hearing his whispery words above the ensuing swordplay and accompanying devastation it was causing around the chamber. "What?"

"Walk wi' me?"

Stunned, she flung out an impatient arm towards Benjamin and Condor. "Do something about them."

Without looking away from her, he gave an indifferent shrug, "Junno an' Bill're seein' t' 'em."

Agitated and mightily frustrated, she enunciated her words. "Do. Something. Now!"

He remained in the open French windows, his attention failing to stray beyond her. "If y'll walk wi – "

"You arrogant bastard."

He hoisted an eyebrow. "Y' ain't t'...."

"Blaspheme," snapped Catherine. She gave a harassed sigh. "All right," she managed through gritted teeth. "I'll walk with you."

It took only two silent, predatory strides for him to tower over her. For her to be assailed by his masculine warm roughness and the tang of the sea that had brought him to her. In spite of herself, she inhaled his presence.

"Your English bride child...."

Bianca got no further. She blanched and retreated when Shadiz rounded on her with a feral growl.

Catherine caught hold of his arm, afraid of what he might do. Her hand closed over hard muscles. It was a mistake. When he turned back to her, the dangerous fury that had threatened Bianca had been replace by an entirely different emotion. Catherine experienced a painful jolt. Neither Shadiz nor herself registered Bianca's surprise gasp at the physical contact Shadiz was not only tolerating, but seemed to be welcoming.

When, with lingering gentleness, Shadiz removed Catherine's left hand from his arm, he looked down at the golden band he had placed on her finger during their wedding ceremony in St. Mary's Church at Whitby. Before he released her, his thumb stroked the wedding ring. Trembling, Catherine watched him walk away, unaware of Bianca's astounded, venomous glare.

A shrill, ear-piercing whistle, recognised by all of the Master's followers, rang out.

"Enough"

Reinforcing his dominant influence, Shadiz drew the broadsword he carried on his back and deftly sliced between the lighter, fast-moving swords.

His skilful intervention put both Benjamin and Condor off their respective strokes. Adding to their disadvantage, Shadiz flicked his wide-bladed weapon broadways, forcing the sweat-bathed antagonists to disengage sufficiently for Junno to capture Condor from behind in a strong restraining grip. At the same time, Bill Todd seized Benjamin, half-turning him away from the Irishman's flailing sword.

Panting, Condor demanded, "Sweet Jesus! Who the hell is this manic?" He tried to shrug off Junno's grip. Only after a curt nod from Shadiz did the big man permit cautious release.

Catherine began to approach the men.

"Stay put, Kore," Shadiz ordered, without turning.

Though she wanted to calm Benjamin for his own sake, she reluctantly complied. Behind her, she heard Bianca snigger.

"So, all right. You're bleedin' frazzled wi' me, brother," Condor said to Shadiz, projecting a hurt expression, "I only did what I thought was best for y'r sweet darlin'." He grinned in the face of Shadiz's jet glare. "Nice to know the pact still stands."

"You will not be standing when I've finished with you," Benjamin shouted, his sweat-bathed face contorted with rage. He continued to writhe in Bill's struggling grip.

When he attempted to raise his sword, Shadiz knocked it away with the broadsword. Bill immediately kicked the weapon away. He kept a prudent lock on Benjamin.

"You murdered my father and brothers!" Benjamin declared, seething with animosity. "And my two young cousins."

Nick Condor's flushed, sweaty features creased into a frown. "I hate to be callous, me boy. Just who're you on about?"

While speaking he had raised his sword a few degrees. Shadiz laid the broadsword over it, bringing pressure to bear. Shrugging, Condor responded by sheathing his weapon.

"They were aboard the Northern Lights two years ago," Benjamin rasped. "They were sailing home from Malta. They had gone there to bring back my cousins after their parents' death. None of them returned to England. Due to your murderous actions."

"Northern Lights, y' say?" said Condor, thoughtfully, looking at Shadiz

"That's right," grated Benjamin. "The ship was bordered by your filthy herd."

Condor ignored him. "Weren't that the one you told me t' find out about when y' sent message wi' Keeble about wanting Sea Witch?"

"An'?" snapped Shadiz.

"I got Pedro to look in ledgers. They're in Portugal," Condor told him.

"Whose in Portugal?" demanded Benjamin, glaring now at both men.

Condor heeded Shadiz's warning look. He cleared his throat apologetically. "Your family, me boy, are toiling in Portugal. Sorry about that. As for your cousins. They must be the young lambs you scared half t' death earlier."

Benjamin appeared sceptical. "I don't believe you."

"Believe 'im. An' me," said Shadiz, tersely. "We'd shipped men out afore Nick found bairns an' brought 'em topside from fire."

Bianca sidled up to Catherine. She gave a nasty laugh. "They're slavers, cretin. Murder would damage their profit. Only he takes lives for sick pleasure."

Shadiz hissed.

Catherine did not allow her hearty dislike of the voluptuous Persian woman to stop her from adjusting her position so that she was standing upon broken crockery slightly in front of Bianca. No matter what the other woman's reciprocal opinion of her was, Catherine sensed Bianca's avid wish to remain behind her. Meanwhile, she tried not to be outwardly affected by the advance of both Shadiz and Condor.

The two men, both impressive in their own right, both came to a grinding halt at either side of Catherine. Realising Condor was about to pull his mistress out of harm's way, she pinned Shadiz with a fixed stare, only to have it collide with a black challenge of his own. He had done as she asked and stopped the fight between Condor and Benjamin. Peripheral vision made her aware Condor and Bianca had not failed to notice how Shadiz had refrained from dragging her away. But then they were not aware as Junno was that he had never treated her roughly, even when she had tried his limited patience.

A restraining hand upon Bianca, Condor looked sideward at Shadiz in the ensuing pause. His usual Irish brightness had been overtaken by serious consideration, not only of the other man's scarred cheek. After a couple of moments, he was the one to march a woman away. Bianca made a show of resisting.

135

Shadiz sheathed the broadsword. A flicker of annoyance crossed his otherwise enigmatic features when Catherine looked past him to where Benjamin was standing. He was clearly trying to evaluate the truth of what he had just been told. Seeing his torment, her heart went out to him.

"Benjamin, why don't you go to Jack and Katy?" she suggested. Looking to where Keeble was standing in the doorway, she added, "Keeble will take you to them."

As if in a trance, Benjamin followed the little man out of the ruined chamber.

Glancing at Bill Todd, Shadiz jerked his head at the door Benjamin had disappeared through.

Catherine gave an exasperated sigh and walked out into the night.

Condor halted his progress with Bianca. He had been utterly taken aback by the manner in which Shadiz, the ice-cold, untameable bastard he knew, had devoured the very sight of Catherine. No menace had existed, only unbelievable vulnerability. Along with the forgotten Persian, his indignant niece and Junno, he watched as Shadiz follow Catherine out into the night time gardens.

Looking over Bianca's head, Condor met Junno's troubled gaze. Mutual understanding passed between the two men. Never having taken to the Irishman on the odd occasions he had encountered him, Junno made an effort to mask his resentment of the other man's knowledge of his cousin. He responded to Condor's quizzical tilt of his head with a reassuring nod.

Out in the fragrant stillness of the night, Catherine was acutely conscious of Shadiz's tall, soundless presence behind her. She plucked at the perceived bitterness of betrayal as if it were a putrid sore. He had married her and then abandoned her on the quayside at Whitby. The grotesque suspicion he had caused her father's death because of his desire to own Fylingdales Hall and Estate gave her ample reason, she believed, to give vent to her churning emotions.

Beneath the lamp-lit covered portico, she stopped abruptly and whirled around to confront him. Only his innate reflex action prevented him from walking into her.

"You are an unfeeling, vindictive, manipulating...."

"Bastard," he softly finished for her, maintaining his undivided consideration of her young, flushed face.

"Absolutely."

She turned and marched a couple of irate paces away before once again rounding on him. "You not only used poor Benjamin against Nick simply because he thought to bringing me here. Oh, yes. I have a very good idea about what takes place alongside the ordinary island life. Why else would I be trapped here at the Casa?" She narrowed her furious gaze. "And, no. No one breathed a word. I maybe young but do not take me for a fool." Without pause, she accused him, "Yet, you have, haven't you? I understand now – really understand." She flung out her arms indiscriminately. "All of it has been bound up in your compulsion to acquire what you consider your birthright. Ye Gods and Little Fishes! If only my father had known the depths of your treachery. He would still be alive. You used him and tossed him away when he was of no further use to you. And you used me. You forced a farcical marriage."

"Farcical?"

She paid no heed to him. "And then shipped me away to France!"

Catherine started to wrench the wedding ring off her finger.

"Don't, " Shadiz whispered, stepping closer to her and covering her hands with his much larger, calloused one. When she continued to struggle against his gentle yet unremitting grip, he added. "Please, Kore."

She swallowed some of her acrimonious heat at his pleading tone. But would not let him see how it had affected her. "Fine," she muttered, ending her resistance. Pulling away from him, she snapped, "I'll keep the shackle on, then."

He flinched. She bit her lip. Nevertheless she continued to glare at him as his long, wild hair fall over his roughly unshaven features while he opened the pouch attached to his low-slung sword belt. Catherine immediately recognised the papers he withdrew.

He held them out to her. "Y' ain't got through 'em all," he stated.

"I saw all I needed to. Down to the last hen and silver spoon Fylingdales boasts."

He pulled out an official-looking document from the rest of the paperwork. "I reckon y' ain't got round t' this one," he said in a neutral tone.

She stared hotly at it, and then switched to his tense features. "What is this? Another of your elaborate ploys."

"Kore, read it." It was not a command.

She was loathed to be influenced by his dark persuasion. Standing tight-lipped, her attention eventually lowered to the document he continued to hold out to her. Hating herself, she snatched it from his grubby hand, which seemed vaguely unsteady.

The neat official script described a lawfully binding contract. Certain details jumped off the stiff parchment and confronted her with the impossible. She read them twice over. And then re-read them again for good measure.

Finally she looked up and laughed in his midnight, barbarous face. "You really do take me for a young, gullible fool," she said, coldly, thrusting the document back at him. "How much did you bribe the lawyer to create the worthless piece of fiction?"

His hard mouth twitched. There was a glint of humour in his black eyes "Isaac'd be real pleased hearin' y' give 'im 'is true worth."

"Ye Gods and Little Fishes! Don't you dare make light of this!"

Shadiz had not taken the document from her. He said, "Isaac the Jew held the mortgage on Fylingdales. I bought it off him."

"It is beyond belief that any part of Fylingdales Hall or Estate would ever need to be mortgaged."

"Unless folk there were dead set on livin' like royalty. How much d' y' reckon the lavish lifestyle Lynette an' his sister insist upon costs? Not to mention upkeep o' 'is small army."

"You have one," she was quick to point out.

"I can afford it."

"Through slavery, no doubt."

Incredibly still, his eyes betraying him, very softly, he asked, "Trust me, Kore."

Once before, he had asked the same of her, when they had

been in the midst of the dangerous North Sea. She had done so, going into a feared black hole. She had emerged with something more precious than gold.

The roiling anger within her painfully tight chest faltered. Had she not named this man correctly on the deck of the Eagle? She had never tried to sew velvet over stone. Only sought to heal the fracture. For, through the hurt, he had pierced her soul.

A prey to confusion, she withdrew from his persistent scrutiny. She sat down on the nearest wrought-iron bench and beneath a lamp's soft glow read the document yet again, just in case an absence of reliable light before had misrepresented the import.

Without a shadow of a doubt, there it was, stated in official language that for eight months Shadiz had held the full hundred percent mortgage on Fylingdale Hall and the Estate. That he was in fact the legal owner with every right to sequestrate the whole if, on demand, the outstanding debt failed to be paid.

By the time Catherine had finished reading the words for the umpteenth time, she was trembling and the neat script was becoming blurred. She slowly lifted her head and looked up at him. "You really are their landlord. The true owner of Fylingdales?" she muttered in wonder. She frowned, mystified. "If that is so why haven't you taken up your legitimate claim?"

A muscle flexed in his scarred cheek. "There's allus Driffield Hall an' Derwent Manor."

Catherine felt seriously unsettled. "They are our neighbours. Nafferton Garth is bordered by Fylingdales Estate, and the estate boundaries of Driffield Hall and Derwent Manor. I...I don't understand?"

For the first time since he had appeared at the villa Shadiz would not meet her bewildered gaze. Half turning away from her, he stood without speaking for some time, contemplating the indistinct garden. The silence stretched between them, disturbed only by the night serenade of the cicada and the sounds of clearing up the aftermath of the swordfight coming from within the villa. Catherine was starting to believe he wasn't going to respond until he turned his head and, seeing her watching him, gave a hesitant smile. She sensed the tension within him and understood when he swung the broadsword off his back he was finding release in movement. He placed the weapon against the nearest fluted column supporting the covered portico. Taking a step backwards, he too rested against the white support, crossing his arms over his shirt, carelessly open halfway to his waist. Catherine's attention was drawn to the moonstone pendent resting against his dark skin, sparkling in the light of the lamps with each quick breath he took.

Scarcely above a whisper, he began, " Sidney Courtney of Derwent Manor ain't any livin' relatives. The old lad weren't keen on 'is place bein' either swallowed up by some greedy treasury official or sucked into Fylingdales. As for Driffield Hall lot. Again, it were a case o' livin' high. An' 'avin' six marriageable daughters. Roger agreed to act as me agent. Y'r da bein' more respectable. Sir Neville about fell over 'issen t' tak' up the offer that meant a way out o' 'is debts wi'out bein' made 'omeless. 'is unknown benefactor would be absent. An old Courtney thought Roger'd be gettin' 'is place after 'is death." He finished with a small, awkward shrug.

Her breath taken away by the revelations, Catherine sat in stunned silence, staring at him. She gave a small breathless laugh. "No wonder my father was the guest of honour at Sir Neville's Christmas ball. And Agnes was permitted to finally announce her engagement." She tried to grasp the significance of what he had revealed "So, in effect, you own all three estates surrounding Nafferton Garth." She raised her shoulders in confusion. "To what end?"

There was a slight change in his stance. His dark features had grown brutally hard. "Lynette approached Isaac about extendin' loan on Fylingdales in order t' purchase both Derwent and Driffield estates by offerin' 'is sister's jewellery chest as collateral, whether she knew it or not. Right from start 'e's been inclined t' Parliament. Though y' would've expected 'im t' look t' king wi' 'is background. I weren't goin' t' watch 'im isolate Roger." There was a brief hesitation before he added, "An' 'is daughter."

"Isolate Nafferton Garth," she muttered. A thought struck her with devastating consequence. "Wait a minute. You do not own Nafferton Garth, do you?"

"Sort o'."

Colour drained from her face. She rose slowly to her feet. "What do you mean…sort of?"

He cleared his throat. "I wed the legal heir," he answered.

"Ye gods and little fishes!"

He grimaced. "Seems t' be plenty o' 'em flyin' about tonight. Lookin' on tother side o' coin. Y' 'eard what Francois Fordor'd t' say, I reckon. You too own…."

"Half of the Continent," she put in, dryly. "And now it would appear half of Yorkshire." The next development in her whirling mind made her protest. "And Formentera! There are things on this island that are suspect, to say the least. "

"There's good mixed in wi' everythin'."

"I would certainly like to see it instead of the villa walls, pleasant as they are."

He remained ominously silent.

Catherine sat down again. It all seemed so extraordinary. And believable, because of Shadiz's undoubted flair for intrigue.

One point was sorely felt. In all of her father's dealings with him, throughout his visits to Nafferton Garth, she had not known of his existence except in tall tales. Not even that the Romany who her father allowed to stay each winter at Nafferton Garth were in fact his relations. Or that it had been his grandmother, for her own reasons, who had taught her about herbal medicine.

Only when through treachery which had led to her father's death had Shadiz entered her life, with devastating consequences. What if the lie of the land had remained tranquil? "To whom had you decided to marry me off?" she demanded.

He swung away from her.

"Rosa wants t' know if y' want owt t' eat?" asked Junno, approaching them

Trembling, Catherine watched the dense veil descend over tormented jet. She jumped up. "I'll go inform her you do," she murmured, wanting to escape Shadiz's overwhelming presence in order to marshal her splintered thoughts.

CHAPTER EIGHTEEN

Discord and Harmony

Catherine and Lucinda agreed to desert the formality of the dining room. They had no trouble in persuading Junno, Keeble and Benjamin to join them and the children in partaking of breakfast outdoors, especially Benjamin who was hoping to become better acquainted with his young cousins. Rosa had taken a little more persuading to forsake tradition, but once she had been convinced, mostly by Jack, Katy and Peter, she fussed around the table set up on the sunny terrace. The food was secondary to the novelty, yet was eaten with far more relish than otherwise would have been surrounded by the tapestries adorning the immaculate white-washed walls of the villa. The sparrows and pigeons came en masse to feed on the crumbs of sweetmeats, almond cakes and garlic and saffron bread, spread haphazardly with preserved cherries. Grapes were popped into laughing mouths and apples pealed to lie fallow. The strawberry water and orange and lemon juices flowed, and so did the spillages.

After a mainly sleepless night plagued by chaotic thoughts, Catherine welcomed the diversion.

In trying to come to terms with what Shadiz had told her the previous evening shortly after his arrival at the villa, one conclusion kept coming to the fore. Although he had remained silent when she had challenged him about who he would have seen her marry if matters in her world had not gone awry, her intuition provided the answer he would not. For despite his vicious ridicule of Richard's immaculate respectability, he must have been aware that it was a quality her father sought for her. After securing Fylingdales Hall and Estate, would he then have handed over his half-brother's inheritance as a wedding gift?

Even though Shadiz was a law unto himself, deep in the restless night, Catherine found herself wondering if her father had been privy to the intentions of his unlikely friend. The suspicion aroused a feeling of betrayal. No doubt her father had only had her best interest in mind. Yet in all matters, he had always respected her opinion. Had he been just another poor soul to fall under Shadiz's mesmerizing influence?

Ever since her father's death her world had spun in tumultuous ways. She was now married to Shadiz. Albeit a wife in name only. A convenience supposedly to protect her. Or had their marriage been a means to merge Nafferton Garth with the three estates he had apparently acquired? What should she believe? He seemed like a wild wind, blowing close, explaining matters to her, giving her an intriguing slice of himself as he had done when, on the quayside at Whitby, he had admitted to having watched her grow up from a distance. Only then to withdraw from her once more. Insisting she sail away from England and himself. Nor could she take any real comfort in his reappearance while feeling torn between the hope he had responded when he had considered her to be threatened or the suspicion he considered his investment to be threatened. Her feeling of being trapped in a poignant labyrinth made her oblivious at times to what was taking place around her.

She was drawn out of her pensive slips by Lucinda's perceptive looks across the jolly breakfast table. Returning to the present moment, she renewed her efforts to partake in the jolly meal with Peter, Jack and Katy.

Laughter stopped him in his tracks. Standing perfectly still, Shadiz listened to what to him was sweet music. When the merriment came to a conclusion, he realised he had been holding his breath. Released from the captivating spell, he took a shuddering intake of warm morning air and moved silently forward, unconsciously adopting the caution he had practised on so many previous occasions. Lacy fronds of tall drooping ferns in a leafy corner a few feet away from the occupied terrace provided shady camouflage.

That very first glimpse he had stumbled upon, eons ago it now seemed, had brought about a shift deep within him. It had spurred him on for a thousand more glimpses. From a distance. Always from a distance. The wraith within the darkest shadows.

At first the overwhelming need was to protect, afraid for her innocence and her madcap adventures. As the years passed and she had blossomed even lovelier in his eyes, his consideration of her had subtly altered. It had made the ache deep with his vile frame a righteous thread to her wherever he might be.

Her father had never condemned him. Roger had not baulked at the suspicion and then the knowledge both of them could not deny. It was he who had grown wary of himself, even more protective.

As always, he could not refrain from watching her. His untouchable wife.

She could put the Graces to shame. Thalia, the flowering. Euphrosyne, joy. Aglaia, radiance. All bound up in Charis, grace itself in spirit and body.

Above all she was Kore. The Maiden who would forever be his soul.

The sensation of being watched made Catherine look up. Frowning slightly, she cast about into the deepest shade within the garden bordering the terrace. The feeling persisted for several moments longer before slipping away. She had not felt threatened. Just the opposite. With that in mind, her heart began to pound and her hand holding a knife began to tremble. She looked around again, catching Junno's concerned eye.

When more dishes were require because all those carried out had been used with gay abandon, Catherine volunteered to collect more despite the polite objections of the busy servants.

With something akin to relief, she turned her back on the laughter and happy chatter of the outdoor breakfast. Upon approaching the dining chamber, her attention was caught by the occupants. A disturbing aspect about the tableau brought her up short in the same spot in the open French windows Shadiz had occupied the previous evening.

Prince Ardashir was sitting halfway down the long dining table. Both his attention and appetite appeared to have become diverted from the tempting dishes set before him. His young servant stood stiffly behind his master's chair, his frightened gaze darting one way then another at the other two occupants.

Judging by the half eaten food upon his plate, Nick Condor had been breaking his fast with the Persian Vizier. As Catherine watched, he fidgeted in his chair. Shadiz was standing beside the long polished table. There was no sign of him having joined the two men for breakfast. He appeared far from pleased about something. Catherine registered his disparaging tone but did not catch the gist of his low-pitched words. Nick Condor's response seemed to be a mixture of resentment and discomfit. Projecting a detached attitude to the two men's obvious discord, Prince Ardashir was studying Shadiz.

In the next moment, Shadiz turned abruptly. For all his glaring displeasure at discovering her presence, Catherine got an impression of involuntary guilt as their eyes locked briefly. Swinging away from her, he fired a single word at Condor before stalking out of the sunny chamber. Condor gave her a long-suffering grin before getting to his feet and following Shadiz in a nonchalant manner that somehow did not ring true.

Prompted by Prince Ardashir's indulgent attention, Catherine stepped into the overly quiet chamber. She thought it best not to mention the exchange she had interrupted between Shadiz and Nick Condor, though she was burning with curiosity. Instead, she politely asked after Ardashir's health.

"I endeavour to defeat the march of years," he replied, the lines in his aristocratic face creasing into a self-depreciatory smile beneath his jewelled turban. After a burst of particularly loud laughter was heard from the courtyard, wistfully, he added, "Oh, what it is to be young."

"Not really," muttered Catherine.

Finding her endearingly vulnerable, Ardashir's expression softened. He made no comment on the haunted look in her lustrous blue eyes. "It would seem your husband is displeased by my continuing presence on Formentera," he observed, quietly.

"So that's what that was all about," said Catherine, looking towards the door first Shadiz and then Condor had disappeared through.

"He is quite formidable," commented the Prince, thoughtfully, looking in the same direction. "Your husband."

"H'm," responded Catherine.

"A wife must honour her husband's wishes," he observed, returning his mild attention to her.

"Even when he sends her hither and thither!" she pointed out, briskly.

Amusement crinkled the corners of his wise eyes.

Catherine excused herself with a polite curtsy and went in search of plates. Making her way to the kitchen, her footsteps slowed when she heard Nick Condor's Irish brogue, thickened by agitation.

"In normal run o' things, y' wouldn't give a flyin' fart about old bastard bein' here, whether it upset Spanish or French majesties. Truth is you want the damn Persian away 'cos Catherine's here. Ever since you arrived you've been like a friggin' bear wi' wolves nipping at its heels. Brother, I've got to say, you're better off either beddin' y'r wife or payin' a visit to sheds if …."

His words were cut off by the sound of something or someone colliding with furniture. Alarmed, Catherine scurried down the long cool passageway. Just as she reached the door of the chamber from where the disruption had emanated Shadiz emerged and collided with her.

Brought up short by her much shorter presence, he reacted quickly, seizing her arms to prevent her from catapulting off his hard chest and onto the tiled floor of the passageway. Even so, their coming together had knocked the breath out of Catherine. While she struggled to get it back, his grip on both her arms intensified. He looked down at her, his expression one of fierce concern. She managed a shaky recovery and squirmed in his overly-tight hold. Whereupon, he released her as if she was burning his hands.

"What're y' doin' 'ere?" he growled.

"I live here, if you recall!" she retorted, still a little breathlessly. It seemed to her, she had told him exactly the same once before at the Lodge.

Despite his great height, Junno moved with Romany stealth.

146

It was only when Shadiz looked sharply upwards that Catherine realised the big man was behind her.

"Watch 'er, dammit," rasped Shadiz, glaring at his cousin.

Catherine bristled at his tone. He made her seem like a recalcitrant child who needed to be supervised like Peter, Jack and Katie. She glared at his broad back as he strode away down the passageway.

Aware Junno would not want her to investigate further, which was confirmed by his discouraging look, even so she walked into the chamber. Junno shadowed her.

It was immediately obvious what had happened. Junno brushed past her and extracted Nick Condor from the jumble of overturned furniture. Concerned about him, her anger at Shadiz soared to new heights. Blood was pouring from the Irishman's nose and mouth. He blinked dizzily as Junno hoisted him up into a sitting position. Catherine knelt down beside him.

"Jesus, that hurt," he mumbled, spitting out blood.

While Junno righted the furniture, Catherine inspected the damage. "You're lucky, there's nothing broken. But you are going to have a few colourful mementoes."

"Ah, sweet darlin'. Why don't I learn to keep me mouth shut around the bas…Beast?"

"I'll send someone with a cloth and water while I go for soothing salve" she said, standing upright.

When she had left them, Junno and Condor said nothing. There was little need.

From the outset the evening meal threatened to be less than convivial. Condor was having difficulty talking because of his swollen face. Bianca kept glowering at Catherine, clearly blaming her for what had befallen him. Although Benjamin had made the startling discovery his father and brothers were alive, the fact they had been sold into slavery only marginally lessened his conspicuous aversion to Condor. The last to enter the dining chamber, Shadiz seemed in no mood to speak to anyone. Taking the chair at the other end of the laden dining table opposite Nick Condor, he gave Catherine, sitting two places away, an enigmatic look. Still smarting from his curt dismal that afternoon, she pointedly ignored him, grinding her teeth because of the involuntary blush in her downcast face. For the sake of the children, she joined forces with Lucinda, Junno, Keeble and Benjamin, who was fast becoming the twins favourite cousin, in managing to keep a degree of cheerful talk alive. Proving himself to be the consummate diplomat, Prince Ardashir chipped away at the frosty atmosphere so that as the meal approached its satisfying conclusion those prone to a stony reserve saw fit to glower less.

It was with something akin to general good-humour, as the twilight deepened, the evening continued outdoors beneath the beeswax lanterns hanging under the covered portico smothered in bougainvillea.

Catherine and Lucinda sat together on one of the wrought iron benches between huge terracotta pots overflowing with sweet scented lavender. Bianca curled up with Condor on a neighbouring bench.

While reclining in the tall-backed wicker chair his youthful servant had carried out for his master, Prince Ardashir conversed quietly with Shadiz. They were the only ones not to have touched the sweet wine from Southern Spain. Shadiz was sitting on the grey flagstones, leaning against the white column nearest to the elderly Persian's chair, his long legs stretched out in front of him. Keeping a dominating eye on Condor's two subjugated hounds, the mastiff was sprawled beside its master. Although he had ordered the departure of the prince, Shadiz did not seem adverse to his company. Catherine had not seen anything of him since their morning's encounter, but shortly before the evening meal she had spotted him from the window of her bedchamber strolling in the garden, deep in conversation with the dignified Vizier.

The children had been allowed to join the adults in the balmy evening. Following an energetic ball game, they along with Junno, Keeble and Benjamin held races with beetles, whether or not the black shiny coated insects were willing participants. Their relatives the cicada kept up a constant chirpy support. When Rosa eventually arrived to announce bedtime, the plump, motherly housekeeper was assailed by the usual complaints and cajolery. Disappointment was lessened by Junno, Keeble and Benjamin becoming the mounts upon whose backs Peter, Katie and Jack could gallop into the villa.

The evening grew quiet without the boisterousness of the children. The adults took their ease in idle conversation. Throughout the evening, Catherine had resolved to pay Shadiz little heed. But finding herself increasingly distracted by his presence, she began to respond automatically to the chit-chat beneath the fragrant portico.

Shadiz was staring into the concealing darkness laid upon the garden during a lull in his conversation with Prince Ardashir. He seemed unaware of the prince's study, though Catherine suspected that not to be the case. The suspicion made her bow her head and her gaze to become even more furtive through her lashes. The rough stubble about his jaw had gone and his long midnight hair was less unruly than before. He even wore a clean cambric shirt. There were no weapons in sight, though she was convinced it did not mean he was unarmed. As she watched, he drew up his left leg and rested his arm upon his knee in a leisurely manner. His right hand was buried in the mastiff's untidy grey coat.

She became fascinated by his idle stroking of the dog. Absorbed in him, for the first time since his arrival on Formentera, she went beyond her issues with him, seeking the man to whom she was married, finding herself twisting the gold band on her left hand. The dark smudges of tiredness remained. There were faint lines of strain around his vaguely slanting black eyes and hard mouth. An unmistakeable consistency, the aura of intelligent authority clung to him. Every inch of his big, muscular body, although appearing relaxed, was that of a powerful warrior. In spite of the soft honey glow of the lanterns, he gave the impression of being elusive, part of the night. She had long since acknowledged the sinister, wild traits no one could curb. Everyone was wary of him to some degree. Yet she had never felt intimidated by him. Just the opposite. When her life had been turned upside down she had looked to him for support, albeit involuntarily at time. Right or wrong, the emotion he generated within her existed beyond her control. Being completely honest with herself, she did not want it any other way.

All at once, Shadiz turned his head and met her centred gaze.

Catherine found it impossible to tear herself away from the intenseness of his obsidian attention. Beneath his seeking directness she found her breath hard to control and her heartbeat accelerate. Once again the colour flooding her cheeks was a betrayal. And when he gave her a slow smile it almost proved her undoing.

A light touch on Catherine's shoulder made her jump. It shattered the emotive spell. She had no idea Prince Ardashir had quit his seat close to where Shadiz was reclining in spite of looking in their direction. The robed Persian was leaning upon his gold topped cane beside her. She rose hastily. A furtive glance in Shadiz's direction revealed faint amusement playing across his dark features. Hiding her rueful reaction, she returned her full attention to what Ardashir was saying.

"Before an old man seeks his rest, I must apologise for being remiss this morning by not thanking you for the consideration you showed me yesterday?" he said, smiling knowingly at her.

"I am glad the potion of feverfew helped relieve your headache?" she answered.

Taking her by surprise, Ardashir lightly kissed her flushed cheek. Before drawing away, for her ears only, he murmured, "Judge him not too harshly."

She gave him a startled look. His gaze warm, he inclined his turbaned head and then headed indoors with his young servant at his side.

Shortly afterwards, Junno, Benjamin and Keeble returned after escorting the children to bed. While Junno and Keeble resumed their seats, Benjamin began to walk away into the night-shrouded garden.

"Where y' off?" demanded the Master.

"See Bill, sir," answered Benjamin, pausing, looking over his shoulder. It was plain he did not want to remain now that Jack and Katy had gone. Briefly his pleased gaze rested on Condor's swollen face.

Shadiz gave a curt nod of acquiescence.

"Tell me," said Nick Condor, watching Benjamin go. "Why is it, lad blames me an' not you for what happened to his family?"

Shadiz dismissed the observation with an indifferent shrug.

"After all, 'tis just business," grumbled Condor. Heaving a long-suffering sigh. he disengage himself from Bianca's possessive grasp. Despite her objection, he stood upright and sauntered into the villa. A few minutes later he reappeared with two Spanish guitars. Halting beside where Shadiz was sitting on the flagstones, he held out one of the instruments and raised a quizzical eyebrow.

Shadiz seemed to hesitate, glancing in Catherine's direction. Her curious expression was met by a rueful grimace. Upon getting to his feet in one fluid movement, he took the proffered instrument from Condor. Whereupon both of the men tuned their respective guitars. Watching Shadiz in particular, Catherine recalled how the chamber at Shannlarrey contained a vast array of musical instruments, also what Philippe had informed her.

After the discord of tuning, there was a moment of expectant silence. The two men looked at one another. Seconds later the balmy night air was filled with the cascading notes of the Spanish guitars. They complimented each other, becoming expert partners in magical harmony.

Catherine was drawn forward on the bench she shared with Lucinda. She was only vaguely aware of Condor's participation. Fascinated, she watched Shadiz's long fingers as they brought the strings of the guitar to vibrant life. Raising her gaze, she saw how playing the instrument was having a relaxing affect upon him. Head bent slightly sideward, his long black hair obscured his scarred cheek. His eyes were half-closed as he concentrated on the intricacies of the music he was creating alongside Condor.

The evocative melody came to its natural conclusion. While the echo played on in the ensuing silence, Shadiz looked across at Catherine, his jet gaze speculative. She responded with a broad smile of approval.

Not to be outdone, Bianca snatched up the tambourine Condor had also brought out of the villa. "Play," she commanded, gliding from beneath the covered portico. Staying within the glow of the lanterns on the flagstones of the wide terrace, she gathered up the full, lacy skirts of her low-cut gown and demanded the music with her dramatic pose.

Condor looked sideward at Shadiz. The Irishmen appeared relieved when Shadiz joined him in playing a flamenco.

Attention was focused on Bianca. She became the interpreter of the vibrant notes of the twin guitars. The tambourine in her outstretched hand complimented their tempo. Although some of her skirt flourishing, hair tossing movements possessed the mannerisms of a flamenco, the whole was performed with sensuous Persian grace. Rather than maintaining a stiff posture, her lithe body twirled and twisted for a man's delight.

Catherine and Lucinda looked at one another and then together raised their eyes heavenwards.

Uncomfortably out of the blue, Catherine experienced a spike of inferiority. She was sixteen, younger than anyone one else present. She felt unremarkably ordinary when compared to Lucinda's dark quiet charm and Bianca's dusky sensuous appeal. Her heart in her mouth, she stole a glance at Shadiz. It was with relief she saw his attention remained exclusively on the music. Unlike Nick Condor. As he played somewhat absently alongside Shadiz, he was watching Bianca avidly.

Junno stopped whittling on a horse for Jack. He put the half worked wood and his knife aside and, much to her surprise, took hold of Lucinda's hand, raising her up onto her feet. There was more than a hint of irritation in the big man's actions. Leading her decisively forward, he looked across at his cousin. Shadiz gave an imperceptible nod. Ignoring Condor's partnering music, he changed his tempo. Instead of the flamenco rhythm, he began to play a lilting Romany melody, the type Catherine had heard in their encampment at Nafferton Garth.

Robbed of Bianca's alluring contortions, it was Condor's turn to appear irritated. Thwarted by the smooth alteration in the music, she had halted in mid-spin and was glowering at the Romany couple who were performing the measured tread of their tribal heritage. While Bianca marched back under the portico and flung herself down on a bench, Condor, on the other hand, became intrigued by the rarely heard chords of a secretive race. After a few moments of listening intently to Shadiz's expert playing, he attempted to emulate the distinctive flow of ethnic musicality.

Catherine was surprised by the light-footedness of Junno but not the grace of Lucinda. It easily rivalled Bianca's, though her movements were far more sedate. The couple matched each other and the music in a manner that served as a reminder of when she and Shadiz had dance together in honour of Tom Wright in the library at the Lodge. The lump in her throat was for the passing of her dear surrogate father. The ache deep within was for that moment of closeness she had shared with Shadiz. Just like the husband and wife were presently experiencing.

She had no idea the wistfulness imprinted on her young, fine-boned face was what prompted Lucinda to break away from Junno. Approaching Catherine with the same lightness of movement she had shown in her dancing, Lucinda urged her to her feet and then drew her into the impromptu dance. Holding both Lucinda's and Junno's hands, Catherine was unsure of what steps to take while trying hard to follow their encouraging lead in the tribal dance.

After several minutes of Junno unobtrusively observing Shadiz, his ardent hope was rewarded by movement behind Catherine. Due to her concentrating on the dance steps, she failed at first to registered the diminished tempo of the music. Only when the Romany couple's rhythmic movements slowed did Catherine look up from her shuffling feet and register Lucinda's expression.

She swallowed convulsively as the powerful, masculine height and warmth she would have recognised anywhere drew close behind her. She began to turn to face Shadiz, but he put his hands gently on both of her arms to prevent her from doing so. He held her away from him by mere inches as his hands slid down her arms and his fingers entwined with her much smaller ones. Thoroughly disconcerted by his towering nearness while looking straight ahead at Lucinda and Junno's noncommittal features, she felt Shadiz turn slightly.

"I'm tryin' me best, brother!" exclaimed Nick Condor. "Settle for summat I know, will y'."

Still without speaking, Shadiz started them moving in a shadow dance of Junno's and Lucinda's traditional lead they were adapting to Condor's playing, influenced by his Celtic roots.

Unsure of herself, Catherine surrendered to Shadiz's

considerate guidance. As one, they circled Junno and Lucinda, went forward to meet them and then swept past them. Repeating the movement twice over, the meagre distance between her back and his chest became non-existent.

After another, and what turned out to be the final gliding sequence over the terrace, Shadiz and Junno changed their holds on the young women, and spun them around several times. Catherine laughed giddily and was glad of Shadiz's support as he and Junno signalled the end of the dance by holding their respective wives by their waists, lifting them high and then placing them lightly back down on their feet facing them.

Uncertain and speculative, Lucinda and Junno looked across at the couple sharing the flagstone dance floor with them. Engrossed in one another, Shadiz and Catherine were clearly oblivious to the haunting conclusion of Condor's playing. A hush fell on the terrace lit by the ornate lanterns.

Holding his silent guitar, Nick Condor caught Junno's eye. Both men were aware of the risk. Yet Junno, after glancing at his motionless cousin, shepherded Lucinda into the villa, despite her reluctance. Following the big man's example, Condor silenced a thoroughly disgruntled Bianca with a stern look. Forgotten, Keeble melted into the night.

Catherine's world had narrowed to Shadiz. The warmth of his possessive hands around her waist burned through her thin, silk gown. His dark, harsh features softened while he continued to stare down at her. Emotional tension sparked between the few inches separating them. Holding her expressive gaze, he slowly bent to her. The heady sensation experienced by both of them as he took possession of her lips shuttered their eyes. She felt his heart beating a wild rhythm that matched her own as she slid her hands up the loose front of his cambric shirt and locked them around his neck beneath his long black hair. He deepened the kiss with exquisite tenderness.

It was with the greatest reluctance, they drew apart slightly. His breathing ragged, he leant his forehead against hers. "Kore," he murmured, softly.

Trembling, Catherine wanted desperately to seize the precious moment; to break down his reserve she sensed he was struggling to keep in place. At the same time, she was fearful of doing anything that might precipitate the return of his remote and chilling courtesy. Inwardly bemoaning her lack of experience, she caressed his neck, loving the unrestricted feel of him. Her tender touch produced an intense response, solving her dilemma. He gave a low moan. His left hand swept up her back and became buried in her long fair-white hair. This time his kiss quickly grew ardent. She matched his crushing desire, melting into his worshiping hardness until they had deprived each other of breath.

Both inflamed, he kissed her forehead, her eyes and then lay his badly scarred cheek against her soft, flushed one. "Monisha," he breathed huskily against her hair, "Forgive me."

Catherine moved a fraction so that she could look up into hot jet a hair's breadth away. "For being here?"

"For wreckin' y'r life."

Catherine would have protested, but he rested a finger upon her mouth, stroking her burning lips.

"For what it's worth, I berate mesen every day for becoming known t' y'," he confessed, his big body crowding hers.

His whispery words stung her. She wanted to take away the pain she saw in his honest gaze. "Do not say that. I will never, ever, regret knowing you."

He stood without speaking for several moments, searching her young, open features.

"And do not believe, if matters had been otherwise you could have easily married me off to Richard," she added, firmly.

A muscle flexed in his scarred cheek. Without replying, gathering her close beneath his shoulder as if he dare not let her go, he guided her to one of the wrought iron benches at the far end of the deserted portico. Instead of sitting beside her, he went down on one knee before her. His hands gently caressed her arms. "That was afore I believed y'r father when 'e said y' were stubborn. Afore I saw for mesen y'r courage." His ghost of a smile faded. "An' the way y' care for any poor sod."

"I'll never regret feeling the way I do about you," she told him, her voice unsteady.

He probably had no idea his grip on both her arms had tightened like an unguarded vice.

"I don't want t' 'urt y'."

She was racked by grief at his self-condemnation, because it was so cripplingly real in those mesmerizing black eyes. "I told you once before how I have come to feel about you. And you…. "

"Said y' were my soul."

"You left me alone on the quayside at Whitby. Sent me away."

His hands retreated from her arms. He placed them on the bench at either side of her.

"For y'r own safety." Sighing, he looked downwards for a heartbeat. Looking back up again, immured in wretchedness, he whispered, "I ain't able t' trust mesen."

She reached out a shaky hand and touch his moonstone pendant. It rested on the mat of hair beneath his open shirt. For a second his eyes closed and his lids tightened a fraction.

"Through this, I have known when you have been hurting. I have called you back when you thought to go from me. Because I knew I could not live without you being in this world." She felt the heat of him through the white stone and the dark flesh on which it rested.

There was a noticeable tremor in his right hand as it rose to where her jet pendent rested upon the Flemish lace of her blue gown. "An' I've been tortured more than one time by the sense o' peril the stone's given me." His tone was edged by roughness. "I'd kill any bastard who'd 'arm y'."

"You have done so."

Shadiz looked unrepentant.

While he was approachable, she thought to make a request. "Can I not return to England? If not to Nafferton Garth then back to the Lodge?"

His slight movement was subtly regretful. "T'ain't safe, Kore."

"I don't like it here," she said, flatly.

"I know y' ain't 'appy 'ere on Formentera. But the island's safest place now we reckon there's some sod planted wi' us by Lynette. T'ain't just Lynette, though, who'd use y' against me. The bloody war in England threatens y'."

"You profess to have…feelings…for me," pointed out Catherine. She was beginning to feel quite desperate. "Yet refuse to be truly my husband." He flinched. She continued, nevertheless. "And that is in spite of making it plain to all and sundry I am yours. Then, of course, there's your parting shot at Whitby. Why is Junno guarding me against you?" Why don't you trust yourself?" She took a shaky breath before answering her own question. "The tale you told in the winter's cavern on the moors. You were naming yourself Want."

Shadiz looked away from her. He stared into the middle distance, saying nothing.

Catherine regarded the man knelt before her, her husband in name only. He was as multi-faceted as a hard diamond. With a damning, living history. Yet she loved him with every fibre of her being.

He did not pull away from her persuasive touch as she turned him to once again face her. Instead, he covered her hand with his and drew it to his lips and kissed her palm. "You would not hurt me," she said, with quiet conviction.

Kore." Her name was spoken in a manner that matched the plea in his black eyes.

Tears stung her eyes and rolled down her cheeks made warm by his kisses. "You have special names for me. And yet I must use the one all call you by. Why can I not lay claim to your given name? Tom told us…. "

Immediately, with a lightning reaction, he covered her mouth with two fingers. It was the heart-rendering torment in his reinforced plea that took her breath away.

"Forgive me, Kore," he muttered in a strangled whisper.

He rose and left her.

CHAPTER NINETEEN

Waking Nightmare

Coward. Animal.

It was in his perverse nature to seek the night and the waves. Wraithlike, he moved along the path leading down to the shore. He was desperate to escape the excruciating drumbeat in his head. All the while, self-hatred chiselled the words into his entire, loathsome being.

Coward. Animal

Coward for not being honest with her. She deserved to know she had named him aright. The Fair Maiden in the tale from his own blood-stained lips, who had no idea how the miracle of her love had tied her to an animal.

The mastiff looked up at him, sensing his strange mood. It sat on its spiky haunches and watched him strip off and wade into the sea. The faithful dog whimpered softly as his master was swallow up by the stygian blackness of sea and night.

A reassuring hand ruffled its ears.

The black, watery void tossed her around as if she was a piece of jetsam. It threatened to overwhelm her, making the struggle for survival arduous. Not only her own. She battled against the glutinous murk for it was imperative to cling to the thread of torment in order to resist the terrifying pull of purgatory.

Catherine came awake with a nerve-shattering jerk. Gasping for breath, disoriented, she sat bolt upright and looked about her wildly, half-expecting her chamber to be overflowing with the morass of her nightmare.

Her head hurt abominably. So much so, even the mellow candlelight hurt her eyes. Despite the balmy night, her entire body felt numbingly cold – except for where her pendant rested. Beneath inscribed silver and jet her flesh was being slashed by hot coherency.

Catherine shot out of the chair by the window, calling for Junno. She was running towards the door when it was thrust open and the big man rushed in, sword in hand. He was tripping over Keeble's own hasty entrance. A second or two later, Nick Condor ran into her chamber, shirtless, also sword in hand.

"The sea," Catherine, exclaimed, frantically, "The darkness. Oh, God. Help him!"

The men were confused. Fastening her night robe, Lucinda pushed through their arrested knot. She took hold of Catherine, trying to calm her uncontrollable tremors. "Easy. Easy, goodlo. Take a breath. That's it. Now, start again," she urged.

"Shadiz is lost in the sea," Catherine explained, rapidly, gripping scorching jet. Her desperate gaze rested on Junno's large, round face. "Not like Whitby. Not like then." In her distress she missed Lucinda's flushed reaction. "There is something very wrong. Headache. No. More than that."

"The waking nightmare, dammit," muttered Condor.

Junno cast a sharp, inquiring look in the other man's direction.

"Whenever he goes to the sheds," Condor explained, succinctly, glancing at Catherine.

The big man was glad the grim statement did not seem to have penetrated her preoccupation with Shadiz's plight.

"Sweet Jesus. He could be any damn place," pointed out Condor in frustration.

Catherine fought down panic. She forced herself into a passing semblance of calmness. Continuing to grip her pendant, she closed her eyes. And reached out beyond the chamber, the villa, the walled grounds.

In awe of the Romany pattrimishi, afraid to lose Catherine to its potent spell, Lucinda gripped her tightly.

Catherine's eyes flew open. "He is close."

"How the hell she doin' that?" muttered Nick Condor, looking uncomfortable.

Junno ignored him. His anxious scrutiny remained on Catherine. "Y' reckon around 'ere, Rauni?"

"Yes. The sea. Find him, please."

Condor stood in mid chamber, muttering to himself. The expectant attention of everyone turned upon him. He burst out, "Below us! Playa Eulalia. I'll bet y' a pouch of florins that where we'll find him."

Catherine would have been hard on the swift departing heels of the two men if Lucinda and Keeble had not joined together to prevented her from leaving the chamber.

"What this? English bride child fretting her absent husband from her bed?"

The sardonic, accented voice broke through Catherine's strenuous rejection of Lucinda's and Keeble's detaining persuasion. All three looked towards the doorway where Bianca was standing, contempt on her beautiful face. She was wearing a fringe shawl that hardly covered her nakedness.

Speaking heatedly in the Romi, Lucinda marched forward. She pushed Bianca roughly backwards and slammed the door shut in the Persian woman's furious face.

Turning back into the chamber, in no uncertain manner, she told Catherine, "Forget the chikly dunnick!"

Condor disturbed the sleeping villa by demanding torches. Wielding the hissing light in order to chase away the concealing darkness, the two men dashed through the gardens. They encountered Benjamin and Bill Todd.

"What's amiss?" asked Benjamin.

The big man was loathed to spare the time to explain. "Guard 'em," he ordered in passing. Leaving the two men staring after him, Junno followed Condor through the ornate gateway leading out of the gardens.

Wath materialised out of the darkness.

"Y' seen Shadiz?" Junno demanded.

"I saw 'im leave," the older Romany replied, blinking owlishly in the flickering light of the torches. "'e was...I sent Tomas after him."

160

"This way," said Condor, locating the tortuous path down to the shore. "Whose Tomas?" he asked over his shoulder.

Prompted by his own worries, Wath tagged along with them. "About best tracker. Even Master finds 'im 'ard t' notice." He glanced sideward at Junno. "Summat didn't seem right," he added in their language.

Halfway down the rocky slope, Condor halted. The two men with him were forced to followed suit.

"What?" snapped Junno, impatient with the delay.

"Thought I heard summat," answered Condor, looking off to his right.

"Y' did," confirmed Wath.

"'is dog," exclaimed Junno.

Guided by the fretful barking of the mastiff, the three men covered the remaining distance down the slope at breakneck speed. While racing across the fine sand, heading to where the rustling, pale surf lapped upon the indistinct shore, the large grey dog ran up to Junno. It then raced back to pace the shallows, an agitated shadow.

Condor had anticipated correctly. Junno cursed. He thrust his torch at the Irishman. Simultaneously he and Wath dropped their weapons and pulled off their boots. Realising they must act quickly, both men plunged into the midnight sea to be followed by Condor. He waded out from the shore until the water was lapping high up his broad chest. Rocked by the waves, he held both torches aloft in an effort to shed light where it was most needed on a moonless night. The orange glow revealed that the youthful rescuer was in as much danger as the man he was trying to save.

Tomas might be considered a remarkable tracker. Unfortunately, the young Romany was an indifferent swimmer who could barely keep himself afloat let alone someone suffering from a crippling malady. While powerful strokes brought salvation closer, the torchlight garnished relief deeper than the sea from which he had yet again emerged spluttering, stubbornly dragging his burden up with him.

Fortunately for Tomas, just when his strength was in danger of giving out altogether, the lifesaving skills of the two men who reached him were far more superior. Wath fished him out of the reflective water just before he was about to disappear beneath its surface for what would surely have been the last time. The older Romany had to prise his hands away from Shadiz. Even then, Tomas weakly fought to maintain the grip that had kept the Master alive until both Junno and Wath shouted at him in their language. After which, Junno took on the courageous youth's burden. Heading back to shore with his limp cousin, his guts as cold as the Mediterranean, the big man marvelled at the way the slightly built lad had managed to support Shadiz's vastly superior weight.

Back on dry land, Shadiz coughed up seawater and moaned, otherwise he remained motionless where Junno had placed him on the beach. The mastiff had stopped its barking, but was no less anxious. It sat beside its master and whimpered. Tomas was shivering uncontrollably. He struggled through chattering teeth to explain, "Dog... barkin'. Summat...wrong. Found...floatin' Tried...from goin'...under."

"We need to get 'em back to the Casa," said Condor, crouching between Shadiz and Tomas, dripping wet himself.

Junno hesitated. Condor looked up at him. The big man came to a decision. He turned to Wath, and said, "Take Tomas." And to Condor, he added, "Find wood. Get a fire goin'."

Condor was slower to react than Wath. A vaguely challenging look passed between him and Junno. A second later the Irishman inclined his head.

During the hours they sat on the shore watching over Shadiz as the worrying malady racked him, though nothing was said, the two men came to a mutual understanding. It was the worst Junno had witnessed, but he accepted he had not been present during all of his cousin's debilitating attacks. His misgivings regarding the Irishman had fade away by the time he recalled Nick Condor's apt description when they had been in Catherine's chamber.

'Wakin' nightmare.'

Condor grimaced. It was with fire lit regret he looked to where Shadiz lay upon the sand, calmer than before but still oblivious to their presence. He took a deep breath. "He told me to prevent him from going any time to the sheds."

"Where y' keep folk y' sell into slavery? Women?" For once there was no condemnation in the big man's tone, only heartache.

Wrapped up in his own haunted thoughts, Condor nodded. "It's been bleedin' hard. An' friggin' painful."

Silently distressed, Junno stood up abruptly. He roamed around the crackling fire both men kept feeding at regular intervals with brittle driftwood. Eventually halting close to where Shadiz lay, one arm thrust over his scarred face, the big man bent and picked up something from the sand, highlighted by the warming blaze. He looked with idle curiosity at the strange organic shape. He was about to toss it away, when Nick Condor asked him what he had found. Junno shrugged. "Nowt much," he answered.

"Can I see?" asked Condor, getting to his feet.

"You sailors're a superstitious lot," the big man remarked, trying a little humour.

Condor's eyebrows rose, but he was grinning nonetheless, "An' you Romany lot ain't?"

He sobered, frowning suspiciously, as he examined what Junno considered to be nothing more than an odd shaped piece of driftwood. He then put it up to his nose and sniffed. Immediately he recoiled.

Junno was suddenly on the alert. With a sinking feeling, he recalled his cousin's strong links with the Moslem world. "Is it…?"

"No," replied Condor, staring at the object in his hand as if it had sprouted horns all of a sudden. Distracted by it, he added, "Catherine'll probably know what it is…but then again, it's mebbe better she doesn't."

"What the 'ell're y' on about?" demanded Junno, alarmed. He had found her weeping heartbroken and Shadiz missing the previous evening. He was certain, under the present circumstances, she didn't need anything else to add to her unhappiness.

Still staring at the twisted manifestation in his hand, Condor explained, "Me Grannie O'Toole used herbs, much like Catherine." He winced. "Well mebbe not quite like Catherine." He looked up at the big man. "Old lass went up in flames. It were after she'd given a body who crossed her some of this." He throw the object of their mutual study into the fire. The two men stepped back as

163

the flames hissed ominously and grew in luminosity and strength. While the heightened blaze lit their wary faces, Condor went on, "The poor sod she gave it to went mad. Killed the chief's family. All ten o' 'em. Warriors all."

Junno swallow hard. "What the 'ell is the damn stuff?"

"Mandrake. Y' heard of it?"

Stood beside the blaze, Junno went cold from the top of his shiny bald head down to his sandy toes. The hairs on the back of his neck were standing painfully on end. His thoughts flew back to earlier in the year when he had tracked Shadiz on the wintry moors. Shadiz had left the cavern they had taken shelter in after escorting Catherine to her father's grave. Close to where he had found Shadiz laying in the snow he had glimpsed something very much like the root he had come across on the shore. He hadn't recognize it then, but now his suspicions were playing havoc with him.

Condor had got his answer by the big man's demeanour. Junno looked as if he had been punched in the guts. The Irishman sat down again beside the fire which had settled down. "Where'd he get it from?"

Junno settled beside him, looking across at Shadiz's unmoving form. "Not Catherine, that's for sure."

Nick Condor kept the vigil with Junno until Shadiz began to stir in a more normal manner. Without a word, Condor got to his feet, briefly touched Junno's shoulder and then walked away across the shore, heading towards the steep slope leading up to the villa.

The fire on the beach the two men had sat beside all night while Shadiz remained oblivious had been reduced to glowing embers. Taking its place was dawn's burgeoning radiance of a new day. Increasingly the tranquil sea was becoming flushed with spectacular hues from the sun rising over the distinct horizon. Junno was able to view the glittering daily birth without flinching. Shadiz was looking to his left, to an unaffected part of the quietly stirring Mediterranean.

Neither of the two men had spoken. Junno had not even looked towards where Shadiz was sitting some distance away, giving his cousin the time he needed to pull himself together.

Eventually, Shadiz got to his feet. He stood with his back to Junno, gazing out to sea. The faithful mastiff rose and stretched, remaining close to its master. At length, in a whispery tone, he said, "It weren't meant."

Junno stood up and went to stand beside Shadiz. "Rauni realised y' were in trouble." Glancing sideward he saw his cousin's black eyes were no longer dilated. He also caught sight of the painful reaction to his quiet words that were meant to reassure.

Junno ended the elongated pause. "Y' seen Mamma lately?" he asked, casually. "She be all right?" He was, after all, a caring man and had not seen their grandmother for some time.

Shadiz continued to look to the west. "As far as I know," he replied, distractedly.

They fall silent again. There was no doubt in Junno's mind that Shadiz was trying to come to terms with the present situation. Yet he was totally unprepared for his cousin's curt announcement. "Tonight I'll sail for England."

Junno's surprise gaze jerked around to him.

"I'll deal wi' Lynette an' old bitch once an' for all."

"An' then what?" asked Junno. When Shadiz did not answer, gently he said, "Y' wouldn't 'urt Rauni."

Shadiz half-turned and met his compassionate regard. "Stay vigilant, simensa."

CHAPTER TWENTY

One More Day

Although everyone remained seated around the table, breakfast had more or less finished. What little conversation there had been during the first meal of the day had been mostly for the benefit of the children. Having satisfied the grown-ups by exhibiting healthy appetites to sustain their play in the grounds of the villa, Peter, Jack and Katy were chafing to be out in the sunshine.

The young trio were pleading for release when Shadiz entered the chamber. Young and old alike fell silent. An air of uneasiness settled on the chamber.

As was often the case, Catherine had sensed his approach before his soundless appearance. Even so, she barely had time to brace herself against the thrill of his presence before those intense black eyes found her. She feigned mild interest, tinged with a rosy glow.

After the trauma of the previous night, she had sought out Junno when he had finally returned to the villa shortly after dawn. Comforted by her sense of Shadiz's recovery, she still had questions for the big man. However, he had been annoyingly vague about events in the midnight water, and what had followed.

Shadiz made his silent, predatory way to where Catherine was sitting between Lucinda and Katy half way down the table strewn with the remnants of breakfast. She half-turned in her seat as he reached her, and forced a calm look upwards to disturbing heights. Shadiz stood without speaking. Judging by his enigmatic scrutiny of her, encroaching upon a scowl, she was convinced he had arrived to berate her for sending the men after him the previous evening. While striving to maintain her composure, ready to defend herself, she was aware of the heightened, watchful tension of both Junno and Condor.

"Ride wi' me?" Shadiz asked, very softly.

It was the last thing Catherine had expected. The painful thumping of her heart in her breathless chest made a calm response difficult. "I...would love to."

When his gaze eventually shifted from her uncomfortably flushed face, she was relieved he did not expect to escort her outdoors immediately for she was sure her shaky legs would have difficulty supporting her. She watched as he surveyed the present company he had previously ignored. His alert cousin, who upon hearing Shadiz's requested had not relaxed. Unlike Condor, who was looking amused. Lucinda appeared as anxious as her husband. The Persian's speculative attention remained on Shadiz. Behind him, his nervous servant looked ready to bolt. The rest, Benjamin, seated as far away from Condor as possible, Keeble and the children all seemed nervously engaged with the situation Shadiz had brought about by his appearance.

The corner of his hard mouth twitched in a rueful grimace before acknowledging the others in a surprise invite. "All o' y'."

When the children realised what the day offered their joy outweighed their wariness of Shadiz, and they scampered away. The adults were slower to show their approval. Lucinda certainly looked unconvinced by the compromise, but said nothing. Junno's gaze on his departing cousin's broad back was full of wistfulness.

"Come on, big fella," said a grinning Condor upon pausing beside Junno. "Lets go play chaperon."

While the excited children were being helped to mount the sturdy Connemara ponies Nick Condor had shipped from his native Ireland to Formentera, he prevailed upon Shadiz to wait for Bianca. The Persian princess usually never rose until late in the morning. Eventually putting in a hasty, irritable appearance, she pushed the female servant away who was trying to adjusted the long, sheer jacket she wore over baggy silk breeches and a shorter, sleeveless jacket that left her mid-drift bare.

Shadiz, his patience exhausted, started to lead the way through the villa's tall, ornate gates. Riding beside him on a bay mare very

167

much like her own horse Twilight, Catherine heard Bianca's shrill complaints, but was more interested in exploring the island.

Since the evening Lucinda, Peter and herself had arrived at the villa in a closed carriage none of them had seen beyond its walled grounds. The sound of the sea had been ever present, especially during the hours of siesta and the night. Riding at a leisurely pace, Shadiz's big grey horse closest to the cliff edge, the golden shore and the glittering sea were revealed below the broad, grassy track. They were soon passing several low buildings grouped around a small courtyard adjacent to the villa's much grander one. Junno had previously described to Catherine and Lucinda where the Master's men, both Gorgio and Romany, were quartered. Not that there were many there at present. Most were acting as escort led by Bill Todd and Wath. Even on Formentera where he held sway Shadiz clearly looked to Catherine's safety.

Condor was heard attempting to mollify Bianca as she rode in sullen silence beside him, not least because of her position far down the column due to her tardiness. Even her uncle rode at a sedate pace in front of her on a chestnut mare, his robes stark white in the sunshine, the magnificent jewel in his red turban glinting within its bright rays.

Benjamin and Keeble were riding behind the giddy children while Junno and Lucinda rode before them. Benjamin was not the only one convinced the Master would head in the opposite direction to Formentera's main harbour. He was relieved that the children and the women, with the notable exception of Bianca, would not pass through La Sabina.

He had visited the busy harbour where most of the Master's corsairs dwelt a couple of times following his leader's boisterous reception upon his return to the island. Unlike most of the Master's men, he did not frequent the rowdy taverns and kept well away from the busy whorehouses. He had become familiar with the quayside warehouses full of merchandise taken from captured shipping, especially those holding the poor wretches – men, women and children – who had had the dire misfortune of being waylaid at sea. The sight of them made him feel sick to his stomach. He was outraged on one occasion when he had witnessed the captives being herded together in the market square for the benefit of those traders in doomed flesh who were regular visitors to the notorious island. He had got into arguments with both their overseers and disgruntled bystanders. Only the fact he was known to be one of the Master's English lieutenants had spared him from a thorough beating.

Thoughts of his family tortured him. But at least they were alive. Against all the odds, he did believe Shadiz when he had assured him they would be released. For it seemed the Master's authority was far-reaching.

Ignorant of Benjamin's relief, Catherine's attention was presently taken up by her immediate surroundings. Riding beneath a cloudless blue sky made the world seem a better place. She glanced at Shadiz. That and the company. Before long, he led them away from the beauty of the wild shoreline. Henceforth they rode inland through a landscape that was a paradise of gentle, wooded slopes, lush greenery and terraced wheat fields.

Watching her keen interest in their surroundings, Shadiz explained, "The island was known t' Romans as 'Fragmentary' 'cos o' its abundance of wheat. Its named nowadays 'cos Forment is local name for wheat."

"The Romans seemed to have been everywhere," Catherine responded, happy that he had broken his silence, even though it had not been an unpleasant one.

"Damned Norsemen, also," he said, with a faint smile. "Y'll see as we go along some o' islanders are tall an' blond. It's due t' Norsemen bein' in command o' island for hundreds o' years."

Catherine looked across at Shadiz. "You would make an excellent historian," she pointed out.

He grimaced. *"An' all world's a stage. An' all men an' women merely players. They've their exits an' their entrances."* he quoted in a whispery, noncommittal tone.

Catherine quoted the next line of Shakespeare's verse. *"And one man in his time plays many parts."*

"Well said: that was laid on wi' a trowel."

Catherine laughed at his ironic tone.

They began to encounter clusters of one or two storey,

169

white stone dwellings where dark-haired, sun-baked children stood and stared in awe, pigs ran away squealing and chickens fled from under the hooves of the horses while dogs snarled but kept their distance from the mastiff and Condor's two dappled hounds. During their passing through the random villages, the people they encountered greeted Shadiz with great deference, akin to that given to any lord of the manor in England. With a jolt, Catherine realised that was precisely what he was on the island. Although Nick Condor took charge in his absence, even he, along with everyone else, deferred to the Master. She was glad to see him reciprocate with politeness whenever he was given a respectful bow or curtsy on their sojourn.

Leaving behind a lazily turning windmill and its large, respectful family, Shadiz briefly rubbed his temples.

"A residual of last night?" Catherine asked, quietly.

He scowled at her across the small protective gap between their mounts. "Junno...."

"Never said anything of importance. Nor has Nick."

"Kusi bunii."

She raised her eyebrows in elaborate shock. "I shudder to think what that means."

"Little witch," he translated.

"Not really when you consider it was you who gave me this," she replied, holding up her jet pendant.

The same dense colour, his eyes lingered on the polished stone before they returned to her sapphire gaze. "Aye," he murmured. They rode on in silence.

Unable to resist the temptation, Catherine regarded the defined outline of his barbarous, scarred face from out the corner of her eye, hoping he wouldn't notice. In truth she found it hard to believe he was riding beside her. His long black hair was not quite in its usual wild tangle. He was once more respectable in cambric shirt and breeches. There was very little stubble about his jaw. His gold earring gave a shiny reflection of someone swallowing convulsively. Although he did not wear the broadsword on his back, the curling sword was at his hip. She suspected he had other weapons secreted about him.

"Will I do?" Shadiz asked, barely above a whisper, continuing to gaze straight ahead.

She might have known he would register her study of him. "As far as I can tell," she commented, berating herself for being so rosily flustered. A regrettable condition which deepened as he turned his head and looked at her.

"You will." His expression had softened considerably. "Y' look beautiful, monisha. In the blue gown y' wore at Whitby. At St. Mary's."

Catherine regarded him with surprise.

"What?" he said in a mild exasperation. "Y' reckon I'd not recall 'ow 'y looked when we romered?"

She needed no translation. "No. Yes. I thought...." she stammered. "Oh ye gods and little fishes!" She took a deep calming breath, immeasurably pleased by his acknowledgement of the day they had married. "For what it is worth, you looked quite...er... dashing that day," she told him, self-consciously.

"Dashin', eh!" he echoed, amused. "I've been called many things but that's first time I've 'eard that one."

"That's the first and last time I compliment you," she retorted, scowling at him.

"It probably will be," he responded in a half-whisper.

Their leisurely progress was halted when they encountered a herd of goats blocking the narrow track they were currently following. Having become a little bored, Peter, Jack and Katy made ungainly dismounts from their docile ponies and thoroughly enjoyed helping the apologetic old goat herder to persuade his wayward charges into a sloping meadow. Catherine also dismounted to admire the wild flowers growing in amongst the long gently stirring grasses in the meadow; those not being trampled underfoot by energetic children or eaten by the goats. While Shadiz looked on, a leg thrust casually over the big grey's saddle, the old goat herder proudly showed Catherine a patch of pink orchids, rare even in the Balearic Islands.

Lucinda collected the children and Junno helped them to remount. No one approached Catherine but Shadiz. Having slipped down from his own mount, he took hold of her by the waist and lifted her back onto the patient bay while she talked enthusiastically about the flowers she had just seen.

They continued on their easy progress, eventually coming across a diminutive waterfall splashing into a small lake, around which grew tall, elegant lilies. The morning's heat was steadily rising. The horses and the dogs drank from the clear, crystal water. So did the people, cupping their hands. Even the aristocratic Persian. He seemed to find it something of a novelty. When a number of the men began to skim smooth, round pebbles across the lake's bright, reflective surface, the children sought ammunition for them from around the water's edge, getting soggy in the process. Before long they were having a go themselves with varying success.

Bianca remained close to the convenient flat boulder Prince Ardashir was sitting upon and viewing the activities with far more appreciation than his beautiful niece. Arms folded, she looked disgusted when Lucinda proved herself adept at skimming stones. And malevolent when Catherine decided to try her luck.

Unfortunately, instead of skimming the water with the stone Peter had found for her, she inadvertently skimmed a succession of ankles. There were roars of laughter from those not hit by the wildly erroneous shot and good-natured grimaces in response to her profuse apologies.

When Peter produced further ammunition for her, everyone backed off until Shadiz approached her from behind and captured her in a loose bear hug before she could throw a second time.

Unable to suppress laughter, Catherine's indignation was feigned.

"Y'll bring down me men faster than bloody Crop-Ears," he remarked, dryly.

Surprise at his amused action registered on the faces of those watching before their attention was quickly directed back to the children.

While Shadiz and Catherine watched together as the children tried hard to master the skill of skimming stones, he did not release her. Relaxing into him, she was acutely aware of the steady rise and fall of his chest.

"Y' enjoyin' day?" he softly asked, rubbing his chin on the top of her head.

She looked up at him over her shoulder and smiled. "Very much. Thank you."

As her eyes met his, the people enjoying themselves at the lake's rippling edge melted away. Without speaking, she turned fully to him. Upon placing her hands on his chest she felt his heart beating in time with hers. His arms became gently possessive. There was several uncounted moments of tender honesty. When the world intruded, he walk her back to the waiting horses, keeping her in the shelter of his arm. Just like the children, Catherine was loathed to leave the lakeside.

Feeling uncomfortable in the heat of the late morning, Catherine tossed the long, single plait woven expertly by Lucinda over her left shoulder. "If I'm to reside in a warmer climate, I might just have a trim," she muttered, irritably.

"Y' won't," commanded Shadiz, forcefully.

Taken aback, and a little put out, she confronted his fierce gaze.

In the next moment, his hard mouth twitched into a crooked grin. He leant sideward in the saddle and taking hold of a wayward strand of her fair-white hair rubbed it between his fingers before tucking it behind her ear. Of their own accord, the horses continued their unhurried pace down the stony track. Disturbed by their passing, a bird flew out of nearby bushes screeching.

Cursing, Shadiz controlled the startled grey, at the same time seizing the reins of Catherine's smaller bay even though she was already soothing her jittery mount.

"Y' know, brother, you'll have to get this courting lark sorted," commented Nick, grinning, urging his horse past them.

"Develesko Mush!" Shadiz growled.

Catherine burst out laughing.

Apparently a midday meal before siesta had been arranged.

Upon their arrival at the Casa Berberia, while their horses were led away and their substantial escort catered for, they were welcomed by their host, Don Miguel Berberia. Even Shadiz exchanged a respectful bow with the portly Spanish noble, the only other substantial landowner on Formentera apart from himself.

Don Miguel failed to prevent his astonishment from showing briefly on his lined features when Shadiz introduced his wife. Formalities dispensed with, the elderly widower led them to a lavish meal spread beneath a shady portico overlooking flowerbeds bursting with colour and heady scents. The splashing of fountains and softly dripping stone basins added to the perfect atmosphere.

The abundance of food and wine was consumed in a companionable manner. Sitting beside her, Catherine was pleased to see how at ease Shadiz seemed. Afterwards, she and Lucinda settled the sleepy children in one of the chambers Don Miguel had ordered to be prepared for his guests during the siesta. Upon being shown to her chamber, when she got the chance without causing offence she escaped its darkened confines.

Being more accustomed to England's variable climate, Catherine found the obligatory drowsing through the hottest part of the day irksome. Her one concession to the heat while wandering around the garden was to take periodic respite beneath wreathed arches and large drooping ferns.

Wandering down a stone flagged path that was leading her around the rear of the white stone villa, she heard voices. At first she thought they were coming from another part of the garden, then realised they were drifting through an open window above her head.

"I not understand what sees he in England child."

Catherine heard Nick Condor speak but his words were indistinct. She did catch Bianca's sharp retort. "You defend brat!"

Angry with the Persian woman, herself and the world in general, Catherine rounded the corner of the villa at an infuriated pace. Before she could stop herself, she stumbled into the bench upon which Shadiz and Prince Ardashir were sitting beneath a close-knit group of palm trees. If it had not been for Shadiz's quick reaction, she would have landed in the Persian's lap.

On his feet, he kept hold of her arm. Her apology to the prince was cut sort by his sharp inquiry, "What's up?"

"Nothing," she answered, just as sharply.

"Really?" he snapped, brows raised. "Folks swear my looks can kill. Yours were doin' a bloody good imitation."

"I am perfectly well, " she emphasised, trying to free herself from his persistent grasp.

"Y' seen Bianca?"

"No," she denied, hastily. Strictly speaking she was telling the truth.

He glowered at her, darkly dubious. "Y' ain't tired?"

"Not really." She certainly wasn't going to admit she could not rest knowing he was somewhere close after all the weeks of wanting him to be so. In an effort to make light of his interrogation, she turned her attention to Prince Ardashir and politely curtsied.

"Now why the 'ell doesn't she do that t' me?" complained Shadiz, releasing her, but remaining close.

"Possibly because your manners need polishing," she retorted.

He snorted.

Smiling at their banter, the Persian rose. "I shall leave this debate. I for one need rest." Before walking away, leaning on his gold-topped cane, he addressed Shadiz, "You will consider what I have mentioned to you?"

His expression unreadable, Shadiz gave a curt nod.

Catherine switched from the Persian's stately departure in the company of his attentive servant to Shadiz.

"What?"

"Don't tell me," she said, dryly. "He has asked you to help rule Persia?"

"Y're definitely a kusi bunii," he commented, returning to the bench.

Full of curiosity and not a little apprehensive, she sat down beside him. "Is it true?"

Shadiz gave an exasperated sigh. "Accordin' t' 'im. They've a boy king who needs strong backin' that ain't swayed by rival factions," he explained.

"You are considering the offer?" She held her breath, waiting for his answer.

He shrugged. "I've matters t' sort out. Unless y' want t' live in me 'aram?"

What was spoken in jest struck a subtle chord with both of them.

"H'm. Could I be chief wife?" she remarked, hoping to disguise her true reaction with flippancy.

He took hold of her left hand and, raising it to his lips, kissed her wedding band. "Y're chief an' only wife," he commented, very quietly. Keeping hold of her hand, caressing the ring with his thumb, he put his right arm about her shoulder. She lay her head on his chest. For a while they remained thus in silence, acutely conscious of each other.

Eventually, his voice scarcely audible, he informed her, "I'm leavin' tonight."

Immediately, she sat bolt upright. "But, you've only just arrived!"

He seemed uncomfortable yet his words were emphatic. "Summat need sortin' in England."

"Lynette," Catherine stated. And then went on to argue hotly, "I'm safe here."

"An' the war?"

"To Hell with the war."

Though he looked vaguely amused, he started to rebuke her, "Y' ain't t'...."

"Blaspheme," she dismissed, annoyed. "You would make a saint do so!" A thought struck her. "That is what this day is all about, isn't it. I'm surprised you didn't go without telling me."

He avoided her accusing stare.

"You were going to, wasn't you?" she exclaimed, jumping angrily to her feet. "I hate you!"

"Per'aps it'd be better if y' did."

His low-pitched words sliced through her burst of anger. She saw the effort it took to utter the words that were not meant lightly. The sudden lump in her throat threatening to choke her, she watched as he looked downwards, ploughing a brutal hand through his midnight hair while a gamut of emotions played across his dark features, more used to displaying the harder traits of his dangerous character. She took a ragged intake of breath. "I'm sorry. I could never hate you whatever you did." After a moment, she murmured, "Have done."

He looked up, a haunted shadow in his black eyes. Then, his

176

gaze growing warm, he held out his hand to her. "Come 'ere," he urged, softly.

Without realising, she had already drawn nearer to the bench. Upon placing her hand in his, he pulled her gently back down beside him. "Kore," he whispered into her hair, holding her close.

She swallowed hard, fighting the tears. Making a fist, she aimed a desperate blow at his chest.

"What were that fer?"

Catherine reared up. "You had better come back to me."

Laughing softly, he bent towards her so that when he spoke next she could feel his loving breath upon her upturned face. "Y' little Amazon."

He gathered up her long plait and closed the slight gap between their lips. They finally shared the kiss that had smouldered between them during the day.

It was only when she was drifting off to sleep in his arms that she realised he had not given her an answer.

Shadiz watched Catherine sleeping.

"Ay me! For aught that ever I could read,
Could ever 'ear by tale or 'istory,
The course o' true love never did run smooth."

CHAPTER TWENTY-ONE

The Sum of All Fears

"Kore! Develesko Mush."

From the depths of despair Catherine grasped the lifeline out of nightmares.

"Kore. Wake up, dammit."

Her eyes flew open. Relieved to be in the waking world, with Shadiz, she clung to him trembling, her breathing ragged. He held her fiercely close, trying to soothe her.

"She's bad dreams," said Lucinda, a faint accusing note in her quiet voice.

"Aye. I got that," rasped Shadiz into Catherine's disarranged hair. He pulled back slightly in order to look down at her flushed, tear-stained face, which appeared to everyone heartbreakingly young. "'ow long this been goin' on?" His demand was moderated, full of concern.

"Since y' took Rauni t' wild man an' made 'er go t' 'is weird pool in Stillingfleet," pointed out Juuno, forcefully.

"Develesko Mush. Why didn't y' tell me?" Shadiz demanded, his low-pitched voice contrite.

"By carrier pigeon?" Catherine replied, managing to sit upright within his tight, embracing scrutiny. She grinned sheepishly at Lucinda and Junno. They smiled back at her but continued to appear troubled.

"What they about?" asked Shadiz.

"That's just it. I can never recall. As if…Oh, I don't know…." All she really knew to her cost were the ghastly emotions the dreams evoked. Even though she felt the one she had just endured had been particularly vivid its contents remained shrouded, just beyond her reach. Along with the inevitable aftermath of her frequent dreams came a reoccurring thought. Did their contents contain an omen she instinctively shunned?

Shadiz gently cupped Catherine's face and, despite the watchful presence of Junno and Lucinda, he bent and brushed her mouth with a light kiss. As if he had read her thoughts, he whispered, "I'm the one that's cursed. Not you, my monisha."

Catherine shook her head, refuting his admission.

When the two young women had gone away to rouse the children from their siesta, Shadiz and Junno stood in silence. Not only the heat hung between them.

At length, Shadiz expelled a regretful sigh. "What the friggin' 'ell 'ave I done t' 'er, simensa?" he questioned, not for the first time.

Junno was far too compassionate to berate a tormented soul, especially one whose sinister hardness had been cracked open. "Y' love 'er."

"I ain't touched 'er."

Junno turned his head and looked directly at his cousin. "Even if 'y did, y' wouldn't 'urt 'er."

Nick Condor strolled around the verdant corner of the villa, a silver goblet in his hand. He frowned when he came across the two men. "You two look full o' joys o' spring," he remarked, dryly.

Shadiz glared at him. Junno scowled at him.

"As I said, you two look…"

"I'm leavin' tonight," stated Shadiz.

The burly Irishman cocked his head to one side. "I don't have to ask why," he remarked.

Shadiz's glare became deadly.

"Pressing business elsewhere," Condor added, in a conciliatory manner. His sidelong glance caught Junno's worried expression. Looking fully in the same direction as the big man, Condor asked, "What d' y' want me t' do about Benjamin's family? I don't want him to come tiptoein' up on me one night 'cos you ain't sorted 'im out."

Shadiz commanded, "I want Raffael t' sail *Cristobala* t' Portugal, wi' lad an' bairns aboard. Supply Raffael wi' documents an' funds to ransom Benjamin's lot we sold t' Bartolomes Faraone. After that, Raffael's t' sail t' England. I want a couple o' 'em from Lodge t' escort the lot o' 'em t' their manor near Richmond. I'll take some o' men I sent t' Shannlarrey back wi' me t' England."

"And the Persian?" quizzed Condor, guardedly.

Shadiz cast him a cold, meaningful look. "Negotiate 'is safe passage t' France or wherever the 'ell the old man wants t' go."

Condor gave a resigned nod, at the same time sighing regretfully.

"Peter's goin' t' miss 'e's playmates," commented Junno.

"Keeble'll make up for their absence," suggested Condor. "Little man's good at keeping bairns entertained."

The two men continued the conversation until they noticed Shadiz's black eyes were abstractedly open in thought.

"Looks like the Liffe is overflowing," remarked Condor, broadening his Irish brogue.

"Where are we going now?" asked Catherine as they remounted their rested horses and rode away from Casa Berberia. They had left Prince Ardashir behind to enjoy the company of Don Berberia a little longer. Shadiz had arranged an escort and their host was to provide a man to guide the newcomers to the island back to the villa. "The children would very much like to visit the sea?" she added, persuasively.

"We're off t' waves," Shadiz informed her. "I want t' see a wreck."

"A wreck?"

"Aye. The *Samson* was driven onto a reef in a storm a bit ago, while I was away."

Catherine was immediately reminded of the stormy night when the Eagle had almost succumb to the same fate in Mercy Cove. The merchantman would surely have done so and her crew perished if it had not been for Shadiz's suicidal battle against the raging elements.

"Did anyone perish?"

He met her haunted gaze, and clearly tried to lessen the impact of his answer by his considerate tone. "A few. Them as panicked afore Nick could get t' 'em."

"I see," she murmured. Lost in memories that were far from pleasant, it was a while before she realised he was watching her.

"Tell me about that night?" he urged, quietly.

It cannot have been hard for him to read her thoughts. She realised they were plain on her sun-bronzed face.

"Humour me," he added, without heat.

"If you had not marched me off to see Garan, you might have learnt more at the time," she pointed out.

He did not respond to her curt tone. They rode on in silence. Behind them the others chatted amiably. Once again, Junno and Lucinda were riding close to the children, as were Benjamin and Keeble. Condor and Bianca were behind them. Their escort brought up the rear with no great effort.

Meanwhile Catherine debated with herself how to narrate one of the most harrowing nights of her life. Or even to do so. She glanced at Shadiz's harsh profile, wondering where his interest lay.

He turned towards her. "I ain't about to persecute the innocent. I know 'ow bloody persistent y' can be."

Grimacing at his comment, she began, "I had a bad feeling about what was happening that night. I don't know why. I just did. When I asked Mary if she knew the way to Mercy Cove she told me she didn't but that Billy did. We sought him out, but he was too frightened of what you might do if you discovered he had guided me there. Then, as I recall, Keeble arrived in the stables. He realised what I was trying to do. I gave him the impression I was worried about Bob and his crew. Which I was. But...I had started to feel the warmth of the stone." Her hand rose unconsciously to her jet pendant. "It was Keeble who came up with the idea of telling the sentries at the Lodge that he and Billy were providing extra rope you had ordered, and suggested Mary and I leave the Lodge when the women from Glaisdale did. We met up with him and Billy on the outskirts of the forest."

"An' went to Mercy Cove?" Shadiz asked in a neutral tone.

"Yes. We rode double on the ponies." After a slight hesitation, Catherine added, "By then the jet stone had begun to burn me."

Riding past orange groves, they exchanged a long, absorbed look.

At length Catherine wrenched her gaze away from him afraid her pounding heart would burst otherwise. "When...when I knew you to be safe," she continued, diligently viewing the track ahead, "I wished to remain...close."

No words needed to be spoken between them regarding her determination to wield their link through the Romany pendants. Shadiz knew very well what she had done to safeguard him on a stormy shore and in the depths of a rock pool.

"Billy suggested we go to his family's cottage," she went on. "But I did not wish to put anyone else in jeopardy of your wrath. After we had found somewhere to curl up, Keeble went to see what was happening further along the cliffs."

"It'd take 'im a bit," suggested Shadiz.

Catherine turned in the saddle and looked to where the little man was riding his pony between Peter and Jack. He returned her gaze, appearing concerned. Realising she might be giving the wrong impression, she gave him a quick smile. He responded with his usual lopsided grin.

Shadiz watched their exchange. His expression worried Catherine. "You said you wouldn't..."

"What's done is done," he murmured, barely above a whisper. "'e guards y'."

"Yes, he does, bless him," she responded, a little happier.

After a pause, he said, "An' next day goin' back t' Lodge, y' run into Lynette."

"H'm. We did," she responded, shame-faced. "I still feel responsible for what happened." The memory of the ferocious clash when the Master and his men had rescued her and those with her from Lynette and his force remained a painful one. Another memory struck her, this time making her grateful. "You are right when you say Keeble guards me. He was the one who challenged Lynette. He informed him you were close. It was a gallant attempt to worry Lynette."

"Did it work?"

"I'm not sure," she answered, reflectively, "Perhaps. We soon seemed to be on our way to Fylingdales Hall."

Not long afterwards, they emerged from a grove of pines and

came within sight of the sea. The children hailed the glittering Mediterranean with glee. They would have urged their ponies to put a spurt on but the adults tempered their eagerness to be by the sea with caution as they made their way along a narrow track that twisted down a steep, rough slope to the shore.

Immediately upon their arrival in the small, picturesque bay, the children dismounted recklessly and ran towards the sea, kicking up the fine, warm sand and calling to one another. They were followed at a more leisurely pace by Catherine, Lucinda, Benjamin and Keeble. While the escort took care of the horses, Shadiz called Condor and Junno to him. The three men were setting off towards the southern end of the bay where the baked carcass of the Samson rested at a crippled angle upon an outcrop of rocks when Bianca started to follow them.

"Stay put," Shadiz commanded, over his shoulder.

"Would be different if I was your pathetic child bride," muttered Bianca, in her native tongue.

Shadiz slewed fully around. His dark features holding a chilling, murderous promise, in two lethal strides he was upon her, taking her unawares not only by his swift action but also by the way he growled at her in her own language. He seized her slender neck a second before Condor reached his side.

"Let me deal with her, brother," said the Irishman, persuasively,

He knew better than to try and restrain Shadiz. And was relieved when Junno came up behind him, speaking in the Romi. When Shadiz thrust Bianca away, Condor caught her as she stumbled backwards in the sand. The red marks on her neck showed how vicious Shadiz's grip had been on her.

"Watch the bitch," warned Shadiz, in a dangerously low voice, "Or so 'elp me, I'll wrin' 'er friggin' neck." He turned and walked away with Junno.

A few minutes later Condor re-joined them. Bianca had masked her shock at Shadiz's brutal response with haughty disdain. She had railed at Condor and then took horse and rode away in a monumental huff.

"I know she's a right bitch," he said, falling into step with the two men, "But she's a bloody good ride."

Shadiz did not respond to his attempt at levity. He met the other man's pacifying sideward look with black-eyed menace. "Keep 'er away from Kore."

Condor nodded. He knew the name. What was more, he was beginning to understand its significance. Amazingly, it meant that the Beast did indeed possess a heart when all along there appeared to have been a noticeable lack.

The three men stopped a short distance away from the partially exposed grey serrated rocks and viewed the waves washing over the bare bones of what had once been stout timbers that had voyaged around the Mediterranean.

"As you see," said Condor. "There's not much left of her."

"Y' salvage owt?" asked Shadiz.

"Most o' crew and a good half of her cargo."

Shadiz nodded abstractedly. He stood without speaking for a long time. looking out to sea.

Condor, realising Shadiz had wanted Junno with them for a reason, cast a quizzical glance in the big man's direction. Junno lifted his massive shoulders in an unhelpful shrug.

Eventually, Shadiz turned to Junno and asked, "Y' remember evenin' o' Tom's funeral, when folk were at Lodge?"

The big man nodded.

Shadiz then included Condor in the conversation, explaining, "We 'eld what y'r folks'd call a Wake for Tom Wright. Every sod an' their grannie came." Again he turned to Junno. "D' y' remember comin' into library as lot from Mercy Cove were leavin'?"

"Aye. Earlier on, they'd asked me where y' be," replied Junno.

"They found me," murmured Shadiz. "Wi' summat, at time, I ain't took much notice o'."

Junno was loathed to point out that at the time it had been due to a preoccupation with Catherine. Never one to easily disguise his thoughts, he was aware his shrewd cousin knew what he was thinking. But chose to ignore it.

"Matt Pearson brought Sammy t' see me," continued Shadiz, low-pitched, "Between us we managed t' drag out o' 'alf-wit that on the night Eagle nearly went down in Mercy Cove, 'e were stood wi' bairns when someone came up behind 'im an' told 'im 'e'd t' go up t' Fylingdales 'all an' tell 'em Catherine Verity were on the cliffs somewhere." He glanced at Condor. "It were summat you said that got me thinkin'. After that night at the Lodge, I talked t' Pearson again. 'e told me 'is wife were stood lookin' after bairns while they were watchin' what 'appened wi' the *Eagle* in Cove. 'e joked about 'er bein' a mother 'en keepin' 'em safe . Well if that were so, she'd o' seen someone get up close t' Sammy. I asked 'er an' she ain't seen anyone."

"Y've said 'ow stormy it were that night?" pointed out Junno.

"Aye, but there were a full moon. There'd be enough light for 'er t' see a grown-up wi' bairns."

"Call me thick as Blarney Stone," put in Nick Condor, "But I don't get what...oh! Jesus Wept. It must've been a body small enough t' go undetected among the wee ones?" Startled, he began to turn and look to where the children were frolicking with the adults close to the sea.

"Don't," commanded Shadiz. In a more moderate tone, he added, "We're just takin' a look at what's left o' ship."

"Y' ain't suggestin' Keeble's traitor we've been after!" exclaimed Junno. He rubbed his bald head, shiny under the hot sun, and then shook it in disbelief. "Y' must o' got it wrong." Yet, he knew his clever cousin seldom was wrong.

"I talked t' Kore on way 'ere," said Shadiz, his barbarous face unreadable, "She said 'ow, after Eagle an' 'er crew'd been made safe, Keeble volunteered t' go scout the cliffs t' see what was goin' on."

"Enough time to get to this Sammy an' send 'im up to the Hall," put in Condor, thoughtfully. Having known Keeble longer than Junno, he, too, was finding it hard to believe Shadiz's assumption. However, having lived on his wits for so long, the intuition that had kept him alive thus far meant he was ready to take note of the cold feeling the incredibly astute Master, the only man he would follow, had seeded in his guts.

It took a gutter rat to know one.

"Tom Wright'd recognised 'im if Keeble come from Fylingdales? Surely?" pointed out Junno, scowling, perplexed and unhappy.

"T'ain't nailed on," replied Shadiz. "Tom'd 'is own farm an'

185

was a steward o' estate. What if Keeble'd been in different world. In 'all. Even if Tom'd seen 'im on occasions, it'd be from a distance. More'n likely, Keeble'd not be rag arse we know. 'e could've been dressed in summat like an' from distance would've...."

"Looked like a child page," suggested Condor. He, too, scowled, bewildered. "Why would he remain loyal to this Lynette for all years he's been with us? What the hell would cause him to keep up such a devious game? If that's what he's about?"

He was made uneasy by Junno's troubled expression.

There was a brief pause. Shadiz met his cousin's pained challenge. "Elizabeth," he murmured. To alleviate Condor's perplexity, he added, "Me 'alf-sister,"

"You've a sister!"

There was another brief pause. "I did," replied Shadiz, tonelessly.

"Oh, Sweet Jesus Wept!" exclaimed Nick Condor.

He turned in disgust and walked quickly away from the other two men, and then stopped and swung back around. "You crazy bastard," he fired at Shadiz. "Y' did t' 'er what y' did to my Louise. Ain't you?" he accused through gritted teeth. "How the friggin' 'ell could you do it? T' y'r own sister...half-sister, whatever the 'ell she was." His gaze narrowed. "I should've killed you after what you did to Louise. Put y' out o' y'r fuckin' misery."

When Shadiz approached him, Condor stiffened, ready to defend himself. However, Shadiz simply halted beside him and looked out across the placid Mediterranean. In a barely audible tone of voice, which chilled the Irishmen to his very core, he said, "Why d' y' reckon 'e's 'ere? Protectin' Kore."

Awareness dawning, Condor looked past Shadiz to where Junno was standing.

The big man ignored him. "Where does all o' this leave us?" he asked, succinctly, trying to turn the attention of the two men back to the alarming, hard to believe possibility of Keeble being the traitor they had sought.

Nick Condor took a calming, repressive breath, aware of Shadiz's wild closeness. "Alright, then, brother. I'd say y' gettin' y' just deserts. You've t' leave y'r wife. Who y' love. That's obvious in

short time y've been 'ere. Jesus, why the 'ell y' come to Formentera!"
When no answer was forthcoming from the fathomless man beside
him, he knew he was on the right track. He asked, " So. Are you off
to take Keeble back with you to England?"

"No," replied Shadiz.

"Why not?" asked Junno and Condor in unison.

"Y' givin' 'im benefit o' doubt?" asked Junno, upon a hopeful
note.

"No," replied Shadiz, grimly. He switched from scanning the
sea to the two men. "I ain't goin' t' do owt that'll set Lynette off."

Realizing his cousin's intention, Junno moved across the sand
to stand at the other side of Shadiz to Condor. "Y' goin' t' make
move on Fylingdales?"

Shadiz nodded. Despite ordering the men with him not to pay
too much attention to the others in their party further along the
beach, he looked directly to where Catherine was playing with
Katy. The two men standing at either side of him were accustomed
to his hard, dangerous manner. Definitely less so to the momentary
glimpse of pure longing. "Watch the little bastard. Never leave 'im
alone wi' Kore. By same measure, y' ain't t' give 'im cause t' be
suspicious. An' don't mention owt o' this t' Kore. I'll take bulk
o' men back wi' me. They're kickin' their 'eels 'ere most o' time,
anyways." He turned to Junno. "I want Tomas t' stay on 'is tracks
wherever Keeble goes."

CHAPTER TWENTY-TWO

To Have And To Hold

Eyes shaded against the afternoon's glorious radiance, Catherine stood where the golden shore yielded to the azure, surf-curling sea. She was uncomfortably aware of wayward strands of her braided hair sticking to her hot neck and the gliding moisture between her breasts.

Bianca had left the company in a huffish manner. Not long afterwards, Nick Condor had rode away in pursuit of her. When Junno rejoined them after going with Condor and Shadiz to view the wreck of the Samson, he along with Benjamin took Peter and Jack swimming. Catherine envied the men and boys their freedom. She was unsure of Shadiz's whereabouts until she caught sight of movement beyond where the two boys were being ferried out into slightly deeper water.

Captivated by the rhythm of his powerful strokes, she was reminded of the precious occasions when those strong arms had embraced her. Yet what pained her was not simply the ache deep in her soul. It was also the unfamiliar ache in her body. A potent mixture of the two culminated in the heightened longing for her husband.

Before she had set sail from Whitby, Shadiz had informed her that he had charged Junno not only to be her protector against a hostile world, but also himself. A barrier he had put in place at the start of her dwelling at the ancient Lodge, his headquarters deep in Stillingfleet Forest. What was preventing him from surrendering to the tender desire she had experienced in his few caresses troubled her. She understood he was responsible for many dark deeds. Some she could only guess at. One Richard had made bitterly plain. Slicing through her second hand knowledge, compassion made her want to discover what had caused him to commit such heinous crimes. It taxed her constantly.

Yet not today, if she could possibly help it. The last one it would seem with Shadiz for goodness knew how long. She sought a diversion from the despondent thought.

"What're y' doin'?" demanded Lucinda, scandalised.

Unabashed, Catherine continued to remove her shoes and stockings. "We're going to cool our toes in the sea, are we not, Katy?"

The dainty, auburn-haired girl did not share the boys' enthusiasm for the sea. She had refused to join them while they had frolicked in the shallows. Instead, she had taken pot-shots at them with pebbles from the shore.

Lucinda continued to berate Catherine for her improper conduct. She darted a nervous glance at the men lounging amongst the horses tethered under a stand of trees upon the summit of the grassy slope bordering the shore. Their escort had given the two young women a measure of privacy in the absence of any perceived threat.

Catherine sauntered about in the shallow waves, trying to persuade Katy to join her. The girl maintained her aversion to entering the water. Lucinda had taken firm hold of her hand by way of support while viewing Catherine's conduct with much disapproval. Nevertheless, Catherine was enjoying the coolness of the waves lapping around her ankles. Only when the sand beneath her bare feet began to slope downwards into deeper water, obliging her to hitch up the skirts of her blue gown, did she begin to feel a little self-conscious.

Junno and Benjamin were waving to her. She failed to hear what they were calling across the intervening distance. It was only when she turned around to look at Lucinda and Katy did she realise just how far she had strayed from the water's edge. Her sense of well-being was further shattered when the sand beneath her began to erode at an alarming rate. When her grinding feet failed to find purchase in the shifting sand, she did a very good impression of a demented windmill. When the edge of the disturbed, sloping seabed gave way completely beneath her frantic presence, the realisation that she was going to disappear beneath the waves was made worse by the knowledge she could do nothing to save herself. The next terrifying moment, she plunged backwards. As the water closed over her head, she tried in vain to fight the downward drag of her gown.

What little air remained within her was squandered by her panic-stricken thrashing about beneath the waves. Her fight for life simply resulted in her ears, nose and eyes being assail by the agitated sea.

All at once, strong hands gripped her. Giving her no room to manoeuvre in her fearful state, they propelled her upwards. Catherine broke the surface with powerful help, clinging like a limpet, spluttering and gasping for breath. And was immediately subjected to a torrent of abuse.

"Develesko Mush. What the friggin' 'ell d' y' reckon y' doin'?" Shadiz demanded, fiercely.

Overcome by her inadvertent diving experience, Catherine managed to respond with a weak mixture of shame and resentment. Only when his painful grip on both her arms relented and, treading water for both of them, he pulled her against him in a rough embrace, his concern resulted in a teary reaction against his bare chest.

He began to undo the laces of her gown.

"What are you doing?" she asked, startled.

"Lightenin' ballast," he replied, adroitly stripping her of her gown.

While she continued to remonstrate with him, Shadiz tossed the garment, heavy with water, to Junno. His action made her aware of the big man's closeness. He had tried to reach her, but Shadiz's response had been lightning swift, clearly borne out of desperation. Not far away, appearing worried, Benjamin was supporting the boys in the sea. They both appeared shaken by her mishap.

"We tried warnin' y' about that ledge, Rauni," Junno told her.

"I failed to hear you," murmured Catherine, feeling utterly ridiculous.

When Junno swam back to Benjamin and the boys, Catherine

narrowed her eyes against the glaze of the sun on the ruffled surface of the sea in order to see the mirage-like figures of Lucinda and Katy on the distance shore.

"Y' feelin' better?"

Her attention returning to Shadiz, she gave him a small, rueful nod.

"Y' not t' try owt like that again," he growled, giving her a slight, watery shake.

The unfortunate incident had proved one thing, she realised, while trying not to squirm beneath his scolding glare. It had shaken not only her composure.

Although she dare not loosen her grip on Shadiz, her closeness to his rippling body made her acutely conscious that he was clothed only by the water. Nor did the fact she now wore only her drifting linen shift help matters.

His expression made it plain he had read her thoughts and that he, too, was affected by what existed beneath the glistening surface of the sea. Careful to maintain his hold on her, he altered his position at the same time placing her hands on his shoulders. When she was safely resting upon his back, he began to swim with her towards the shore.

Catherine found it an exhilarating experience, and soon forgot her nervousness of the sea, even of their state of undress. She was enjoying the flow of cool water over her and the fluidity of his strong body beneath her, to such an extent, she asked, "Could we continue a little longer out here?"

Shadiz did not respond immediately. Catherine was unsure whether he had heard her request or was ignoring it. It was only when he started to change direction, taking care she did not slip off his back, was she certain of his silent acquiescence. Henceforth, he shadowed the shoreline. When they approached the reef upon which the Samson had run aground he gave the poignant carcass and serrated, grey rocks half submerged by the restless waves a wide berth.

It was plain what had manifested the rocky outcrop. Some time in the past coastal erosion had dislodged the steeper parts of the slope above the shore. The resulting landslide had effectively blocked one end of the bay.

Carried on Shadiz's back towards the more random jumble of boulders beyond the reef, Catherine was enchanted by the sight of a tiny, picturesque cove. The narrow arc of beach was enclosed by pine covered slopes. She exclaimed in delight upon seeing a wild dog and her pups. Only to cry out in dismay moments later when she glimpsed a small, brown body struggling in the sea a few feet from the shore.

Reaching forward, she exclaimed into Shadiz's ear, "One of the pups has got out of its depth!"

"Y' don't've t' deafen me. I see it."

"The mother hasn't noticed. We have to do something or the poor little thing will drowned."

Beneath her tense body she felt the hesitation in his movements before he swam to a cluster of large, smooth boulders. Upon drawing alongside, he began to slide her off his back. The action immediately induced panic in Catherine.

"I can't swim!" she cried, floundering against him.

"Kore, stand up," he said with amused, exaggerated patience.

Moving gingerly, her feet made contact with the stony seabed. The measure of sea lapped around her waist. "Oh, very funny," she muttered.

Even so, Shadiz did not release his guiding hold on her until he had made sure she was wedged into a crevice between the slick boulders before responding to her urgent pleading. From her watery niche, Catherine watched him scoop up the half-drowned pup and wade the short distance to the beach. Her jolting view of his rear nakedness was overtaken by concern for the small soggy bundle he lay on the sand. She abandoned her safe position and risked the perils of the placid waves to move towards where he was kneeling beside the squirming pup.

A fierce growling was the first indication that its mother had become alerted not only to her offspring's plight but the presence of humans.

Catherine was alarmed by the sight of the large shaggy dog bounding across the beach towards Shadiz. Having straightened, he was in direct line of attack from a dangerous maternal instinct. And, for once, she was convinced he wasn't armed. Without turning, he calmly put out an arm, warning her to halt in the shallows. Just as its mother reached within a few feet of Shadiz, the whimpering pup struggled to its feet.

Shadiz stood quite still, his head turned away slightly from the bitch's wild-eyed glare. Convinced the dog was going to attack, Catherine was about to deflect attention away from him when, bristling menacingly, the bitch halted and sniffed her soaked, trembling offspring. The next moment, she grabbed it by the scruff of its neck and ran away towards the rest of her advancing litter.

Not until the small family had disappeared into the pine trees did Shadiz move. Looking in the same direction, Catherine was slow to follow his example. That was until something began nipping at her toes. Responding to her fearful exclamation, he slewed round and raked the sea beyond her for signs of danger. Seeing nothing out of the ordinary, he scowled at her rapid, splashing passing.

Safe on the beach, Catherine explained in an agitated rush, "Some thing was trying to eat my feet."

"Like as not a crab no big than y'r thumb nail," he remarked, dryly.

"It was starting to crawl onto my foot," she retorted. "It was definitely bigger than any of my nails." Indignant, she sat down in the sand. She used the emotion to conceal her response to his nakedness. Apparently, not well enough.

Shadiz abruptly turned away from her and crouched down at the water's edge.

Silence grew heavy between them.

Catherine fought the desire to creep forward and trace the scars that criss-crossed his back and disappeared under wet strands of his long black hair. They lay tantalisingly beneath the more recent indelible marks left by roasting flesh. The curiosity she had harbour ever since she had treated the burns across his back following the fire at Ijuimden earlier in the year got the better of her. "You have suffered under the lash?"

He shrugged his naked shoulders. "A galley slave needs thick skin," he responded.

She could never imagine him being anyone's slave. "You

are referring to the time when Nick and yourself fought before becoming allies? He explained the result."

"That. An' times afore."

"Oh?" She waited for him to reveal more, but was thwarted by his guarded silence. In spite of her best efforts to concentrate on their idyllic surroundings, as he was apparently doing, her attention kept returning to him. Her heart beat faster at the sight of the moist glow on his dark-skinned, warrior's body.

To her dismay, her voice shook slightly while observing, "Nick said most sailors, including himself, are not the best of swimmers. You, on the other hand, are an excellent swimmer?"

"Sink or swim," he muttered, dipping a hand into the waves lapping around him. "Seamen're a bloody superstitious lot. They reckon if they learn they'll tempt Fates."

"I see very little logic in their way of thinking," Catherine commented, glad she had got him talking. "How did you learn?"

"As I said, sink or swim."

Catherine frowned, registering the bitterness. "I don't understand."

"I got slung overboard," he said in a matter-of-fact tone of voice.

"You were what?"

"Some o' crew used me when I were young. There's never any women aboard. Another ship-board superstition."

Realisation dawning, she was glad he could not see her heighten colour, some of which was caused by outrage on his behalf. .

"In end, I struck back. That's when cap'n got rid o' me. While 'e weren't around somebody slung a small barrel overboard. It kept me afloat until I got 'ang o' bein' in sea."

"What happened to you?"

"I was hauled aboard the Bey of Algiers's galley."

"How old were you?"

Shadiz shrugged. "Eight. Nine. I ain't sure."

"Don't you know how old you are?"

"Tom told me."

Catherine's heart clenched for him and for the loss of Tom. "And me," she said, quietly.

She got to her feet, hesitated, and then slowly approached him. "Tom only meant well when he spoke to me about your…origins," she pointed out, coming to an uncertain halt behind him. "For the one he loved above all others. A wayward one, it has to be said. Yet, well worth his sentiments."

Startling her, Shadiz abruptly straightened in one fluid move. "We'd best be gettin' back."

Catherine reached out to him.

"Don't!"

Stung by his sharp rejection, she twisted away from him, exclaiming, "I'll not trouble you further. I'll make my own way back."

Shadiz was upon her before she had ground two irate strides in the soft sand. He seized hold of her arm, forcing her to turn and face him. "Y' goin' no bloody place wi'out me," he rasped, glaring down at her.

"Oh, really," she retorted, attempting unsuccessfully to wrench free of his relentless grip. Her young, fine-boned face infused with stormy colour, her blue eyes accusingly narrowed, she blasted him with feelings that would no longer remain pent up. "You go nowhere with me. You simply dispatch me wherever you please. What is more, you have the arrogance to expect me to submit to your whims like a meek and mild goodwife. Well, I am heartily sick of your variable moods. By one turn of the hour glass you dally with me. And the next you shun me. Ye gods and little fishes! Are you even listening to me?"

He was paying attention to her.

The way her small breasts were defined by the transparency of her wet shift. How her rosebud nipples thrust forward with the intensity of her anger. Jet black, his intense gaze slid lower, past her slim waist to the pubic shade visible at the juncture of her long, shapely legs beneath the clinging material.

His sensual study of her doused anger and caused a thrill of anticipation to surge through Catherine. Inevitably there was the resentful melancholy of a ripe woman not harvested. "I am not even permitted to call you by your given name." She took a deep breath, and went against the imperative grain Tom had emphasised.

"Sebastian."

His head came up immediately, his attention snapping at her in such a disconcerting manner a chill of apprehension shot though her. She tried in vain to free herself from his grasp that had suddenly become a bruising shackle.

He gave her a brutal shake, which rattled her teeth and sent her dizzy. Before she could collect her scattered wits, he thrust her away with such force she landed heavily in the sand, her breath knocked out of her. She was stunned by his harsh treatment. It seemed inconceivable to her that the man who had shown her unique consideration, even if it had been stretched at times, now could look upon her with such feral menace.

Truly afraid of him for the first time, she froze, watching in horror as his black eyes became marbled by sinister lust. Realising she was confronted by the merciless savagery others had witnessed...before their deaths, she scramble backwards in the sand as he advanced upon her.

Catherine came up hard against a boulder, scrapping her shoulders on its sharp indentations and tearing the back of her shift. She cast about wildly for means of escape. Too late, Shadiz had stalked her down with terrifying intent.

His nakedness was secondary to the hardness of his manhood, that had nothing to do with finer feelings and everything to do with violation. Inconsequential to the unbelievable plight in which she found herself, a detached part of her wondered how many wives were routinely raped by their husbands?

Shadiz loomed inescapably large over her. Hard muscled and broad shouldered, blocking out the sun, he ruthlessly knocked aside her valiant attempts to defend herself. Try as she may, she was powerless to stop him from ripping open the front of her wet shift, exposing her virginal nakedness..

A despairing sob escaped her. "Why are you doing this to me? You gave me the jet partner to your moonstone. You said I was your soul. You call me Kore."

She had no idea what part of her heartfelt entreaty brought his brutal attack to a shuddering halt. Breathing raggedly while she dare not breath at all, he remained poised over her. Trembling uncontrollably, she saw the perverse, lustful malevolence that was fixated upon her falter. In the elongated seconds he stared down at her confusion was gradually replaced by dawning recognition in his dilated black eyes. To be swiftly hounded by agonised horror.

Pinned to the chafing rocks, her fingers wedge in the sand, Catherine watched Shadiz stumble away from her and then collapse onto his knees a few feet away. She remained where she was, weak with relief at her reprieve.

Shadiz startled her by emitting a cry that sounded as if it had come from a tortured animal. He raked both his hands through his long wet hair before bending double until his forehead slammed against his knees in such a vicious manner it made her catch her breath, and hold onto it.

Catherine began to tremble even more. Shadiz was shaking violently. He started to mutter wildly. What he said was lost on her with the exception of the name he alone called her. Identifying the other name frightened her. Gianca. His mother, who had died giving birth to him at Fylingdales Hall.

Her head demanded she make her escape while she could. Yet, even as badly shaken as she was, her heart insisted she give solace to the essence of the man struggling against the grotesque malady that flawed him. She administered herbs to cure physical ailments. Surely, if she gave unstintingly of her love, it might just bring about a measure of comfort? Or lead to her rape and death.

The insistent drumbeat of her heart grew loud in her ears. Her hands shook as she pulled the two halves of her ripped shift together. She crept forward over the sand and knelt cautiously beside Shadiz.

He had begun to rock backwards and forwards, grinding a pit in the sand, in a manner Catherine found at once terrible and tragic. His fists were balled. White knuckles appeared in danger of bursting through taut skin. The way his arms were twisted in a curious knot across his chest gave every appearance of him attempting to hold within the infernal compulsion he had previously exhibited towards her. While her jet pendant burned her damp skin, she saw how his rapid breathing was vibrating his moonstone pendant. When he lifted his head and looked at

197

her, the sight of blind torment blighted what little breath she possessed.

"Run!" The painful strain in his barely recognisable voice was evidence of a man fighting inner demons. " To…Junno."

Pierced to the very core of her love for him by his horrendous struggle, Catherine reached out to him.

The moment she touched his hot flesh a pall of darkness descended upon her. She recalled the weird phenomenon happening to her once before, on the deck of the Eagle. But that was of little comfort.

Sunlight returned. Although possessing none of the brilliance or warmth of a Mediterranean climate, nevertheless, it took a few moments for Catherine's eyes to become accustom to the harsh light. And for her to comprehend that the beach she found herself standing upon was more rugged and windblown than those of Formentera. Below a low-slung hovel, squatting on a short, grassy cliff, children laughed and played some kind of excitable game on the pebbly shore. In their midst was a slim girl with long fair-white hair much like her own. Her home spun beauty surpassed the coarser features of her younger playmates. Yet the family likeness was easy to discern.

Watching them dash happily about beside the beating sea, she experienced a deep foreboding. It soon gained credence. Overwhelmed by the act of merciless lust, she shunned the seascape behind closed lids. When her conscience forced her to unlock her vision, time had shifted. The children had vanished. Only the fair-haired girl remained.

While Catherine struggled to comprehend ravished death, she became aware of two shadows on the seashore.

One was barely distinguishable. Catherine got the impression it was being held fast by the other, Stygian entity. She felt an intuitive sympathy for the insubstantial Shade. She sensed grace, dignity and a tragic anguish. Then, in the next moment, she was consumed with dread when the denser shadow turned and soul-piercing malice wafted towards her.

Afraid, Catherine sought the protection of her jet pendant. The images dissolved. Re-emergence into Mediterranean glory dazzled her.

She recovered with difficulty from the traumatic vision, eventually realising she had severed her contact with Shadiz. Tears misted her vision as he cast around blindly for her. Upon seizing her trembling offering, he carried her hand to his heaving chest and held it there with desperate possession.

It was incredibly difficult to witness the violent tremors wracking his big body. She had no idea what he was muttering. Bending towards him, she had to strain to discern his halting translation. "Y' did it again. Made cannon fodder out o' barricade."

"Oh, my love!"

Catherine wrapped both her arms around him. After the briefest of hesitation, he responded by leaning into her soothing embrace. Nevertheless, through clenched teeth, he muttered, "Y' must go."

Disregarding his warning, a memory stirred in the turmoil roiling within her.

She recalled the time Shadiz and herself had been forced to take refuge in a smuggler's niche on board the Eagle earlier in the year when Francois Lynette's men had boarded the vulnerable merchantman in the wintry North Sea. In an effort to distract her from the dangerous situation in which they found themselves, Shadiz had spoken to her about her life growing up at Nafferton Garth, her father's manor close to Driffield. The extraordinary knowledge he had exhibited had had a calming influence on her.

Nowadays, she possessed a reasonable suspicion of how he had come to know her so well, without her having any knowledge of him. That in turn gave rise to an inspirational thought.

"Were you close when I climbed the water wheel at Loftsome Bridge and ended up falling head first into the mud? I never did see who pulled me out. Mind you, I was unable to see anything at all with a face full of mud!"

At first his response was one of confusion that tightened his sweat-bathed features. When comprehension dawned, his poignant change of expression and the way he gently squeezed her hand caused emotions to clog up her throat. She was briefly unable to speak.

Catherine would have far rather learned the true extent of his knowledge of her before her father's untimely death in different circumstances. Yet the halting disclosures her careful prompting was rewarded with made her strive in each precious moment. He informed her about the time her father had proudly shown off his week-old daughter, and confessed to experiencing an odd feeling when he had looked upon her. Even explaining how her father had commented on the way his baby daughter had become curiously animated.

In due course, the queer, intense chafing against himself lessened. He grew less alarmed by her presence. More contrite. Those times she found herself battling against the irrational spasms by wielding the magic of her name special to him thankfully came to an end. Before long all that remained of the demon that had claimed him was intermittent shudders.

Eventually, he was able to look fully upon her, and give an awkward half-smile, half-grimace. Instead of replying to her latest probe, in coherent Latin he murmured, "Whom God would destroy. He first sends mad."

Catherine immediately changed her approach. She started to challenge his intellect.

In French, she quoted, *"He knows the world and does not know himself."* And, quoting Aesop, *"Beware you do not lose the substance by grasping at the shadows."*

Back and forth between them pertinent quotations or the philosophy of ancient thinkers were weighed against each other. While their wits fenced, Catherine was obliged to call upon every morsel of her learning, and still he outflanked her, to her immense relief. Following her lead, surpassing it, he gradually pulled himself together. Catherine smiled hesitantly up at him, feeling suddenly self-conscious. She was relieved to see the weird density had gone from his black eyes. Only now there was another form of torment within jet.

"I could've.... "

Quickly, she placed a gentle hand across his mouth. "You did not. What is more, I don't believe you ever would."

They remained on their knees, facing one another, Guilt was etched into his barbarous features. He took hold of her hand and brushed her knuckles with a light kiss. "It can't remain unspoken," he said, barely above a whisper. "I raped Lucinda. An' would've done more if Junno'd not responded t' 'er screams. Peter's more 'is son than ever mine." He gave a confessional sigh. "An' there's been others."

"The girl on the beach? Mary's friend?" she asked, her voice unsteady.

He slowly nodded.

"Elizabeth?"

A difficult expression flittered over his features, before they tightened in anticipation of her denouncing him.

He nodded.

Catherine bit her lip. "Why?"

She was confronted by a self-loathing so profound it stole her breath away.

Shadiz raised his naked shoulders in a helpless gesture while slowly shaking his head. The way he was bleeding pain and excruciating vulnerability made her quietly weep. He wrenched his ashamed gaze away from her and looked towards the sea. When he spoke, she could not understand his barely audible Romi words.

"My love?"

"Want, the beast within," he murmured, referring to the tale he had told her in an ancient cavern during a snow storm. "Or 'cos I'm a Posh-Rat."

"You are wrong. You are the man I love."

His attention shot back to her, the wretched hope of hopelessness.

Catherine took a deep, calming breath. Was love a weed to be plucked from thorny ground? "There is something terribly wrong. That is plain. But, God help me, and I could do with him to make sense of this, do you really believe I would turn against you? My beloved husband."

Tears glistened in Shadiz's black eyes.

Still in possession of her hand, he pulled her up with him. "We need t' go back."

She took a step closer to him. "Let us stay awhile."

"No," he muttered, adamantly. In desperation.

Catherine resolved not to be denied. The first part of the healing process had been to engage his mind. The second part was to appeal to his body by offering her own.

Reaching up and capturing his dark, scarred face in both her hands, his irregular breath fell upon her upturned face. She felt the turmoil within him through their closeness. Saw in his regard an anxious resistance.

She was once more acutely aware of his nakedness and that her torn shift was revealingly open. Her conduct had never been so bold with anyone of her own age let alone a worldly-wise man twelve years her senior. A formidable, complex man, whose tall, powerful maleness she found unique. Her husband.

When she started to pull his head down towards her, persistence gradually splintered determination. Even so, there remained hesitancy on his part when she pressed her mouth to his, and coaxed a response with her lips. Until the helpless lover in him found her tantalising innocence irresistible.

Upon drawing apart slightly, his unlocked ardour lingered on her lips. She smiled up at him, revelling in his sea-salt, musky scent. "I want to touch you," she said, shyly.

His smile was tender. "Y' touch me deeper than anyone ever will, monisha."

Gently taking hold of her hand, Shadiz kissed her palm. Then he spread her hand beneath his over the moonstone pendant laid upon his damp skin. Held fast by his softened gaze, Catherine experienced the raised beat of his heart, matching her own, all the while conscious of his painful caution.

Before she lost her nerve, she slipped her hand from beneath his and began to slide it slowly downwards. He immediately halted her light-fingered progress upon the rapid rise and fall of his muscular chest. A plea had entered his black eyes. She ignored it. And, confident he would no longer exert harmful pressure on her, gradually extracted herself from his faltering grip. Free once more to roam upon him, her fingers combed through the thick mat of his chest hair. By the time her exploration began to follow the curling trail beyond his navel, Shadiz was trembling. Catherine feared her legs would collapse under her if he removed his arm from around her. When her hand came into contact with crisp hairs, she was rendered motionless by blushing inexperience.

Shadiz's sweat-bathed face reflected someone caught within the hell of not yielding to the lure of heaven. The impasse was broken by his tortured sigh.

His slight movement caused Catherine's hand to brush against the head of his aroused manhood. Both of them jerked upon the involuntary contact.

For an elongated second, she fully expected him to withdrew from her. But he failed to do so. Swallowing convulsively, she gradually splayed her fingers. Her tremulous action caused him to inhale sharply. Clearly unable to stop himself, he guided her diffident caress along his swollen shaft. The intimate touch branded her own body with a throbbing need.

Shadiz moaned. This time it was he who initiated a kiss that engulfed both of them with intoxicating passion. Still clutching him, her hand was sealed within their ardent embrace.

Although her bare breasts were against his naked chest, Catherine wished suddenly to divest herself of the clinging shift and be completely skin to skin with him.

Shadiz appeared bereft when she pulled away from him. The dull light of shame was beginning to seep into his gaze. Until, rigid, he watched as she shrugged the ripped shift off her shoulders. It landed in a soggy pile at her feet. His gaze locked with hers, he slowly shook his head as if she were persecuting him.

Catherine stepped back into his tense shadow. Experiencing the heady sensation of his body heat against her own nakedness, her aching breasts brushed against his heaving chest.

"Kore," he muttered, hoarsely.

He cupped her breast while loosening her braided hair, shaking it free down her back. Bending to her, he kissed his way from the jumping pulse at her neck to her other breast. When he took her into his mouth, she held him close, experiencing the exquisite thrill of his tender pull upon her ripe nipple down to her sandy toes.

Aching in places she hadn't known existed made her want more from him.

Entwining her fingers with his, she drew them away from paying court to her breast with the intention of enticing him down herself. But he resisted her invitation. Raising his head, his expression was one of desire harnessed by uncertainty.

"It seems only fair," she responded, breathlessly.

He gave a soft laugh which was more of a husky growl.

"Only you, Kore," he murmured, bending to her once more.

He kissed her jet pendant with reverence. The black stone jerked between her breasts when his mouth descended with loving ferocity on hers. His fingers gently untangled from hers. There was a protest blossoming on her captured lips until she felt his hand skim over her stomach, causing a thousand butterflies to run riot.

Very gently, he parted her thighs with his knee.

Catherine wrapped her arms around his neck and leaned her forehead in the shelter of his shoulder, surrounded by the scent of his male desire. His hand travelled down her spine beneath her long wet tresses and then cupped her buttock. Solicitous, he kissed the top of her head, nuzzled her hair while running his right hand through her other soft hair. When his long fingers probed her virginal bud with tender care, she gasped at the powerful sensation that tore through her. And when he began a slow, sensual rhythm, her shuddering response caused him to thrust slightly against her.

Their simultaneous moans were cut short when Shadiz abruptly captured her lips in the most unrestrained kiss he had given her so far. Consumed by a desperate longing, Catherine eagerly complied as his tongue demanded entrance into her hot mouth. Melting into one another, they aroused one another by the sensuous friction of their naked passion.

Even so, gritting his teeth, he gave her one last opportunity to spurn him. "I ain't able t' trust mesen."

Her shaky response was simple. "Trust my love for you."

That gave him adoring pause

She rose up on her toes and kissed away the incredulous tear as it ran along the ridges of his scarred cheek.

He sank down onto his knees before her. Breathing hard, he

looked up at her young, flushed face. And answered her questioning gaze. "You've t' be ready for me."

While his hands lightly caressed her hips, he spread her legs in order to seek her sensitised entrance. Her senses began to spin out of control at his worship of her womanhood. Gasping, inflamed beyond anything she had experienced before, she dug her nails into his shoulders.

Catherine was becoming completely overwhelmed by his erotic courtship. Rising off his knees, his demanding mouth traversed her body, lingering on her breasts. Without hesitation she took him into her hands. Her urgent persuasion upon his shaft and sac drove him over the edge. His heightened need matching hers, he lifted her off her feet. Upon wrapping her legs around him, she heard his soft groan as the virginal wetness he had aroused smeared his chest. Holding her close against him with a gentle strength that made her feel safe, he lowered her down beneath him. The soft, warm sand became their marriage bed.

CHAPTER TWENTY-THREE

Hitched To A Baggage Wagon

It was with growing consternation that Benjamin finally approached Junno and Lucinda. There was an unmistakable division between the normally happy couple.

Coming to an uncertain halt a few feet away from them, their heated words were lost on him. Before he could seek a diplomatic translation, Tomas's dash across the sun-drenched beach grabbed everyone's attention. Even the two Romany appeared mystified by the lean youth's garbled tidings upon his stumbling arrival.

Irritated by his struggle for breath, hands on knees, Tomas bent almost double. In an effort to stave off the growing concern, tinged with impatience, by which he was surrounded, he flung out a directional arm. Junno and Lucinda seemed to comprehend the desperate action. Benjamin remained confused.

Ever considerate, Junno gripped the youth's shoulder. "'Tis alright, lad."

Tomas managed to straighten and speak in rasping gasps. It was then that Benjamin understood his urgency. He had heard the two names.

Ignoring Lucinda's accusing glare, Junno was watching the dark thoughts flittering across Benjamin's handsome, sun-bronzed face. "Who told y'?"

Benjamin swallowed. "Richard warned me."

"Aye. Bastard would," muttered Junno.

Lucinda lost patience with her husband's loyal tardiness, which in her opinion had gone on for far too long. She seized Tomas's arm and jerked him around in an attempt to force him to retrace his footsteps in the sand. He looked over his shoulder at Junno, desperately seeking approval.

The big man gave a resigned nod. Already holding Shadiz's clothes, he gathered up Catherine's gown from where Lucinda had spread it out on the beach to dry. "Round up folk, an' wait 'ere," he urged Benjamin, starting to follow Lucinda. Registering the younger man's troubled expression, he added, "'e won't 'arm Rauni."

Benjamin appeared unconvinced.

Tomas was soon approaching the landslip that had cut off one end of the sweeping bay they had occupied since arriving at the sea. The looming pile of smooth, grey boulders, stretching down to the water's edge, rested precariously upon one another. Glancing back to make sure Junno and Lucinda were following, Tomas led the torturous way through the narrow passageway he had located between the rocky obstacles.

"'ow much did y' use?" Junno asked, suddenly. "At Whitby?"

"Not enough," retorted Lucinda.

"Y'd a bagful?"

Lucinda made it plain she considered her husband's interrogation to be ill-timed. There had been plenty of opportunities since she had slipped poison in Shadiz's ale when he had been well-gone in his cups to seek details of her murderous attempt. She stopped so abruptly in the rock passage he almost walked into her. "What's wrong wi' y'? Y've guarded 'er all this time. An' now when 'e could be doin' Catherine in, y' ain't bothered about 'er!" Before he could answer, she gave an aggravated sigh and hurried after Tomas.

Junno pursued her. "I've guarded Rauni for 'im, not against him, no matter what 'e reckons." When she failed to respond, in a softer tone, he added, "I ain't blamin' y' for owt y' did. I never would. Y' did what y' thought was right for 'er."

"Wi' good reason," Lucinda snapped, without turning around. She was silent for a few more determined strides. Then, in a different tone of voice, she admitted, "I didn't get time t' use it all."

"Why not?" asked Junno. When he saw Tomas's shy interest in their conversation, he smiled encouragingly at the youth. "This way?"

"Aye, tother side o' those last few rocks," Tomas answered, striding ahead, back into the brilliant sunshine.

Junno tugged at Lucinda's arm, slowing her down. "Why not?" he repeated.

She would not be easily diverted from her self-imposed mission to save Catherine from Shadiz, and dragged him along with her, retorting, "Keeble and some o' Gorgio entered Bagdales's common room." After a slight hesitation, she added, "I was afraid o' little man recognisin' me. So I fled."

"What did y' do wi' rest o' stuff?"

His sharp demand startled her and made her angry. "What's it matter now – when Catherine is in danger?"

Junno brought her to an abrupt standstill. "Tell me what y' did wi' rest o' stuff y' stole from Mamma Petra's 'erb bag?" he reiterated, sternly. "Nightshade, weren't it?"

Realising belatedly they had halted in the cool shade of yet more overhanging boulders, Tomas did so too. He stood and watched them, full of curiosity.

Despite her overwhelming need to find Catherine and Shadiz, biting her lip, Lucinda had grown tense. "There were rubbish in the alley. I threw the rest away. I'd not used much. I didn't know what else t' do."

"Was anyone around?" Knowing he was frightening her, he gave her a gentle smile. "I just want t' know, that's all."

A sense of urgency churning inside her, she recalled her guilty flight. "Some bairns playin'. I was scared they'd get it, but daren't go back. I was scared o' bein' known."

"An' do y' reckon y' were?"

"I ain't sure," she said, abstractedly. "It were only Keeble I saw comin' out o' tavern as I went round corner." She squirmed free of his slackened hold on her arm. "Please, we've got t' find Catherine. Now."

Thoughtful, Junno nodded.

Moving swiftly away from him, Lucinda muttered, "Anyway, I ain't robbed Mamma's bag."

It took a moment for him to realise what she had said, but by that time Lucinda was running well ahead of him.

When he emerged from the haphazard barrier of boulders, the big man found Tomas seemingly loathed to cross the small, isolated cove. He was a consummate wraith. A nosy one, at that. He knew the secrets of countless folks. And was the best source for the Romany women who practised dukkereriben, fortune telling, on the Gorgio. Nevertheless, he had lost his nerve while watching the Master with the girl all knew he favoured. And had bolted back to Junno.

"No!"

Lucinda's horrified outburst struck fear in Junno's massive chest. His blood ran cold. For months he had protected Rauni. Had his trust in his cousin's special feelings for her been misplace, causing her to suffer?

He started past Tomas at a self-condemning gallop. Smaller, nimble and just as desperate, Lucinda easily outpaced him across the beach. Both husband and wife were spurred on by the sight of Shadiz bent over Catherine, straddling her as she lay beneath him, his hands at her throat.

The increased weight suddenly bearing down upon Catherine caused her breath to leave her in a painful whoosh. The heavy pressure on her chest was alleviated immediately such was Shadiz's reaction. He reared up, taking her with him. Before he swung her behind him, she glimpsed his murderous expression.

Catherine's dizzy thoughts fled to the previous aggression he had shown towards her. Ashamed after the precious intimate act they had just shared, she quickly became even more uncomfortable with herself upon realising he had not only placed her behind himself to keep her safe but also to defend her modesty, careless of his own.

The mystery of why such an action was necessary went a long way to being solved when she glimpsed Lucinda sprawled in the sand. What alarmed Catherine was the way the Romany woman's frantic resolution ensured a swift recovered from Shadiz's hefty blow. Springing back on to her feet, only Junno's urgent arrival prevented Lucinda from launching another ill-advised assault. Spitting fury at Shadiz, she found it impossible to escape her large husband's timely restraint.

Upon Catherine moving slightly, Shadiz put an arm behind him pinning her at his scarred back. Nevertheless, she managed to address Lucinda's wild accusations. "He has not raped me. Our pendants had become entangled."

"Y' would say that. Y'd defend 'im whatever bastard did t' y'."

Already dangerously angry, it was clear that if Shadiz had not been trapped in his protection of Catherine's nudity, his retaliation to Lucinda's charges would have been savage, which would have brought him into conflict with Junno.

As it was, the big man, fearing for his wife's safety, tried to calm her down. But she would have none of it.

"Please, Lucinda," cried Catherine, adding her own persuasive efforts to Junno's. She was as much upset by his anxious struggle as Lucinda's near-hysterical behaviour. Despite what she had tried to do to Shadiz, over the past weeks Lucinda had become like a sister to her.

"Enough."

Shadiz's harsh command forced a brittle silence.

Locked against his back, Catherine felt his tense restraint. "Look, I'm sorry about what I done t' y'. All I can say in mitigation is out o' wrong I did y' got two rights. A good husband an' a son t' be proud o'."

Squirming to see around him, Catherine saw Lucinda's and Junno's shocked expressions. It was easy to surmise that up until that moment, Shadiz had shown no remorse for raping and almost succeeding in strangling Lucinda.

Catherine lay her cheek and a gentle hand upon his naked back.

"An' now my wife needs t' bathe," he stated, turning to face her. He picked her up in his arms and, still shielding her with his own bare body, started walking towards the sea.

"Let us make an honourable retreat," Shadiz quoted. He grimaced. "Though I do come wi' bag an' baggage," he added, low-pitched.

"I'll lighten the load," Catherine assured him.

CHAPTER TWENTY-FOUR

The Ache of Suspicion

The icy tendrils crept up on Catherine shortly after leaving the isolated cove where Shadiz had made love to her, tenderly mindful of her until the passion, devoid of evil or sin, had consumed both of them. As the stealthy coldness gained strength, she attribute its cause to her time spent in the sea and, despite Lucinda's solicitous efforts, the dampness of her gown.

When she began to shake uncontrollably, concerned about her, Shadiz took her onto his own mount and held her close. By the time they reached the villa, Catherine was experiencing pains throughout her entire body. By then, everyone who had accompanied her and Shadiz on the excursion around the southern part of Formentera were worried about her worsening condition.

While carrying Catherine up to her chamber, Shadiz called for the only physician on the island to be summoned. His urgency also summoned Nick Condor from mollifying Bianca. Upon discovering the reason for Shadiz's uncharacteristic distress, the Irishman rushed away to collect Senor Alvis himself.

By the time he returned with the short, plump, unnerved physician, Catherine was sweating profusely yet icy cold, almost paralysed with pain yet could not keep still. Only Shadiz's desperate embrace was stopping her from causing herself harm.

Matters were not helped by Senor Alvis's inability to diagnose symptoms he had not encountered before. When his best solution was to prescribe a goodly dose of bloodletting, Shadiz promptly dismissed the Spaniard, not wanting to make worse Catherine's deathly paleness.

It was while the physician was escaping from Catherine's chamber and Shadiz's fury at his ineffectiveness that the Persian surprised everyone present by his appearance. His regal influence, more potent than usual, was felt by everyone except Shadiz who was more taken up by Catherine's alarming plight.

Prince Ardashir's solicitous gaze focused on her. Eventually, his attention switched from her writhing in Shadiz's arms to Shadiz. When Shadiz responded with a fleeting glare, the Persian continued to survey him fearlessly.

"I would ask to speak with you alone," Prince Ardashir said, quietly.

"I ain't interested," rasped Shadiz, his anxious attention fixed on Catherine.

"I have questions for you," persisted the older man, undeterred. "They might assist your wife."

Shadiz's black head came up sharply. His long hair fell away from his barbarous face, taut with anguish.

"Say what y' want," he growled.

"For your ears alone," stressed Prince Ardashir.

Shadiz swore. Then brusquely dismissed everyone from the chamber, even though they were loathed to leave while Catherine was in such dire straits.

When the Persian was alone with Shadiz and Catherine. He moved to stand beside the bed, leaning on his gold-topped cane.

"Well?" rasped Shadiz, his jet gaze not leaving Catherine.

"This afternoon you consummated your marriage," stated Ardashir, tonelessly.

"What the 'ell 'as that got t' do wi' owt!" Shadiz demanded. "Or you."

"The joining has everything to do with her malady," replied the Persian. "I come to point this out. To offer a solution."

Shadiz came suddenly off the bed to stand tall and menacingly over the diminutive Persian. "Don't fuck wi' me, y' bastard. Just 'cos y' want y' freedom."

Appearing unmoved by the younger man's threatening behaviour, Prince Ardashir spoke soft-voiced. "There has been a difficulty between yourself and Catherine. You are a virile man, therefore the difficulty lies elsewhere. Certainly not with your wife, for she plainly has great love for you. As you do for her.

212

There is a difficulty beyond your comprehension. At the moment it manifests itself in a fit of pique."

Shadiz scowled. Yet his manner was evasive. "What the bloody 'ell're y' on about."

The Persian gave a regretful sigh. "You were right to send away the physician. He is of no use to counteract what Catherine suffers."

After a deep pause, Shadiz looked away from the Ardashir. "Y're on about sorcery," he muttered.

The low-pitched words sounded like a confession. Ardashir understood that despite Shadiz's undoubted strengths, he was vulnerable to such wickedness. With that disturbing knowledge in mind, the Persian trod carefully on the younger man's raw emotions. "You have the misfortune to know of such deeds?"

Shadiz briefly closed his eyes. For several moments he stood without speaking. A bleak, forlorn air settled upon him as he returned to where Catherine lay restless on the bed, oblivious to his presence. He caught her flailing arm in a gentle restraint.

For one glorious moment, he had thought himself free of the curse. He had dared to believe he could live happily with his wife. Believed that the demon had been slain by her love for him. In reality, all he had done was to expose Kore to an insatiable vengeance. He slowly shook his head at his own stupidity.

"I ain't able t' escape her vengeance."

"You must seek her out and confront who ever plagues you," urged Prince Ardashir.

Shadiz gave a brief, sinister laugh. "Each time she drags me down into Tartarus I fail t' vanquish the bitch."

For all his years of dealing with human foibles, the Persian's composure was shaken. "Of whom do you speak?" he asked, determined to keep his tone of voice even.

Continuing to stare down at Catherine, Shadiz spoke in a harsh whisper. "Gianca. My dead mother."

He knew the moment he uttered the words he was giving the Persian ammunition to use against him in Europe and beyond. He looked down at him, waiting to be condemned.

Ardashir responded to the glaze of torment and regret in those incredible black eyes with an expression of sincerity. "I shall hold your trust close to my heart," he promised. For he knew this hard to fathom man gave his trust sparingly, if at all. He attempted to give reassurance, which in its substance offered little comfort. "Be assured, whoever does this to your wife, resides in the world of the living."

Shadiz looked unconvinced.

"If I go away will it stop?" he asked in a resigned, painful whisper.

"I believe so," answered the Persian. "First, though, we must protected your wife."

He urged Shadiz to call Lucinda back into the chamber. She came readily, followed by Junno, Condor and Keeble. Their concern plain, all of them immediately scrutinised Catherine's worsening condition.

Ardashir approached them, speaking to Lucinda, his tone a mixture of command and courtesy. Upon him outlining what was required, her dark eyes grew wide with shock. There followed a moment's stunned silence. Having grasped the significance of the Persian's comprehensive request as well as his wife, it was Junno who looked to Shadiz for approval of Lucinda's errand. The anxious big man received a curt nod without Shadiz's attention straying from Catherine.

"Have a care in whom you confide," warned Ardashir, as Lucinda turned to leave the chamber.

"I'll go wi' 'er," said Keeble.

"I'll see she gets what's needed," assured Condor. While leaving the chamber, he was heard to ask Lucinda the reason for the assortment of items the Persian wanted.

Upon their speedy return, Condor remained in the corridor, guarding the door of Catherine's chamber along with the prince's young servant. Ardashir directed Lucinda and Keeble to set the candles they had brought around the bed where Catherine remained feverishly restless. Lucinda had already explained to Keeble and Nick Condor that the white candles were for purity and the blue ones for cleansing.

Meanwhile, Junno watched Shadiz retreat from the bed to

stand in the farthest corner. He had never seen his cousin look so defeated. Tears sprang into the big man's eyes at the same time as a sorrowful knot lodged in his throat.

Under Prince Ardashir's quiet guidance, Lucinda wafted around burned sage in a further attempt to cleanse the warm air. After which, making her fearful, she was called upon by the Persian to ignite the fumitory she had brought to the chamber. She was uneasily aware the pale, gossamer smoke, in conjunction with the candles, expelled evil spirits. Trembling, she obediently pushed a double hazelnut under Catherine's pillows in the knowledge the amulet protected against evil intentions.

Ardashir had begun to softly chant, presumably in his own language. If Shadiz understood the foreign mantras, he gave no indication, his stoic attention remaining on Catherine.

When Ardashir gestured for Lucinda to spread the bracken around the bed she had collected, her resolve almost faltered. She looked desperately at Junno to see if he realised the sweet-smelling plant was believed to give protection – because witches had a strong aversion to the plant. He inclined his bald head in encouragement and acknowledgement to her. Therefore, moving around the Persian as he continued to chant, she dealt with the wormwood and tormentil, while cringing at the thought both herbs were renowned for their magical powers to keep black witches at bay.

By the time Lucinda had completed her disturbing tasks she was quietly weeping. She paused and cast a look towards the corner of the chamber where the shadows of evening were creeping upon Shadiz's motionless presence. For the first time in a long time there was no guarded fear or animosity in her gaze.

It was of no consequence. Lucinda was convinced Shadiz was oblivious to her compassionate regard, or anyone else's.

She wanted desperately to go to Junno and have him gather her into the safety of his arms. Instead she went and stood at the opposite side of the hushed chamber. The big man met her sad, troubled gaze with loving understanding.

Lucinda's attention was caught by Keeble. The little man was sitting cross-legged on the floor behind Junno. He was staring downwards, the expression on his long, ugly face one of anxiety.

215

Yet Lucinda got the vague impression of anger roiling within his twisted body.

The only sign of the passing of time was the deepening of the shadows and the reliance on the comforting radiance of the white and blue candles around the bed where, thankfully at last, Catherine lay quiet.

Prince Ardashir stopped chanting. He sat down heavily in the nearest chair, emitting a ragged sigh, clearly exhausted by his demanding vigil. Lucinda hurried to him with a goblet of water. He thanked her and then looked around for Shadiz. Lucinda and the others in the chamber followed his concerned gaze.

"She sleeps peacefully," said the Persian. "Undisturbed by spite of spleen."

Many miles away, across sea and land, in wooded seclusion, a rasp of thwarted malevolence was carried on the wind.

The door was opened quietly by Nick Condor, anxious to know how Catherine was faring. Prince Ardashir's servant crept into the silent chamber behind him. Seeing his master's weary condition, he would have gone to the prince, but Condor prevented him from doing so.

Shadiz was walking slowly forward.

Everyone regarded him expectantly.

He came to a halt just beyond the circle of light and the sweet-smelling herbs around the bed. He stared at Catherine, on his barbarous, scarred face a tapestry of gut-wrenching misery, overwhelming regret and soul-deep, unfettered love.

Accustomed to the Master's formidable, icy reserve, those present were all affected by his torment.

Except Catherine.

Eventually, Shadiz gradually turned away from her sleeping, oblivious form.

He looked to where the Persian was sitting. The older man met the jet-black gaze. His own grew wide with surprise and his brow creased by sorrow as Shadiz unexpectedly salaamed to him with the deepest respect.

Then, unable to resist one last, despairing glance at Catherine, Shadiz walked quickly from the chamber.

Many miles away, across sea and land, in wooded seclusion, a sigh of sinister triumph was carried on the wind

Part Two

Winter

I remember, I remember,
The house where I was born,
The little window where the sun
Came peeping in at morn.

CHAPTER ONE

Lastly Stood War

York stood resolute within a wilderness. It had been the prospect of a siege which had warranted the wilful devastation around the Royalist's northern capital. Blacken stumps were all that remained of ancient woodland. Fields and meadows had been laid waste to prevent them from offering succour to the locust descent of the enemy. Cottages stood eerily empty, devoid of home comforts. The country folk, along with their livestock and premature harvests, had been gathered within the city's strong Roman walls.

A regretful sigh escaped Sir Thomas Fairfax's pursed lips. The scourge of war would forever remain a source of remorse for the slender, noble Parliamentarian commander. His moderate, scholarly air sheathed his renowned military expertise, an attribute which at times he struggled to equate with his desire for a peaceful existence.

There was an abiding loyalty and a genuine respect for him within the army he jointly commanded with his less popular father, Lord Ferdinando Fairfax. Soldiers and troopers alike readily acknowledged his passing as he allowed his white mare to amble through their numerous ranks squatting on the mutilated earth around York.

On 20th April they had rendezvous with the Scottish Army, commanded by the Earl of Leven, close to Wetherby. By the 22nd the combined muster of sixteen thousand foot and four thousand horse had laid siege to York. Within days sprawling encampments had become entrenched on both sides of the river Ouse, barely a mile from the city's grey-stone walls. At the same time great battering pieces had been placed at regular intervals around the substantial four mile circuit. From the outset Sir Thomas had sought to spare the ancient Minister, dominating the skyline of the besieged city, from the determined offensive.

In June the Eastern Association commanded by Lord Manchester had marched North to join the fray, thereby adding to York's defiant woes by increasing the number of besiegers by six thousand foot, a thousand cavalry and twelve cannons.

Sir Thomas hoped the afternoon's counsel of war he was riding to through the pleasing afternoon sunshine would prove more productive than the ones he had attended of late. Instead of the picked-over gristle of a stale siege, he and the other commanders now had the meaty prospect to chew over of Prince Rupert's advance North.

The Scottish Lord Leven, though not a man of much education, was well versed in the ways of war, having spent thirty years in the Dutch and Swedish armies, attaining the rank of field-marshal in 1635. Gaining considerable wealth during his military career abroad, he had decided to retire to his native Scotland; only to be called upon to lead the Army of the Solemn League and Covenant.

Baillie, a fellow Scot, had written of Leven, '*Such was the wisdom and authority of the old, crooked soldier that all gave over themselves to be guided by him.*'

The shrewd observation reflected Lord Ferdinando Fairfax's attitude to their present mission. Sir Thomas had been forced to accept that his father would far rather follow than bear the onerous burden of true leadership. Although they had raised an army together of which his father was the general, it was he, Sir Thomas, to whom their captains looked for direction.

Lord Manchester, a mild-mannered man, was renowned for the way he considered the welfare of his men. His military skills, though courageous, were limited. However, he did have the support of his Lieutenant-General of the Horse, Oliver Cromwell.

All of the Parliamentarian commanders were united in their determination to break York's spirit of defiance. Yet unlike his fellow besiegers, whose response to the prospect of Prince Rupert's advance was to pour scorn on his military prowess and extraordinary swift marches, Sir Thomas readily appreciate a man of worth, even though he be the twenty-four-year-old foreign nephew of King Charles and termed a dangerous enemy.

Dwelling on the possible strategies Rupert might consider, Sir Thomas was struck by a thought. He turned in the saddle to engage the two young men riding slightly behind him. "Have either of you heard tidings of Benjamin Farr of late?"

Both Jamie and Jonathan Muir shook their heads. "No, sir," answered Jamie.

The two brothers had grown up with Benjamin in Swaledale. Upon the outbreak of the Civil War their loyalty had been given to Parliament, and given unstintingly to Sir Thomas upon joining his staff, whereas their lifelong friend had chosen to defend the King. Both brothers respected their friend's contrary allegiance. What they had found hard to understand was Benjamin's willing presence with the notorious, gypsy mercenary, the Master. Only the fact that he had been instrumental in reunited Sir Thomas with his wife and daughter after they had become separated from him after the battle for Selby had they had cause to think better of Benjamin, and the Master for his surprising protection of the women.

When an argument between several soldiers broke out to their left and looked as if it might turn nasty, Jamie and Jonathan simultaneously put spur to their mounts and flanked Sir Thomas.

Smaller than his brother, curly-haired and muscular, fiercely ready for any eventuality, Jamie's hand rested on his sword hilt. Slender, his straight brown hair tidied neatly with a leather throng, his manner reserved yet alert, Jonathan looked towards the commotion half-lost from view within the narrow, haphazard rows of makeshift huts which characterised the living quarters of the three armies. Only the commanders and their officers occupied campaign tents when not on duty.

Siege warfare had elements of tedium. Commanders were obliged to keep their men occupied. But the daily grind of patrols when there was no prospect of engaging the enemy or the hours spent in hot, gritty trenches on the look-out for a target upon the Roman-constructed battlements made for a humdrum existence. Only the sweaty work of the gunnery crews penetrated the city with any meaningful reward. Even so, their constant bombardment played on the nerves not only of the hard-pressed inhabitants of York.

Sir Thomas took little heed of the disturbance in his vicinity. He was fully aware that after almost two months his men were running short of money, arms and clothing. His Foot was commanded by experienced field officers whom he trusted to keep order among the predominately young soldiers.

His thoughtful gaze rested upon the waste land beyond the cluster of besieging allies. "He will come," he muttered.

Both Jamie and Jonathan looked questioningly in his direction. "Benjamin, sir?"

Sir Thomas shook his head slowly. He had recalled a hill top encounter and his own observation were Prince Rupert to endeavour to relieve York. Who the Prince would call upon to assist in such a difficult undertaking.

A dangerous, protean nomad.

Upon his arrival at Lord Leven's headquarters, Sir Thomas resolved to keep his own counsel regarding one possibility that might impinge on the strategy of isolating York. The sight of the painted taffeta flag of the Scots, bearing the Cross of St. Andrew's, fluttering proudly in the light breeze and the formidable, kilted Highlanders standing guard, though familiar to him, caused him to feel uneasy.

Jamie and Jonathan Muir accompanied Sir Thomas through the laced-backed entrance of Leven's impressive tent and into its cool interior, illuminated by several candle lanterns and furnished with masculine comforts the common soldiers who endured campaign squalor could only dream of. As he had done during other counsels of war, discretion being paramount, Jonathan acted as Sir Thomas's secretary. Jamie melted in to the shadowy background, guarding his commander's back, still not prepared to put too much trust in the warring Scots within England.

As time passed Sir Thomas grew bored and slightly irritated by his fellow commanders' bickering. Lord Leven and his General of Horse, David Leslie, Lord Manchester and Oliver

Cromwell, and his own father Lord Ferdinando, who had been the last to arrive at the counsel of war in the Scottish camp, all vied with one another to determine the tactics the notoriously unpredictable Prince would employ in an attempt to wrest York out of their tight-fisted grasp. All were unanimous in their belief that whatever strategy Rupert decided upon would fail against their united, superior might.

Only when David Leslie pointed out Rupert's ignorance of conditions within York due to the capture of several messengers who had paid with their lives for their daring efforts to escape the besieged city, did Sir Thomas take renewed interest in the discussion. Yet, keeping to his resolution, he failed to point out that perhaps it would be wise to be on the alert for someone attempting to get into York.

"What about Rupert's gypo mercenary?"

David Leslie's curt query gave Sir Thomas an unpleasant jolt. He eased forwards in the leather chair he occupied next to Lord Manchester.

"Damn heathen snapped at our heels all the way from Newcastle," observed Lord Leven. He was lounging in a wicker chair covered by a green and black plaid. There was a hint of respect in his thick Scottish brogue.

Leslie gave a derisive snort. Sitting straight-backed on a carved stool, the chagrin he harboured against the man he had encountered while reconnoitring the landscape around York prior to the devastation of spangled greenery and shady woods showed on his thin, peevish face. He glanced at Sir Thomas, knowing the older Englishman had witnessed his humiliation by the gypsy.

Sir Thomas failed to respond to what amounted to a challenge. He was aware of Jamie's step out of the shadows, and gave an imperceptible shake of his head.

The momentary tension was ended by Manchester's chief scoutmaster clearing his throat. Always ready to give his men a hearing, Manchester gave Watson, the burly Lincolnshire man standing alongside his leather chair, a nod of acquiescent.

"The gypsy's been quiet of late. "

"Bastard's up to something," snapped Leslie, thrusting his elbows on his knees in a decisive manner.

"He could be keeping low," continued the Scoutmaster, his knowledgeable manner undisturbed. "According to reports, where we reckon gypsy's mainly based around North York Moors, Francois Lynette of Fylingdales Hall has increased his force with recruits from France. That's what might be keeping him in check."

CHAPTER TWO

The Ache of Suspicion

Catherine lay back against the soft cushions in the chair which had been carried outdoors for her by servants who had expressed their gladness at her steady recovery. Eyes closed, she listened to the lyrical birdsong, underscored by softly splashing fountains. The ceaseless whisper of the sea was carried on the soft breeze. It gave an evocative reminder of what lay beyond the stone walls, smothered in blazing-red bougainvillea, enclosing the extensive gardens around the pristine white villa.

Enjoying the restful atmosphere beside cascading willows, Catherine basked in the sun's warming rays. The fiery beasts chasing away the remnants of a brutal cold malice were helping her to recovered physically. Her spirit, on the other hand, would take far longer to mend after what had been practised upon her.

From her first waking to find Shadiz gone, coupled with the haunting malevolence that had assailed her through spiteful feverish images, Catherine had suspected the origin of the malady which had affected her so horrendously. In the following days, what she had come to sense was not mysticism. It was pure sorcery.

In doing so, she had realised who she was up against, and resolved to fight the potent malice, for Shadiz's sake.

Lucinda suspected the truth. Junno was slowly coming to terms with his wife's suspicions. He trusted her.

Why hadn't Shadiz trusted her? Instead, he had left her bereft.

Catherine hurt all the more because of the tender intimacy she had shared with Shadiz on the shore.

Unlike those who had fallen victim in the past to the mindless depravity, including his half-sister, his deep-rooted feelings for her had made it possible for her to reach beyond the sinister flaw that had at first threatened her.

No longer restful, Catherine's disturbing thoughts strayed to the beginning of the year, when her and Shadiz had been aboard the Eagle. She had done everything Mamma Petra had taught her in an effort to bring Shadiz back from the brink of death after he had been burnt in a fire at Ijuimden. Throughout she had felt the weight of the White Witch's presence. And when all her efforts had seemed in vain, there had been no doubt in her mind that Mamma Petra's weird influence had increased tenfold, incredibly over distance, implanting within her the drastic means to save Shadiz.

Only later had she learned the blind, old Romany woman, Mamma Petra, the matriarch of the tribe her father had welcomed each winter to Nafferton Garth, his estate close to Driffield, was Shadiz's grandmother. The White Witch who had gone against Romany tradition and taught her, a Gorgio, how to heal with herbal remedies.

Tom Wright, dearest Tom, her surrogate father during her time spent at the Lodge deep within Stillingfleet Forest, had warned her shortly before his death about Mamma Petra having some kind of hold over Shadiz. His fatherly instinct was proving devastatingly correct.

With that in mind, during Lucinda's vigil at her bedside, Catherine had broached the subject of Mamma Petra. Before she had accompanied Catherine as well as Junno and Peter to France and then to Formentera, Lucinda had been the blind, old Romany woman's hard-pressed servant. Since leaving Mamma Petra in England, Lucinda had definitely flourished.

It was clearly because of her freedom from the old woman's oppressive manner that Lucinda had been prepared to agree with Catherine's suspicions, and to give further insight into Mamma Petra's conduct towards Shadiz.

Lucinda had explained how Mamma Petra had taken great pains to seek him out. Upon her eventual success, Shadiz had been taken into his mother's Romany tribe. He had disappeared a couple of years later.

Catherine experienced an aching disquiet while wondering about Mamma Petra's influence upon him during childhood, and throughout the following years.

Troubled by her reverie, she sighed and opened her eyes, dazzled by the afternoon sunshine.

"I'm sorry. I didn't mean t' wake y'."

Her eyes watery, Catherine squinted upwards. "No, you didn't," she responded, sitting up, surreptitiously wiping away the glisten of tears while avoiding Lucinda's compassionate look.

Both Junno and Lucinda, having discovered their fears for Catherine had been miraculously unfounded, had been quick to apologise for their ill-timed and ill-judged descent upon Shadiz and herself in their private moment in the secluded cove. She had accepted their apology. Shadiz had been much slower to follow suit.

"Y' must be feelin' warm. You've pushed off y'r blanket," commented Lucinda, sitting down on a nearby bench surrounded by earthenware pots filled with sweet smelling lavender.

Junno joined them. He appeared worried. "Y' seen Keeble anywhere?"

"'e was off t' get bairns lemonade last time I saw him," answered Lucinda.

"He's done an excellent job of keeping Peter occupied since Katy and Jack left with Benjamin," observed Catherine.

Peter had been most upset when he had learned his playmates, Jack and Katy, were to leave Formentera with their cousin, Benjamin Farr.

The twins' parents had died in a boating accident while on Malta. Benjamin's two older brothers and his father had gone to the island of the Knights of St John to escort the children back to England. During the return voyage their ship had been waylaid by the piratical exploits of Shadiz and Nick Condor. Benjamin's family had been taken off the defeated ship before the youngsters had been discovered. The adults had been sold into slavery. The twins had been taken to Formentera to live at the villa before anyone had realised the family connection.

For a long while, Benjamin blamed Condor for his family's

misfortune, believing his father and brothers to have been murdered. Yet Shadiz had been just as complicit in the fate of his family.

Ultimately, it had been Shadiz who had ordered a vessel from the corsair fleet to sail to Portugal, with Benjamin and the twins on board. The captain of the *Sirius* had originally been entrusted with a missive from the Master claiming the men back, along with generous funds to compensate for the loss of their servitude on a plantation in the south of the country. Upon Benjamin being united with his father and brothers, they would all then sail for England.

At the last minute, Nick Condor had decided to undertake the mission himself.

On the day Jack and Katy had departed with Benjamin, Peter had gone missing. A search had immediately been launched in the villa and throughout the garden. It had been the Persian Vizier, himself a victim of Formentera's corsair plundering, who had discovered the Romany boy, curled up under the velvet-draped seat he favoured in the cool shade of tall palm trees. Thereafter, everyone had made great efforts to keep Peter entertained. At Junno's request, two of Rosa's grandsons visited Peter most days.

Catherine, Lucinda and Junno caught the drift of children's laughter. Relieved that Peter had found two more playmates, the adults shared indulgent smiles.

Catherine grew serious, even dared to be a little hopeful. "Is there any word?"

Junno was loathed to disappointed her yet again. "No, Rauni. Not since he sailed on the Fortuna."

Lucinda placed a comforting hand on Catherine's arm.

Smiling stoically at the young Romany woman, Catherine was once again made aware of a notable change in Lucinda's attitude. Whereas before, she would have been hard-pressed to disguise her relief at Shadiz's departure, she now appeared regretful. Certainly, when Lucinda had described the way Shadiz had been affected by her illness and his self-imposed banishment from Catherine's bedside, her eyes had filled with tears.

Forcing down the surge of misery, Catherine's speculative gaze

230

rested on Junno. "How did Mamma Petra discover Shadiz?" she asked, aware as she spoke of Lucinda's keen study of her husband.

After a brief hesitation, the big man crouched down between Catherine's chair and the bench his wife was sitting upon. The bright rays of the sun polished his bald head as he plucked at the grass. "She knew o' 'im o' course bein' wi' Tom Wright an' his wife. She also knew when 'e were taken from Fylingdales t' York. 'e were never let out into the city, so it was only when me dadrus learned o' the few searches for 'im that Mamma realised 'e'd escaped from the grand house in Petersgate. It were Imre who come across 'im in a tavern, Dark Horse."

"Do y' know what she said when Imre told 'er o' Shadiz's whereabout?" asked Lucinda, looking at her husband's bowed head.

Junno looked up at her. Frowning, he shook his head.

"Imre is my oldest brother," she told Catherine. Switching her attention back to Junno, she went on, "Mamma said t' 'im Shadiz belonged in whorehouse."

Both shocked, Junno and Catherine stared at Lucinda. "Imre kept 'is eye on Shadiz, without sayin' owt more t' Mamma. That was 'ow 'e knew Shadiz'd escaped from the place. 'e were in Dark Horse when landlord an' 'is sister paraded the two whores who'd 'elped 'im t' get away around the tavern naked an' let every sod've a go at 'em."

The three of them were silent for a time, digesting the unpleasant facts of Shadiz's past.

At last, Catherine asked, "How old would he be?"

"'e were about four or five when 'e was taken from Fylingdales," answered Junno, grimly.

"'e'd not be much older when 'e started livin' at the tavern," put in Lucinda.

"An' about six or seven when 'e got away from there," said Junno. "Mamma sent our kakoes, uncles, including me dadrus, searchin' for Shadiz. as they travelled around the foros, markets and fairs."

"They eventually found him," stated Catherine, apprehensive about the outcome of their search.

"Aye," responded Junno. He gave her a lop-sided grin full of memories. "'e weren't too pleased. But 'e stayed wi' us for a year or so."

"Mamma drove 'im away," said Lucinda. When her husband switched from Catherine to her, giving her an uneasy look, she added. "Y' know its true. She was obsessed wi' 'im. Still is."

Junno sighed and raised his massive shoulders apologetically. "'twas just she wanted t' know 'im better."

"It were more than that. An' y' know it!" challenged Lucinda. "What about them times she'd keep 'im alone close by 'er fire in woods." Lucinda turned to Catherine, adding, with fierce superstition. "Still does given 'alf a chance."

Junno rose to his full, impressive height, saying nothing.

Catherine's ripe suspicions had solidified into a firm belief. "Shortly before he died, Tom told me he was sure Mamma Petra possessed some kind of hold over Shadiz."

Clearly uncomfortable, Junno nodded. "'e started comin' t' 'er every so often." He took a deep breath and then expelled it, as if he was ridding himself of unwanted thoughts. In the next moment he gave the two young women a forced smile, muttering, "I must go find Keeble."

Frowning, Lucinda stood up. "'e always seems t' be wantin' t' know where Keeble is these days." She shrugged away the observation. "I best go see what bairns're up t'. You rest." She began to move away along the garden pathway in the opposite direction to that taken by her husband.

Glad of Junno's departure, Catherine called softly to Lucinda. When the young Romany woman turned back to her, she asked, "Does Mamma Petra prepare drinks for Shadiz when he visits her?"

"Allus," answered Lucinda, her expression also answering Catherine. "Alone, wi'out me 'elp."

Having spent years with Mamma Petra, caring for the tribe's Pura Dai, even before she had married Junno, and assisting the old woman in her role as White Witch, Lucinda knew just as much as Catherine about herbs with healing properties; and those that were spell seekers.

★

Resembling a page on a mission, Keeble, dwarf-like and stooped, carried a silver tray of robust mugs destined for Peter and his two new friends. Halfway along the cool, whitewashed passageway he passed a door stood slightly ajar. Already taking care his uneven gait did not cause the brimming golden fruit juices to spill, upon hearing light feminine voices, his short footsteps slowed even more, coming to an eventual halt.

He recognised one of the voices coming from within the chamber as belonging to the Persian woman, Bianca, Nick Condor's exotic mistress. An expression of furtive interest on his large, ugly face, he glanced towards the arched doorway at the end of the passageway that led out into the sunny gardens and then, being a consummate ear-dropper, yielded to curiosity and shuffled closer to the intriguing crack.

Alluringly accented words and their vicious sentiment were easy to distinguish.

"Stupid bitch has anyone at her beck. They fawn on her. English rose. Bah! Even now, she sits outside if mistress in this place. She should be gone from Formentera not Shadiz."

There was a murmur of devoted agreement.

Keeble heard other, masculine voices coming his way. His mind calculating, his expression wholly innocent, he continued down the passageway.

★

Catherine was of a mind to follow Lucinda down the stone flagged path edged with red and yellow roses to where the children were playing in another part of the garden. She was prevented from doing so by the arrival of Prince Ardashir. Although his greeting was given in his customary dignified manner, Catherine got the impression it was of consequence to him that he spoke with her. Rising from the curtsy she always felt his graciousness warranted, she gestured for him to be seated in the chair she had just vacated. His young servant bobbed down on the ground beside his master while Catherine sat down on the bench close by.

"Your health is much improved," commented Ardashir, smiling. "I am please to see this be the case."

Catherine responded with a grateful smile. "Once again, I must thank you for your consideration on my behalf."

Though Lucinda was well-versed in the use of medicinal herbs, having served Mamma Petra since she was quite young, she had explained to Catherine how the Persian had shown incredible insight into what had taken hold of her, and how he had combated the strange, dangerous malady with an extraordinary expertise, employing herbs, white and blue candles, and a chant foreign to Lucinda.

Creased slightly against the glow of the late afternoon sun, his shrewd attention rested on Catherine's young face, once again becoming bronzed by summery radiance having lost the pale, almost translucent pallor.

"You miss him," he stated, sympathetically.

The knot lodged suddenly in her throat made it difficult to speak. She nodded.

"That is good. A wife should always look towards her husband's return."

Catherine managed a controlled answer. "I wonder if he will ever return."

"Love has many strands," answered Ardashir, kindly smiling. "With time, they form a bond that cannot be broken."

Catherine looked down at her tightly clasped hands. After a moment, she lifted her head and, tears on her eye lashes, regarded the Persian. "Lucinda has described how Shadiz did not approach me while you sought to aid me. Also, afterwards, when he knew I was over the worse. He left Formentera."

"Are you aware of Gianca?"

She was taken aback by his inquiry. "I…I heard him utter her name when he was injured and consumed with fever," she replied, shakily.

"She was his mother?"

Catherine swallowed convulsively. "Yes. May I ask how you come to be aware of her?"

Ardashir was thoughtful. "He believes her to be the cause of your distress."

Catherine covered her mouth with her two trembling hands.

"Rauni?" called Junno, approaching her with wide, urgent strides. "What be amiss?" He scowled at the Persian as he sat down on the bench next to Catherine and put a comforting arm around her.

"I was explaining to Catherine how her husband labours under the impression his mother haunts him," said Ardashir, calmly.

Junno stiffened. A shocked expression crossed his round, honest features.

"Junno?" murmured Catherine, regarding him expectantly.

He gave her an awkward half-smile that was more of a grimace before he threw Ardashir a warning, accusing glance.

The Persian remained perfectly serene. "I am of a mind she deserves to know what you hold within."

In the pause that followed, it was plain Junno was struggling for some kind of a response. Eventually, with reluctance, he met Catherine's pleading gaze.

"I can't make 'ead nor tail o' it, Rauni," he admitted, regretfully. "'e talks o' 'er, Gianca, 'is ma, as if she's cursed 'im. Aye, as if she 'aunts 'im. As if, no matter 'ow 'e tries…'e ain't able t' get rid o' 'er. Slay 'er, like 'e reckons 'e did when she birthed 'im."

A sob was wrenched from Catherine.

Junno drew her close. "I be sorry t' cause y' 'urt," he muttered, unhappily.

"Please do not be sorry," she answered, brokenly. "Shadiz is the one who is hurting." She was beginning to comprehend the burden he had kept locked away from her. The guilt she was suddenly experiencing was intensified when a thought struck her. She slowly sat upright.

"Elizabeth, his half-sister. Lucinda. The other women." She closed her eyes, for a moment unable to continue. Junno tightened his compassionate hold on her. Eventually, she added, "He believed he was saving them from Gianca"

"The belief he placed you in danger when the malady struck after he had claimed you as his wife caused him to step away from you while the healing took place," explained Ardashir, quietly. "And why he left the villa and the island before your awakening."

"'e's allus wanted t' protect y', Rauni."

Catherine slowly nodded. Her hand rose to her jet pendant. "He found it impossible to sever the connection," she murmured.

That evening, after a difficult dinner, during which conversation had been kept alive for Peter's sake, Catherine retired early. She dismissed her maid with a pleasant excuse.

It was therefore with a resigned sigh she responded to the soft knocking on the door of her chamber. Lucinda popped her head around the door she had half-opened. Seeing Catherine halt in mid-chamber, with a quick, apologetic warning, she opened the door wider to reveal the Persian and Junno standing in the shadowy corridor.

Leaning on his gold-topped cane, Prince Ardashir stepped forward. He bowed to Catherine. Straightening a little stiffly, he said, "Forgive the intrusion. It would be most inappropriate to enter your chamber in the absent of a chaperon. Understanding this, I prevailed upon Junno and Lucinda to accompany me. Besides, what we may speak of could well impinge upon them." He gave Catherine an ingratiating smile. "May we enter?"

"Of course," she answered, graciously. She glanced at Junno as Ardashir entered her chamber. The big man gave the impression of being suspicious of the Persian's motive for wanting to visit her. Nevertheless, he kept his own counsel and went to stand by the open window while Catherine invited Prince Ardashir and Lucinda to be seated.

Sitting down herself across from the Prince, she waited for him to instigate the conversation, aware both Lucinda and Junno were uncomfortable about the situation.

"Your husband is an extraordinary man," began Ardashir, his grey, considering eyes on Catherine. "A true leader whose potential lies surely beyond that of a corsair general." He looked to where Junno was standing beside the gossamer hangings, stirring slightly in the soft evening breeze coming through the open window. "Would you not agree?"

Junno's answer was guarded. "Aye. But what Shadiz does is up t' 'im."

236

While the Persian Vizier's shrewd attention lingered on Junno, Catherine studied him, curious about the reason for his visit. Why had he brought Lucinda and particularly Junno along with him? For, despite his courteous declaration, during her recovery, he had been a regular visitor to her chamber, often unaccompanied, .

On such occasions, he had entertained her by speaking about the vast, ancient country of Persia, its courtly politics and the country's young Shah.

Responding to Catherine's interest, the Prince had spoken eloquently about the ancient rulers of his country, Cyrus the First who had built the first world empire, Cyrus the Great who had extended that empire into Arabia and Palestine and Darius whose military might had conquered Egypt and Libya. With regret, he had described Persia's dark ages, when a succession of invaders, Alexander the Great, the Arabs and the aggressive Mongols and Timurids had each in turn brutalised the country. Throughout the people of Persia had struggled to maintain their identity.

The Prince had gone on to explain that it was nearly three centuries later, at the end of the sixteenth century, that the military confidence and shrewd diplomacy of Shah Abbas had brought about stability between warring factions and a political independence. Both were of vital importance to Persia, for the Ottoman Turks lay to the west and the Uzbegs to the east.

Catherine received part of the answer as to why Junno was present when Ardashir once again outlined Persian history.

Including Catherine and Lucinda, he went on to speak glowingly of Persia's capital Isfahan.

How the city was situated in the country's richest oasis and flanked by tall-peaked hills. Set like a rare jewel in the heart of Persia, how its climate was less harsh than elsewhere. Describing how the majestic river Zayandeh Rud, Giver of Life, flowed through the city where gifted craftsmen and artists had created palaces, mansions, mosques and broad avenues and wide verdant areas. Shah Abbas's patronage had made Isfahan a most exalted place, combining all aspects of royal, secular, religious and commercial life into a montage of wonders that could easily rival anything the West had to offer.

The Prince let them digest his picturesque description of his city for several moments before he began speaking again.

"Upon Shah Abbas's death it was essential his successor be sufficiently able to support his impressive advancements. Unfortunately, due to him leaving only female offspring, the new Shah, Abbas's nephew, is an eight-year-old boy. Although well supported by myself and my family, there is a vital need for a trustworthy, protective force, immune to any internal dissent while guarding the young boy Shah, Isfahan, the trade routes important to the country and the borders that lay next to hostile powers."

Catherine grasped the significance of Ardashir's carefully chosen words. Her attention snapped to Junno. He stared back at her with a matching expression of startled comprehension. Then they both switched to the Prince. The calm gaze of a statesman met their united scrutiny.

"I don't understand," complained Lucinda, alarmed by Catherine and Junno's manner.

"He wants Shadiz," Junno explained, without taking his attention from Ardashir.

The Persian smiled reassuringly. "I have spoken to him at length."

"An' I bet y' ain't got a straight answer!" observed Junno, grimly.

Hit by another inspirational thunderbolt, Catherine muttered, "Wait a minute."

She ran swiftly though how Prince Ardashir had been taken prisoner by Nick Condor while sailing on a diplomatic mission to the French court. Thereafter, he had been living quite comfortably on Formentera, well-liked and respected by all at the villa. Much to Condor's chagrin, instead of sanctioning a ransom, Shadiz had ordered his release. A safe passage was presently being arranged for one of their ship to sail to a French port in order to discharge the noble Persian from their highly dubious keeping.

"Ye gods and little fishes!" she continued, scarcely able to believe what she recognised as the truth. "You made certain you would be waylaid in the Mediterranean. Alright, you were hunted by Nick Condor, but you knew Shadiz was associated with him. Unfortunately, Shadiz wasn't on Formentera. No wonder you were not in a hurry to have a ransom demanded for your release. You were happy to remain on the island until Shadiz returned, knowing Condor needed his approval for your ransom. When he did return that was your chance... *to speak to him at length.* "

Her heart beat a rhythm of fear while recalling her glimpses of Shadiz and Ardashir strolling together in the garden, deep in conversation. Rising panic was suffocating her breathing. She felt overwhelmed by agonising desertion.

"He will go. To the other side of the world. In an effort to get away from me," she exclaimed. She looked around wildly for succour. For someone to tell her it wasn't true.

Seconds later, she felt her jet pendant grow warm against her cold skin. Knew it was answering his moonstone, which had alerted him to her distress.

"You will go, but the link will still remain to torment!" she cried, barely aware of Lucinda and Junno closing about her.

Lucinda put an arm around Catherine's trembling shoulders, desperate to console. Junno went down on one knee before her and took hold of both her wringing hands. He spoke urgently to her, trying to reached past her near-hysteria. "Rauni, calm down. Please! Y' don't know for sure whether Shadiz'd go to Persia."

Catherine shook her head, tears blurring her cringing vision.

Junno half-turned in Prince Ardashir's direction. "Damn y'. Don't y' reckon Rauni's got enough to deal with?"

Ardashir ignored him. He rose from the chair opposite Catherine and approached her. Halting between Junno and Lucinda, they gave way reluctantly to his silent command. Bending forward, he gently placed his hands at either side of her damp, stricken face. "You will heed me, anyna," he said, in a soft, compelling voice. "You are the key that unlocked his heart. He roams not far from the half of him. Be at peace."

Catherine stared into the wise, grey eyes. They had taken on a strange compulsion, from which she could not break free. She felt the terrible panic that had threatened to consume her slowly recede. After a few moments of meeting his gaze, she found she could breath easily again.

"He left me," she murmured.

Ardashir looked to where she was gripping her jet pendant. "He is always with you in heart and soul. As you are with him." He gave her a reassuring smile. "I foresee difficulties ahead. Yet do not underestimate your entwined destinies."

He straightened stiffly. "There was a point when I envisaged you slipping away from my care in spite of my effort. In those moments your husband held you to him by force of will. I know not what *his* chant be while he clung to his pendant akin to yours. It reinforced his determination to not let you go from his world, bleak though he considers it to be. He kept your beloved light burning within it. As for him leaving you. He sought to protect you from the demon. She continues to torment him for her own sake. In this world, not the other."

"What are you?" asked Catherine, shakily.

"I am Mage," answered the Persian, quietly. "As my father before me, and his father before him. On through the centuries."

"A witch?" muttered Junno, cautiously. Lucinda had moved closer to him.

Ardashir's attention remained on Catherine's young, open face. "What is your saying? It takes one…."

"To know one," finished Catherine.

CHAPTER THREE

The Dwarf and the Princess, The Druid and the Witch

Bianca's maid answered the knock on the door at her mistress's off-hand bidding. Silver tray in hand, Keeble ignored the pretty young girl's increasingly desperate efforts to detain him at the door and, slipping past her, hastened into the lavish, perfumed chamber.

His determined entrance earned him a haughty scowl from Bianca. She reclined upon a silk couch. A small round table inlaid with golden filigree and mother-of-pearl stood close by upon which was a silver dish half-full of sweet-meats. Her flimsy attire rippled around her voluptuous body in the light breeze coming through the open, full length windows.

Keeble glanced towards the balcony. Having reassured himself it was unoccupied save for the heady scent of jasmine, he turned his attention back to the Persian woman as she addressed him in accented impatience.

"I order no sherbet." She gave him a brief, disdainful appraisal. "From your hand especially. I not to know how your mistress took hand in preparation?"

Before answering her, Keeble placed the silver tray holding the goblet down on the exquisite Persian carpet, one of many scattered around the chamber. Straightening, he met Bianca's indignant glare. "I don't come from my mistress. I come for my mistress."

"You speak in riddles, dwarf," she snapped.

Though his heart was beating hard in his misshapen chest, he answered her calmly, "'Tis y'sen, m'lady, needs a riddle solvin'."

"And what riddle would be that?" responded Bianca, a faint gleam of interest entering her almond eyes, defined by artfully applied kohl.

Before continuing, Keeble looked to where the maid was standing next to where the door stood ajar.

Realising the twin threats he perceived, Bianca dealt imperviously with both. Only when the maid had been vouched for and the door closed did he turn back to her with an imperceptible sigh of relief, keenly aware of the risk he was taking.

"'Tis plain y' entertain no likin' for my mistress. 'Twould please y' t' see her gone from Formentera." He took a deep breath. "I've a solution for y'."

Her dark gaze sharpened. He had her narrowed attention as she slowly sat up and swung her shapely legs off the couch. Yet her mellow voice possessed the sting of continued disdain. "That be what?"

"Y'r 'elp t' ship 'er away from 'ere. There'd be reward from them folk who'd keep 'er safe in England. She needs t' be protected. The Master values Catherine now. But I fear the future. So y' see…. "

"I indeed do, dwarf." murmured Bianca, thoughtfully.

Keeble was overwhelmingly relieved she was contemplating his suggestion. For he would do anything to keep his Catherine safe from the Master.

He experienced a pang of guilt.

There had been times when the unusual man had reminded him of Lord Richard, his father. And he had to admit for quite a while he had begun to admire the Master. But above all was Catherine's safety. He had to avoid by all means anything happening to her, as it had done to his dear Elizabeth. Even if it meant inviting the Master's lasting, deadly wrath.

★

There was the very vivid impression that the seasoned wood was alight. Fortunately, it was but an illusion. One that from time to time brought back unwanted reminders of when the world had indeed gone up in smoke.

The big-wheeled, ancestral vardos of a proud people, cautiously independent, held a thousand memories; some good, some not.

Resembling their ancestors who followed the teaching of the prophet Zoroaster in Persia long before Christ walked the earth, men and women sat around their portable hearths. Nowadays they found solace in Christ as well as the lingering reverence of flickering flames that banished the velvet darkness of night.

Women sat in convivial groups, among them young mothers with their babies in their laps or discreetly at their breasts. Salt and pepper older women reclined with them, or had settled in senior clusters. They remained close to the sleeping children.

Separated by dominate measures from the women who remained close to their sleeping children, the men sat around their own fires, engrossed in pipe smoking discussions. On their fringes, holding their own animated conversations, were the boys who had recently graduated to manhood.

The nocturnal air was still and balmy. Women had shrugged off their colourful shawls and men raised their mugs in shirt sleeves. Tethered horses cropped the grass free of the harness after a day of labour, bringing their masters and their families to the whispering brook within a thinly wooded hollow. The many slumberous dogs were disturbed only now and then by troublesome fleas.

It was therefore with utter shock that the Romany reacted to their visitors.

Their reverie was shattered by the ghostly white figure and the brown shadow who had come among them with eerie silence, women clutched their offspring, making them whimper and men, after rearing up, became paralysed by superstition. Likewise, the dogs, the sentinels of the tribe, made no murmur, simply watched in rigid wariness.

Of all those settled within the hollow only the old woman beside her own fire, ringed protectively by her tribe, seemed unimpressed by the approach of the white-robed figure. She tilted her head to one side, disturbing her long grey plaits, and through sightless eyes gazed towards Garan with deep fissures of contempt.

She remained seated as the Druid from Stillingfleet Forest came to an unhurried halt a few paces away from her. "Ye allus was one for thy cutting o' a figure," Mamma Petra observed in her own language. "A charlatan wi' a fat-bellied pig."

Faithfully by Garan's side, Myr growled low in her throat. Even though he knew it was for his sake that she responded to the deliberate insult, he gently touched her leathery side with his long staff. Harbouring aggressive silence, the long-tusked boar glared beadily at the old Romany woman.

"She ensures peace reigns," said Garan, mildly.

Mamma Petra gave a contemptuous snort. "A wild man o' trees wi' 'is pet."

Again, Garan lightly touched Myr's side, sensing her increased hostility to the old woman.

"A rogue priest, despised by thy brethren."

He had come in the full knowledge he would be exposed to her vindictiveness. Appearing to pass off her sour thrusts as a compliment, he inclined his head.

"What dost thou seek?" she demanded, irritably.

"For you to leave them alone. Both of them."

A damning emotion flickered over her deeply lined feature. Its aftermath lingered in the tightness of her thin lips. Her sunken, sightless eyes narrowed. "Thou darest t' rule me!"

"Above anyone else," responded Garan. He was immune to what she practised on others. He leaned forward on his staff. "I know you. I know what you have done to him. You will not meddle, witch, with his last chance."

Mamma Petra rose unaided to her feet. "He be mine. Not that absurd child's."

Garan smiled. "Be warned. That absurd child has got a heady whiff of your foul stench."

She gave a smug, wicked laugh. "She be nought match for me."

"Really?" murmured Garan, raising his bushy brows.

"Thee sought 'er, " accused Mamma Petra.

"I simply gave her a nudge in the right direction. Unlike the sharp prods you have given her in the past."

Mamma Petra responded to his plain speaking huffishly.

Garan advanced upon her. Tall and thin, he bent to her much smaller, black-garbed figure. Mamma Petra stood her ground, waving an impatient hand to halt the men who, attempting to conquer their fear of the white-robed Druid, had embarked upon a hesitant shuffle towards their Pura Dia.

Garan spoke for her ears alone. "I could not save the mother. But I managed to wrest the babe from your talons. You have punished him enough for your lack of foresight. It ends."

Mamma Petra stiffened.

CHAPTER FOUR

Dawn Patrol

Martin Wedgwood, one of the more professional defenders of York, was uncomfortably aware he was leading a patrol consisting of a bunch of amateurs in what had become known as the 'Achilles' Heel' of the besieged city.

The vulnerable King's Manor, in better times the residence of the Governor of the North, and its grounds sloping down to the River Ouse, had come under attack from the Crop-Ears on the 16th June. A successful counter-attack by the grimly determined defenders had ensured the L-shaped, red-brick Manor had remained in the possession of the Royalists. Yet due to its position, projecting just beyond the robust city walls, there was always the likelihood of a furtive reprisal from within its verdant precincts by the equally determined enemy .

So why the hell, thought Wedgwood, not for the first time, had he been given orders to lead members of the Citizens Volunteer Brigade around one of the most dangerous quarters was beyond him. The only advantage in their favour was that dawn was breaking, giving their surroundings a misty, ethereal reality.

If Wedgwood was feeling unhappy about the hazardous situation, it was nothing compared to what Robert Dickinson was experiencing.

What seemed like a century ago, he had been pleased to join the Citizens Volunteer Brigade, and proud to be elected the leader of his district's Brigade. Never in a million years had he expected to be called upon to help defend York against his fellow countrymen, and the damned Scots.

As Dickinson and his pinch-faced companions prowled around the neglected grounds behind Wedgwood, stumbling across those areas that had suffered badly during the battle for ownership of the King's Manor, they gripped their muskets as they had their mothers, aiming them at anything looking vaguely suspicious in the burgeoning light of a new morning they hoped to live through.

When out of nowhere shots from unseen muskets suddenly split the eerie atmosphere like a flight of angry bees, the entire Volunteer Citizens Band adhered to their brief training at the rear of Matt Cartwright's smithy and met mother earth at terrific, lung-punishing speed. Dickinson thought to leap-frog over Cartwright's bull neck and leg it. He was not alone in wanting to beat a hasty retreat.

Martin Wedgwood's teeth-grinding call for discipline prevented a mass exodus. What followed was not what he had envisaged.

"We've 'ad it," wailed Robert Dickinson.

When further pot-shots Dickinson's loud despair had invited came to a ragged end from Crop-Ears secreted in the mist-wreathed foliage, Hugh Harvey, a more adventurous soul, muttered, "'ad it, me arse. Come on, lads. Afore bastards reload."

None of the 'lads' wanted to be singled out for criticism later. United in their panic-stricken bravado, deaf to Wedgwood's desperate commands, they jumped up and scampered in the direction Harvey had gone, praying hard that their headlong dash would manifest leafy camouflage before the phantom muskets rang out again.

Cursing roundly, Martin Wedgwood had no option but to follow his recalcitrant charges. To his surprise he made it to the bushes they had ploughed through without a musket ball whistling past his ear, or worse. Starting to emerge from the prickly cover, he saw the reason for his continued existence. And cursed a second time; very quietly. He was in the process of melting cautiously back into the depth of the bushes when he was halted by the barrel of a musket being jabbed into his back. Thereafter he followed the direction the musket's sharp prod indicated and before long was standing among the corralled members of the Brigade, like them having been roughly disarmed.

Hugh Harvey was looking remorseful. He had been quickly surrounded after skidding to a halt too late to warn those he had urged to join his wild charge. As a result, John Foster had jabbed his musket into George Harvey's recoiling back, causing the latter to do a queer jig, and Robert Dickinson had swiped Matt Cartwright over the head with his weapon, a feat in itself.

The six Crop-Ears appeared vaguely triumphant and, more worrying, dimly ready to extract revenge for their own onerous duties. They discussed what action to take in front of their subdued captives, none of it pleasant. When Wedgwood tried to intervene, aware his men were ready to fold in sheer terror, he received a vindictive blow to the head from the butt of a musket that sent him reeling down on to his knees.

Stunned, he was therefore unaware of what happened during the next few minutes. When his senses returned sufficiently for him to once again take in his surroundings, to his amazement he discovered the tables had been turned; or so he hoped. Climbing dizzily to his feet, helped distractedly by Matt Cartwright, he saw that the Crop-Ears who had captured them were now all sprawled on the dewy grass in conditions they would not rise from. In their place were silent men who radiate a much harder menace through the clinging mist.

Despite a blinding headache and a cold feeling in the pit of his stomach, Martin Wedgwood straightened his shoulders and stepped forward. "I'm Captain Martin Wedgwood. To whom do you give your allegiance?"

"T' me." answered a distinct voice in a deep whispery tone possessing hard-edged authority.

★

Miles before the market town of Skipton came into view, the tight pack of dust-stained riders encountered the Royalist Army of Prince Rupert. Men, horses, armament and the inevitable baggage of an army on the move had flooded Ribblesdale and leaked into Wharfedale. In overlapping contingents they had gathered in fields and meadows, thronged villages and manor houses.

Inevitably, the multitude was wary of an unknown band of riders. Especially a well-armed one.

Restraint ensured the continued progress of the Master's men. At the mention of their leader's renowned title the wariness they repeatedly encountered was replaced by rampant curiosity, only to be in turn replaced by disappointment upon discovering the legend was not accompanying his men.

Riding at the head of his half-brother's men, alongside Danny Murphy, Richard Massone had come to the sour conclusion by the time the outskirts of Skipton was reached that the Master's star hung high over the Prince's army.

The riders from the Lodge negotiated the rowdy bustle that had descended upon the market town, swelling its inadequate lanes. Eventually, they reached the north side of the town where the formidable castle stood on a rocky outcrop. The semi-circular moat protected the east, south and west approaches. To the north the sheer drop to the gorge of Haw Beck was the best defensive measure. Approaching the well-guarded southern gatehouse, flanked by powerful drum towers, the Master's men encountered the same active suspicion they had elsewhere on their journey.

Richard's patience was wearing thin. "No, the Master is elsewhere," he informed the captain of the guard. "It is for that reason we have arrived to see Prince Rupert. I am a member of his staff."

After a few moments of humming and hawing over his dog-eared credentials, Richard and Danny Murphy were allowed access into the castle.

The rest of the Master's men went off in search of the huge field kitchen, where they had been told was a roasting fire and large pots of ale to slake their dusty throats.

Upon entering the Conduit Court in the heart of the substantial castle, Richard was hailed by a booming voice.

"Well met the Archer!"

Heads turned in the direction of the two newcomers. Keen interest rested on the long bow slung across Richard's shoulder and the quiver of arrows hung at his waist. The dour ruggedness of Danny Murphy also drew speculative looks.

"Goring, " responded Richard without enthusiasm.

Lord George Goring met them beside the ancient yew tree growing in the middle of the sunny, open-air courtyard. The flamboyant cavalier gave Richard a hearty slap on the back. "How goes it in the east?" As he spoke, he looked over Richard's shoulder. In his customary effusive manner, he cut across the younger man's answer to his first question, asking a second, "Where is the Devil?"

"I've come to inform Rupert of his whereabouts."

The sharpness of his tone caused Goring's blue eyes to widen and his bushy brows to elevate in an elaborate manner.

Aware of Murphy's critical gaze, Richard muttered, "Forgive me, sir." It was his turn to cast an inquiring look over another's shoulder. "Is the Prince in residence or out in the field?"

"He's presently discussing matters with Sir John." Goring gave a mischievous wink. "I'm supposed to be attending. Come, I'll escort you."

While leading the two men through the boisterous atmosphere within the Great Hall, crowded with the Prince's senior officers and those of Sir John Mallory, the Governor of the Castle, Goring explained how prior to the siege of York, Lord Newcastle had sent out his cavalry. Goring, his General of Horse, had subsequently joined Prince Rupert's army.

Leaving the hall after he had exchanged ribald comments with a couple of his hard-drinking cronies, he led Richard and Murphy up a dark, narrow stairway. Entering a small chamber flooded by sunlight, it took the three men a couple of moments for their eyes to adjust to the warm brightness. Eventually the black shadow advancing upon them materialized into an agitated secretary.

Attired in puritan black, his greying hair neat, the Prince's secretary appeared more like a sober parliamentarian when compared to Goring's attire of ruby-red doublet, bronze breeches and the scarlet sash around his ample middle. Nonetheless the fellow carried a certain air of authority about his short person. When he chastised Goring for his tardiness at joining the Prince's discussions, Goring cringed overly at the curt politeness and offered his profuse apologise before turning aside and pulling a comical, long-suffering face at Richard.

When he and Danny Murphy started to follow Goring to the

door of the Prince's chamber, his secretary blocked their way. "You cannot enter, I'm afraid, gentlemen."

"Jesus, Thomas. Do your eyes play you false?" roared Goring, grinning, "Neither of us knows one of the gentlemen in question. Yet surely, methinks, your well enough acquainted with Lord Richard of Fylingdales."

Goring's good-natured teasing served to ease Richard's ire at not being immediately recognised by someone he had worked with on the Prince's staff. The contrite, belated greeting also lessened the feeling of having fallen deeper into the pit of his half-brother's shadow.

"You have changed somewhat since leaving to join the Master's company," observed Thomas Huntly, scrutinising Richard.

"Joining his *brother*," stressed Goring, playfully.

"Half-brother," Richard muttered.

After he had vouched for Danny Murphy, Goring ushered both of the men into Prince Rupert's presence.

Like the anti-chamber, the larger main chamber Rupert was using for his war cabinet was drenched in sunshine. It came pearling through the mullion windows and brightly polished the fine veneer of the two tall settles and court cupboard stood against the tapestry covered walls. Dust motes drifted in shafts of warm sunbeams around the carved chairs occupied by the men studying the maps spread upon a large oaken table in the middle of the chamber.

Sir John Mallory surveyed Richard and Murphy with a quizzical frown. Sir Charles Lucas, Goring's Lieutenant-General of Horse, looked mildly annoyed at Goring. Upon switching his attention to Richard, smiling recognition blossomed. Lord John Byron's customary dark-eyed glower accompanied his waspish remarked aimed at Goring for his tardiness.

Goring took immediate measures to appease his transgression with an overly deep, courtly bow to the Prince, the only man standing.

Tall and powerful, his dark handsome features reflecting his austere, reserved character, the King's twenty-four-year-old nephew was already a veteran of countless skirmishes and battles, both on the Continent and more recently in England. Having began his military career at an incredibly young age, he had grown into an outstanding leader. As his uncle's General of Horse, commander of the largest Royalist army, his achievements during the Civil War had given good cause for the Parliamentarians to fear him. More recently, he had been charged by King Charles to raise the siege of York, despite the walled city being surrounded by three armies.

Richard and Danny Murphy bowed to the Prince. Thereafter, Richard moved forward, responding to Rupert's recognition, and the tail-wagging welcome from the Prince's large white dog, Boy. Meanwhile Murphy remained in the background along with the lesser personal on the Prince's staff.

The Prince's stern, expectant gaze bore into Richard. "Where is he?" he demanded.

Richard stifled the urge to cough. His chest hurt abominably after the hasty ride to Skipton from the Lodge. He was once more acutely conscious of the affinity between the Prince and Shadiz. It could be discern not only in their unusual height and strong physique. Both fiercely self-contained men were charismatic leaders with far-reaching reputations.

Richard held himself tensely while the attention of the chamber was upon him. He took a deep breath to relieve his aching lungs, unsure how Rupert would receive the message he was about to impart.

"Shadiz has gone to York, sir."

Following an elongated moment of astonishment, an air of uneasiness settled on the men.

"To what purpose?"

Goring shot a foul curse at Byron. It seemed to have little affect. Byron merely shrugged his broad shoulders, his dark features impassive. "Just picking up on the unspoken thought," he added.

It was only the Prince's impatient gesture which obliged Goring to remain angrily silent.

"After receiving your dispatch, sir," explained Richard, "he decided to go straight to York instead of first seeking you out here at Skipton."

"Mayhaps, the gypsy had a passage through their ranks."

This time it was the Prince who chastised Byron, with a thunderous glare worthy of the Master.

He slammed a fist into the map-covered table, before striding restlessly around it and the occupied chairs. "I must have tidings of how York fares," he muttered, running an agitated hand through his long black hair. "To understand the condition of the inhabitants and the damage done to the city. What support if any can be relied upon. All messengers have been intercepted, so I am told. I cannot lead an army blindly to an impasse. It is imperative I understand the enemy's formation before York." Eventually, he halted, adding, "I could not entrust such a task to any other."

"Devil take it, sir!" exclaimed Goring. "You have consigned Shadiz to his death."

Both Lucas and Mallory looked as if they agreed with the dramatic statement.

Richard attempted to reassure the Prince, though it galled him to speak the truth. "Sir, he saw no great hardship in what your dispatch tasked him with."

The loud camaraderie within the Grand Hall below seeped up into the difficult atmosphere in the chamber.

Rupert stirred from difficult thoughts, gesturing to Richard. "Sit," he commanded. "You look weary."

By the time Richard had pulled out one of the tall-backed chairs around the table and thankfully descended into it, Lucas, his kindly face anxious, was handing him a goblet of wine.

Rupert was once again consulting the various maps scattered over the oval table. "He will prevail," he muttered.

"The Devil takes care of his own," remarked Byron.

"On this occasion, let it be so," retorted Rupert. He tapped the map showing the landscape around York. "Gentlemen, we journey to Knaresborough," he announced, decisively. He looked up at Richard, and asked, "Do you believe it possible to get a message to Shadiz, to alert him to our next destination?"

Richard was unsure. "We have a couple of his Romany guides with us, sir." He turned in his seat and sought Danny Murphy's opinion. "Would they be able to alert him?"

Murphy nodded. He put down the goblet of wine he, too, had been offered, and looked towards the Prince. "Wi' y'r permission, sir. I'll deal wi' it."

"You have it." replied Prince Rupert.

After a significant look at Richard, which the other man understood with bad grace, Murphy left the chamber.

CHAPTER FIVE

Erosion of Faith

Henry Potter was saddle sore and weary.

For once, the familiarity of the North York Moors did not hold the welcoming promise of destination. Instead, his guts were flooded with disquiet. He drew rein upon the moorland rise. While the hooves of his mare stirred the distinctive scent of burgeoning heather, his gaze roamed over the undulating, hazy purple wildness before settling reluctantly on the granite magnificent of Fylingdales Hall.

His disquiet spiked upon surveying the opaqueness of the mansion's tall, regimented windows. The deepening shadows of dusk gave the ancestral façade a forbidding appearance. He sighed. It could just be the illusion of his dejected thoughts that made the present unpalatable.

The tragic death of his youngest sister in child birth had probably brought about the clinging melancholy. Or perhaps, while he had been away at Saltburn attending her funeral, distance had brought into clearer perspective current matters at Fylingdales Hall.

He sat forward in the saddle trying to stretch away his stiffness, absently patting the sweat-stained neck of his tired mare. Age suddenly came upon him, burdening him with memories that had the potential to beat him down.

Upon recalling his youthful pride at being accepted as a guard at the Hall, he dwelt for several minutes upon the harmony of Lord Richard's stern, tight-reined, scrupulously fair regime. For the first time in a long while, Gianca entered his retrospective thoughts. The beautiful, charming Romany had captivated Lord Richard. Her death in child birth had shattered his heart, that had been given to no other, despite his marriage some years later to Lady Hellena, Potter suspected.

He sighed once more, regretfully over the plight of many would-be mothers. Lost in his reverie, he recalled the baby Tom and Janet Wright had taken in and raised as their own. Heartbreakingly for them, the young child had been sent away to York upon the impending birth of Lord Richard's legitimate son. He had always wondered why Lord Richard had not married Gianca. It had been obvious he thought enough of her not to care about her lowly origins.

Inevitably, his thoughts dwelled on the fateful night when the spurned child, having grown into a towering youth bearing his dead mother's image, had returned to his birth place.

No one really knew what had taken place in Tom Wright's cottage, but they had certainly been made aware of the consequence when Shadiz had carried his father into the Hall. There was one incident in particular Henry Potter recalled during that stormy night. After Shadiz had viciously evaded all Lady Hellena's hysterical calls to prevent him from leaving Fylingdales, Potter had witnessed the lad's fleeting backward glance at his dead father.

Yet whatever leeway that look had given him in Potter's estimation had been nullified by the rape and murder of Shadiz's own half-sister on the moors within sight of the Hall. Such a heinous act had hardened irrevocably Lady Hellena's resolve to see the rogue gypsy annihilated.

Having risen through the ranks of Fylingdales' retainers, after Lord Richard's untimely death, Henry Potter had found himself serving his French widow, but answering directly to Francois Lynette, Lady Hellena's brother. Upon her request, Lynette had resigned his impressive position with the Knights of St. John at Malta in order to become the custodian of Fylingdales.

Prompted by Lady Hellena's deep, abiding hatred of Shadiz, the schemes hatched by the aristocratic brother and sister, including several attempts to capture Catherine Verity, who the gypsy reputedly loved, had all failed when pitted against Shadiz's maddening ingenuity. The biggest failure, of course, had been of Henry Potter's own making. He had allowed the Eagle to sail away from beneath the *Endeavour's* cannons earlier in the year because Richard Massone, the present estranged Lord of Fylingdales, had convinced him that Shadiz, his supposedly hated half-brother, was not on board the merchantman when no evidence of him could be found. Later, when it become known he had been duped, Potter had felt the heat of Lynette's wrath and particularly Lady Hellena's. From that time onwards, the French woman had not spoken a word to him. Only Lynette's appreciation of his talents as a commander had kept him at Fylingdales, especially after Shadiz's murderous dismissal of Lynette's favourite, Gerald Carey.

Since then matters had moved on. With the gathering of Parliamentary forces in the North, including the invading Scots, the advantage appeared to have turn slightly in favour of those at Fylingdales Hall, staunch supporters of Parliament, though rumoured in the household to be of the Catholic persuasion.

Eventually, sighing in weary resignation, Potter urged his mount forward.

Before long, he was riding through Guy's Keep. Erected by the founder of Fylingdales, centuries later the ancient Keep had been cleverly incorporated into the Hall, which had been built from the same gritty, grey stone farmed from the surrounding moors. His mare needed little urging to turn sharp left down the narrow passageway that arced around the base of the Keep.

Entering the stable yard, the sight of a figure swaying in the light breeze turned Potter's guts. Anger flared, burning away the need for rest. He dismount with an agility of a man half his age. At the same time several of his men hurried out of the long stable block.

Consumed with rage, he pointed to the oak tree, soughing its regret at being used as an implement of death. Hung by the neck from a rough piece of rope thrust over one of its thick branches was a young servant of the Hall. "What the hell's the meaning of this?" Potter demanded.

His sergeant-at-arms, a tall, muscular fellow with unruly red hair and beard, answered him from within the agitated group by which Potter was being quickly surrounded. Upon further examination, Potter realised all of the men were sporting trophies from an aggressive dispute.

"Bastards accused young Colin o' stealin' from 'em," explained Bob Malcoms, voicing the same ire Potter was experiencing.

"Colin'd do nowt like that, 'e weren't the sort," put in Allan Fisher, a small tough-looking man, standing next to the big sergeant-at-arms.

The other men nodded. They were being joined by more of their fellow retainers from different parts of the large courtyard.

Potter gestured at the grotesque figure of the young servant. "For pity's sake cut the poor wretch down."

While several of the men did his bidding, Malcoms explained, "We tried stoppin' bastards, sir." His gruff voice was filled with the bitterness of failure. "'alf o' 'em were sloshed. But that dint stop 'em."

"And Lynette?" asked Henry Potter, grimly. "Where was he when all this was going on?"

Bob Malcoms shrugged. The silence of the crowd of men was condemning.

Gazing down at the dead youth laid on the cobbles, Potter's mouth compressed into a tight, repressive slash in his fiercely constrained features. At length, he ordered, "See to young Colin," he ordered, starting to move away. "While I make certain nothing like this happens again."

"I'll come wi' y', sir," said Bob Malcoms.

"I don't need anybody at my back in this place," snapped Potter.

His sergeant watched him walk away, not at all put out, understanding his commander's outrage. It matched his own, and that of the men around him. Stalwarts of Fylingdales, they moved forward in unspoken accord, shadowing the man they regarded as their leader far more than Francois Lynette.

The sickeningly familiar rowdiness assaulted Henry Potter and those men he knew were at his back upon turning the corner of the stable block. Their silence a stark, vengeful contrast, they approached the old coach building. It had been turned into a barracks for the men who had arrived from France after the abortive attempt to snatch Catherine Verity from the gypsy's chateau. The survivors, a mixture of hired mercenaries and men-at-arms from the family estates in Normandy of Lady Hellena and her younger brother, had licked their wounds at Fylingdales after being repelled by the Master's men guarding Shannlarrey, assisted by reinforcements commanded by Nick Condor. The corsairs' timely arrival had tipped the balance against the aggressive onslaught. Following Lynette's glacial reception after their defeat, the foreigners had been kicking their heels and generally making a nuisance of themselves on and off the Estate while awaiting his next call to arms.

Henry Potter did not trust himself to walk mildly past the elaborate Elizabethan building presently housing the Frenchmen. He veered off to his left. Reaching the wrought iron side gate leading into the elegant Quadrangle, he encountered the leader of the Frenchmen strolling through the leafy archway along with several of his men.

His path effectively blocked by grinning, drink-fuelled disdain, Potter had no option but to halt his disgruntled pace. Glaring at Jean de Morgut, he was aware of his own men moving up fast. They reluctantly answered his gesture to halt a few paces away from boastful sneers.

"You strung up anymore young pages?" demanded Potter.

The large, brawny Frenchman regarded the smaller, grey-haired Englishman. His devilish grin did not touch his cold brown eyes shadowed by bushy brows. "A young thief, mon ami."

"I've known that lad since childhood," retorted Potter. "He was no thief. And certainly did not deserve to die by the rope. It was plain murder. Does Lynette know of your foul deed?"

"No doubt he will when you run to tell tales."

Whatever else the Frenchman uttered, not comprehending very much of the fellow's language, was lost on Potter. Yet he bristled with deepening anger when the foreigners around him burst into gleeful mockery. He shouldered his way through them. Their nasty merriment floated after him as he walked stiff-backed into the Quadrangle.

He was aware of the looks of anticipation resting upon him from various directions while making his way across the beautiful, verdant expanse, filled with the music of cascading fountain, the fragrance of roses and the evening song of birds. Servants and those men-at-arms he had not encountered since his return to the Hall stood witness to the outrage he made no effort to conceal.

Several maids curtsied to him before moving aside, eager to give him access to the great hall. A cursory glance told him they had been weeping. Of late, the female servants were constantly at risk from the large pack of Frenchmen. No one had envisaged an horrendous injustice to be practised on one of the pages.

"Ah, Potter. You have returned just in time."

Potter turned round to see Francois Lynette leaving the Dowager's Solar. Changing direction, he approached his handsome, fair-haired leader. The atmosphere in the hall was subdued. Those few people present within the regal splendour looked on with the same anticipation Potter had experienced in the Quadrangle.

Though he had not given much thought to Lynette's frame of mind, concerned mostly with his own, he was shocked by the suave Frenchman's broad smile.

"I trust all went as well as could be expected at Saltburn?"

"I've come from one untimely death to find another here at the Hall," Potter pointed out, forcefully.

"Ah, mon capitaine," sighed Lynette. "You are referring to the young thief."

"Colin Sawyer was no thief," Potter stated.

"I was not in residence at the time of the unfortunate incident," responded Lynette. He raised a dismissive, jewelled hand, adding, "Enough of that for now. Your return is providential. Come, we have a newly arrived visitor."

Silently fuming over his need to pursue the thorny matter, Henry Potter followed his leader to the door of the Dowager's Solar. He had no interest in who was visiting Fylingdales Hall, expecting whoever it was had arrive to discuss the progress of the war, especially the ongoing siege of York. Instead, he had a mind to engage Lady Hellena about Colin's death. Surely she would have objections to the demise of one who had served her well?

Yet upon entering the elegant, candlelit Solar all thoughts of the page's cruel end fled his mind. He stopped and stared at the newcomers, only vaguely aware of Lynette's triumphant laughter or Lady Hellena's satisfied smile.

Henry Potter had never expected to see the little, crooked man at Fylingdales. Yet he was swiftly forgotten at the sight of the lovely young girl with long fair-white hair. Potter's guts turned over, assailed far worse than anything before.

Between them, sister and brother had somehow succeeded in bringing down the wrath of a devil on Fylingdales Hall.

CHAPTER SIX

Heathen Hope

In an ill-tempered effort to conserve the dwindling stock of candles, Lord Eythin sat with furrowed brow close to a cracked window through which poured splinters of early morning sunlight. The tough, robust Scotsman, in command of Lord Newcastle's bid to hold York for King Charles, was not the only one in the gloomy chamber trying to juggle lists of rations, from biscuits and beans to powder and shot, supplied by struggling quartermasters. The view they would soon be surviving on stale air and hurling rocks at the Crop-Ears stubbornly entrenched around York was gaining credence by the day. Not the best way to maintain morale.

Isolated from the rest of the country for nearly two months, those trapped within the besieged city had no way of knowing whether their increasingly desperate situation was going to be relieved any time soon by fellow Royalists. None of the messengers dispatched by Eythin had been successful. The entire city had been made aware of the successive failures of brave volunteers by the malicious retaliation of the enemy.

The door of the chamber was suddenly flung open with a lack of decorum that immediately captured Eythin's scowling attention. Diverted from the heavy silence of disquieting paperwork, the bowed clerks held fast to their quills while bracing themselves for tidings of fresh hardships. That was, until they saw the newcomer's bubbling elation.

The young scribe dragged an older, coarse-featured man into their quizzical midst. "Tell his lordship!" he exclaimed in soprano excitement.

Robert Dickinson rattled out his precious message. His own highly excitable state overriding the nerves he would have ordinarily experienced within Lord Newcastle's noble establishment.

Rising slowly to his feet, Eythin got the gist of the garbled tidings. Around him, incredulous, hopeful grins were blossoming.

"Show me," commanded the gruff Scotsman, heading for the open door.

He hurried from the handsome, medieval house in Petersgate, where he had been billeted with Lord Newcastle since the start of the siege when occupation of the King's Manor had become far too dangerous. Following Dickinson's eager, guiding lead, Eythin struggled against false hope, acutely aware of his burdensome responsibilities.

The two men skirted the pile of jagged stones torn away from St. Michael-Le-Belfrey Church by the latest Crop-Ears' bombardment. There were more signs of the enemy's determined attacks in Duncombe Place. Several houses had been reduced to rubble. Accustomed to the war-torn city, Eythin's mind was elsewhere, buzzing with speculation.

An embattled tactician, there had been occasions when he had dared to construct some kind of relief from the brutal impasse of siege. What quarter that precious ray of hope might issue from had remained the same. He would have gone down on his knees in the miraculously untouched Minster had he thought the Lord would invest divine intervention in a heathen.

Yet someone had. Rupert, perhaps? For no rules of engagement seemed to apply to the Prince's strange mercenary. He waged his own form of warfare, slipping through the enemy like a black ghost.

Turning out of Duncombe Place around yet another shattered corner, Eythin caught sight of the Gypsy. His height meant he stood head and shoulders above the men gathered around him at a respectful distance, clearly in awe of what he had achieved. His physique was brutally muscular, yet dangerously athletic. In spite of his wild, long midnight hair and rough attire, he reeked of charismatic authority.

His hasty strides slowing, Eythin was in no doubt the Gypsy was aware of his approach. The veteran Scotsman registered the subtle shift which ensured the Gypsy's back was not turned on the men around him or his own sober advance that masked his inner elation.

Shadiz looked sideward. Eythin felt the chill of jet eyes upon him, making him trip over broken brickwork.

"Well, if it ain't the slug-a-bed," Shadiz remarked, whispery, strolling across the short distance between them.

"I'll have you know, I've been up since the wee hours going through damned supply lists," Eythin retorted. "How the hell did you get in?"

Shadiz shrugged. "Fairy dust."

"More'n like Jock-a-Lurk," muttered Eythin. "You come from Rupert?"

"Aye."

"God help you getting back to him."

"*Work out y'r own salvation wi' fear an' trembling,*" quoted Shadiz, with sardonic detachment. He walked away, surveying the scarred buildings they were surrounded by.

Martin Wedgwood and Robert Dickinson trailed behind Shadiz and Eythin, glad no one had ordered them elsewhere. Sir Thomas Glemham, the Governor of York made a flustered appearance in Davygate, staring in amazement at Shadiz. Henceforth, both he and Eythin were subjected to a rigorous interrogation while trying to keep up with the rapid pace set by their early morning visitor. It soon became apparent to the two men that Shadiz's knowledge of York meant he required no guidance. Indeed, he made shortcuts neither of them had encountered before even though they had laboured for weeks in the besieged city.

Every magazine in York was scrutinised. Also arms and ammunition stacked ready for an emergency in various command posts. It was quite obvious the store Eythin had assiduously built up prior to the siege had dwindled considerably. During each visit, Shadiz spoke to the soldiers, men of the Citizen Volunteer Bands and anyone else possessing tip-bits of useful information.

On his way around York, he inspected the Bars of the city and how they were locked down against attack from the besiegers. Talking to the respective companies on guard, between the defensive thunder of the cannons mounted atop of the solid, imposing gates, he learned how Bootham and Monk Bars faced the forces of Lord Manchester. Walmgate and Fishergate stood firm against the forces of the Fairfaxes. And Micklegate continued to defy the Scottish Army commanded by Lord Leven.

Shadiz went onto inspect the various cannons positioned in the wider streets, great ponderous beasts ready to snarl at invaders if the walls of York should be breached. Other, smaller armaments had been placed in four barks slung across the River Ouse from Skeldergate to the opposite bank close to warehouses containing valuable foodstuffs. Only the main, eighteen foot wide stone bridge over the Ouse close to the King's Staith, where ships had docked since ancient times, stood firm. Both Lendal Bridge and Skeldergate Bridge had been torn down. Even the much smaller Foss Bridge over the murky tributary of the Ouse had been demolished, obliging Shadiz and the commanders with him to take a short boat trip to the eastern quarter of the city.

He took little notice of the churches in the that area, St. Denys' boasting the oldest stain glass in York, or St Margaret's with its fine Norman porch bearing the signs of the Zodiac. His interest was centred on the Red Tower along the city wall north-east from Walmgate Bar. Unlike the churches, which had sustained only minor damage, the Tower, holding a good defensive position, showed evidence of sustained attacks. Once again, he listened to what the men manning the outpost had to say about their experiences.

Returning to more populated areas where often the upper stories of houses on opposite sides of narrow streets almost met, Shadiz was shown at junctions of thoroughfares how ditches had been dug and great, protective banks thrown up. Hogsheads filled with soil ranged for barricades.

Tidings of his presence in York had spread like wildfire. He had become the '*Pied Piper of Hope*'.

It had not taken long before his passage through the city had become thronged with siege weary people. Many had been drawn away from ramshackle camps they had set up in the forlorn remains of their devastated homes and businesses. Haggard faces had taken on sunny expectation. War haunted children skipped along beside their parents, happy again because the grown-ups declared their ordeal would soon be at an end because of the Master's appearance.

At first Eythin and Sir Thomas had been unsure how Shadiz would respond to the constant pressure of the inquisitive crowds. At times, particularly through the narrower streets, the two men along with Wedgwood and Dickinson found themselves carried along by rampant eagerness, which never really seemed to interfere with Shadiz. As they progressed through the battered city with the Gypsy they came to realise and admire the leadership skills not of a rogue mercenary but a highly intelligent man with a genius for command, including the ability to instil morale in soldiers and citizens alike.

Eythin, Sir Thomas and Robert Dickinson were beginning to feel the strain of the fast-moving morning. They viewed the lofty Clifford's Tower with misgivings. Only Martin Wedgwood managed to follow Shadiz's fluid ascent up the many wooden steps set into the steep, grassy mound with alacrity. By the time the older men arrived, breathing heavily and sweating copiously in the warm sunshine, Shadiz was already engaged in informative conversation with the commander, Sir Francis Cobb.

The detailed inspection of the thirteen century quatrefoil keep culminated in the well staircase being taken up to the ramparts where a strong platform had been constructed to hold two demi-culverins and a saker.

Moving around the ink-black guns and precious, diminishing ammunition, shading his keen gaze against the rays of the late June sun, Shadiz took advantage of the excellent vantage-point to scan the damaged panorama of York. Although the Minster remained intact, many of the spires of lesser churches had proved to be prime targets for the relentless enemy. Upon their collapse they had frequently penetrated the roofs of surrounding buildings. There were yawning gaps in narrow lanes where only the jagged walls of cottages remained. Substantial dwellings in prosperous streets had not escaped the Crop-Ears' demoralising bombardment. The rubble strewn aftermaths had opened up new inroads to the lay-out of the city.

Eventually, Shadiz turned his attention outwards. The once fertile land around York was now little more than a wasteland reaching to the ancient Forest of Galtres, several miles away in the hazy distance. Here and there were signs of vegetation struggled to re-establish tenuous life along the ragged evidence of burnt hedgerows, but for the most part the landscape remained barren whilst trampled upon by the determined might of three armies.

Walking beside him around the parapet, Sir Francis was able to give Shadiz a more detailed view of the forces encircling York than the one he had received from within the city.

The handsome features of the young, aristocratic commander of Clifford's Tower showed clear signs of siege fatigue, and the hope that the formidable man beside him would be instrumental in ending the hellish nightmare he, his soldiers and the inhabitants of York had suffered for far too long. He pointed out where the Northern Army of the Fairfaxes, father and son, stretched from Fulford to the remains of Yearsley Bridge over the Foss to the east. How Lord Manchester's Eastern Association continued from the wrecked bridge around the grey stone wall to the forward lines of the Scottish Army of Lord Leven. The Scots spanned the biggest area, occupying the opposite bank of the River Ouse until completing the besieging circuit with the fringes of the Northern Army.

To begin with the presence of the vast combined enemies had aroused a brave defiance within Lord Newcastle's Army, York's various garrisons, the Citizen's Volunteer Bands and the majority of citizens. However, as time had dragged by, cut off from the rest of the world, the interminable, deadly blows from the iron fist that gripped York had become a daunting feature of besieged life, in some cases weakening the resolve of those experiencing it and, fortunately, strengthening the defiance in others.

In his continuing quest to get as true an impression of the state of York as possible from all quarters, Shadiz sort the experiences of the soldiers of the Tower's garrison, particularly as they had a bird's eye view of the enemy from their lofty perch. Their only complaint, combined with resigned shrugs, was in regard to their shrunken diet. Like the civilians, the soldiers had been reduced to one meal a day. Their daily ration comprised of a penny loaf and a mutchkin of beans, washed down by a prudent measure of ale. At a time when few were lucky enough to have eggs costing three pence each, for most of the chickens had had their necks wrung, and butter at two shilling, from cows that were quickly going the same way, most people were resigned to the constant pangs of hunger whatever their duties.

What almost proved the undoing of the flagging older men accompanying Shadiz was his decision to conclude his exhaustive exploration of York with a tour of a large part of the all-encompassing wall.

Groaning inwardly, Lord Eythin and Sir Thomas climbed the worn stone steps up to the narrow walkway to Baile Hill. The remains of the Castle of Old Baile, erected by the Normans, once housed a garrison of five hundred soldiers whose duty was to help subjugate Yorkshire. The present-day rough stone shell was being manned by a Band of Citizen Volunteers to prevent a Crop-Ears' incursion into York.

Moving on in Shadiz's purposeful wake, Eythin and Sir Thomas looked on enviously as Robert Dickinson left them with the well-timed excuse to join his Volunteer Band.

Martin Wedgwood continued to keep a few paces behind Shadiz. By now, the older men were struggling to maintain the rigorous pace. The three men kept a cautious eye out for incoming shots over the battered wall. The threat did not appear to concern Shadiz.

They had gone as far as the Tower of Tofts, just beyond Micklegate Bar, when they came under fire from an enemy gunnery crew stationed like their encircling fellows mid-way between the mass of the combined armies and the city walls. It was with a rapid thought for self-preservation that Eythin, Sir Thomas and Wedgwood took cover against the tall, gritty wall as a fiery whooshing flew overhead in a blind search for a target. Shadiz, meanwhile, exposed to the accompanying musket fire, calmly established the source of the cannon belch. He pointed out to the nearby gunnery crew on the Tower of Tofts in which direction they should send their answering fire before moving on. Straightening from undignified crouches, the other men hurried after him, at the same time casting wary glances over the indented parapet.

They suffered another bout of nerves upon taking a ride on a flimsy raft back across the River Ouse where Lendal Bridge had once stood.

Matters did not improve when Shadiz halted to view the irreparable damage done to Marygate Tower, which backed on to the courtyard of the King's Manor. They were quick to explain how in early June the Tower had been blown up by the Crop-Ears and, though the enemy's attempt to overrun the area around the deserted Manor had been defeated, it remained a dangerous place to linger. Martin Wedgwood testified to such wise advice having had an early morning encounter with a band of Crop-Ears. Only the intervention of the Master and his shadowy men had ensured a fortunate outcome.

Sighs of relief were expelled during the eventual descent at Bootham Bar. Back within the city walls, no long fair game for pot-shots, the men bypassed the glorious Minister founded by King Edwin shortly after his convertion to Christianity by Paulinus in 627. The three men accompanying Shadiz entertained the impression they were on their way to the house in Petersgate where, according to the message conveyed to Eythin halfway through the morning's rigorous sojourn around York, Lord Newcastle awaited Shadiz with grand annoyance at the affront to his rank.

Eythin, Sir Thomas and Martin Wedgwood, and Lord Newcastle, were about to be disappointed. Shadiz turned unexpectedly right into Stonegate.

Throughout, the soldiers and civilians of York, whether or not he spoke to them, had all fallen under the spell of his charismatic presence and all respected his aura of authority. The other, forbidding aspects of his character had been less noticeable. Upon entering Stonegate, the men around him suddenly experienced the full force of Shadiz's hitherto restricted menace. They were glad it was not directed at them, but became anxious for the plump, grey-haired woman who was the formidable, likeable landlady of the Starre Inn.

Shadiz stalked across the lane.

Maggie swallowed hard and shifted the baby in her arms, but stood her ground as he approached her. All morning she had been hoping the dreaded meeting would not take place.

"What the friggin' 'ell are y' doin' 'ere?" he demanded, towering ominously over her.

Despite her resolve, Maggie flinched. Her head bent slightly in defence, she braced herself to meet the dark, thunderous expression and the fierce black eyes.

"All right, I be sorry. But you've t' understand…."

"What?" snapped Shadiz in an icy whisper.

Maggie felt shaky and her cheeks were burning red. It didn't help matters that she had communicated her apprehension to the baby in her arms. Throughout the short time it took to coax a halt to the fretful wailing, she failed to allow Shadiz's aggresive scowl not to unnerve her.

Rocking the whimpering baby, she explained. "I got t' thinkin' after y'd gone that night afore this bleedin' siege. If this place should go down t' those bastards out yonder Skelton'd be a prime target for 'em cos o' 'is size an' all." She forced herself to meet his black glare. "Y' know I'm right. Surely. Skelton's mebbe twice size o' every bugger else, except you, o' course. But wi' 'im bein' soft in head, them bastards've a field day wi' 'im." She shrugged. "So I stayed instead, and sent 'im off wi' Marianne an' all bairns I could gather up t' go to Nafferton Garth, as y' said."

Shadiz did not look convinced.

"Besides," continued Maggie, persuasively. "Bairn wasn't well enough t' travel." She had explained to him during his nocturnal visit to York several weeks earlier to deliver ammunition to Lord Eythin how the baby girl's mother had died destitute. Known throughout the city for taking in waifs and strays, including at one time a five-year-old Shadiz, it had been natural for her to nurse the baby back to health. "An', anyway, Isaac be dyin'," she added, less of an excuse and more of an unhappy declaration.

"'e ain't in St. Leonard's Hospital, or any o' tothers," pointed out Shadiz, looking down Stonegate to the Jew's bow-windowed shop.

"I weren't goin' t' see 'im carried off t' one o' them 'ell-'oles," responded Maggie. There was a hint of approval in the cold black gaze as it slewed back to her. "If y' been t' 'em, you'll o' seen they're full o' sickness as well as wounded."

Leaving Eythin and Sir Thomas watching him curiously from the head of the rowdy crowd, boiling in the brilliant sunshine, Shadiz headed to the well-known shop with the three golden balls above the door. Having gently put the sleeping baby in the arms of one of the serving girls who had poured out of the Starre to catch a glimpse of Shadiz, Maggie set off after him, sweating at the waddling pace she was forced to endure to keep at least ten paces behind him.

By the time she entered the Jew's property, Shadiz was already in the chamber at the rear of the shop where Isaac lay on an old velvet couch covered by several blankets despite the stuffy heat prevalent in the entire building. Stopping at the foot of the couch, she watched as Shadiz looked down at the Jew. Ravished by illness, he was clearly not destined to live for very much longer. Shadiz went down on one knee on the flagstone floor and quietly spoke the old man's name.

Isaac's eyes, set deep in a skeleton head gradually opened. Thin, worn drapes had been drawn across the small window in the sparsely furnished chamber. It was by the light of the flickering candles that recognition slowly filtered into the dying man's gaze. Isaac tried to speak and failed until Maggie had held a goblet of water to his cracked lips.

"I knew you would come," Isaac managed, hoarsely. Even in the throes of death, he knew not to reach out to the man knelt beside him. "I have waited."

Shadiz smiled.

Stood at the other side of the couch, Maggie clapped a hand across her mouth. Tears sprang into her watchful eyes.

"A wonder flags weren't out. 'Twould seem every sod reckoned on my arrival," remarked Shadiz, in gentle amusement. The persistent, jaunty hoards crowding his route around York had been quick to tell him so. More seriously, he asked, "Where's the Nubian? Hadia?"

Isaac took a difficult intake of breath before speaking. "I…I sent him to France…to Philippe. With all your documents while York was free still."

"The Nubian took a lot o' persuading," put in Maggie, quietly.

An emotion stirred in Isaac's shrivelled features. "I did correct?"

Maggie became tense, looking from the Jew to Shadiz. Relief washed through her as Shadiz nodded, smiling. Once more appearing years younger.

"She told me…you wed."

"She's allus been biggest gob in York," observed Shadiz.

Though his tone was moderate and his sidelong glance lacked ice, Maggie's fleshy features grew rosy.

"I wished for you…and your wife…to be secure."

Shadiz's barbarous, dark face softened. His hard mouth quirked briefly. "She'd take me guts for garters if she knew where I be."

Isaac tried to smile, but failed. Instead, he took a ragged breath. Then he did reach out. "I glad you came…."

Maggie need not to have worried. Shadiz made no move to shift away from the hand on his arm. Indeed, much to her surprise, he covered the wrinkled hand on his arm with his own hard, healthy one until Isaac's went limp. By then she was blinded by silent tears.

CHAPTER SEVEN

Rubble and Rabble

The large crowd bristled with anticipation when Shadiz emerged from Isaac's premises. He was being met in the middle of the lane by Eythin and Sir Thomas, with Martin Wedgwood trailing behind, when there came the alarming herald of yet another assault on York. The all-too familiar, air-shattering boom of a cannon brought about a momentary, fearful hush. To be swiftly followed by pandemonium as people scattered before the incoming missile struck.

Having received the baby back into her arms, Maggie had little time to respond to the danger before Shadiz took her and the baby down to the ground. He deftly cushioned their landing, and then protected them with his own body against the flying debris caused by the impact of the Crop-Ears' bombardment.

The harrowing aftermath of the destructive blasts had become a daily occurrence in York. The uninjured picked themselves up from the latest onslaught and tried to brush away the clinging dust of devastation. Breathing in life, they cringed at the moans of the injured and the wailing of the bereaved.

To Maggie's surprise, Shadiz had sheltered her and the baby without crushing either of them with his superior weight. He helped her back onto her feet without commenting on her lively string of curses.

She was making sure the baby was not affected by the gritty dust clouds clogging the warm, bright atmosphere in the damaged lane when she heard a short, ironic laugh. Looking up, she realised it had come from Shadiz. Mystified, she followed his line of sight to the shattered remains of the Starre Inn. Her heart sinking, she was grateful that the people who would normally have been inside had

273

vacated the tavern upon Shadiz's appearance in Stonegate. Looking around, she realised the young serving lasses were creeping tearfully back to her, all shaken by what had just happened in Stonegate and the loss of the Starre.

"Well, y' ain't much option now," Shadiz remarked, turning back to her.

Upon him giving an ear-piercing whistle, two Romany quickly emerged from the chaos Eythin and Sir Thomas were trying to dispel. They both nodded in response to whatever Shadiz had said to them. Turning to Maggie, he commanded, "Y'll go wi' Liata an' Dyalt. They'll get y' out o' York. An' t' Nafferton Garth."

"An' lasses?" she pleaded. "They've no folk." .

"Aye," muttered Shadiz, signalling to his men.

Maggie looked at the forlorn ruins of the Starre Inn, and then back at Shadiz.

"For god's sake, watch y'rsen," she urged.

It was what she used to say to him, years ago, whenever she had sent him on an errand, knowing the young gypsy lad was a magnet for trouble.

Shadiz's hard mouth twitched briefly into a crooked grin, reminiscent of the response she had usually received.

"God's nawt t' d' wi' it," he muttered, as he watched his men lead the women away.

★

Having left the soldiers who had arrived hard on the heels of the Crop-Ears' strike in Stonegate to deal with the aftermath, Eythin and Sir Thomas escorted Shadiz the short distance to the stone-built mansion in Petersgate where Lord Newcastle presently resided. Both men, similarly dust-splattered like Shadiz, were of the opinion the morning's excursion around the hard-pressed city had been well worth the tremendous effort. They had thought themselves to be acquainted with all aspects of York's plight, but Shadiz's insatiable hunt for details had revealed discrepancies in their knowledge. It had also shown up how little they had hitherto attributed to the quite extraordinary Gypsy.

No sooner had the men entered the cool of the oak panelled entrance hall of the mansion than they were confronted by the quarrelsome reception committee awaiting Shadiz.

He cursed.

Leaving a disgruntled silence weighed down by caution behind him, Shadiz followed Eythin and Sir Thomas into the chamber where Lord Newcastle was holding court, only to be confronted with more of the same. The exception being that the men allowed into Newcastle's presence was of a higher standing, with, it seemed, even more need to make themselves heard.

Eythin and Sir Thomas had experienced the silk of a notorious cloak, now the two men witnessed the abrasive side. They exchanged a surreptitious grin when the elite of York were persuaded by Shadiz's presence that their consideration of Newcastle's nobility should modify their complaints and demands. As for Newcastle, a stickler for protocol, his perceived slight at the gypsy's blatant lack of respect was radiant. Especially when Shadiz spoke to Eythin.

"Where's ledgers y' were on about?"

Uncomfortable, Eythin glanced at his commanding officer.

Newcastle continued to lavish his aristocratic displeasure on Shadiz.

Half-turning, Shadiz addressed Newcastle directly, "D' y' recognise my authority as Rupert's agent?"

The low-pitched, forbidding demand silenced the last mumbling slivers of contention in the chamber. It forced Newcastle to resign himself to the inevitable. He nodded curtly at Eythin, making his acquiescence an excuse to retreat with a lofty air from Shadiz's brutal glare. Only when the gypsy was following Eythin into the smaller chamber used by the clerks did he return his affronted gaze to the disappearing broad back.

A little while later, glad to escape Newcastle's tirade, Ethyin entered the chamber into which he had ushered Shadiz. Tray in hand, he paused against the door he had quickly closed against the speculation rampant in Lord Newcastle's regal domain.

The tough, stocky Scot found Shadiz sitting cross-legged on the floor, surrounded by documents and ledgers. Positioned around the shelf-lined walls of the chamber, young and old, the clerks waited nervously with even more paperwork describing York's deteriorating condition for Shadiz's consideration.

Eythin set the tray of frugal fare the city could spare for their would-be saviour on a small table beneath the open windows. "Well," he muttered, gazing down at the other man's bent, black head. "What d' y' make o' it?"

"Lookers-on many times see more than gamesters," came the eventual reply. Shadiz gestured to the nearest clerk. Without hovering too close, the fellow delivered more evidence of dwindling food stocks for his perusal.

Wanting to speak plainly, Eythin dismissed the clerks. After they had trooped out of the chamber, hiding their relief, he demanded, "Can we expect relief from Rupert?"

"D' y' reckon I've come on a whim?"

The barb found its mark. Shadiz looked up at the contrite Scot. "You've viewed York for yoursen. God knows me old bones know about it." Eythin admitted, wearily. "Fact be, truth's staring ye in the face. Place is living on borrowed time."

From being cross-legged on the floor, Shadiz rose to his full, commanding height in one fluid movement, causing the much smaller Scotsman to take an involuntary step backwards.

"There's allus byways an' furrows," remarked Shadiz, reaching for another doom-leaden ledger from the nearest table.

"Aye, I'll give ye that. But the damn Crop-Ears're making their own blasted in-roads."

Looking up from the ledger he was consulting, Shadiz gave Eythin a calculating look. " Y' don't reckon Rupert'll turn up in time."

Eythin shrugged, avoiding the other man's black-eyed scrutiny. "When ye explain how matters stand with us...."

It was common knowledge that Rupert and Eythin had not been on the best of terms ever since the professional Scot was a commander in the Swedish army. He had been criticised for not supporting the young Prince during a skirmish at Vlotho on the Weser. Rupert had made no bones about who he held responsible for his three years imprisonment in an Austrian fortress.

"Let water run under the bridge," advised Shadiz, in a shrewd, whispery tone. "If you don't keep faith, the whole blood edifice'll collapse around y' ears. One thing I've learnt today. It ain't that preening popinjay yonder whose binding the strings."

"Well, I'm grateful for the thought," muttered Eythin, aware that such an endorsement from Shadiz was praise indeed. Nevertheless, he continued to appear troubled. "Three armies, though," he emphasised. "Three armies Rupert would've to deal with to get to us in York."

The quarrelsome clamour from the larger chamber, which had been a persistent background during the two men's conversation, seemed to be growing in aggravated intensity.

Glaring at the door that separated him from the crowd of officials gathered in Newcastle's audience chamber, Shadiz swore. "Go sort bastards out, afore 'eadless chickens run riot."

As Eythin headed resignedly to the door, Shadiz called after him, "Jamie."

The Scotsman paused and turned around.

"Keep that bloody popinjay from doin' owt daft."

Eythin grimly nodded.

When he returned sometime later in the hope of persuading Shadiz to meet the impatient officials, he found the chamber empty. He stared pensively out of the open window.

CHAPTER EIGHT

Folly Of Self

The Scotsman emerged from the campaign tent. Disgruntled, his wide strides thrust him into the late afternoon sunshine. Momentarily blinded by the warm glow after the lantern-lit dullness of the spacious tent, his sudden appearance and brisk pace caused him to collide with a man sauntering past Lord Leven's headquarters. It took less than a heartbeat to disengage, and another to continue on their separate ways.

The Scotsman took a few purposeful strides, persisting in his foul mood, before the full, staggering relevance of the brief encounter dawned on him. Even then, disbelief in his own judgment took him a stride further away from the man going in the opposite direction. Convincing himself, he came to a shuddering halt, grinding his heels into the summer dust.

David Leslie's frantic gaze raked through the varied activities in his vicinity. In all of the Scottish encampment's sprawling complexity only one stray intrusion was at once unfamiliar and yet recognisable. He gestured wildly at an exceptionally tall, powerfully built man. "That's the gypsy. It's Shadiz. *Get him!*"

Men well-acquainted with the infamous name sprang to their feet, responding to their duty while actively harbouring the same disbelief their commander had fought against.

No matter the boldness the notorious gypsy Master had demonstrated previously in his exploits against them, surely he wasn't likely to venture into their camp in broad daylight?

Whatever the degree of madness, the shrill exclamation from Lord Leven's Cavalry General began a mad episode the like of which could only be created by someone of Shadiz's ilk. A past

278

master at the bizarre art of mayhem, his unfortunate confinement promised all manner of wicked diversions.

The fighting men of Scotland, the flowers of the thistle, grimly followed Leslie's dashing lead. His glare was fixed unswervingly on Shadiz's disappearing back.

The infuriating fiend was presently sprinting effortlessly down one of the narrow, dusty alleys between the rows of tents, and waving in a most friendly manner to perplexed bystanders. They were soon being drafted into the chase as the main body of pursuers surged past.

Arthur Lilly, the sour Lowland cook temporarily attached to Leslie's cavalry, was preparing the evening meal. An indifferent affair, which even he did not relish. He cursed as the heat from the bubbling cooking pots combined with the heat of the June day was causing him to sweat profusely.

During the next frantic moments, Lilly's tough hide leaked a good deal more. But nowhere near as much as the innocent flesh of his general helper and pot washer. The young lad from Aberdeen was the last poor soul to catch sight of the oncoming storm and the first to encounter Shadiz at his most devastating. Lilly watched, whiskered mouth agape, as his general helper was hurled into a large pan of beans and swiftly emerged howling.

Merry as a spider in a turnip patch, Shadiz followed up the callous prank by unexpectedly pivoting and giving the astounded cook a hearty whack on his ample backside with a sizzling pan. With a hot arse and a bull bellow in his raw throat, Arthur Lilly, disregarding every command Leslie shrieked at him, took to his unscathed heels.

By the time Shadiz made a rapid departure from the field kitchen, there was no longer a field kitchen. He had dispensed with all the wooden dishes and spoon and every drinking vessel. His impeccable aim had temporarily kept his pursuers at bay.

They swarmed after him, en masse, kicking aside deflated bannock loaves, slipping in squashed cheese and giving the spilt beans a wide berth.

Eventually arriving at the cattle pen, Shadiz confounded the Scots by releasing the nervous animals, and riding an irritated cow straight through their panting ranks. They sprang hither and thither, avoiding him and the herd he had stampeded while emitting oaths best not heard by their straight-laced clergy.

The antic came to a bone-jarring end when dear old Daisy decided enough was enough and deposited her merry rider in the dirt.

Shadiz was quickly back on his feet and nimbly vaulting over straggly bushes. He descended among soldiers involved in illicit gambling. Stern-faced, he duly chided them, while they stared at him with a mixture of guilt and bewilderment. Then he was gone as fast as he had arrived. In the next moment, the entire pack of sweaty, irate hunters crashed through the bushes and were ploughing into the gamblers.

Makeshift tents collapsed. Men fought their way out of them.

It was decided by someone not entirely carried away by the breathless farce to split their lumbering, unsuccessful herd into several search parties. One such hopeful band quickly managed to get lost in the maze of small, rough tents, and was coolly directed by a tall, dark man speaking in a passable Scottish dialect. The hapless soldiers got the message, eventually. They did not get their man.

Yet another gullible band, warily trotting down another alley between tents, upon hearing a shrill whistle turned together and promptly felt together the hard edge of a pike. They went down like so many cracked sticks.

"St...st...stop or...or I...I fi... fire!"

Shadiz skidded to a controlled halt, placed a hand solemnly on his heart and replied, "Fa...fa fancy th...th that."

The flustered, dimpled-faced soldier kept true to his word and discharged his wavering musket; unfortunately, in the direction of his compatriots, putting an immediate, self-preserving curb on their headlong charge.

Shadiz, meanwhile, had vanished.

He took temporary refuge in the cool shadow of wagons pulled up in a convenient triangle. Bent over, hands on knees, recovering from the mad escapade, he cursed his folly.

The next moment, a very genuine smile spread across his sweat-bathed features.

After he had felt impelled to leave Kore, to keep her safe from the vengeful bitch that preyed upon her when he was near, the following weeks had become endless. He had roamed Stillingfleet Forest and sought the waves on isolated shores. To no avail. Yet, in a moment, the recent agony had been swept away by the sweet sensation of her presence.

"Forgive me, Kore."

He had hurt her. It was surely because of the cowardly way he had left Formentera she had chosen to maintain the distance from him. Now he welcomed with an open heart her displeasure at his arrogant folly.

"Alright, monisha. *A wise man'll make more opportunities than he finds.*"

But then, all at once, she was gone. Leaving him bereft.

★

The footsteps paused at the door of her chamber. Catherine heard the murmur of voices. Then all was silent again except for an occasional rasping cough. So it was the turn of the man with the bubbling chest to guard her chamber. Over time she had come to recognise the characteristics of her guards.

The first few had brought a sense of foreboding to her door, making her glad it was also locked against them. There was the one who constantly rolled dice, practising, he had told her through the solid oak, for the time she would be given to the winner. Then there had been the one who invariably muttered to himself about such a mundane duty, and promised she would suffer for the humiliation. Worse of all had been the one who murmured at the other side of her locked door what he would do to her if given half the chance. All had spoken with foreign accents.

Then Henry Potter had come to her chamber, and apologised for the harassment she had suffered. He had assured her that from then on his own Fylingdales men would guard her door, and, if she was in need, she could rely upon them. Henceforth, he had been a frequent visitor, always ensuring her welfare. Having seen his initial shock and horror at her presence at Fylingdales Hall, despite their close encounter upon the North Sea earlier in the year, Catherine felt she could trust him. Quickly growing to like him, she was grateful for his presence whenever Lady Hellena or Francois Lynette put in an appearance. Both were remarkably civil to her, and at pains to emphasis her safety was in no doubt. Nevertheless, they kept her under lock and key.

Catherine believed it to be Henry Potter who had sought permission for her evening walks. He made a point of accompanying her around the Hall's substantial grounds. They were always undertaken surrounded by Potter's men. Their presence made her feel safe from the less desirable company at Fylingdales. Among their rowdy numbers she had no doubt were those Potter had dismissed from the door of her chamber. She wondered at what cost to himself. The realisation that the foreigners among the more militant of Lynette's followers had taken part in the attack on Shannlarrey made her even more thankful for Potter's convivial company and his protective brigade.

Catherine strolled across the beautiful chamber and sat down on a velvet stool by the window. She stared out across the Inner Quadrangle below her chamber, but took little interest in the emerald lawns between meandering stone-flagged paths, the colourful, aromatic flowerbeds and the crystal fountains.

Her anxious thoughts remained on Shadiz. She was cross with herself for being overwhelmed by her sense of his danger enough to seek him through their connection of the pendants, his moonstone, her jet. Sitting by the tall window she forced herself to remain aloof and not to allow her plight to infiltrate through to him. She had made the decision not in anyway to alert him at the beginning of her abduction.

Catherine felt not so much abandoned, more a prey to betrayal.

Given past events, she could understand how Shadiz would have believed he was protecting her…from something he did not fully comprehend. Even so, the hurt festered. If he had just trusted her as he had done on the seashore.

Instead, he had taken his sinister burden away from her, and returned to Yorkshire.

Then there was Keeble's betrayal.

He, too, had been adamant that he was trying to keep her safe – by taking her to Fylingdales. Not necessarily to use her as bait to snare Shadiz, unlike Lady Hellena and Lynette's intention. The little man had declared his action was in order to protect her from Shadiz. He had admitted to her that he had come to admire and respect Shadiz. Then he had gone on to explained how he had been Elizabeth's page at the time of her rape and murder by Shadiz, her half-brother.

Yet again betrayal made a cruel kind of sense. It did not prevent her from ignoring Keeble's pleas for forgiveness. Above all, the future outcome of his action, how it would affect Shadiz, terrified her.

Catherine remembered little of the actual abduction. In her chamber in the villa on Formentera, she had taken a goblet from Keeble, as she had countless times before, having no reason to suspect his intention. On that particular evening, he had put a sleeping potion in the rich Burgundy wine.

All she recalled upon immerging briefly from the foggy blanket laid heavily upon her senses was a woman's familiar accented voice, saying, "Take English bitch. Do with her like what wish you."

★

Catherine's sudden withdrawal troubled Shadiz. For a couple of seconds, he held his moonstone pendant tight in his fist, putting the milky white stone to his lips. Had she forgiven him enough to acknowledge his waywardness?

Shadiz resolved to end the madcap episode. He could hear the commotion he had instigated heading his way from different directions. The first to make a heavy-breathing appearance was a group of burly Scots. The rest of the sweaty hunting gangs quickly followed.

Intellect would not outfox their encompassing numbers. Nor would agility. Therefore he fell back on his years of Spartan experience.

The resolve would also ensure the pendants remained dormant.

Shadiz stood casually at ease, hands lightly on hips. His calm, black survey sent ripples through the surrounding hostility. Made nervous by his legendry presence, swords were gripped a little tighter. The triggers of loaded muskets were inched backwards.

David Leslie put in a panting appearance. "I want the bastard alive," he commanded with breath he could ill-afford to use loudly.

Accompanied by several hefty Highlanders, he swaggered through the crowd to stand triumphantly in front of Shadiz.

"Ah, gypsy. What say you now?" Leslie grated, desperately trying to control his rapid breathing. He was acutely aware that the other man, though wet with sweat, was breathing with maddening normality. "Who is cock of the midden, think you now, eh?"

"Aye, well," drawled Shadiz, grinning nastily. "You're still in a rare old flap."

The smug smile instantly vanished from Leslie's thin ruddy face, dripping with sweat.

"Search the bastard," he ordered, glaring at the amused prisoner.

The growing crowd of men looked on in a more relaxed attitude as the Highlanders move up to Shadiz. His leather jerkin was pulled aside and his thin shirt ripped open. He stood tight-lipped while the rough search produced his dagger, apparently his only form of weapon.

The narrow-bladed weapon was passed on to Leslie. He weighed it thoughtfully in the palm of his hand. "How many have you used it on? Or have you lost count?"

"There's one I should've."

Leslie looked up, malevolently grinning. "Your loss, gypsy. My gain."

The sinister ice from the slanted black gaze beat down Leslie's regard. Concealing his defeat and determined to extract retribution, he commented with a sneer. "You would appear to enjoy trinkets."

One of the dour Highlanders responded to Leslie's curt gesture. While his fellow countrymen seized Shadiz, he wrenched the silver pendent from around Shadiz's neck.

Shadiz went viciously berserk. It took even more of the massive, strong men to restrain him.

David Leslie took great delight in Shadiz's response. In an effort to fuel the other man's frustrated rage, he tossed the silver moonstone pendant to one of his captains. "Here, Alex. Give it to that doxy you've been after."

Laughter burst through the expanding crowd of soldiers and troopers. The growing number of their compatriots forced to struggle with Shadiz failed to appreciate the jest.

CHAPTER NINE

Consequences Of Others

Henry Potter knocked politely and then, worried about the lack of response, entered the guarded chamber, closing the door behind him. He was confronted by the sight of Catherine striving against a bout of apprehension. She looked endearingly vulnerable. Helplessness swept over him. Silently cursing the scheming Lynette and his vengeful sister, he moved swiftly across the chamber to where she was sitting on the stool close to the window.

Catherine caught sight of his stricken look, and tried to bring her flaring intuition under some kind of control. She was scared out of her wits, but not for the reason Henry Potter had surmised.

The kindness he showed her could not lessen the heat of the jet pendant locked in her fist.

*

Sir Thomas Fairfax regretted his tardiness. Though he entertained no great liking for Lord Leven's Cavalry General, he hoped he had not inconvenienced the young Scotsman.

Upon his belated arrival at Leslie's canvas headquarters, he found the immediate vicinity deserted.

Unsure what to make of the odd development, he walked his fine white horse through the Scottish camp. Put on the alert, Jonathan and Jamie Muir flanked their leader. Eventually they came across two dejected-looking figures sitting amidst unbelievable damage and loose cattle grazing on ruined food.

"What has transpired here?" demanded Fairfax. "Where is Leslie?"

Arthur Lilly and his quivering helper got to their feet. "General's captured a spy, sir. Over yonder," replied Lilly, pointing west.

It did not take long for the three riders to encounter the large, boisterous crowd of soldiers. When they dismounted, the Muir brothers closed about Sir Thomas. Together, they shoulders their way through the men baying for blood until they came across the so-called spy and his massive torturers.

His suspicion confirmed and his hope quashed, Sir Thomas gave a brief, regretful sigh. In the next moment his noble features grew uncharacteristically hard.

His presence continued to go unnoticed such was the excitable, concentrated din. It was as if the Scotsmen had been given the ideal outlet for the frustrations incurred by the past few weeks of siege warfare. Sir Thomas briefly surveyed their steaming mood and found it to be an ugly sight. Jonathan and Jamie remained protectively close.

It was Shadiz, lifting his head and focusing with difficulty, who made his tormentors aware of disapproval in their midst.

David Leslie half-turned reluctantly.

"We do not employ conditions of war to satisfy our personal grudges," rasped the Englishman, striding forward.

While the two commanders glared at one another across a gulf of conscience, the large, powerful Highlanders, uncertain whether to continue the punishment they were inflicting upon Shadiz's ribs, relaxed their brutal lock upon him. A resentful hush had fallen on the surrounding soldiers.

"Welcome to Tartarus. *Chevalier sans peur et sans reproche.*"

"Shut up, gypsy," snapped Leslie.

The Highlanders gave Shadiz a vicious shake.

Sir Thomas cringed inwardly. It was plain Shadiz was suffering for his audacity. "Where is Lord Leven?" he demanded, turning back to Leslie.

The Scotsman shrugged. He suddenly grinned. "Aren't you interested to hear the bastard's confession. Even he cannot resist their arms. They require no instruments to make a man spew all. Their strength is their weapon."

Sir Thomas said nothing. Nor did his grim expression alter.

Continuing to gloat, Leslie said, "Rupert will leave Skipton on the morrow. He intends to take up a battle stance betwixt here and Wetherby. He has with him a force in excess of twenty thousand."

Sir Thomas Fairfax switched from Leslie to Shadiz. The barbarous features gave nothing away. Yet Sir Thomas fancied he caught a glint of fathomable emotion in those weird black eyes.

"He gave you such information?" he muttered, highly sceptical.

Leslie gave a scornful laugh. Smugly, he replied, "Bastard wished to keep some of his ribs intact." An impatient mutter rippled through the surrounding crowd. The Scotsman went on, "Spare a moment in the future for the reports of your scouts. It is known that there's been plenty of movement by Rupert's lot around Skipton. The gypsy was attempting to penetrate our lines in order to inform Newcastle when to sally forth from York at our backs."

Sir Thomas looked away from Leslie's thin-faced triumph, sickened by the vindictiveness. Turning away, he saw how Shadiz's fierce glare was fixed on a young captain twirling what appeared to be a pendant.

"A council of war must be called," announced Leslie.

Shadiz sagged in the brutal arms of the Highlanders. They jerked him upright in a harsh manner, causing Sir Thomas to flinch.

"Put on y'r considerin' cap, Good Thomas," suggested Shadiz, "Afore they crack me like a bloody nut. Friggin' Titans!"

In the next couple of minutes Shadiz was rendered speechless.

Sir Thomas Fairfax loathed Shadiz's trial by the mob, and was certainly mistrustful of David Leslie's motive in the matter. His sharp command was almost drowned out by the vehement cheers of the Scotsmen. The Highlanders did however curtail their ruthless punishment and looked towards Leslie for direction.

"You're too damned soft," Leslie remarked. Nevertheless, subjected to the older commander's stern warning, he relented, and indicated to the Highlanders that they should desist.

Leslie reiterated his call for a council of war as Sir Thomas approached the prisoner and his massive guards. "For the love of God, let the wretch lie," he commanded.

Once again the powerful group looked to Leslie for direction.

Busy dispatching messengers to gather the other commanders of the combined forces for a council of war, he gave them a curt, distracted nod.

Released none-too-gently from the Highlanders' grip, Shadiz landed heavily on the rough ground. He remained there unhindered, apparently beaten into submission. Therefore, Fairfax and the Muir brothers, David Leslie and the Highlanders were all taken by surprise when Shadiz shot to his feet. At the same time, he snatched up his dagger from where Leslie had tossed it. He advanced with predatory speed and murderous intent upon the young captain who had received his moonstone pendant from Leslie.

The young captain was the one most taken by surprise. He had been uncomfortably aware of Shadiz's menacing glare upon him, but while the gypsy was securely detained he had felt no reason to be overly worried. Seeing Shadiz laid prone on the ground, he had thought himself safe, and turned his back on the prisoner to show off the newly acquired piece of jewellery.

Those men gathered around him abruptly broke off from their companionable banter, but their warning shouts proved too late. Wielded with vicious determination, the dagger sank deep into the young captain's back. Tumbling forwards, the pendant was ripped out of his lifeless hand.

With the moonstone secure in his fist, Shadiz went down fighting against the overwhelming odds that descended upon him.

Registering Leslie's deadly instructions to his countrymen, Sir Thomas Fairfax acted upon his instinct for honour that abhorred rough justice.

Desperation to succeed ensured he roughhoused his way through the violent melee, supported by the Muir brothers. He located Shadiz in its savage midst, and smashed the hilt of his pistol down upon the back of his head. Henceforth, his commanding presence and the aggressive protectiveness of Jonathan and Jamie Muir prevailed.

The three men had one thought in common. Never had they imagined themselves to be protecting the Master.

★

Joshua Watson mopped his sweaty brow in nervous haste. Not only was the spacious command tent uncomfortably warm despite the lateness of the hour, the occupants he was addressing were contributing to the difficult atmosphere in unspoken accord.

Lord Manchester's tall, wiry scoutmaster, whose long, sharp features had earned him the nickname of *Ferret*, cleared his throat and looked towards his leader. Manchester offered an encouraging smile. Sitting beside the genial Lord, his Lieutenant General, Oliver Cromwell, wore his habitual dour expression.

"Well, speak up, man," urged Lord Leven, impatiently.

The Scottish veteran warrior, sitting at the head of the improvised conference table, wanted answers to a deadly puzzle. "Where the hell is Rupert bound fer?" he demanded.

Watson cleared his throat once more, and then continued with his report. "I've received clear evidence that Rupert is leaving Skipton and heading in Wetherby's direction. It looks very much like he intends drawing us away from York to confront us in that area. As the gypsy confessed to."

David Leslie made a satisfied noise. He sat back in his canvas chair, arms folded, grinning at Sir Thomas Fairfax.

Though seething inwardly, Sir Thomas ignore the Scotsman's malicious smirk. He was well aware the only reason Leslie wasn't berating him for putting to an end Shadiz's defiance after he had murdered one of Leslie's captains was due to the prospect of treating the allied armies to a comprehensive execution that would see Shadiz suitably reduced.

Sir Thomas's grim expression had nothing to do with the information Watson purported to have gathered. And everything to do with the debt he had to repay. Had it not been for Shadiz's protection of his wife and daughter after they had become separated from him following the battle of Adwalton Moor, goodness knows what would have happened to them.

Much to Sir Thomas's frustration, the meeting in Leven's campaign tent dragged on without any viable tactics being agreed upon for combating the advance of Prince Rupert while needing to remain at the locked gates of York.

In the end his patience wore too thin to remain in the humid atmosphere, stirred only by indecision. He was also annoyed with Lord Ferdinand. Yet again he had been obliged to apologise for his father's absence, pleading indisposition while knowing full well he would be partaking with his cronies the store of wine he had brought with him to the siege.

Sir Thomas escaped into the fresh air of summer's twilight. Jamie and Jonathan Muir followed him with the same relief as their leader, and were ready to escort him to wherever he was destined. Sir Thomas had other ideas, and sought to dismiss them. He was already walking away when, keeping pace with him, they questioned his order .

Appreciating their loyalty, he slowed his pace. "I do not want you with me," he declared.

"Sir, it is not safe for you to be alone," pointed out Jamie.

Though the objective of the Parliamentarian and Scottish armies were the same, the atmosphere was certainly different in the Scottish contingent towards the English. Worryingly, only slightly less so to the English commanders..

Before Sir Thomas could refute the plausible observation, Jonathan stated, "You are going to see Shadiz, sir."

Sir Thomas halted, with a resigned sigh. "I am," he admitted. "And I do not want either of you involved."

"In what, sir," questioned Jamie, switching from his leader to his brother.

Sir Thomas maintained Jonathan's understanding gaze. He gave an appreciative smile. "I am immune. You two are not."

"What the hell is he about to do?" demanded Jamie, watching Sir Thomas walk away, resentful of Jonathan's restraining hand upon his arm.

Both brothers were well aware of the protection Shadiz had given Sir Thomas's family.

"Give him a minute," advised Jonathan, calmly. "Is that a scribe over there?"

Shadiz came to his senses abruptly.

He startled Sir Thomas even though he had braced himself

against such an inevitable eventuality. It was the full onslaught of the searing black eyes and the raging agitation that caused the momentary lapse. Recovering swiftly, Sir Thomas went down on one knee beside the other man sprawled on the ground.

"Be still," he commanded. "You are watched." At the same time he unobtrusively pushed the silver moonstone pendant at Shadiz.

He instantly locked it into his fist. Fighting for composure behind shuttered eyes, he remained achingly silent.

Conscious of the two watchful Highlanders at the tent's entrance, Sir Thomas sat back on his heels.

Presently, Shadiz asked, "What seek y' 'ere, Good Thomas?"

"Are you in a mood to confess further?"

The long-lashed curtains rose on the black eyes, revealing pain-masked amusement. Shadiz raised his head, and groaned. "Who the 'ell cracked me bloody 'ead? You?"

As he spoke, he looked past Fairfax at the Highlanders planted like two great oaks across the closed tent flap.

"There are two more outside," Sir Thomas pointed out, wary of Shadiz's appraisal of his captors. In hushed tones, he added, "Have you taken leave of your senses? What the devil possessed you to walk through the entire Scottish army – in broad daylight for goodness sake!"

"I would've paid y' a visit, only I were short on time," replied Shadiz.

"And most assuredly long on foolishness," commented Sir Thomas. He was unable to resist the temptation, knowing the Gypsy's extraordinary capabilities. "Has your sojourn taken you inside…"

"Troy," interposed Shadiz. He stared into the middle distance, lit by two idly flickering candle-lanterns, and quoted, "*Famine and Fire he held, and there withal He raised towns and threw down towers and all.*"

There was a distinct pause.

Sir Thomas, his sincere, noble features greatly troubled, eventually admitted, "They will not believe me." He had gained Shadiz's full attention, and felt uncomfortable because of it. "They will just not credit a vagabond with resilience," he observed.

"D'y reckon a vagabond can alter tide o' events?" mused Shadiz, "Even t' save 'is own worthless skin."

"That, my wayward friend, is quite typical of you," muttered Sir Thomas, fiercely. He sighed impatiently. "You really have no conception. *Il connaite l' univers et ne se connaite pas!*"

"I was 'urtin'," retorted Shadiz.

"So I've been informed," pointed out Sir Thomas, "Now, what has taken weeks to achieve they are very close to throwing away. On your confession."

"Thank Devil for Cassandra," remarked Shadiz.

"It is all an unimportant game of chess to you," replied Sir Thomas, curtly.

Shadiz did not answer immediately. He moved stiffly into a sitting position on the rough ground, one arm tucked inside his filthy, torn shirt, cradling his ribs.

The Highland guards immediately paid even closer attention to him.

Shadiz opened his right fist slightly. "This ain't unimportant t' me."

Frowning, puzzled, Sir Thomas looked down at the silver-edged, moonstone pendant, unable to understand the cynical Gypsy's intense emotion attachment to the strangely inscribed piece of jewellery, almost barbaric in its charm.

"'Tis all there ever was. An' the only thing remaining," murmured Shadiz.

Sir Thomas looked up at him, but a disturbance outside the prison tent drew his attention away from the other, enigmatic man.

The attention of both men was focused on the tent entrance when Jonathan Muir lifted the flap and strode into the dingy interior, carrying writing materials.

The two Highlanders caught hold of him before he could progress further.

"As I explained to your two colleagues outside, Sir Thomas ordered me to find paper and ink, and bring them hither to record any useful details from the prisoner," said Jonathan, looking earnestly in the direction of his leader.

The flicker of anger in Sir Thomas's face was quickly stifled by enforced approval.

293

Released with ill-humour by the two large men, Jonathan moved forward and knelt close to Sir Thomas. Unlike Sir Thomas, who had used his commanding position to refuse the Highlanders' demand to relinquish his weapons, Jonathan had been forced to surrender his. However, upon casually shuffling the papers he had brought with him, he revealed what else he had managed to bring into the tent.

Anxiety passed over Sir Thomas's set features as he glance at Jonathan's innocent countenance.

Of the three men, Shadiz was the one who seemed most at ease. "Good Thomas," he said, barely above a whisper, "I appreciate y'r visit. Now go. Y' ain't t' play treachery for the carrion-crow."

Jonathan stared at him as if he was seeing him for the first time.

Sir Thomas remained silent, his brow moist, his gaze direct until, uncharacteristically, Shadiz looked elsewhere.

There was less than eight years difference in their ages, yet Sir Thomas had always seemed the much older, certainly more sedate man. In spite of everything, the fate that divided them was regretted by both men.

"My first encounter with you," began Sir Thomas, speaking quietly in French, "left me wondering what kind of devil you were. My second made me realise I would probably never decipher the mystery. By our third meeting, it became clear to me that the outrageous reputation and the despicable cruelty clothed intelligent depths.

"In as many languages as I could give tongue to, you would repay me with a fluent response. And, yes, retaliate with an obscure language I am never likely to come across again. That would be only a small part. You are a man who has come from goodness knows what squalor who would feel at ease, I doubt not, with men of learning.

"As I said, I do most assuredly detest both your detached and passionate violence. But I also find vindictive waste detestable. They, my most illustrious colleagues, would squander you in the vilest possible way before all armies at the earliest opportunity. In this matter my thinking deviates from theirs.

"You showed great compassion to my wife and daughter. I am bound to honour that response."

Genuine surprise, an infrequent visitor, lingered on Shadiz bruised face. "Ave Caesar; morituri te saluting," he muttered.

"Macte nova virtuous, puer, sic itur ad astra, " answered Sir Thomas.

"Ah," murmured Shadiz, beginning to grin. "It ain't goin' t' play 'oly 'avoc wi' Gabriel's Conscience, then?"

"Indeed not," said Sir Thomas, firmly. He looked questioningly at Jonathan, knelt close by.

The serious young man inclined his head. Quietly, in French, he explained, "Jamie, my brother, is laid low at the back of the tent with cloak and weapons."

Shadiz switched from Jonathan to Sir Thomas.

The older man replied to the jet-eyed query. "I came with a vague intention. Be glad the brothers mutinied against my explicit orders." He took a deep, regretful breath, adding, "Yours has to be a lonely task."

"I've 'ad plenty o' practise," assured Shadiz, ominously.

Sir Thomas and Jonathan both experienced an unpleasant thrill of apprehension at the animalistic menace in Shadiz's brief appraisal of the two Highlanders.

Shifting his disturbing black gaze back to his visitors, Shadiz issued a low-pitched command. Jonathan looked expectantly at Sir Thomas, who gave a confirming nod. Knowing his leader was glad he was being dismissed, after a brief hesitation, Jonathan rose, leaving the writing materials on the ground.

Watching his loyal captain head for the tent's opening, Sir Thomas's relief was short-lived.

Shadiz was on his feet in an instant and surging forward while the two suspicious Highlanders were occupied with Jonathan's approach. In the next pounding heartbeat, Sir Thomas glimpsed the flash of a dagger in the lamp light, and held his breath, paralysed by mixed emotions.

Shadiz pushed Jonathan out of harm's way. At the same time, he pierced the heart of the nearest Highlander. Withdrawing the blood-soaked weapon, in one expert move he swung towards the second Highlander whose lumbering forward momentum caused the dagger to sink up to its hilt in his heart. Like his fellow countryman, he died instantly.

In an effort to avoid alerting the other two Highlander guards outside the tent, Jonathan had caught hold of the first Highlander Shadiz had killed. In an attempt to lower the Scot down to the ground, slender yet strong, he was pulled erratically downwards by the Highlander's superior weight. Shadiz experienced the same difficulty with the other dead Highlander.

"Bleedin' Titans," he was heard to mutter.

After scrambling back onto his feet, Jonathan helped Shadiz drag the two hefty guards deeper into the tent.

"Go," commanded Shadiz.

Jonathan was loathed to leave his leader alone with the man who had shown such comprehensive violence. Once more, he was dismissed with relief and, this time, with a mute assurance that all would be well.

Having concealed how unnerved he was, Sir Thomas stood his ground as Shadiz walked over to him with that dangerous, feline gait.

"You must leave," he urged. "Remain free."

Shadiz gave him a sidelong look he was unable to identify.

"I intend to."

"Let us part friends, whatever the world dictates," said Sir Thomas, steadily.

"Aye," agreed Shadiz, giving the older man a genuine smile.

Sir Thomas was given the impression he was about to receive a handshake.

"An' in the name o' friendship, allow me t' provide y' wi' an explanation," murmured Shadiz, laying the senseless figure of his supposed enemy on the already littered floor. "*Knight without fear and without blemish.*"

CHAPTER TEN

War Breeds Strange Bedfellows

The sentries on guard at the east gate of Knaresborough Castle did not at first recognise the tall figure. Only when the big white dog padded silently out of the shadows between flaring torches did they realise Prince Rupert was approaching them, not in his usual quick-stride, no-nonsense gait, but rather with a restless saunter.

Acknowledging hasty salutes with a curt nod, Rupert walked beneath the archway spanning the two semi-circular towers at either side of the main gateway.

Once free of the castle's precincts, shunning the common thoroughfare, he strolled along the steep track lancing like a well-festered scar down the rocky shoulder of the promontory upon which the ancient fortress was situated.

Dwarfed beneath the lofty shadow of its formidable neighbour, the prosperous cluster that was Knaresborough slept embedded in the cloaking night. Beyond its false normality, camp fires burned at frequent intervals, giving bright notice of the Prince's Royalist Army gathered along the banks of the River Nidd, and ensconced in every nook and cranny of the accommodating, pastoral landscape.

Unlike the massed humanity, but in conjunction with the many sentries, Rupert remained sleepless. He had come out into the night seeking solace from the demands of maps and dispatches in his chamber, ironically close to the King's Chamber.

He approached the base of the steep incline, where the foliage grew dense and chaotic. His chosen path was leading him towards the murmuring drift of the river, a moon-haunted, silvery wraith, when he realised Boy had gone off on his own. The usual soft whistle brought forth the dog, and a shadow matching his own uncommon height. An instinctive reaction, his hand had gone to his sword hilt before he registered Boy's friend-welcoming manner. Holding fast on steel, Rupert held his breath in anticipation.

"Y' just strollin' or lookin' for summat?"

The whispery question caused Rupert to grin. "An illusive wraith," he quipped in immense relief.

Even in the soft, moonlit darkness of the June night it was impossible to discern features, only the outline of the man of whom he had asked the impossible. Unlike his officers who had politely derided him for such an action, he had taken comfort in the extraordinary man's abilities. And now he was rewarded by a return that promised the golden nuggets of future success.

The two men spoke little as they ascended the rocky track's narrow gradient up to the castle. Rupert was full of questions, but reined in his eagerness, knowing something of the man beside him and, as always, wary of his scant knowledge.

It was the shocked stares of the sentries as they entered the revealing light of the torches around the main gate that caused the Prince to look sideward at Shadiz. Whereupon he cursed roundly, not least because the guilt that had ridden him for the last few days spiked painfully.

Shadiz merely shrugged as his array of bruises and ragged appearance was scrutinised. *"A wise man'll make more opportunities than he finds."*

He said nothing further while Rupert led the way to his own chamber. Upon entering, while Shadiz lowered himself down onto the long, cushioned window seat, the Prince called for his servant.

In the next turn of the hour glass, Shadiz was brought food and water, upon refusing wine. A physician was summoned from his bed to minister to his hurts.

When Shadiz was in a slightly better condition, and had eaten his fill, when the two men were once again alone, Rupert could not contain his avid desire for tidings of the enemy and how York was faring.

"Were you able to penetrate York?"

"Aye," replied Shadiz, low-pitched.

Relief immediately flooded Rupert's handsome face. "You

298

had difficulty doing so? Or upon leaving?" he queried, once again surveying the other man's bruises.

A hint of rueful amusement crept around the purple-red marks on Shadiz's tribal-dark face. "Difficulty came when I bumped into an acquaintance," he remarked.

Rupert frowned. "Who?"

"David Leslie," came the nonchalant reply.

Rupert stared at him in astonishment. "David Leslie? The Scot?"

There was a brief, loud knock on the door of the chamber.

At the Prince's impatient response, several men almost fell over themselves to get into the chamber.

Goring let out a joyous whoop. "Goddamit, you did it!" he bellowed.

A second later, the newcomers grasped the significance of Shadiz's appearance.

"The bastards!" declared Goring, outrage replacing his cheerfulness at Shadiz's return.

Sir Charles Lucas's quiet smile of relief had slipped away, leaving shadows of concern. On the other hand, a narrowed speculation had entered Lord Byron's gaze, set firmly on Shadiz.

Richard, standing a little apart from the other men, was prey to mixed emotions upon his half-brother's return. He had been awakened from a restless, haunted sleep with tidings of his arrival at the castle. Briefly meeting Shadiz's black glance, he hoped any information acquired for Prince Rupert was worth the obvious effort.

And so it proved. Ignoring the reaction to his beaten appearance, Shadiz furnished the expectant men with a detailed account of York's plight.

Articulate and dispassionate, he conjured up every aspect of the siege of the city on their respective mind's eye. In so doing, giving a disquieting insight into valiant efforts and relentless destruction against the backdrop of a hard pressed summer until the men could see within York's battered walls, smell the acrid smoke emitted by her hot, clamouring cannons and feel the mounting dread of the trapped citizens.

Yet his impressive narration did not end with dwindling stocks of foodstuff and ammunition, full hospitals, ruined houses and shattered lanes overcrowded with the increasingly desperate homeless.

When Shadiz began speaking about the respective camps of the enemy laying siege to York, English and Scottish, the enthralled men found such knowledge difficult to comprehend.

"It would be most interesting to know how you came by such information," drawled Lord Byron. "Or have you been sent back to us with misinformation?"

There was immediate uproar in the chamber.

While Richard and Lord Lucas edged towards Shadiz, Goring took up an enraged stance close to Byron. Meanwhile, Rupert placed himself between Shadiz's menacing retaliation and Byron's threatening defiance.

"This man has done what I doubt no other could do," rasped Prince Rupert, glaring at his cavalry officer.

Byron retreated only in so far as his loyalty to the Prince would stretch. "I would respectfully ask, sir, how it is your gypsy mercenary comes to us with such precise knowledge."

Shadiz forestalled Rupert. *"Allah hath granted to every people a prophet in its own tongue,"* he quoted in whispery ice.

Rupert turned to him. "You did not just 'bump' into David Leslie?"

"An' a few other Scots," replied Shadiz, dryly.

"You were taken!" exclaimed Goring, horror stamped upon his rosy features.

"Y' win the overflowin' tankard," commented Shadiz, ending the stunned silence.

Richard studied his half-brother. He wasn't alone.

Those around him were also looking searchingly at the tall nomad who it seemed possessed no apparent allegiance, only loyalty to his own mercurial traits.

The candlelight in the quiet chamber flickered upon harshness in barbarous features, and sinister detachment in cruel, slanted eyes.

"Their scouts report o' y'r movement around Knaresborough,"

Shadiz explained, in a soft, chilling tone. "An' now reckon y'r 'eadin' for Wetherby."

Rupert scowled. "Why would they consider such a move? I intend relieving York."

"I told 'em."

Rupert's scowl deepened. He cut short the apprehension of his commanders with an irritable gesture. "What else did you inform them?"

"That y'r army's strength's up t' twenty thousand. That y'r seekin' t' do battle an' racin' t' claim 'igher ground around Wetherby. That Newcastle's got wind o' what y' about an' plans t' break out o' York at Micklegate an' cross Ouse at Skeldergate so 'e can back y' wi' Goring an' 'is troopers."

"They believed you?" demanded Rupert.

"I give 'em what I caught bandied about in their own camps," replied Shadiz, with a slight shrug. "Apparently no sod can withstand 'ighland muscle," he added, ironically.

"Yet you could," remarked Byron. "And escaped them, to boot. How...."

He said no more beneath the Prince's chastising glare.

"No bastard's muscle tak's kindly t' steel," snapped Shadiz, bestowing a look on Byron that made it plain he wanted to demonstrate upon the other man.

While the rest of the men anticipated another clash between Shadiz and Byron, in the midst of them, Prince Rupert stood deep in thought for a further moment before observing, "You have an alternative?"

Rupert followed Shadiz to the maps strewn on the table and stood beside him as Shadiz traced the route he proposed over consecutive maps of North Yorkshire.

"From Knaresborough strike north. Cross the Ure an' then Swale at Thornton Bridge. That way y' march down the east bank o' the Ouse, reaching York by a northly direction wi' the river between y' an' Crop-Ears."

Attuned to Shadiz's tactics, Rupert put forward, "Meanwhile, a substantial detachment of Horse make it appear they are the vanguard of the army by being in the Wetherby area. They will not only maintain the ruse, through their presence we will be able to ascertain whether or not Leven, Fairfax and the rest have taken the bait and abandoned their siege of York." He thumped the table in triumph. "By the devil's horns…it's a viable scheme."

"Your highness," drawled Lord Byron from the other side of the littered table. "Would you not find it wise to consider that the devil maybe leading us into a hellish trap?"

Retaliation was immediate. Shadiz forestalled Rupert, his commanders and Richard in a manner that left all of them shaken.

For his part, Byron's shock at the flying dagger missing him by the narrowest of margins caused him to stagger backward against a tall oak cupboard.

"Y' either get that bastard out o' me sight or I get out o' y'rs," rasped Shadiz.

His swarthy features consumed with smouldering fury, Byron straightened, vigorously brushing away the humiliation of his scramble to protect himself.

"You are dismissed," commanded Prince Rupert, his narrowed gaze on Byron.

Taking his cue from Rupert, it fell to Goring to extricate the disgraced lord from the chamber. Before closing the door on Byron's stiff back, Goring glanced across at Shadiz and merrily winked.

"It is fortunate he ducked," observed Rupert, turning back to the maps.

"I never miss," retorted Shadiz, retrieving his dagger.

The Prince exchanged a glance with Richard. Switching back to Shadiz, he asked, "You will take lead on the endeavour to free York?"

"Y' sure I won't lead y' over Rubicon?" retorted Shadiz.

Rupert surveyed him fearlessly. "War breeds strange bedfellows."

His confident attitude was greeted with sardonic humour.

CHAPTER ELEVEN

Manoeuvres In The Dark

It had been a long day, followed by an equally long night. Now, presently laying prone beneath bushy camouflage, waiting for the next relentless development in the unfolding strategy, Richard kept his long bow and quiver of arrows close.

Benjamin Farr lay beside him, deep in the dewy undergrowth.

He had made a surprise appearance in Knaresborough during the disciplined scramble to prepare the Royalist Army to march to a destination to which only Prince Rupert's senior officers were privy. Also the Master and his men.

Their leader was riding with Rupert, guiding the main body of the army on a tortuous route that entailed crossing the rivers Ure and Swale, the objective being to relieve York by way of Boroughbridge and Thornton Bridge. The Master's Romany scouts, his tribal will-o'-the-wisps, were the proficient eyes and ears of the army, forging ahead in all directions. Meanwhile Lord Goring had been dispatched with several regiments of cavalry to deceive the Parliamentarians and Scots into believing the prince intended to take up a battle ready position close to Wetherby.

The Master's men had been split into three groups, commanded by Richard, Benjamin and Danny Murphy, respectively. They had swept the land, dealing with any pockets of enemy soldiers or troopers they encountered.

Shortly before dawn, deep within the devastated landscape around York, Richard's and Benjamin's companies had combined within the eerily deserted camps of the Crop-Ears and their allies the Scots. Upon being joined by Danny and his company, they had heard about the store of four thousand pairs of new shoes, found by a party of Romany.

Coming within sight of the Ouse at Poppleton, three miles north-west of York, they had spied the bridge of boats spanning the river, guarded by Lord Manchester's dragoons. As they had kept watch a large contingent of dragoons reinforced those already present. More worrying, the newcomers had brought with them two cannons and positioned one facing away from the river and the other pointing over the broad flowing Ouse.

The unexpected development posed a possible threat to Rupert's deceptive path to York. Unsure how best to proceed, Richard had sent a messenger to Shadiz with the approaching army.

Richard, Benjamin and Danny along with their men had taken up surveillance beneath ragged shrubbery capping an otherwise barren hillock while the Romany accompanying them had disappeared into the desolate locality to gather information.

Awaiting tidings from either the scouts or his leader, Richard stretched as best he could beneath the thorny bushes. He looked across at Benjamin.

Pleased as he was to see Benjamin again, after he had disappeared into the Mediterranean with Shadiz, Richard had found his friend subtly changed. He had quickly detected a hard-edged reserve that had not been apparent before when they had both served on Prince Rupert's staff and later when they had resided at the Lodge in Stillingfleet Forest.

Desperate to have tidings of Catherine, Richard had expected Benjamin to acquaint him with events, instead he received a succinct response which left him no wiser and more than a little annoyed. His humour was not improved by Shadiz's present attitude, more curt and brittle than usual. It made him suspect there was an underlying reason.

"Y' any good wi' flame throwing?"

Richard and Benjamin jumped, twisted around with one accord, and would have, with one accord, roundly berated anyone else who had crept up behind them.

As it was, they were obliged to accept Shadiz's customary soundless approach. They were, nevertheless, surprised by his appearance. It made them suspect the Royalist Army was fast approaching the Ouse, and the dangerous obstacle they had discovered at the river.

"Y' demonstrated distance a while back," commented Shadiz, moving up closer to the two men.

It was a reference to when Richard had shot a cluster of arrows to which a rope had been attached across the storm swept shore in Mercy Cove for Shadiz to follow to the Eagle, stranded on a reef.

Richard bristled at his half-brother's far from complementary tone. "What would you have me do?" he retorted.

Shadiz gave a low bird-like whistle.

Almost immediately one of his Romany scouts appeared beside him. Shadiz murmured to the newcomer. In response the Romany briefly drew away the cover over a candle lantern.

"Reckon y' could set off a fireworks display?"

Realising what their leader had in mind, the men concealed in the ragged bushes returned their attention to the River Ouse.

The soft, late June night was giving way to a grey dawn. A thin, gossamer mist drifted over the smooth leaden surface of the river. It clung in random places to the gently stirring bridge of boats stretching from the nearest west bank to the furthest east bank of the river.

Above all, the men took particular notice of the newly-arrived cannons, primed no doubt to deter any hostile approach to the bridge of boats from either east or west directions. Beside them, ready for use, were neat piles of cannon balls and squat barrels undoubtedly filled with gunpowder.

The only real advantage was the slack attitude of the guards, gaining more momentum with the daybreak. Though there were many, and well-armed, their united belief that both their own and the Royalist Army were engaged elsewhere made them vulnerable to a surprise attack. A speciality of the Master and his men.

"You want me to loose fire arrows at the barrels?" muttered Richard, weighing up the difficult angles.

"That's idea," challenged Shadiz. "Y'll need t' shift y'rsen."

Richard gave his half-brother a smouldering look. It penetrated dawn's increasing light.

He strung his powerful long bow, careful not to let it come into contact with the moist ground, aware of the bird song, deceptively similar to the dawn chorus.

While reaching for an arrow from the quiver on his back, a Romany materialised beside him. His nerves already fraught with the thought of the shot he was about to take, Richard scowled at the older, muscular man who had caught him unawares. His attitude changed to one of wary interest when the Romany wordlessly took the arrow from him and began to wrap a piece of cloth around it.

Shadiz had disappeared for a while, but now suddenly reappeared beside Richard. "Y' set?"

Richard nodded. Whereupon, Shadiz gestured to the Romany with the candle lantern.

Shadiz, Benjamin and Danny shielded the two Romany as they sought between them to ignite the poised arrow.

Richard briefly shied away from the burst of heat. He then drew the bow, mindful of the closeness of the flames. Whatever the cloth had been soaked in fuelled bright death.

The five men around him parted the bushes in order to give Richard the opening he needed for a clear aim.

By the time the enemy soldiers realised the flaming arrow, fanned by rushing air, was heading their way, the only defensive option left to them was to flee amidst cries of alarm.

Few succeeded before the barrel of gunpowder close to the cannon pointing over the river exploded with a thunderous roar.

Yet Richard had little time to contemplate his achievement. Almost immediately the two Romany had his next flaming arrow ready for an even more demanding shot.

Richard blocked out the turmoil the explosion had caused and the way the Master's men, led by Danny Murphy, were racing over the bridge of boats, taking advantage of the surprise attack on the Crop-Ears.

He concentrated on the other barrel of gunpowder, half concealed by the cannon aimed towards the east. Obliged to stand clear of the concealing bushes to adjust his aim, there was no chance of him defending himself.

The burning cloth was uncomfortably close to his hand as he maintained the tension on his bow while further perfecting his shot. Releasing the arrow up into the brightening sky, he watched the blazing trajectory descend on the required target on the other side of the river.

He was suddenly slammed down onto the ground. Musket fire buzzed like a swarm of angry bees past were he had just been standing a moment before.

Getting his breath back, coughing, two things became apparent.

Squirming around, Richard saw Benjamin and the two Romany who had helped with the fire-arrows were reloading muskets before firing a second round at a group of dragoons. They had regrouped away from those in disarray who were nonetheless trying to hold their own against the Master's men.

Squirming back around, he realised it had been Shadiz, sprawled out next to him, who had ensured his safety.

The next explosion rent the already confused atmosphere.

Though Richard's shot had been slightly off target, the arrow had penetrate the ground close enough to the barrel to infect the ripe wood and subsequently the combustible contents.

It brought to an end what remained of the dragoons' reckless defence. Those in a condition to do so, ran for their lives.

Richard got to his feet alongside Shadiz. He brushed the damp soil off his doublet. "Thanks," he muttered, looking sideward.

Shadiz walked away.

CHAPTER TWELVE

Unique Return

Richard and Benjamin walked out of Prince Rupert's command tent. Both men hesitated, wondering how best to carry out their task. There was a certain urgency about it, but both were unsure how best to proceed. It was close to midnight. The large, sprawling camp centred around the prince's headquarters, crowded with men and horses, was for the large part slumberous after the swift march from Knaresborough. What had just been decided meant the respite would be shortlived.

"Right," said Richard. "You go that way, and I'll go this way."

"He's probably with the Romany," suggested Benjamin.

Richard made a disparaging noise. "He would trust no other to watch his back."

Commanders from every section of the prince's army had attended the animated conference in Rupert's tent. Shadiz had said very little, except to add his distinct voice to those who denounced the prince's intention to engage the Parliamentary Armies of the Fairfaxes and Lord Manchester and the Scots in battle. Nor had he been alone in wanting the relief of York to be a sufficient blow to the combined enemy. Yet Rupert had remained adamant, referring to the letter his uncle, the king, had dispatched, post haste to him from Worcester. In it Charles had stated:

If York be lost I shall esteem my crown little less. But if York be relieved, and you beat the rebels' army of both kingdoms.

While the commanders had been considering their respective roles in the upcoming battle, Shadiz had left the tent without a word to anyone.

Standing in the shadows at the rear of the impressive, lamp-lit campaign tent, Richard and Benjamin had watched him go, swaying slightly with exhaustion, red-eyed from lack of sleep. It was anyone's guess how long Shadiz had gone without sleep.

Having remained in order to inform Shadiz what had transpired in his notable absence, they had been sent by Prince Rupert to look for their leader after he had received an imperative message from Lord Newcastle in York.

The two young men started to move away in different directions.

"If we can find the Romany," said Benjamin, over his shoulder, "we should find Shadiz."

"True," replied Richard. A few paces away, he paused. "You quite sure you are not troubled?"

Benjamin sighed irritably. "Not that again," he answered, walking away.

"Just asking," muttered Richard, frowning, stifling an urge to cough.

Benjamin had been walking for some time, feeling rather like he was looking for a needle in a haystack, at night. He was trying to avoid stepping on inert figures when a shadow came out of nowhere.

"Easy, there, Gorgio Farr," cautioned the shadow.

Benjamin curbed the movement towards his sword. Taking a breath to calm himself, he explained, "I'm looking for Shadiz."

"Why?"

"There is trouble in York."

"Let 'em get another!"

Benjamin was about to object when another, taller shadow materialised next to him. Even clothed in darkness, Shadiz's authority could not be mistaken.

The Master spoke in the Romi, whereupon the indistinct Romany melted away into the night.

"Well?" demanded Shadiz.

"Prince Rupert asks you go to York, sir. The soldiers there are refusing to march to the prince's aid in the forthcoming battle, " explained Benjamin.

309

"What's that got t' do wi' me?"

"Lord Newcastle is very much against the prince's plan to engage the Crop-Ears and the Scots. And now the soldiers have mutinied. Lord Eythin set the ball rolling...."

"Eythin?"

"Yes, sir," confirmed Benjamin. "Apparently he was the one who brought up the matter of arrears of pay after the siege. The men won't budge until they hear from you, sir."

"Develesko Mush," rasped Shadiz. He set a fast pace through the camp.

In silence, Benjamin kept pace with him.

"What y' doin' 'ere?"

The brusque demand caught Benjamin off guard. "The prince said to...."

"Y' know what I mean."

Benjamin sought to marshal his thoughts. When his leader gave him a sidelong glance, penetrating despite the darkness, he said, "I am no longer welcome elsewhere."

"Wi' y' family?"

"Yes," responded Benjamin, quietly.

"Cos o' me." It was a statement.

Benjamin's response was guarded. "They believe me to have become... wayward." More candidly, he added, "Yet, my 'waywardness' ensured their freedom. With your assistance, sir."

They walked on in silence until Rupert's headquarters, flooded by torchlight, came into view.

Shadiz halted so abruptly, Benjamin had taken a couple of steps forward before he realised. He stopped and looked back at his leader.

"Y' still loyal to t' 'em?"

A lump came suddenly into Benjamin's throat. He swallowed convulsive beneath Shadiz calculating scrutiny, and then drew himself up. "Yes, sir. Always."

"Y' loyal t' me?"

The whispery question took Benjamin by surprise. He was held fast by the mesmerising black eyes of his leader. He slowly nodded. "Yes, always."

Shadiz challenged him further. "Divided loyalties?"

"No, sir. Shared loyalties."

A rare shadow of a smile lasted barely a heartbeat on Shadiz harsh, battered features. He started walking again. "She'd be pleased wi' that."

For a couple of moments Benjamin remained where he was, wondering if he had heard right. Then, with his own hint of a smile, willingly followed his leader.

Thirty minutes later, Richard and Benjamin flanked Shadiz at the head of the Master's men and a strong detachment of the Prince's Lifeguards as they rode into York.

The regimental colours turned the heads of the citizens celebrating the relief of their wounded city. At first they believed Prince Rupert had come to see for himself the damage York had sustained during the prolonged siege by the combined armies of the Crop-Ears and the loathed Scots. When it became known Shadiz was once more in York, he was hailed as the returning hero throughout the often devastated streets. Upon reaching the grand house he had visited previously in Petersgate, close to the undamaged Minster, Richard and Benjamin accompanied their leader into the mansion crowded with dignitaries, church leaders and an assortment of other people who thought themselves to be of worth to York.

Shadiz's powerful, chilling influence silenced all present in the regal chamber. Even Lord Goring's hearty welcome died on his thick lips. Richard and Benjamin, along with everyone else watched as Shadiz crossed the chamber, caught hold of Eythin's arm and, without pause or word, conducted the startled Scotsman through the nearest door.

"You bear witness, gentlemen, how this youthful prince insults me," complained Lord Newcastle. "Not only does he stay away. He sends a gypsy-vagabond to lord it over me." He emitted a huffish sigh. "After I have defended York these many weeks."

"You forget most conveniently, sir," rebuked Goring. "If not for that gypsy-vagabond, you and Eythin and every sod else would still be trapped in York!"

"Must I therefore, say you, be grateful to…that?" countered Newcastle with a condemning sneer.

For the next few minutes, conversation was spasmodic and abstracted. Richard and Benjamin, sharing Goring's outrage at Newcastle's conduct, remained apart from the rest of those present.

Before too long, Shadiz thrust open the attention-burdened door and with brusque courtesy gestured for Eythin to proceed him back into the flood of candlelit interest. It was obvious from the older man's demeanour he had experienced the sharp edge of Shadiz's disgust at the way he had stirred up trouble among the defenders of York by suggesting arrears of pay would not be forthcoming anytime soon. It was equally obvious he had just made another enemy.

As Shadiz came abreast of him, Newcastle rose with a grand show of dignity from the seat he had flung himself into when Shadiz had disappeared with Eythin.

"Your behaviour is obnoxious. Yet, what can one expect from something Rupert has seen fit to fish out of the gutter."

The atmosphere in the crowded chamber was vibrant with tension. No one stirred, their attention riveted on the lord and the gypsy.

Shadiz had halted. He surveyed Newcastle's thin, aristocratic features with narrow eyes. When he began to speak, his voice was low-pitched and brutal. "Where's that chivalry attributed t' y'r position in life, *milord*? Or 'as y'r noble sense o' duty deserted y' altogether?"

Newcastle had gone stiff with rage. "I am…" he began to splutter.

Shadiz slashed across his outraged splutter. "Aye. The selfish utterance. The eternal declaration of self-interest. As a leader of men shouldn't y'r duty come afore petty dislikes and imagined slights? As a nobleman shouldn't y'r allegiance t' y'r king come afore any reservation y' might 'arbour about 'is emissary? Knowing 'im t' be no courtier. Right or wrong, Rupert's out there already bleedin' for Charles, while y' an' Eythin, in the freedom given y' by 'im, brew a mutiny that ill-suits York after her valiant defiance.

"Look y' into vulgar channel o' life occasionally. Even there respect's earned." Whether he realised it or not, Newcastle had backed away a few paces from Shadiz. "You dare to lecture me," he

312

muttered. He had developed a pinched look around his mouth and nose.

There was feral danger in Shadiz's smile. His black eyes glittering, in a whispery tone, he murmured, *"From the gods comes the saying, 'know thyself.'"*

★

Upon catching sight of Shadiz, Sir Thomas Glemham, the embattled Governor of York, breathed a sigh of relief. He tried to make himself heard above the clamour of the argumentative citizens clustered around the devastation wrought by the siege, but before the soldiers loyal to him had grasped his command, the large contingent of horsemen was already forcing the large crowd to fall back away from their formidable progress along Tower Street between Clifford's Tower and the King's Staith on the east bank of the River Ouse.

Sir Thomas was struck by the commanding presence of the Gypsy. The unmistakable impression was a reminder of when he had escorted Shadiz on a fact-finding tour of York during the siege. He appeared to have subjugated Newcastle and Eythin. The two men were riding grim-faced and tight-lipped at either side of him at the head of the column. Sir Thomas witnessed the upsurge of tension in the two commanders as they surveyed the hostility seething around the tall mound upon which Clifford's Tower was situated. He considered it to be of their making. His attention remained hopefully on Shadiz.

Obeying Shadiz's bidding, the combined escort of Prince Rupert's Lifeguards and his men came to a halt. They remained mounted, sword drawn and glinting in the profusion of torchlight while Shadiz swung a leg over his mount's neck and dropped easily down from the saddle. He responded with a curt nod in passing to Sir Thomas's expression of gratitude that was more of a regretful grimace. Behind him, Eythin and then more tardily, Newcastle dismounted and joined the Governor. Standing in a semi-circle of protective soldiers, they watched the Gypsy make his unhurried way towards Clifford's Tower,

313

doubtful he could quell the siege-hardened soldiers in their present volatile mood.

They were engrossed in talking boldly amongst themselves about the lack of pay. Their discontent at being denied their rightful dues for striving with blood and guts to defend York had led to a hostile reaction upon being ordered to march out of York in support of Prince Rupert's Army.

Unnoticed, a dark shadow, Shadiz passed through them. He emerged from the rowdy throng and strolled up the high, grassy mound surmounted by the historical landmark. Coming to a leisurely halt halfway up the impressive, Roman-constructed mound, he stood at ease without speaking, hands on hips, looking down at his boots.

It took only a few minutes for him to be spied by many in the large, agitated crowd of soldiers. Thereafter, recognition rapidly spread causing a hush to fall on the gathering.

"Well I'll be damned," muttered Lord Goring.

When the attention of the entire gathering was upon him, Shadiz's lifted his head slowly. His dark, barbarous face in the abundance of torchlight gave nothing away.

Those in the escort, commanders and common folk, certainly the soldiers, all regarding him expectantly.

Shadiz's cold black gaze travelled over the mosaic of upturned faces.

"Well, 'ere I am," he began in a voice that reached to the river but was neither overloud or strident. "But, I ain't no bloody miracle-worker. What in God's name d' y' expect me t' do about y'r dues? Money-chests be empty. An' there ain't much y'r commanders or mesen can do about it. So, think again, me prattlin' pretties. So, go ahead, carry out y'r threat. Wreck the rest o' place. Finish off what Crop-Ears an' Scots started. Sour them efforts against all the odds that've made y' talk o' Yorkshire."

It was not what Lords, Sirs or well-to-do commoners wanted to hear. Newcastle hissed his displeasure, Eythin swore and Sir Thomas bit his lip in vexation. Aghast, Richard glanced at Benjamin. He frowned at his friend's expression. He had no idea that Benjamin had heard the Master address a society of corsairs in Formentera, overjoyed at their commander's return. Benjamin was in no doubt of the night's outcome.

Adding to the general sense of unease beyond the ragged fringes of the soldiers, Shadiz continued in the same vein. "Develesko Mush, don't tell me y' really expected t' get rewarded for all the sweat an' guts y' put into defendin' York? Ain't y' learnt yet y' dirt under nobs' thumbnails? Dirt they're quick t' get rid o' when they feel safe again. If the bastards toss y' a promise that's all y' likely t' get. If y' live."

"He is sanctioning their mutiny!" exclaimed Lord Newcastle.

For the first time, there was a hint of regret in the distinct, hypnotic voice.

"Even if y' were t' go meekly back t' war right now, I doubt y'd get y'r just rewards."

A heartfelt murmur of agreement rippled upwards to the leaden heavens.

All at once, Shadiz ripped into the emotional atmosphere. "O' course. Y' do realise, if y' ain't off t' stir y'rsens them poor sods y' toiled t' keep from comin' under Crop-Ears' lash'll be slaughtered? Along wi' them working on lines o' battle out yonder on Marston Moor. They've got families just like y' lot. An', aye. More'n likely they ain't got their dues, either.

"They're goin' t' be up against same bloody Crop-Ears an' bleedin'Scots you lot faced down, day after day. If y' think about it, you're leavin' 'em t' finish off battle bastard started wi' y' comin' t' York. Aye, an' y' still be strugglin' t' survive if it weren't for 'em answerin' Rupert's call t' march t' York.

"Jesus, don't y' want a chance t' score against them renegade bastards who think theirsens better than y'rsens cos they reckon they've got a Righteous God on their side?

"I come t' York for Rupert. 'e wanted t' know what state y' were in. 'im an' all 'is men know o' y'r bravery. It were clear t' me when I were 'ere you lot'd be well able t' use the kind o' courage y'd shown 'ere t' support 'im against the enemy. 'e marched men none-stop from Knareborough to raise the siege. An' now their lookin' t' y' t' repay 'em by fightin' alongside 'em. They ain't 'eard yet you've mutinied against 'em."

315

Shadiz set his head on one side. When he next spoke, his voice held a quizzical note. "Or am I sellin' all o' y' short? I know the rattle o' coins in y'r breeches's pocket is good t' 'ear. Yet, so is feelin' o' freedom. An' a life to be lived in peace. Y'll own none o' that if y' don't act now, regardless o' owt else.

"Rupert's men needs every last one o' y' that survived the siege. In same way, y' lot recently had need o' them.

"T'ain't in me power t' give you wages. I wish it were, for I recognise an injustice when I sees one. No. This y' must do for the spirit o' fellowship. For, as I say, did y' not expect y'r brothers-in-arms t' do same for you?"

It was very quiet in the thronged vicinity of Clifford's Tower and the Ouse after Shadiz had finished on a challenging note.

Once again, men had come under the magnetic spell of his many-faceted character. The emotional atmosphere had undergone a remarkable change. It became clear he had been successful in binding men to him.

A cheer went up, followed by another, and another. Soon the torchlit soldiers were unanimous in their change of heart.

Shadiz held up a hand for silence.

Following the obedient response, he challenged, "What say we take fight t' the bastards!"

The battle cries rose around the ancient, stone Tower.

Sir Thomas Glemham murmured, "The man is unique.

'Give the urchin 'is due.'

Though his expression remained that of a skilled warrior-leader with a remote and chilling manner, within, Shadiz experienced ironic amusement at the fleeting thought.

He had shied away of late from looking within, too afraid to acknowledge the gut-wrenching sense of emptiness. Since feeling the blessing of Kore's disapproval when he had been trapped in the Scottish camp, he had been acutely conscious of her withdrawal. Yet, bizarrely, he had also felt a closeness he could not access.

Returning to his mount, he was barely aware of the respectful approval by which he was surrounded. Instead, made uneasy by the conundrum, he ran a hand through his long, wild hair.

Richard held the reins of his horse out to him.

"Is something amiss?" he asked, not liking have to raise his voice above the general clamour. The half-brothers were surrounded with the newly raised desire to march out of York.

Accepting the reins of the stallion, Shadiz twisted them absently, seemingly oblivious to the activities he had instigated. He shook his head, not so much in answer, more as if trying to clear his head of some illusive foreboding..

His uncharacteristic manner deepened Richard's infected disquiet.

CHAPTER THIRTEEN

A Different Battle

After Shadiz had quelled the mutinous intentions of the garrisons of York, the rest of the night he had spent in the forefront of the preparations for the march out of the city. His charismatic presence among the soldiers ensured they did not falter in their resolve to support Prince Rupert's army in the forthcoming battle against the combined armies of the Fairfaxes, Lord Manchester and the Scots, commanded by Lord Leven.

All was in readiness to quit the city as dawn crept rosily over the surviving rooftops and the elegant Minister. A messenger from Prince Rupert found Shadiz standing with Richard and Benjamin in neglected gardens close to Bootham Bar where the detachment of the Prince's Lifeguards who had escorted him were preparing to ride out of York.

He was informed Rupert needed him to take command of the reconnoitre to the north of Marston Moor, where the Parliamentarians and the Scots were believed to be belatedly responding to reports of Prince Rupert's formations for battle. Shadiz appeared far from pleased. His only comment as he took his leave of Richard and Benjamin was that Richard was in charge of the men in his absence.

The two young men were not surprised when several Romany materialised out of the early morning mist clinging to the shattered dwellings of the devastated city in answer to Shadiz's soft whistle.

"He seems…distracted," Richard muttered, watching his half-brother ride away. "Have you noticed?" he added, giving Benjamin a quizzical sidelong look.

Benjamin continued to stare straight ahead. "He has many task," he remarked, noncommittally.

Richard turned fully to him. "Dammit! You know what I mean."

Benjamin did not turn his head. "What would you have me say?" he replied, with mild exasperation. Thereafter he maintained a stoic silence.

Richard, coughing slightly, took several agitated paces away. He was becoming increasingly frustrated with the marked difference in Benjamin since his return to England. All the time Richard had known him Benjamin had possessed a quiet disposition. Yet now a definite reserve blocked any real informative discourse Richard was desperate to have with him. It was reinforced by a hard edge to his previous easy-going character. The only information Richard had managed to get out of him was his father and older brothers were not in fact dead and that they had returned to their home close to Richmond. How this had come about, Benjamin was not forthcoming. Richard found such tight-lipped behaviour maddening. He knew very little about the happenings of the last few weeks, and was desperate for tidings of Catherine.

He turned back to Benjamin with a demand which sounded more like a plea. "Look, all I want to know is if Catherine is safe and well?"

He was made suddenly wary by Benjamin's slow turn around and long, hard stare.

"What you really want to know is, how did Shadiz come to leave Catherine at Formentera?" said Benjamin, accusingly. "He left tormented by his love for her. He left because *of* his love for her. Whatever you believe your half-brother to be, he possesses a deep, abiding, unselfish love for Catherine." He took a deep, calming breath. It was the most emotion he had shown since arriving back with the men. "Now, don't you think we should proceed with the task he charged us with?"

Obeying their leader's commands proved harder than they had expected.

Following his departure, Richard and Benjamin, along with many others with the same objective in mind, found the progress out of York to where Prince Rupert awaited them had slowed considerably. It seemed to have become bogged down in the slights

Lord Newcastle and Lord Eythin perceived themselves to have received from both Prince Rupert and Shadiz.

The strong contingent from York, including several Volunteer Citizens Bands, eventually reached Marston Moor at around ten in the morning. After the frustration of the snail's pace they had been forced to endure due to Newcastle's and Eythin's studied tardiness there was an eagerness among them to claim their places within the ranks of the prince's infantry already forming battle-ready positions upon the proposed battlefield.

Unsure how best to proceed, Richard and Benjamin left the Master's men keeping to themselves in the general commotion prevalent on the moor where Prince Rupert had raised his Standard. After a few minutes of aimless wandering, they caught sight of Shadiz's black stallion tethered close to Rupert's field headquarters. Also, several of his Romany, who appeared ill-at-ease in their present environment.

The two young men were drawing close to them when they caught sight of Shadiz. His brutal fluidity gave mute testimony to a rush of fury. His unmistakable manner slowed Richard's and Benjamin's approach.

Moments later, Prince Rupert appeared behind Shadiz.

Richard and Benjamin watched as the prince located Shadiz striding towards the restive stallion, and followed rapidly in the other man's purposeful wake.

Shadiz wheeled to face Rupert, who came to an abrupt halt a few paces away. Whatever passed between the two men was lost on Richard and Benjamin due to distance even though they had drawn closer to where Shadiz and Rupert where standing. Yet, the expressions on both of the men's faces showed their respective irritation. Then whatever Shadiz said clearly took Rupert by surprise.

Shadiz turned away, leaving Rupert staring after him.

Continuing to be watchful and now alert, Richard and Benjamin surmised rather than heard the prince call out to Shadiz. He twisted back around with obvious reluctance.

Rupert's manner had clearly altered. The tension he had carried with him seemed to have dissipated. Whatever he said impacted on

Shadiz. He appeared to take a calming breath. An understanding looked passed between the two tall, extraordinary men. Shadiz's eventual reply caused Rupert to give a rare smile. He raised a hand in a gesture of good-natured farewell. A lop-sided grin creasing his dark, barbarous features, Shadiz inclined his head in a genuine salute to the prince.

After the two men had parted, Shadiz walked the stallion towards Richard and Benjamin, followed by the Romany, leading their own more placid mounts.

"Where's men?" demanded Shadiz, upon coming abreast of his half-brother.

"Just over there," replied Richard, falling into step beside Shadiz, Benjamin at his elbow. "What is happening?" he asked.

Shadiz did not answer. He continued in silence until he reached his men. They gathered dutifully together and awaited their leader's orders.

The Master surveyed them. "Y've a choice," he began in a low voice. "Y' can either stay 'ere an' join the battle against Crop-Ears an' Scots, whenever the 'ell it begins. I won't fault y' if y' decide t'. Or y' can remain wi' me. But, I warn y', I'm 'eadin' t' another battle. "

"You are going to move against Fylingdales," stated Richard, scowling. "Why now? We're expected to join Rupert!"

"If y' would rather sit out one battle for another," retorted Shadiz, "so be it."

"You bastard!" growled Richard, "You know very well what I mean."

Glaring at Richard, Danny Murphy spoke for all of the men, having collected their nods of acquiescence, "We're *all* wi' y', sir. Tis about time place were sorted."

"Why now?" persisted Richard, standing his ground while everyone else prepared to mount. "What reason have you given Rupert for your leaving before the battle?"

"That me wife's in danger," rasped Shadiz.

CHAPTER FOURTEEN

The Personal Battle

Shadiz walked away from the seclusion of a wood south-east of Malton where his men were taking a break from the quick dash to the Lodge. Each hour's ride had seemed endless. The maddening distance appeared to shrink at a snail's pace. They had been forced to circumvent the Royalists, Parliamentarians and the Scots in order to avoid becoming embroiled in an inconvenient encounter. By the time he had reluctantly called a halt within the rural peace of twilight, they had left the warring forces far behind.

The tension consuming Shadiz manifested itself in his impatience strides through the wild grasses and tall bulrushes growing in abundance beside the shallow stream meandering over a pebbly bed. He was pushing his men hard, even more than usual. God help them, whatever he slung at them they gave of their best, especially now when his sense of urgency had infected them. Presently, they were leaving him to himself, knowing how the need to rest the horses irked him.

Coming to an abrupt halt, he flung himself down in the long grass and, elbows on his drawn up knees, drove his hands through his wild hair, staring blankly at the dark ripples in the stream. Then, almost without knowing it, he grasped his moonstone pendant.

He was furious with himself for succumbing to tricks of doubt instead of acknowledging the precious stone's throbbing with a dire warning. Why hadn't he recognised the moonstone's weird potency? Instead he had tried to bury the agonising emptiness by keeping busy with other bastards' concerns.

He was not as adept as Kore at grasping the significance of the uncanny perception. Yet, after he had sensed her brief presence while he had been in the Scottish camp, he should have realised she would not practise a malicious rejection. He now knew with absolute certainty her withdrawal was a protective shield. It left him mortified by his own frigging stupidity!

The insistent demand to journey onwards to the Lodge brought him to his feet. He retraced the path he had beaten down beside the stream, trying to bring his desperate need to protect Kore under control in order to accomplish whatever needed to be done.

The men caught sight of him as he emerged through the trees. Getting to their feet, they could see he was anxious to be gone. In unspoken accord, they returned to their horses.

When the tight pack of horsemen eventually reached familiar territory their progress was hampered by a thick mist upon the North York Moors. Dawn was lost somewhere over the hidden horizon. Until morning advance with evidence of summer they remained warrior wraiths deep within an ages-old silence.

It was the unerring, tribal instincts of Shadiz and his Romany mulesko dud which kept everyone on the right track over the vast, undulating moors, where the leaden sky appeared to have become part of the isolated landscape.

By the time the leafy swathe of Stillingfleet Forest came into view, the mist had dissipated considerably, leaving in its wake tendrils of gossamer vapour drifting around the forest's ancient boundary.

Answering a signal from their leader, the horsemen draw rein a few feet away from the close knit army of sturdy tree trunks. They didn't know what the Master had in mind, but were on the alert, ready to respond to his commands.

Richard, looking extremely pale and exhausted after the swift ride from York's vicinity, was buoyed by the seemingly peacefulness of the forest. He began to say as much, but Shadiz threw him a warning glance.

Shadiz's low-pitched, birdlike whistle brought the Romany among his men to him on foot. He was gesturing for them to scout ahead when a soft breeze emanated from out of the forest. Rustling leaves on bending boughs sounded akin to heralds.

Flanking their leader, Richard and Benjamin both became wary when he held the Romany back with a raised hand. Their tribal instincts heightened, the Romany followed the line of his scrutiny into the dark maze of trees. Richard and Benjamin followed suit. The body of men behind them closed ranks, their hands shifting to their weapons.

The tense pause ended with the appearance of a figure so strange it piqued curiosity edged by superstition rather then an upsurge of aggression.

Nevertheless, oak and elm through which the man emerged seemed to bow down towards him in a protective manner. The huge, brown boar accompanying him dog-like remained slightly in front of him, long wicked tusks aimed at the men and their nervous horses.

"Garan?" muttered Shadiz.

He dismounted, and in a few rapid strides reached where the old man had come to a calm halt.

Benjamin looked questioningly at Richard. He shrugged and shook his head. Yet the incredibly thin, tall man stirred a vague memory, Richard could not quite grasp. His hair and beard were long and snowy white. He wore a robe of pastel green. The staff he was leaning upon was almost as tall as him. In mute company with the Master's men, Richard and Benjamin were struck by his aura of mystique. It had raised the hairs on the backs of their necks.

"D' y' know where she is?" Shadiz demanded without preamble.

Garan's responded with a regretful smile. "I have no reason to offer an explanation."

The countless years had not bowed the willowy slender Druid. Yet tall as he was, Shadiz stood head and shoulders taller and far more muscular, intimidating in his concern for Catherine.

"What y' doin' 'ere?" he snapped.

Garan met the cold, piercing black eyes, his own emerald gaze serene. He sighed a little at the younger man's manner, but fully understood the reason for such harshness. He recognised barely contained desperation.

Richard and Benjamin dismounted and approached their leader, careful to keep their distance from the watchful boar's gleaming white tusks.

"Who is he?" asked Richard, scrutinising the peculiar stranger. Still trying to grasp an evasive familiarity.

Shadiz's attention remained on Garan.

"I foretold of an attack descending on the dwelling of bygone years."

"The Lodge?" queried Richard, scowling.

"Your menfolk believed my utterances through the women's knowledge of me," Garan went on, after Shadiz had silenced Richard with an impervious gesture. "Thus they dispatched the women hence. Small beats of time followed before the hoards descended." Garan shook his head in dismay. "Bark and branch could not stem their onslaught."

"The Lodge is under attack?" exclaimed Richard. "By whom?"

Shadiz rounded on him. "Who the 'ell d' y' reckon?" Answering his own savage observation, he added, "Y'r bleedin' lot, o' course."

"Your menfolk took to the dwelling, snatching at defence," said Garan, bringing Shadiz's dangerously glittering glare back to himself. "Mistress Time and echoing stones give solace to lives fighting doom." Then he stated cryptically, "With fortune, others come to bring aid."

"Probably the men of the moors, the women's families. All are loyal to you, sir," pointed out Benjamin. "But they are no match for…" he broke off, giving Richard an uneasy glance.

"*My lot*, you mean," Richard growled, bitterly. He spoke to Shadiz, though his half-brother seemed absorbed in scanning the forest. "This is none of my doing. You have to believe me."

Shadiz's only reaction was to signal his men to dismount. He ordered them to tether the lathered horses. They had got the gist of what had happened in their absence.

"'ow many, d' y' reckon?" Shadiz suddenly demanded of Richard.

"I tell you, I don't know," protested his half-brother.

"Don't fuck wi' me," growled Shadiz.

Seething with resentment, Richard snapped back, "A good half of Fylingdales men-at-arms, I suppose. And…."

Striding into the forest, Shadiz glared at Richard, keeping pace with him. "And? Dammit!"

"I heard, there's a large band of French at Fylingdales. Some mercenaries. Others from mother's family estates." Richard shrugged. "Perhaps, Francois has mobilised them." Fiercely, he continued, "I just don't know!"

"Or just ain't wantin' t' bloody spew what y'r dear uncle's about," rasped Shadiz, moving purposefully forward.

Gritting his teeth against pent up fury, and a need to cough, Richard almost ran into Shadiz. His half-brother had stopped, catching hold of Garan's lean arm and pulling him to a halt. "Y' 'urt?"

The Druid glanced down at the bloodstains down the left side of his green robe. "Oh, no. Not I," he explained. " Mya took exception to one of the hoards' ground creepers."

Having become close to the boar because of Shadiz's uncharacteristic pause, both Richard and Benjamin stepped back a pace.

Garan chuckled. The boar made a noise in the back of its throat that sounded remarkably like a humorous response.

As the men set off again, while Shadiz was quietly dispatching his Romany mulesko dud, Garan suggested, "Let Mya guide thy brethren."

To everyone's surprise, Shadiz agreed, knowing far more about both the boar and Garan's mysterious capabilities. Immediately, the Romany will-o-the-wisp scouts disappear into the forest with the huge creature.

Though they were a large group lacking the clandestine drift of the Romany, the Master's men knew from the experience they had gained from serving him how to move towards a target with stealth. They had believed themselves to be familiar with Stillingfleet Forest, having lived within its depth for well over a year, but they soon became confused by the strange old man's guidance. They became totally reliant upon his unerring lead between ash and oak, larch and beech. The trees seemed to bend away from their furtive passing while their branches appeared to sway around them concealing their advance. Within a remarkably short time the broad clearing in which the Lodge was situated came into view. The dilapidated roof, its slanting chimneys and the large grey stones of the upper storey appeared untouched. But as they drew closer to the high, irregular enclosing wall smothered in thick ivy, the clash of arms could be heard in the courtyard.

Concealed in the expectant stillness of the forest, Shadiz deployed his men at strategic points for when they entered the courtyard to the front of the Lodge, in order to take as much advantage as possible of their arrival. He was about to gesture for them to advance when one of his Romany scouts appeared at his elbow, delaying the grim onslaught.

Richard, ready with his long bow, Benjamin and Danny on the alert with their respective band of fighters, all keen for the order to attack, saw a rare expression flicker over their leader's dark, scarred features.

Shadiz rose from crouching in the abundant ferns. What he said to the young Romany was inaudible, but seconds later, as the wiry, dark-skinned youth swiftly made his way around them, the men received the warning to engage only those wearing the insignia of Fylingdales Hall.

Garan stood to one side, having been reunited with Mya, while the men poured into the fierce battle taking place in the courtyard. The foliage around the low, slanting arched entrance swayed downwards, concealing the Druid as he peered into the heart of the conflict. He aimed his tall staff at the stinging nettles and the ivy's thick snakelike vines around the edges of the courtyard, seeking to impede those who had brought malice into Stillingfleet.

At first, the newcomers to the fighting were briefly caught off guard by the sight of familiar faces they had not expected to encounter among the more cosmopolitan ones. Wearing confident grins, they turned away from energetic colleagues who had returned to Yorkshire and sought those they had been commanded to engage.

"Nice of you to join us, brother," Nick Condor tossed in Shadiz's direction, while dealing with a couple of vicious opponents. "What kept you?"

"Some other bastard's fight," rasped Shadiz, wielding the broadsword and the scimitar with devastating affect.

It was clear the attackers from Fylingdales Hall, including the

French who had arrive in Yorkshire after the unsuccessful raid on Shannlarrey, had arrived in Stillingfleet Forest expecting to easily defeat the Master's men guarding the Lodge.

What they had not expected was to suddenly find themselves confronted by the same blood-thirsty, multi-national force that had driven them from the chateau. The brutal newcomers had added to the violent mixture by unlocking those infuriated followers of the Master who had taken refuge in the Lodge. Then, shortly afterwards, the Master himself and the bulk of his men had joined the fray.

If that wasn't enough. Henry Potter withdrew those Fylingdales men loyal to him, holding them with no effort to one side of the courtyard.

Though Potter remained expressionless, his men, bearing bloody momentous of combat, showed little sympathy on their flushed, sweat-bathed faces for their fellow Fylingdales retainers who had fallen in whole-heartedly with the swaggering Frenchmen. Indeed, they would have been loud in their vengeful glee if Potter had not silenced them when the remaining, thoroughly trounced French and English were forced to surrender.

A heavy breathing pause followed the ragged cessation of hostilities. The cobbles were slick with blood. Men lay dead, dying or seriously wounded. Though there had been a few notable wounds inflicted on the defenders, the majority strewn about the courtyard were French or the Englishmen who had backed them to their own misfortune.

The prisoners were rounded up and roughhoused towards the area where Henry Potter stood with his followers. He kept them distinct from the small, mixed group of English and French.

Reflecting the serious nature for their reunion, the Master's men greeted in a subdued manner those their leader had left on Formentera to guard Catherine. Meanwhile, the corsairs who had accompanied Condor were taking in their landlocked surroundings.

Junno ploughed through the men to get to where Shadiz was standing with Condor. The two Romany cousins conversed in their language until Nick Condor called a frustrated halt.

"Hey, will you two stop jabbering like two demented banshees. Well, I suppose they be demented. Anyway, that's beside the point. Sweet Jesus, y' got me at it now." He took a decisive breath. "What the hell you on about?"

Junno's renowned good-nature and patience had taken a considerable battering in the past couple of weeks. There was an angry, impatient note in his rumbling deep voice. "I was explainin' 'ow that bitch Bianca an' that little prat, Keeble must o' drugged us so them bastards they bribed could grab Rauni an' sail away wi' 'er, an the friggin' dwarf! When we were fit enough t' realise what bastards'd done, we went after 'em in…galley…galleon…summat like that."

"Galleass," put in Condor. He took up the narrative. "Nasr immediately set sail with Junno, his family and y'r men. And managed to overhaul me in the Rebecca I was sailing to Marseille to take the Persian to Philippe at Shannlarrey. I'd got word he was arranging the Persian's journey to his original destination, the French court."

At which point Prince Ardashir, the Vizier of Persia who Nick Condor had weigh laid and had hope to hold for ransom until Shadiz had ordered his release, appeared leading a couple of the Master's men who had been injured when the Lodge had been first attacked.

The dignified Vizier salaamed to Shadiz. "There was dire need for the voyage to Yorkshire. We sailed thus with the knowledge your wife had been abducted by the small traitor to offer to your enemies," he explained with regret.

"Junno led us 'ere," went on Condor. "We arrived t' find your men bottled up in that ruin an' o' whole herd o' buggers swarming about the place." He looked around, commenting ironically, "Nice place you've 'ere, brother."

Throughout the combined explanations, Shadiz had paced the blood-stained cobbles, fists balled at his sides.

He caught sight of a ragged, bloody heap close to the Lodge. Walking over to it, he crouched down, and for a couple of moments, head bent, lay a gentle hand on the dead mastiff. At least the brute was safely tethered with the other horses.

Thus far, having opened the floodgates on the knowledge something was terribly wrong, his one objective had been to return, to Stillingfleet Forest and the Lodge. Now that the mystical moonstone warning had gained credence in the most horrendous way rage erupted and was given free rein. It became a living entity within him, consuming him, demanding the worse possible vengeance. He was blind to everything, to everyone. Whatever the sacrifice, he would walk through fire to retrieve his soul and slaughter without mercy those who had stolen her from him.

He stood upright. The lethal, sinister expression on his barbarous features gave the toughest warriors in the courtyard a few qualms. His every wide stride was filled with a deadly intention for revenge as he started to leave the courtyard.

"Hey!" Nick Condor called out from the other side of the crowded courtyard. He dashed after Shadiz.

For a big man, Junno moved quickly, desperate to overtake his cousin.

But Shadiz was going nowhere. Thick vines had suddenly sprouted up beneath the lop-sided entrance, blocking his passage into the forest.

Their attention fixed upon Shadiz, the men rooted to the old, chipped cobbles missed the recognition that passed between the Persian and the Druid.

Cursing Garan, Shadiz was about to lash out at the twisted vines with his broad sword when Junno reached him. The big man, bald head and wide shoulders taller than his cousin, seized hold of the front of Shadiz's leather jerkin and slammed him up against the nearest part of the ivy covered wall enclosing the courtyard. The violent action knocked the raging breath out of Shadiz and shook his already bruised ribs. He lost his grip on the sword, but still maintained a fierce struggle, forcing Junno to exert even more detaining pressure.

Condor rushed up to the two Romany cousins. "Sweet Jesus. Will you calm down, brother."

For once, Junno was glad of the Irishman's presence. Yet whatever either man said did not seem to penetrate Shadiz's fury.

"Bastards want me so bleedin' much. They can bloody well

330

tak' me. So long as they release Kore," he rasped between gritted teeth.

Condor tried brutal persuasion. "There's no way them scheming buggers at Fylingdales are going to release Catherine, even if you give yourself up to 'em. We need y' t' start thinking wi' y'r head and not y'r arse!"

"'e's talkin' sense," put in Junno, straining to hold Shadiz against the wall. "Y' just can't deliver y'rsen an' expect Lynette and that bitch t' not keep usin' Rauni against y'."

"An' just think what they could do to her, to bring you down," pointed out Condor, grimly.

Though Shadiz became less agitated, he remained unpredictably tense within Junno's unrelenting grasp. "So, what d' y' suggest? We attack Fylingdales, an' see bastards use Kore as a shield. D' y' want that t' 'appen, for fuck's sake!"

All of the Master's men wherever they hailed from, the wounded and the prisoners spread around the courtyard remained motionless, watching what was transpiring between the three men.

Standing among them, Henry Potter came to a decision. He stepped forward, and immediately caught Danny Murphy's critical attention.

"There is a way to invade Fylingdales without putting Catherine at risk," Potter said into the brittle silence. He had spent a lot of time with her, and was also keen to see she came to no harm. Besides, his disillusionment with the people at Fylingdales Hall meant he was more than willing to help set her free.

Murphy stepped closer to him with a sharp warning. It was Richard, who defended Potter, the man he had known since childhood and respected.

"Let him speak," he urged, moving closer to Potter.

Murphy shadowed Potter and Richard as they walked across the courtyard and halted where Junno and Nick Condor stood warily close to Shadiz after the big man had reluctantly released him.

"Well?" demanded the Irishman.

Henry Potter met Shadiz's piercing glare with an unwavering resolve to follow his conscience. "I volunteered to lead the assault

331

in Stillingfleet Forest with the intention of keeping the French in some kind of check. You'll no doubt know they're the ones who stormed your chateau in France. They came to Yorkshire to lick their wounds and to reinforce Lynette's men-at-arms. Nowadays a goodly count of the men at Fylingdales follow my lead. They are sick to the back teeth of the French and their arsenal of ways. Also Lynette's rogue manner.

"He has no way of knowing what happened here. No one has escaped to inform him. So, it's possible to disguise your men in the gear of the prisoners, and that way penetrate the Hall without causing suspicion." Potter hesitated for a moment before continuing to outline his scheme. "If you arrived as a prisoner it would hold Lynette's attention. Meanwhile, your men could take over the Hall."

After Henry Potter had finished speaking, Shadiz remained ominously silent.

Condor ran a hand through his curly brown hair and rubbed at his unshaven jaw. "D' y' know. It be a grand plan, brother," he commented, hopefully.

Junno slowly nodded, regarding Potter approvingly.

"Why should I trust y'?" Shadiz demanded, in his customary whispery tone.

He now had himself well in hand. Yet everyone before the battered façade of the ancient Lodge understood his icy, intimidating manner concealed a volatile rage.

Potter faced him with apparent composure. "I've no liking for many of your ways. But I fear for Catherine. Four of my most trusted men are presently guarding her…against those at the Hall. I fear for what Lynette and Lady Hellena might inflict upon her to get back at you. I've spent time with her. She is a remarkable young woman, often wise beyond her years. As God is my witness I want nothing to befall her."

An emotion bled through Shadiz's black scrutinising glare. "So be it," he murmured, eventually, after taking Potter's measure for himself.

While the men began to strip the doublets bearing the insignia of Fylingdales from the prisoners and some of the less seriously

332

wounded, Richard walked up to were Shadiz was speaking to Junno and Condor.

"They'll be expecting me to accompany you," he pointed out.

"The conquerin' 'ero," retaliated Shadiz, with pure malice.

"I did not mean it like that!" rasped Richard.

"No doubt it's what y' been prayin' for, *little brother*," Shadiz snapped, walking away.

"Go to hell," Richard flung at his half-brother's back.

Condor started to follow Shadiz. "He's already there, sunshine," he remarked to Richard in passing.

CHAPTER FIFTEEN

Crystal Prophecy

Someone was crying. Despair. Panic. Foreboding, cold as winter's cruel grip upon the earth. Roiling emotions blighted Catherine's fitful slumber.

She jerked awake to discover tears were streaming down her face. Her throat felt tight and aching, as if she had been trying desperately to gain the attention of someone.

The jet pendant she constantly wore was branding her damp skin and searing her very essence.

Catherine finally understood what she had glimpsed in the Crystal Pool the Druid, Garan, had taken her to in Stillingfleet Forest. Why, through elusive dreams, more like nightmares, the prophetic warning had eluded her…because she had not been able to face the devastating truth.

That crystal prophecy was about to fulfil the inescapable demand of fate.

Without a shadow of a doubt, she knew Shadiz was about to give himself up to the revenge those at Fylingdales Hall had craved for years.

Locked within the distance that separated them, she experienced the glutinous thickness of his rage, and sensed his implacable determination to seek her safety, at the expense of his own.

Catherine sat up in the elaborate four poster bed. Tormented by the triangular web of guilt, grief and helplessness, she rocked back and forward. Covering her red, overflowing eyes, she could not bare to look at her grand surroundings. Her silk prison.

She detested herself for what she had brought upon Shadiz. She wished with her heart and soul that his first sight of her at a young age had not instigated an emotion which had ultimately ensnared him in a death trap. She would far rather he hated her.

A gentle touch on her arm made Catherine jump and cry out.

"Y' be alright, luv," soothed a concerned voice.

Catherine dropped her hands from her eyes down to her mouth, trying to stifle a shuddering sob. She glimpsed the middle-aged maid through a watery haze.

"Ee, luv," said Mattie, sadly.

"He's coming," Catherine whispered, brokenly.

Motherly sympathy shone in Mattie's round, fleshy features. The bed dipped beneath her considerable weight as sat down and gathered Catherine into her thick, comforting arms.

Henry Potter visited her whenever he was not occupied with his duties, but it was Mattie Taylor who had become her constant companion. Catherine had soon discovered the down-to-earth, homely maid had no liking for the way life at the Hall had changed, certainly not for the better she repeated often.

There was a discreet knock on the door of the spacious, richly furnished chamber. The leader of the men Potter had put in place to guard her opened the door halfway. The tough-looking, scarred former trooper, like his companions in the long corridor, and many others at the hall, was unswervingly loyal to Potter.

"Everythin' well in 'er?" he asked, gruffly, scrutinising the women.

Mattie leaned further into Catherine, shielding her with her ample body. "It be not too bad, Alex. Lady's just a might upset."

They exchanged a knowing look.

"Dwarf wanted in again a bit ago," he muttered.

Catherine reared up against Mattie. "I don't want Keeble anywhere near!" she exclaimed.

Alex Firth took in Catherine's white, tearstained face. "Tis fine, Lady. I sent the little fu…flamer on his way wi' a flea in 'is ear," he reassured, grimly. He looked at Mattie. "Call if y' need us for owt," he told her, before quietly closing the door behind him.

"Never fear, me luv," Mattie murmured, combing a gentle hand through Catherine's long, tangled her. "Little runt won't get passed Alex, that's nailed on." Her round face reflected disgust.

"Did y' see little sod when 'e brung y' 'ere first off wi' that riff-raff eager for their reward. Proud as punch 'e be! Swore 'e'd done it t' protect y' from Gypsy. Bah! I don't reckon that fella's 'alf as bad as 'em below make out. An' I'm not only one reckons so."

Catherine took a deep breath, gritted her teeth and tried hard to stem the flow of tears, the result of being unable to put a stop to Shadiz's certain approach. She slipped off the bed. Fully clothed, she had laid down, exhausted by sleepless night and her frustrated pacing. To no avail. Her restless slumber had been invaded yet again...by the most horrendous images first seen in the Crystal Pool, and thereafter shunned.

Unable to remain still, she roamed the chamber. Frustration was giving way to anger, at herself, the world in general, but mostly at Shadiz for surrendering himself to Fylingdales's malice.

She was glad of Mattie's sympathetic presence. The small, plump woman with a large heart had taken over from Keeble and the silly girl appointed as her maid. Mattie had ousted both of them, standing up in a coaxing manner to Lady Hellena.

"There's them 'ere at 'all, me luv," Mattie said, conspiratorially, "who are dead set against that Frenchie, Lynette. An' loads detest them 'e's seen fit t' bring over 'ere, wi' their vicious ways. Damn Frenchies. If y'll excuse me French." She giggled at her own joke. Becoming serious, trying to reassure, she went on, "Henry holds sway over most o' lads. 'e'll see no 'arm come t' y'."

"He is coming," stated Catherine, suddenly halting in mid-chamber.

"Who, me luv? Henry?" queried Mattie. "He'll be back soon enough." Though all of them had been careful not to mention in front of Catherine where Henry Potter had gone, Mattie felt sure she was somehow aware of his mission.

"Not Henry." Catherine's hands were buried in the skirt of her gown, her knuckles stark white. "He's coming because of me."

CHAPTER SIXTEEN

I Remember, I Remember, The House Where I Was Born

The substantial company of riders urged their mounts up the steep slope out of Longdrop Hollow, away from the tall hedgerow on one side and the coppice on the other, both looming shadows in the late evening. It was where several weeks previously Francois Lynette had been prevented from abducting Catherine. The memory rested uneasily on those horsemen who had been involved in the rescue.

On this occasion there was a need for far more duplicity than simply being concealed in the obliging landscape.

Due to Keeble's traitorous action, assisted by Bianca, Nick Condor's mistress, on the island of Formentera, the men were now having to extract Catherine from Lynette's grasp within Fylingdales Hall.

Cresting the summit of Longdrop, Shadiz gave the pre-arranged signal. Whereupon, Condor and those corsairs of strikingly foreign appearance, accompanied by two Romany guides, Junno and the rest of the Romany, Benjamin and Danny Murphy with the bulk of the Master's men peeled off in different directions in preparation to converge on Fylingdales Hall. They carried with them a united resolve to make their mission succeed. The alternative would be at the expense of their leader's life.

The remaining horsemen - Potter's men along with several of the Master's men and a few European corsairs - continued to make an impressive company. All wore the insignia of the Hall on their chests with the exception of Shadiz and Richard.

It had taken nerves of steel to await the evening, in order to benefit from the late July dusk their intended stealth required. One advantage of the enforced wait had been the Master's men could rest, as best their anticipation would allow, after the mad gallop from York's vicinity to the Lodge. Likewise, after Nick Condor and his corsairs, along with Junno and the Romany and several of the Master's men had landed at Whitby, they had rode hard to the Lodge and then become embroiled in fierce fighting with the men-at-arms sent by Lynette. They too had rested in Stillingfleet Forest. The wait had given Henry Potter and his followers time to demonstrate their unwavering support for the forthcoming endeavour.

Many of the men taking their ease within the courtyard had watched Shadiz carry the bloody, untidy bundle out into the forest, some not understanding his reason for doing so. Soon afterwards, Junno had followed, afraid of what his cousin might do in spite of the planned mission to Fylingdales Hall to rescue Catherine. The big man had been joined by Garan and the Persian. The three men waited out the time offering quiet patience to grinding impatience, and the sack cloth and ashes of penitence.

Eventually, thankfully, the time had come to confront Fylingdales Hall.

Flanked by Henry Potter and Richard, Shadiz led the way up the steep rise of Massone's Hag. At its summit, the whispering presence of the North Sea heralded the arc of Mercy Cove, barely visible at their backs. Veiled by the deepening dusk, parkland carved out of the rugged moorland stretched before them. Granite boulders alongside their path were earthbound, shadowy sentinels of ancient times.

Their kin had been harvested from the moors, and tamed by the stonemason's chisel into smooth, grey slabs that had united to create Fylingdales Hall. Regimented, tall windows along the imposing façade resembled the many bright eyes of a mythical beast awaiting their arrival .

Riding beneath the murder holes in the lofty, arching entrance of Guy's Keep, Richard looked sideward at his half-brother, taking advantage of the flaming torches wedged into several sconces. He wondered what lay behind Shadiz's expressionless features. When Shadiz briefly met his quizzical gaze, the frozen gleam in his black eyes sent an unpleasant jolt through Richard's churning guts.

The clattered of hooves disturbed the deceptive peace within the outer courtyard. After the men had dismounted, servants come forward to lead the horses away towards the vast stables running the length of the broad courtyard. Henry Potter gestured for two of his men to lead the newcomers to the Hall away in an effort to disguise their identity and their true intentions. It was also imperative Keeble was not given the opportunity to recognise those who had once looked upon him as a friend.

Potter was prepared to silence the gloating of the men stood around, all heavily armed. He soon realised it was the sheer impact of Shadiz's presence that was mitigating their response to his apparent defeat. Like Richard before him, Potter was curious about Shadiz's reaction to being bait in a hopefully successful trap. His surreptitious glance left him no wiser.

It was left to those loyal to Henry Potter to escort him, Shadiz and Richard through the wrought iron gateway into the Quadrangle. Most of its splendour was blanketed by evening's soft darkness. More men-at-arms, their attention centred on Shadiz, their smugness surfacing cautiously, watched his silent progress past a three-tiered fountain. Its dancing water was illuminated by the light coming from the four tall windows at either side of a regal portico entrance. The heavy oak doors were opened by servants shadowed by guards.

Shadiz entered the ancestral Hall, fully armed. The men surrounding him deferred automatically to his purposeful strides across the tiled greeting hall. He ignored the marble busts of Roman and Greek scholars, set on tall fluted plinths, and the place, in his youth, where he had lain his father following his death in Tom Wright's cottage. Upon his approach, the tall carved doors to the right of the grand, horseshoe staircase opened in anticipation of his entry into the great hall.

The last time Richard had entered, a virtual prisoner escorting his disapproving mother, it had been occupied by members of the local gentry, parliamentary commanders and his uncle's senior officers, all enjoying Fylingdales's lavish hospitality.

Things were now very different.

The candlelight was more subdued. An expectant hush had

339

settled on the impressive company of men gathered between the tapestry-hung, oak-panelled walls, beneath the vaulted ceiling.

With Richard and Henry Potter at his heels and the rest of Potter's men keeping pace behind them, Shadiz made his way down the length of the great hall. Normally his charismatic influence was simply a natural part of his striking persona. What Richard experienced, along with everyone else present, was a deliberate exerting of that bewitching mastery.

In a similar manner to the English and French men-at-arms he had encountered in the courtyards, those present in the great hall had been ready to relish Shadiz's enforced appearance at the Hall, believing their fellow countrymen to have been successful in their mission to attack his headquarters in Stillingfleet Forest. Yet, like everyone else who had witnessed his arrive, they simply kept remarkably quiet and watched him pass by.

Eventually, without haste and lacking emotion, Shadiz came to a potent halt before the raised dais.

He surveyed the two people occupying the elaborate tall-back chairs. Also the small man standing between them. Having halted beside his half-brother, Richard glimpsed the flat calm holding within its jet blackness a sinister promise. Swallowing convulsively, he followed Shadiz's unwavering gaze upwards to his mother and uncle. Keeble he felt like spitting at.

Though he had long struggled for this moment, wanting his own retribution for his sister's murder, Richard was shaken by his satisfaction at the response of his family to Shadiz.

The last time, the only other time, Lynette had encountered Shadiz, had been when the other man was far from well, having just overcome a poisoned chalice. Lady Hellena had attended Tom Wright's funeral when Catherine had been at Shadiz's side. Brother and sister had got their wish to have him brought to Fylingdales Hall, only now he was at full strength and without restrictions. Their involuntary reaction seeped through their shared triumph.

Lynette lounged in his customary elegant attire. His gracious manner impeccable, the Frenchman's handsome face portrayed a smile. It failed to reach his wary blue eyes. While her brother studiously maintained his relaxed posture, Lady Hellena had sat forward in her regal seat. Her small hands were clasped in her lap, her knuckles stark-white against the abiding blackness of her gown. Breathing overly fast, she watched Shadiz's with a keen, narrowed glare, serrated by hateful caution.

The tense, silent stillness came to an end when Shadiz drew the broadsword slung across his back. Immediately there was the grind of swords throughout the main hall. An astute watcher would have realised Potter and his men had drawn their weapons in a protective manner to reply to the upsurge of aggression.

Shadiz raised a commanding hand. Incredibly, not only Potter and his men but all of those present ceased any hostile movement. Only belatedly did his men around the hall look in Lynette's direction, with blinking contrition. Given little choice, so as not to appear churlish, Lynette briefly inclined his golden head.

Shadiz lay the broadsword at his feet. Next, he drew the scimitar at his hip and placed it beside his other much heavier weapon.

Lynette was beginning to look pleased with himself. The two men continued to maintain eye contact as Shadiz withdrew the dagger from within his sleeve, the one he had used to kill Lynette's favourite, Gerald Carey. Lynette responded to Shadiz's brutal mockery with a smug smile.

In the next instance, instead of the dagger joining the rest of the discarded weapons on the parquet floor, it flew to its target intensely fast, with deadly accuracy.

Keeble had only a brief moment to express surprise, it wiped the smile off his large ugly face. He jerked backwards and then toppled forwards between the tall-back chairs, the dagger protruding from his heart.

Like a stupefying wind rustling the waves of an agitated sea, the Fylingdales retainers closed about Henry Potter's men, while they at the same time closed about Richard and, to a cautious extent, Shadiz, maintaining a deceptive cloak.

Preoccupied with each other, the two leaders showed no interest in the emotions of lesser men.

Shadiz spoke for the first time, his whispery voice a rasp of blood-chilling ice. "Where's my wife?"

Just as startled as everyone else, but recovering quickly because of his approval of his half-brother's action, Richard's primary concern was for Catherine. "Mother?"

Lady Hellena had grown pale at witnessing Keeble's sudden death at such close quarters. His dying blood had splashed her gown. Appearing determined to retain her composure, she motioned away with an impatient wave of her hand the concern of her women stood to one side of the dais. She spared her son a withering glance before once more fixating on Shadiz.

"Have the girl brought here," Lady Hellena snapped.

Lynette's sapphire outrage surged against the unequivocal demand in Shadiz's cruel, slanted eyes.

"You will get no further with the gutter-snipe until you do," pointed out Lady Hellena, tersely.

Answering Lynette's irate gesture, a trembling page scurried to the door of an ante chamber.

After the torment of being detained, Catherine found no relief upon being finally allowed into the great hall. Mattie walked beside her, quietly supporting her as she had throughout her captivity at Fylingdales Hall. Walking in a semi-circle around the middle-aged maid and Catherine were the four men who had proved themselves worthy of Henry Potter's trust.

Catherine was inwardly quaking with a mixture of anger and rampant apprehension. Her mouth was dry and her hands cold. Yet she held her head high. Her long fair-white hair rested upon her slender, straight back. She moved with grace in a borrowed cerise gown. Outwardly, her young, delicate face reflected serenity.

Approaching the dais, Catherine was only vaguely aware of the numerous people gathered in the main hall. The one man she wanted to see - only not at Fylingdales Hall - stood head and shoulders above the rest.

Held fast by Shadiz's burning jet gaze, her heart beat faster as she drew near to him. It took her a couple of moments before properly taking in his rough appearance. There was a mosaic of purple-red bruises on his dark face and around his neck beneath his unshaven jaw. As usual, his long, midnight black hair was wild over his shoulders and down his back. His shirt beneath his battered leather jerkin looked as if it had been ripped open, and his breeches and boots were dust-stained.

He turned fully to her as she halted a couple of paces away from him. Catherine curtsied deeply to him.

Looking down at her, towering over her, his barbarous, scarred face creased into a loving smile. Upon putting her hands in his outstretched ones, he raised her up and gathered her to him. For a moment he looked past her and gave the woman and the men who had arrived in the hall with her, a brief nod of acknowledgement.

Despite her resolve, Catherine clung to Shadiz as he held her as if he would never let her go again..

"I love you, Kore," he murmured for her ears only.

She drew back slightly to look up at him. "*Now* you inform me!" she pointed out, quietly.

His smile was haunted. "I let it slip in a few ways."

"Only I was too naïve to realise." She went on to chastise him in a tense whisper, "You should never have come here for me."

He bent close to her again, brushing her cheek with a tender kiss. Then, before straightening, softer than a whisper, he quoted, "*It's allus good when a man 'as two irons in the fire.*"

His expression gave nothing away, but his glowing black eyes reassured her. While Catherine grasped the significance of his words, he secured her beneath his shoulder.

"As you can see, Catherine is quite unharmed. Cherished even. Being so young," drawled Francois Lynette, pointedly, sitting forward in his seat. "She has simply been awaiting your arrival, mon ami."

Looking up at the Frenchman, Catherine caught sight of Keeble's inert body sprawled in a pool of blood between the two grand chairs upon the dais. She briefly mourned the pleasant times she had spent with him, acknowledging his consideration. Nevertheless, she felt no remorse for the passing of someone who had betrayed Shadiz's rare trust.

The gentle emotions Shadiz had shown Catherine were replaced by a sparking hostility upon him turning back to Lynette.

Instead of addressing the Frenchman, Shadiz spoke to Richard. "Tak Kore an' y'sen out o' 'ere."

"No," objected Richard and Catherine in unison.

Lynette stiffened. "You presume far too much, gypsy." he objected, with a sneer.

The ornate doors of the main hall were suddenly flung open, interrupting Shadiz harsh response. Nick Condor appeared through them, a large company of fighting men at his back. "Well, that were easy," he commented, brightly.

A fleeting pause filled with mute bewilderment accompanied his swaggering walk. The English and French warriors failed initially to recognise an enemy, believing themselves safe in Fylingdales's superiority. It was only when Junno and the Romany, Benjamin and a substantial group of the Master's men rushed into the hall hard on the heels of the Irishman and his pack of corsairs that Lynette's retainers were galvanised into action.

Shadiz thrust Catherine behind him, angling her away from the dais. At the same time, he hooked his scimitar with his boot and flicked it up into his grasp.

Henry Potter gave Francois Lynette a look, and then, turning his back on his former leader, spread his men around in defensive positions against those they had come to consider as untrustworthy and dangerous in Lynette's employment.

Richard swung his long bow off his back where it had remained since no one had challenged him. He chose his targets repressing his fury that would only have hinder his shots, and took down several of the French mercenaries his uncle had seen fit to bring to Yorkshire. His accurate aim sought those of the English men-at-arms who had taken particular delight in taunting him when he had been detained earlier in the year by Lynette after escorting his mother to Fylingdales Hall following her appearance at Tom Wright's funeral.

The battle for possession of the Hall was viciously contested. Both sides gave no quarter, well aware of the consequences of defeat. If a man went down he rarely got back up again.

A substantial force of Lynette's men-at-arms had gathered in the hall, eager to see Shadiz humbled before their leader. Finding themselves instead fighting for their lives, they believed their strenuous defence would soon benefit from reinforcements. The brutal truth began to dawn on them as their numbers decrease. Those men who had witnessed Shadiz's arrival in the courtyards had been subdued by his furtive packs that had materialised soon after their leader had disappeared into the Hall, and were presently in no condition to help anyone.

The outcome of the retaliatory scheme devised in Stillingfleet Forest brought about a conclusion which soon spread like the toll of a death knell across the hall for the hard-pressed warriors of Fylingdales. Those who had not succumb to the violent episode which had reverberated around the elegant walls and pitched upwards to the lofty vaulted ceiling were driven out by sword point. The dead and wounded were unceremoniously dragged out.

"Well, as I was saying," announced Condor, approaching Shadiz. "That were easy."

Shadiz had joined the fight only when the combatants had threatened Catherine, leaving her in Junno's safekeeping, which had also included Mattie.

Coming to a halt beside Shadiz, the Irishman grinned at Catherine. She couldn't help replying in kind to the infectious greeting.

"Y' were right, brother," he said, swiping at the sweat on his brow with his sleeve. "They were mostly all in here peering at you. *The legendry Master.*"

Becoming serious, he switched back to Catherine. "You be well?"

"Yes, thank you," she reassured. "I am now," she added, glancing at Shadiz.

"I'm sorry for what happened," Condor said, including both Catherine and Shadiz in his apology.

Catherine smiled and touched Condor's arm. "It was none of your doing."

"Perhaps," he muttered, shrugging. He looked up at Shadiz. "I'll deal wi' it."

Shadiz gave him a curt nod. "Y'd better," he warned.

Turning back to Catherine and Richard, he reiterated his demand that they leave the hall. Once again both of them unanimously objected.

Condor gave a long suffering sigh. "Y' know," he said, winking at Catherine. "I reckon they've earned right to stay."

"I'm not leaving you," she said, with absolute conviction beneath Shadiz's jet glare. Whatever was going to happen, she needed to remain at his side.

"Is that so," he retorted.

"Nor am I," pointed out Richard.

Shadiz swore. Nevertheless he once again drew Catherine under his shoulder, and briefly held her so tightly she thought her ribs were going to bend. At the same time as he brushed a kiss over the top of her head, he looked towards Junno and indicted Catherine with an imperceptible nod.

Once again the big man, Catherine's appointed protector ever since she had first arrived at the Lodge, moved up to stand close behind her. She half-turned, placing a hand on his mighty chest, and smiled lovingly up at him. She mouthed the words Lucinda and Peter. He covered her hand with his huge one and bent slightly to her, answering in a quiet rumble. "Both o' 'em safe wi' Bob an' Laura in Whitby."

Catherine immediately breathed a deep sigh of relief. Throughout her abduction from Formentera and her subsequent imprisonment at Fylingdales Hall, she had fretted over the fate of Junno and his family.

CHAPTER SEVENTEEN

To The Winner, The Spoils

Shadiz moved closer to the dais.

Lynette glanced at his tight-lipped sister, and then got to his feet. He had taken no part in the conflict, choosing instead to watch his advantage slip away into a comprehensive defeat from his tall-backed chair. He stepped lightly down from the dais, to come face to face with Shadiz.

Richard had to give his uncle his due for his composure. He viewed the two men with a jaundice eye. One tall, dark and powerfully-built. The other smaller, lighter and slender. Not for the first time, Richard discerned an affinity between his two relations. Both were dangerous characters in their own distinctive ways with defining auras absent in any of those who were watching them closely from around the great hall.

"You never cease to amaze me, Darkness," murmured Lynette.

Nick Condor nearly choked. "Not another one," he spluttered. He quickly sobered beneath Shadiz's brief glare. He cleared his throat. "Beast's like that," he muttered. Diplomatically brightening, he studied the Frenchman. "So this is the fancy popinjay," he commented. His attention switched to Lady Hellena. "An' the dragon bitch," he went on. He awarded her a courtly, mocking bow that hardened the woman's haughty disgust.

"Y' finished?" snapped Shadiz.

He didn't wait for the Irishman's contrite reply. Turning back to Lynette, he stated. "Y' an' 'er walk out o' my 'all, an' go wherever y' please, just so long as it ain't in England."

A unity of similar opinion wafted through the crowded main hall. Condor was the loudest in his objection.

"That's just downright crazy talk, brother!" he exclaimed. He flung out an arm, indicating Lynette. "Mark my words, bastard'll come after y'."

Lynette had taken a step backwards to avoid being swiped by the Irishman's irate gesture. His delicate eyebrows arched, he queried, "Your hall?"

Only Catherine knew that Shadiz was stating the truth and not just a retaliatory strike. Tense, she understood what was about to break upon Lynette and Lady Hellena, and worryingly Richard. For when Shadiz had visited Formentera he had shown her the evidence of his legitimate ownership of Fylingdales Hall and the Estate. She was also aware he could have gone on to reveal his ownership of the manors and estates bordering Fylingdales.

Shadiz gave a wicked grin. "Reckon y' familiar wi' Isaac the Jew o' York. Well o' course y' are."

There was a small pause. A sardonic challenge and a vague defensive reaction.

Lynette's smile had become somewhat forced. His handsome features had tightened and turned a little pale within the candlelight. "You are mistaken," he responded. "I have no recollection of such a person."

"Really?" Shadiz murmured, ominously. "Well, the sword o' Damocle's just split y' bloody skull."

"To what is the gutter snipe referring?" demanded Lady Hellena, sitting forward, gripping the velvet arms of her seat.

"Nothing of consequence," dismissed Lynette. By way of nullifying his sharpness, he half-turned towards her. "He is simply attempting to goad us."

For the first time Shadiz addressed Lady Hellena directly. "An' 'e's simply tryin' t' stop y' from 'earin' truth. 'ow the 'ell d' y' reckon y' been able t' live way y' done – like y' were still at French court – wi' only revenues o' farms? Cos if you'd taken notice, surplus wealth built up over years were soon depleted, not least by his bloody desire to do y'r biddin' an' bring me down."

"He is talking nonsense!" declared Lynette, fiercely. "He seeks to divide us."

Shadiz continued speaking to Lady Hellena. "'e put up y'r jewels as collateral first off. An' then whatever the 'ell else was

348

worth using to secure yet more loans, until it were 'all he mortgage, and then estate."

Lynette swore in foul French, bringing Shadiz's slit-eyed gaze upon him. The gold lace on his crimson satin doublet vibrated with his fury.

"I bought y'r markers off Isaac, an' owt else y' were in debt t' 'im for," revealed Shadiz, with cold emphasis. "I own the bloody lot. An' you're out on y'r bloody arse." He look back at Lady Hellena. "Y' as well."

Lady Hellena was scathing in her disbelief. "Lies. All lies. Not worth the paper they are written upon."

When Catherine stepped forward, Junno shadowed her, keeping a hand on her shoulder.

"You have to accept that he is telling you the truth of the matter," she said, looking at Lynette and then Lady Hellena.

The older woman dismissed her words with a sneering expression and an irate wave of her hand. "You would say that," she dismissed. "You are just as besotted by the gypsy as he is with you."

Shadiz gave Catherine a lop-sided grin. "At least pair's got summat right."

"No doubt that huge, foreign servant of Isaac has spirited the true missive away," commented Lynette, shrewdly.

Shadiz shrugged. "Isaac made the Nubian leave York afore siege. So y' ain't t' worry legal documents're safe," he acknowledged, mockingly.

Richard moved forward, scowling, his tumbling thoughts plain on his thin face, drained of all colour earned in the battle for Fylingdales. "Just how long have you held his debts?" he fired accusingly at his half-brother. "Owned all of this?" he added, taking in the hall with a sweep of his trembling hand. "You conniving bastard!"

Catherine reached out to restrain Richard. She was afraid of what he might do if he gave full vent to his turbulent feeling. Obviously fearing the same in such a volatile situation in which they were presently involved, Benjamin moved up and stood beside his friend, ready to restrain in a more potent manner.

But it was Shadiz who exerted his authority while gently removing Catherine's hand from Richard's sleeve.

"We'll talk later," he said, having turned to his half-brother.

"Most likely after he has despatched your mother and I," put in Lynette.

Richard started to speak, but broke off, coughing.

Shadiz stepped closer gripping his shoulder.

Eventually, Richard managed hoarsely, "Are you planning to get rid of me?"

Shadiz dropped his hand from Richard's shoulder. "I said, we'll talk later."

Richard's troubled gaze shifted to his mother's stony features, then returned to Shadiz. "Whatever she has practised upon me," he said, a sick feeling in his guts. "You cannot do harm to her. She is my mother."

An ugly light flickered briefly in Shadiz's glance towards Lady Hellena.

CHAPTER EIGHTEEN

The Vision Quest

"Before you send us hither," Francois Lynette began, "to have us dispatched." He responded to Catherine's troubled expression as she looked up at her enigmatic husband. "He will exercise caution in your presence, cheri."

It was possibly the truth, she realised, having no illusions.

"She ain't quite tamed Beast yet," remarked Condor, grinning. "Doubt she ever will." He glanced at Catherine, and shrugged. "Sorry, sweetheart."

"He had no qualms about making an example of your turn-coat, Walter Smithson, in my presence while on board the *Eagle*," she pointed out to Lynette.

"He'd no idea you were on deck," muttered Richard.

Catherine decided not to respomd, aware of Shadiz's dangerous silence.

"Be that as it may," continued Lynette in his soft, accented English. Returning his sapphire-blue gaze to Shadiz, he assumed an apologetic tone, " I must confess to being remiss. Circumstances overtook good manners. We have a surprise for you. Would you allow Potter to go and open the door to the right of the dais." He finished on a malicious note, "As Potter is now your man."

Shadiz inclined his head, trading the Frenchman's deceptively pleasant smile with a hard unreadable expression.

Henry Potter felt the attention of the entire hall fixed on him as he made his way to the door Lynette had indicated. Upon opening it and looking into the small ante chamber, he turned and gave Shadiz a startled glance.

Moments later, Mamma Petra emerged, guided by the young Romany woman who had taken Lucinda's place by her side.

351

Behind her, Catherine heard Junno inhale sharply.

At the same time there was an unanimous gasp from the Romany present.

"What the 'ell is she doin' 'ere? demanded Shadiz, scowling accusingly.

"Oh, have no fear," responded Lynette. "Your grandmother came here of her own volition. In fact, she surprised us by her arrival. But, it has to be said, she is no stranger to us here at Fylingdales Hall. Is that not so, Mamma Petra?"

Ancient and slightly stooped, the Romany woman nevertheless had an air of wilful authority about her. Her withered hands gripped her shawl, black on the black of her simple gown. Deep lines had been etched into her narrow, berry-brown face by long years. Her steady breathing worked the long, grey plaits upon her thin figure. Though her sightless eyes saw nothing, her uncanny instincts located where her youngest grandson stood, wanting answers. They looked difficult to supple.

Lady Hellena had no such qualms.

She rose from her seat and, with her brother's courteous help, stepped down from the dais. Whereupon, age met age in a battle of wills. There were the demands of the highway traversed by nomads as opposed to the gilded finery of aristocratic halls and gardens. Beneath the striking opposites of lives, there existed a similar capability for malevolent deeds.

While Mamma Petra's expression had become contemptuous, Lady Hellena's had become one of sneering satisfaction.

"It was not Keeble who alerted us at the beginning of the year to your fascination with the girl," she began, her sharp gaze switching back and forth between Mamma Petra and Shadiz. "Your grandmother appeared here at Fylingdales. It was during such an unusual visit she explained matters. Through her information we also learned the girl's whereabouts close to Driffield. She maintained that whatever scheme we constructed from her disclosure you would evade us. The girl, well, she simply wanted rid of her, by any means we saw fit."

Catherine felt as if she had just received a vicious punched. She had realised that Mamma Petra was not fond of her throughout the

352

time she had been her pupil. What she could not fathom was why the old Romany woman had taught her how to heal with the herbs if all she had wanted was her death?

Had she been trying to change fate so that the results of her apprenticeship were not required...trying to prevent Shadiz and her from meeting. It was safe to assume he would blame her death on those at Fylingdales.

Junno was standing tense and disbelieving behind her. Catherine's primary concerned was Shadiz's reaction to the astounding revelation. She could sense his disbelief, and his contrasting suspicions. He glanced at her, his expression quizzical, as if she could answer the conundrum.

When he addressed his grandmother in a dangerously soft voice, he did so in a manner Catherine could understand.

"Is old bitch speakin' truth? Did y' come 'ere wantin' Kore dead?"

Mamma Petra appeared defiant. "I didst witness what thy passion wouldst cause thee," she exclaimed, reprovingly. "These few months passed hath shown the sight to give truth. Thee hath suffered because of her."

Her former mentor's harsh words made Catherine cringe. There was the undeniable stab of truth in them. Her nearness to Shadiz had almost driven him over the threshold of death on more than one occasion. All Mamma Petra had been trying to do was utilise her weird foresight to save him from such torment.

Shadiz saw it differently.

His black eyes smouldering, he spoke in a savage whisper. "I trusted y' wi' knowledge o' Kore."

"Thou be desperate for me to giveth health back to the child," Mamma Petra retorted. "Look ye what be cost to thee. Lost thyself in cups and dragged to Scarborough Castle's goal to be caged."

"That's no concern o' y'rs!" rasped Shadiz.

Mamma Petra, demonstrating her weird knack of addressing people through blind eyes, fired her bleak attention at Junno, while he stood in an agony of uncertainty. "I hath given utterance to how many times he be almost lost to thee? Fire raged at him in a friendless port over the Northern Sea. Then one of its deep pools didst close about him. After he hath felt her touch, he lost himself in cups of doomed habit."

Catherine was trembling. She was unsure whether it was due to guilt or anger. The latter won out. She said, "It rankled did it not, when upon you clearing away the poisonous fluids at Whitby, I was the one who brought him back not you." Without being aware of what she was doing, she took a couple of steps towards the glaring old woman. Shadiz caught her around the waist, restraining her. She swung inwards to him. "All that she has so adroitly pointed out is true. And I regret every one of the naïve barbs I have inadvertently thrust your way. But, the real reason for her damning soliloquy, of her trying to eradicate me from your life, is her rampant jealousy. She wants you all to herself."

Mamma Petra was about to repudiate Catherine's accusation, with the full blast of her pernicious temperament. She was forestalled by newcomers to the great hall.

"We have need to dismiss the chamber."

Filled with an imperial command, Prince Ardashir's words immediately summoned attention. The assembled company remained motionless, their variegated curiosity piqued within the pall of silence as the Persian Vizier and Garan the Druid approached those people close to the arrogant dais. Garan, the huge boar keeping pace with him, stared pointedly at Shadiz.

His dark features creasing into a faint, puzzled frown, nevertheless, Shadiz gave a brief nod of acquiescence, much to Catherine's relief.

Though she was overwhelmingly grateful for their pivotal assistance in securing Fylingdales Hall, which had nullified any danger Shadiz had placed himself in for her sake, Catherine had begun to feel uncomfortably aware of the Master's men, the corsairs who had accompanied Nick Condor, the Romany and those men loyal to Henry Potter, all being witness to the interaction between Shadiz and Lynette and Lady Hellena. Moreover, she sensed Garan's and Prince Ardashir's entrance meant there were further revelations regarding Mamma Petra's unexpected appearance at the Hall.

"Let 'em tak their fill," ordered the Master, responding to the formidable hint. "Wi' boundaries."

Determined to remain, Condor gave instructions to the massive Negro, who easily rivalled Junno's impressive stature. Catherine recognised him from the corsairs' defence of Shannlarrey. After being told by Shadiz to remain, Henry Potter gave orders to Alex Firth, the man who had been in charge of the protection of Catherine when Potter had left Fylingdales for the Lodge. Benjamin also stayed where he was, obeying a terse gesture from his leader. Danny Murphy and Bill Todd led the Master's men out of the hall, followed by the Romany, leaving only Imre Panin and Wath behind. Before she too left the hall with the men, Mattie gently squeezed Catherine's arm.

Francois Lynette had viewed the proceedings with detached amusement. Whereas, Lady Hellena looked irritated by the arrival of Garan, and the dismissal of the fascinated audience. It was clear she was eager to inflict as much damage as possible upon Shadiz.

The Frenchwoman took everyone by surprise by moving swiftly to a square object resting at the furthest end of the dais. In one quick move, she pulled away the old cloth, revealing a large, rusty chest.

Catherine had a sudden, overwhelming feeling of dread.

At the same time, Garan called out to the woman to desist.

Ignoring his imperative command, Lady Hellena thrust open the lid of the chest.

"Witness the rotting carcass that fouled the earth with you!" she exclaimed in near-hysterical victory.

Immediately, Garan wielded his staff. Of its own accord, the lid of the chest slammed shut on the gruesome remains it held within.

But not soon enough.

Everyone present within the stupefied silence witnessed what the sight of his mother, however fleeting, had done to Shadiz.

Too shaken to protest, he staggered backwards and, continuing to stare in agonised shock at the chest, fell to his knees.

"Mother!" exclaimed Richard, aghast. "For pity's sake."

"The gutter-born had no pity for Elizabeth," retorted Lady

Hellena. "Or your father. The bastard needs to see from where he was spawned."

The woman was ecstatic. Her only regret, had she known how simple sweet revenge could be, she would have taken the loaded chest with her to Wright's funeral, and brought the gypsy to his knees before all those who regarded him with such misplaced admiration.

Thoroughly disgusted by his mother's evil action, Richard started to approach his half-brother. Benjamin put a restraining hand on his arm.

Catherine was only dimly aware of the stunned people around her. Her eyes bright with angry unshed tears, she quickly reached Shadiz and knelt down beside him. Before she could transform her own heart-beating anguish into the vital comfort he was in desperate need of, Garan was beside her.

He leant his staff on the boar's thick back and, despite his ancient appearance, knelt with little effort beside Catherine.

Fearing what his cousin might do in his present shattered condition, Junno, reeling himself from the ghastly revealing, moved closer to Catherine.

Garan put his hands on Shadiz's rigid shoulders. In a soft, hypnotic voice, he attempted to penetrate the tragic mesmerised plight. "Hear me. Hear my words. The apparition conjured within sight of forced blindness was never the shade of your mother. I carry her within memory. Gianca seeks only protection against ill-will practised by her own source. She giveth her life unto you, and would never in any gossamer light drift with malice, only love and pride, and dismay at the source of influence that directs your lack to feel her honestly."

Shadiz remained helplessly transfixed. His chest was heaving, his breath coming in ragged gasps.

"Look at Kore," commanded Garan.

Shadiz began to slowly shake his head in painful denial.

Few realised Prince Ardashir's deliberate movement in front of the chest. Among them, Potter was fascinated by the Persian's weaving of intricate patterns in the air, while uttering an incomprehensive chant.

Shadiz blinked, long and hard. With his crippled view blocked, his frozen horror melted into uncontrollable trembling.

Garan reiterated his command, filled with a strong compulsion.

Haunted vulnerability dominated Shadiz's jet-black gaze when he gradually sought Catherine.

Garan spoke quietly to her, "Give unto him your healing touch, in a manner performed while braced upon the deck within a traitorous sea."

Catherine had no idea how Garan knew about the time on board the Eagle, at the beginning of the year, when concern for Shadiz had prompted her to reach out to him. By doing so, she had inadvertently entered his Haden vision of his dead mother. And become convinced such a grotesque apparition was a recurring occurrence.

Yet, now, was not the time for the whys and the wherefores.

"Your mother discovered the one true emotion in a difficult landscape. You have done same," stated Garan, his voice continuing to hold that soft, compelling note. He took hold of Catherine's hands and placed them on either side of Shadiz's face, continuing, "Rejoice in Kore's love and reject the evil that has scarred your mind for its own sake. Knowst beyond all harm the evildoer hath come to their ruin."

Garan shifted backwards to give Catherine sole access to Shadiz. The Druid glanced briefly to where the Persian was now standing, close to Mamma Petra.

"My dearest love," Catherine murmured, her lustrous blue eyes maintaining his black plea. She felt Garan's calming, inspirational brush against her inner struggle. She took a deep breath.

"Do you remember when it was Bob's daughter's birthday. You took us sailing out of Whitby harbour and within sight of the golden shore. I wanted so much to stroll in the sunshine on that shore with you." Catherine removed her right hand from Shadiz's battered face. He reacted like a blind beggar before she had the chance to secure his hand in hers.

She was about to continue her difficult coaxing when she heard Garan's barely audible instruction.

Obeying gratefully, she went on, "Let us find that golden shore now. You and I. First, though, in the same manner we have journeyed through the trial of months, we must venture through the long, winding cavern within the cliffs." Shadiz's hand tightened around hers. "Believe my deepest love has set you free from all the malicious harm done to you. Trust me. As I have trusted you."

Shadiz's anguished dense gaze continued to cling to Catherine's look of love.

Prompted softly by Garan, she took them through the rugged darkness by way of reassuring words, until the opening of light was soothingly described. Catherine drew Shadiz out of the cavernous depth and into the utterance of sunlight. She focused on creating stepping stones of words down to a peaceful sea, and brought the healing warmth of nature alive beside the freedom of the waves to cast out the coldness of delusion.

But then for a second she froze herself, balking at Garan's guidance. However, within the vision she had woven for Shadiz, she could already feel the presence behind her.

Catherine turned slowly.

The woman stepped hesitantly away from the Stygian bleakness of the cavern Catherine and Shadiz had just exited. She gave the impression of being overwhelmed by the warmth of the sunlight, raising her arms in adoration of the renewal. Her white gown appeared to shimmer in the brilliance. Midnight black hair fall in lustrous waves down to her waist. She was beauty personified. Tall, slender and graceful.

Tom had been correct. Shadiz possessed his mother's jet almond eyes.

Catherine felt the weight of the woman's regard. She tugged on Shadiz's hand, both physically and mentally.

His response glistened in his eyes, locked with Catherine in the main hall and stood hand in hand with her on a manifested shore.

A timeless moment stretched between mother and son. An understanding. A deep soul healing. A release for both.

A soft, benign chanting was heard, from where Catherine was unsure. Her attention was captured by a beautiful sunbeam. It floated upon the shore, and then held still, waiting.

Gianca smiled at her son.

Shadiz reciprocated in kind.

Catherine realised there was no need of words. The vision she had instigated with Garan's help had taken on a life of its own. She watched with Shadiz as the soft, golden sunbeam enfolded his mother.

Richard, along with everyone else, had been prey to a plethora of emotions. One became uppermost in his thoughts as he watched his half-brother do a lovely thing along with everyone else.

Shadiz took hold of both of Catherine's hands and with infinite gentleness placed them on his chest, over his heart. Matching her glow of love, he murmured, "Y' will always dwell within me, Kore. Y' my heart, my soul."

At that precise moment, when the attention of everyone remained upon Shadiz and Catherine, Francois Lynette decided to strike.

Intensely fast, so that none could impede his intention, he lunged at Shadiz with deadly purpose and struck with the dagger he had unobtrusively taken from Keeble's lifeless body.

The unexpected movement captured Junno's protective instinct. Bellowing a warning, he scooped up Catherine. At the same time, the big man gave Shadiz a mighty push. On his knees still, Shadiz reacted instinctively, going with the blow from his cousin. By doing so, instead of the dagger finding its intended mark deep in his back, the weapon ploughed into his left shoulder.

Nick Condor, also reacted to Junno's warning. Swearing obscenely, he rushed forward and ran Lynette threw with his sword.

The Frenchman had only time to look towards where Shadiz had gone down, muttering, "I promised...bring you down...your own...dagger."

Lady Hellena screamed as her brother fell dead in a growing pool of his own blood upon the floor of the great hall.

Richard stared for a couple of moments at his uncle, who had sought to usurp his place as lord of Fylingdales Hall, and felt absolutely no emotion whatsoever.

Then he turned away and, concerned, went to his wounded half-brother.

CHAPTER NINETEEN

Witch's Brew

Shadiz staggered to his feet, trying to remove the dagger from himself. Failing, he demanded, "Get bastard out."

Garan and Prince Ardashir approached him appearing similar to two physicians pondering on how best to tackle a difficult patient.

"I ain't asked for a discussion," growled Shadiz through clenched teeth. "Just get bastard out!"

Garan carefully extracted the dagger from deep within Shadiz's right shoulder, with Prince Ardashir observing, and Junno holding onto his cousin's left shoulder and arm. While the men were attending to him, unable to help herself, Catherine moved closer to Shadiz. She placed a comforting hand on his thigh, which he covered with his free hand. His attempt at reassurance became more of a pained grimace as the Druid and the Persian between them ensured there were no remnants of his shirt or jerkin remaining in the nasty wound.

The fresh flow of blood soaked Shadiz's already morbidly dyed shirt, also running down his arm and his battered jerkin. He had been mainly stoic throughout, possibly because of Catherine's presence. Richard and Benjamin cut away their wounded leader's shirt and jerkin, trying hard to cause as little pain as possible. Shadiz took intakes of ragged breath, wincing several times. Junno was obliged to widen his stance in response to Shadiz's increased need for support. By the time Richard and Benjamin had finished their cautious task and Shadiz was bare-chested, the extent of the bruising he had sustained during his ill-advised sojourn into the Scottish camp was revealed.

Catherine looked at his wound with a keen healer's eye before bending and ripping a broad strip of linen from her petticoat. Prevailing on Shadiz, he bent towards her while she bound the material tightly around his shoulder in an attempt to stem the flow of blood. She was about to urge him to let her attend to the wound properly when she saw his gaze was once more on the chest containing his mother's remains. Thankfully, there was now an absence of the horror that had previously gripped him. Simply a haunted regret.

The Persian had also noticed where Shadiz's attention lay. He gave a quiet command. Imre Panin and Wath picked up and carried the chest with the greatest respect across the hall and into the ante chamber in which Catherine had waited for Shadiz's arrival.

While concern had been centred on Shadiz, Lady Hellena had stumbled over to her dead brother. On her hands and knees beside him, she hysterically denounced his death as another vile murder perpetrated by Shadiz.

Irritated by her bitter grieving, not least because of how Lynette had struck at Shadiz, Nick Condor snapped,. "Will ye shut up, woman. Jesus, y' sounding off like a banshee caught in a Jesuit snare!"

Coughing slightly, Richard went to his mother and tried to raise her up onto her feet. She thrust him away, exclaiming, "I disown you! You are half of that...."

"Mother, shut up," interrupted Richard, dragging her unceremoniously upright.

She fought him, her wild-eyed stare raking over Shadiz. "I'll inform the great Master something he never knew," she spat out.

Catherine was about to voice her own impatience with the French woman, whose accent had become so pronounced it was difficult to understand what she was saying, when Shadiz gathered her beneath his uninjured shoulder. "Let 'er spew it out, whatever it be," he said, repressively.

Richard grimly hung onto his mother's arm, despite her efforts to escape him.

"One night I found your *father* drunk, weeping for your mother," Lady Hellena began, her shrill voice filled with a lifetime of hate. "That was when he told me how he'd gone himself to her, your grandmother, when your mother was trying to birth you. He begged her to help her daughter. Got down on his knees to her. Said he would do anything she asked if she would just attend the difficult birth as she did with many other women." Her over-bright, vicious gaze shifted to Mamma Petra. "She refused. She said her daughter was already gone from her. That she was a... didik ..."

"A didikoi," muttered Junno. He glanced at Catherine, informing her, a catch in his deep voice, "A Romany gone from the tribe."

After a slight pause, Shadiz stirred from Catherine's side. Looking up at him, she realised he was sweating profusely.

He ignored Lady Hellena's manic smirk. Instead, he approached Mamma Petra. "Is she speakin' truth?" he asked in an overly soft tone.

Mamma Petra's thin, lined face creased into unyielding damnation of what she would forever consider her daughter's betrayal. "Gorgio wanted troth for Gianca. I wouldst not giveth him my chikni. Still without romered, she didst join with him."

"My father wanted t' marry my mother?" said Shadiz. Something in his tone made Catherine look at him, but his hard expression gave nothing away.

"Develesko Mush," he rasped. "So what the old bitch an' y' are sayin'...my father wanted t' marry Gianca, but y' wouldn't agree. An' then, when she was 'avin' me...y' wouldn't 'elp 'er."

For the first time since being revealed at the Hall, Mamma Petra expression held a measure of contrition. "The drukkerebema playeth me false," she exclaimed, fiercely. "Fate didst not show me the mark of thy worth."

Junno stepped to Shadiz's side. "Y' never breathed a word o' any o' this," he said, regarding his grandmother, appalled.

"My reasons were none," she answered, defiantly.

"Y' ain't thought t' tell 'im? That 'e might deserve t' know?" he fired back at her. An honest, simple man, who loved easily, the big man was devastated upon finding out that someone he had held in high regard was being shown to be deceitful, wilfully wrecking lives.

362

Whatever Shadiz said to him in their language caused him to turn away abruptly. He went to stand beside Catherine.

"Did y' really want Kore's death, puri daia?" Shadiz demanded.

Lady Hellena gave a short, nasty laugh. "You slaughtered the wrong person," she flung at Shadiz. "Keeble had come to a possess an annoying regard for you. He only wished to keep the girl safe from your less admirable traits. It was her, your grandmother, who maintained the demand for her death."

Shadiz continued to regard Mamma Petra while the blood seeped steadily through the improvised bandage around his shoulder.

"I didst not wish thy blood of kinship diluted," she revealed, finding Catherine with her blind eyes. "She be of thy mother's wanton ilk."

Her scornful words drew a harsh response from Shadiz before Catherine had the opportunity to defend herself and his mother.

"You it be who named me Posh-Rat. Me blood's already tainted."

Garan stepped forward. "You saw fit to taint the mind of him. Is not that so?"

Beside her, Junno heard Catherine draw in her breath sharply. Frowning, he glanced down at her before returning his keen attention to his grandmother.

"Tell me," said Garan, addressing Shadiz. "When you called upon her, be I right in my belief she persisted in giving up to thee a cup she herself prepared?"

Scowling, Shadiz nodded.

"From whence she sought you out after you fled from York in young days?"

"Aye," muttered Shadiz, his drawn expression quizzical. "What o' it?"

It was clear to all those waiting for Garan to answer that he found it hard to impart the truth. Placing a hand on the great boar faithfully beside him, he gave the younger man, towering over him, a sad, regretful smile. He stated, "She scarred your mind with her brews."

The resulting silence possessed a collective shock.

Understanding his cousin's sudden need, Junno made no move to prevent Catherine from stepping lightly to Shadiz's side.

He looked down at her as if only she could unravel the evil practised upon him. "I don't... understand?" he muttered.

"Lucinda and I have spoken together about our suspicions," Catherine explained, softly. "She found it odd that Mamma Petra would allow no one else to serve you. Moreover, when you visited her, it seems she always demanded to be in relative isolation with you." She faltered, aware of what impact the truth was having upon him. Especially after what he had already suffered during a momentous evening.

It was Garan who took on the onerous burden of informing Shadiz how he had been used by Mamma Petra. "Your grandmother, once she had found you, a young drifting soul within a brutal, uncaring world, should have known value for your existence. Instead, what in you she discovered was means to vent her spleen."

"'ow?" Shadiz's voice was barely audible.

Catherine gripped his arm, attempting to pour loving support into his big, tense body. She found she could not leave the revealing of the despicable truth to Garan alone. "There are certain plants which cause the mind to become susceptible to unreal thoughts, images and...suggestions."

"Such as?" murmured Shadiz.

"You suffered the affects of mandrake, I would call," explained Garan. "Offered in certain amounts, given within time, reasoning is carved into the givers's desire. In truth. Your grandmother poisoned your mind with her cups."

"Why?" Shadiz was staring with blank dismay at Mamma Petra.

Her head come up and to one side. She gave a weird smile. "I wanted her to know eternal suffering for what she didst. I callth her back to be a shade between life she betrayed and death she deserved. Thou hath been that channel. Her bones may lie in the chest but her soul doth know no rest. You answered her call each time to cleave a soul and offer it up unto her. So she knowth their everlasting loathing."

After several extremely difficult moments, Shadiz whispered brokenly, "I killed for 'er."

"*Not* for your mother," stated Garan, emphatically. "Placed within you was the orb of your grandmother's twisted vengeance."

Shadiz said something inaudible. Then, to Mamma Petra, he said, "I come t' y' cos y' give me sleep I got nowhere else." He took a shuddering intake of breath the source of his pain coming not from his wounded shoulder. "Only what y' were doin' was… poisonin' me bloody mind."

Yet, still, the old Romany woman looked unrepentant. "Gianca had to knowth punished. The need be cast upon thee to…"

Junno cried out. "Y've no idea what y'r wickedness done t' 'im. D'y even care!" Tears were streaming down his large, round berry face. "I see y' no longer, old woman. Y' be gone from me." He uttered the formal words in the Romi, turning his back on her, looking instead with a heart full of despair at Shadiz.

Mamma Petra made a subtle move, starting to sign with her withered hand.

The Persian gave a prudent warning. "Watch her. She has power remaining to cause harm."

When Benjamin, Henry Potter and Condor started to close about the old Romany woman, he warned them against the move. Instead, he held up his hand in a particular manner towards Mamma Petra while he told Shadiz, "On Formentera when Catherine was taken ill. After you and her had surmounted with the love you possess for one another the barrier forged with evil. Your grandmother had sufficient power to create a spell that defeated distance. Her spite would not be quelled until her black art drove you from your wife's bedside."

It was what Catherine and Lucinda had come to suspect. Vindication mattered little now.

Shadiz appeared totally crushed. An anathema to all present.

Yet no one could heal him like Catherine, with the one thing he held dear above all else. With a tearful sigh, careful of his wound, she put her arms around his waist.

Shadiz drew her closer still and, bending to her, buried his face in her long fair-white hair.

Eventually, ending the thick silence, Nick Condor asked no one in particular, "What we gonna do wi' bleedin' witch an' bloody harridan?" He regarded Lady Hellena and, especially, Mamma Petra with suppressed violence.

"Myr!" warned Garan, suddenly.

He took everyone by surprise, except for Catherine and Shadiz. They followed the Druid's stern gaze to the huge boar, understanding the reason for what was clearly a reprimand.

Eventually Shadiz lifted his head. He was about to speak when Catherine quickly cut him off. "Don't you dare say it."

He gave her a sad smile. "Tis only thing I can say. That an' I love y' wi' whatever's left in me."

Catherine gave him a far more confident smile. "Y' sellin' y'rsen short."

Her colloquial message along with her look of absolute love, made a genuine smile blossom within his troubled darkness. He gave her a hug, which she halted by drawing away from him, saying, "I must attend to your wound."

CHAPTER TWENTY

Not Again!

Nick Condor repeated his question, "What's happening with the two harridans?"

This time, Shadiz answered, "I ain't wantin' their blood on me 'ands."

"You could allus let me take care o' them, brother," suggested Condor, a mischievous gleam in his green eyes that matched his wicked grin.

Shadiz gave the Irishman a long-suffering glower, accustom to his antics.

Mamma Petra took everyone by surprise as she subsided onto the floor of the hall. She had been standing for much long than usual. Ordinarily, she would have received far more consideration. Following the disclosures of her crimes, and her lack of contrition, those around her simply viewed her weak attempt to sit upright.

Junno appeared on the verge of giving into his charitable spirit and going to the aid of his discredited grandmother.

Catherine went instead, the healer in her unable to refuse succour despite the old Romany's evident hatred. Mostly she wanted to stop Junno from having to deal with someone who had mortally wounded his admirable goodness.

Her good intention received a nasty rebuff. In the end, Junno was obliged to help his grandmother back on her feet and to sit down on the velvet topped stool supplied by Potter.

Condor, in his jovial manner, was still trying to persuade Shadiz to allow him to deal with the two women. Richard, on the other hand, saw nothing humorous in his dubious suggestions. Benjamin and Henry Potter and then Garan and Prince Ardashir entered the discussion, followed by Junno and the two older Romany. Between them, the men were striving to bring their bruised leader back to life.

Grateful though Catherine was for their efforts, uppermost in her mind was the need to attend to Shadiz's shoulder wound, which by now had soaked her strip of petticoat in blood.

She was about to step forward in a brisk manner when all at once she was dragged roughly backwards. The next moment she found herself on her backside and smothered in the aroma of violets. But it wasn't the cloying perfume she recognised that bothered her so much as the feel of Shadiz's wickedly curving scimitar pricking her throat.

'*Oh, no! Not again!*'

On this occasion, however, she was not being held hostage by a bear of a man as she had been in Van Helter's shop in the Dutch port of Ijuimden. Therefore, outraged, she pitted her young strength against that of her elderly captor.

Due to their attention being centred upon him, the men saw their leader suddenly frown and raise a hand to his moonstone pendant, glittering on his bare chest.

Shadiz twisted around. Locating Catherine, he froze for an arrested heartbeat. Then, he took a cautious step forward. "Kore, stay put. Y' ain't t' fight 'er," he commanded, softly.

Behind him, the men reacted, but Shadiz gestured sharply for them to remain where they were. When Richard would have moved past him towards his mother, Shadiz seized hold of his half-brother's arm in a distracted manner.

On her knees at Catherine's stiff back, Lady Hellena crowed victoriously. Catherine could feel her trembling exultation. Furious to the point of recklessness, she squirmed against the woman, trying in vain to break what felt like an unnaturally strong hold on her.

"Kore, be still, dammit!" commanded Shadiz, in the tone of voice no one disobeyed.

Resentfully, she heeded his warning, but not before the sharp edge of his scimitar had pierced beneath her chin. She felt a trickle of blood running down her neck.

Lady Hellena was breathing excitedly. "Yes, gutter snipe. You demon from Hell. You will not prevent her death. *An eye for an eye.*"

Shadiz stood perfectly still and silent, his jet-black gaze not deviating from the woman threatening Catherine.

"I'm going to cut her from eye to eye," warned Lady Hellena. *She'd heard something very similar before!*

Catherine was getting fed-up with history repeating itself. She was having a few qualms about the present declaration. It sounded rather maniac.

Richard tried unsuccessfully to rip himself free of Shadiz's detaining grip. "Mother, for the love of God, stop this," he beseeched.

"Ah, yes," she muttered, smiling, appearing pleased with herself. "*An eye for an eye. A tooth for a tooth.* I see now. I'll take you back. First you must avenge your father and your sister. The ideal opportunity, do you see?"

Richard began to cough. He hit his chest impatiently. Hoarsely he muttered. "Father and Elizabeth are long gone. Let them rest in peace. We must journey beyond all this hate. Can you not understand what such vileness has done to so many lives?"

"I know what I'll do to that bitch's life," rasped Condor, stepping up to Shadiz's wounded side.

Shadiz growled a warning.

"He's powerless!" exclaimed Lady Hellena, laughing shrilly. "We have the gutter snipe at our mercy." She looked around briefly, in the process moving the scimitar against Catherine's throat.

Catherine hissed at the stinging cut. "So help me," she muttered, fiercely.

"Get your bow," ordered Richard's mother, suddenly decisive. "The ridiculous thing now has a valuable purpose." When Richard looked towards Shadiz, she shouted, "You will do as I say."

Nevertheless it was his half-brother's grim nod that Richard obeyed.

Her thin lips set in an aggressive tight line, Lady Hellena waited until Richard had picked up his bow from where he had left it near the dais. "And an arrow, you dolt," she snapped. When he was in possession of both, she added, "Make it ready, Now!"

Once again, it was Shadiz who gave Richard leave to do so.

"I command you. Not the gutter snipe. Now prepare to shoot," his mother ordered.

Responding to the queer intenseness in her tone, a mutter spread through the men standing tensely immobile and watchful around Shadiz.

Her tone had further alarmed Richard. "Shoot at what?" he asked, guardedly.

"At what?" Lady Hellena chuckled gleefully. By design or by malice, she once again nicked Catherine's neck with the weapon held tightly in her eager grip.

"Ye gods and little fishes!" Catherine hissed.

Shadiz captured her narrowed gaze. He quelled the agitation at her helplessness with a reassuring look, before returning his black glare to the woman holding her with the dangerous fury of an avenging wife and mother.

"You are in love with the girl, are you not?" stated Lady Hellena.

Mustering his well-worn patience, Richard answered, "Please mother, release Catherine. She has done you no harm."

"See, I am correct!" she declared, with fierce joy.

"Catherine is wed to…" he began, tersely.

"Not if you wield the bow against him," broke in his mother, satisfied with her own vengeful logic. "Then I will allow her to be your lady."

Another mutter rippled through the men now clustered around Shadiz. He held up a commanding hand to subdue the railing against their enforced inaction. His attention did not stray from Lady Hellena.

"I will certainly not use the long bow upon Shadiz," stated Richard, unequivocally. "I do not shoot unarmed men, whoever they may be."

His mother snorted in disgusted. "For years you have yearned to annihilate that bastard gutter snipe," she reprimanded. "Now is your moment."

Richard was about to fling his long bow away when Shadiz briefly caught his eye. Richard wavered in his defiant gesture as Shadiz gave an imperceptible shake of his head.

Lady Hellena shot Shadiz a glance consumed with wild-eyed hatred. She then turned an accusing glare onto her son. Both men were keeping a wary eye on the scimitar levelled at Catherine's already bloodied neck. She announced, "You have a choice. You either use the bow on him. Or I shall use this strange weapon on the girl."

"Like hell, you will!" exclaimed Catherine, struggling to break free.

Lady Hellena sliced into her neck, making the men, especially her son, understand hers was not an empty threat. Blood stained the Flemish lace on Catherine's borrowed gown. She gritted her teeth, seething with painful frustration.

"Kore," murmured Shadiz, gently. "Let the rat see the hare."

Glaring at him, she snapped, "Do you really have to talk in riddles right at this moment?"

Shadiz gave a lop-sided grin. No humour reach the smouldering rage in his dense black eyes.

Richard spoke into the hostile silence, anguish in his low tone. "How can you offer me such a cruel choice, mother? Has your mind finally been turned by your consistent loathing?" He was rapidly coming to the harrowing conclusion.

She was impatient with what she perceived to be his prevarication. "You have no choice in the matter. You love the girl. And you hate the other half of yourself. Sever the treacherous link you have fought against."

When Richard, trapped in an agonising quandary, began to cough, his mother poured scorn on what she termed his weakness.

Catherine felt sympathy for him, while continuing to watch him with bated breath.

The notched bow ready in his hands, Richard switched from Catherine's young, expressive face to Shadiz's darkly enigmatic countenance.

"She will use the weapon on Catherine," he said in desperation, "before anyone can reach her."

"I know," replied Shadiz, calmly.

Nick Condor swore fluently.

The men were become increasingly restless, only held in place by Shadiz's imposing authority.

The half-brothers shared their first sibling exchange.

With the greatest reluctance, Richard raised the bow, his despairing gaze locked onto Shadiz's sustaining influence.

Unable to withstand the horrendous tension, Junno began to move protectively around his cousin, followed by Imre Panin and Wath. Condor immediately took safeguarding steps at the other side of Shadiz. With one accord, Benjamin and Henry Potter joined the Irishman.

Garan and Prince Ardashir remained a few paces away. The Druid held up his staff. The Persian raised both his hands, long fingers spread wide. Oddly, the attention of both rested on Mamma Petra and not what was taking place elsewhere in the main hall.

Much to the dismay of the men, Shadiz moved with sudden purpose to occupy a willing space. Continuing to uphold Richard's resolution, he held out his arms, though it clearly pained him to move his left one, in a gesture of surrender.

Catherine heard someone laugh in exultation. And another give a despairing cry. She realised it was herself. She call out in rampant desperation to Richard, in an effort to distracted him while intending to throw herself upon the scimitar at her throat.

The men rushed forward at the same time as Richard drew back the bow, aiming at Shadiz.

By unspoken accord, they split up. Slightly younger, Wath outran his fellow Romany, making a valiant effort to reach Shadiz. Benjamin outpaced Henry Potter and even Condor and dashed towards Richard, trying to reach him before he fired the ready arrow.

Richard was already swinging away from his half-brother when Benjamin intercepted him. Knocked off balance, Richard's aim went astray. The arrow pierced Mamma Petra's thin chest at the same time as she flung herself at Lady Hellena.

Shadiz had easily side-stepped Wath. Junno and Imre Panin were pulled up short a hair's breadth away from Shadiz by the sight of their wounded matriarch. But then, recovering swiftly, with Wath following, they started forward when Lady Hellena, screaming with hysterical rage, scrambled back onto her knees thrusting wildly at Catherine.

"*Move, now!*"

Catherine did not need telling once never mind twice by Shadiz, who was also moving fast himself. She fled on hands and knees away from the woman's maddened wielding of the curved weapon. She was vaguely aware of Benjamin behind her, trying desperately to subdue Lady Hellena's murderous efforts.

Three things seemed to happen at once.

Shadiz reached Catherine and scooped her up out of danger. Lady Hellena rearing upwards, thrust forward with the scimitar. Her demented attack was brought to a shuddering halt as Nick Condor's dagger struck her hard from behind with ruthless ferocity.

While Shadiz was placing her on her feet away from where the woman had fallen, Catherine caught sight of Richard approaching his mother.

Shadiz surveyed the damage Lady Hellena had done to Catherine's neck, clearing the blood from the various cuts with a gentle hand.

Catherine smiled up at him. "I'll live," she assured him, shakily.

"The old bitch won't," said Condor, halting beside Shadiz.

They looked to where Richard was kneeling beside his mother. Catherine tried to go to comfort him, but Shadiz pulled her back against him. "Y' ain't off anywhere near 'er."

"But, she's dying," objected Catherine.

"I don't bloody care," muttered Shadiz.

"So's tother one," pointed out Condor.

Their attention was drawn to where Mamma Petra lay. Junno, Imre Panin and Wath were all crouched around her.

Instead of going over to his grandmother, Shadiz, a possessive hold on Catherine, Condor at his heels, walked to where Richard was kneeling beside his mother. Benjamin stood beside him, offering quiet support.

Garan had already made it plain that nothing could be done for either of the women.

"Suppose two o' them'll battle it out in Hell or Heaven, whichever they land in," remarked Condor.

Unremorseful, he shrugged beneath the reprimanding glances of both Catherine and Benjamin.

Shadiz gripped Richard's slumped shoulder. Richard look up at him, tears in his eyes. "She's gone," he murmured. Getting to his feet, he added, "I am not sure why I am mourning her passing. I am uncertain whether she would mourn mine."

"She was y'r mother," replied Shadiz, low-pitched. "I've learned such a person should be...valued."

When Catherine touched Richard's arm in a comforting manner, he gave her a forlorn smile.

Turning back to Shadiz, he said, "I did not aim for your grandmother. My intention was to skim my mother's arm. I thought the shock of such an action would force her to release the weapon, and Catherine."

"Great shot for a deflection," commented Nick Condor.

"*I* was deflected," retorted Richard He coughed, and then cleared his throat impatiently. "Anyway – who the hell are you?" he demanded of the Irishman.

Nick Condor introduced himself. While he did so with an elaborate flourish and a courtly bow, Richard's astounded gaze swung to Benjamin.

It was Junno coming up behind them who interrupted Benjamin's curt explanation.

"She's askin' for y'."

When Shadiz failed to respond to the big man's silent plea, pushing aside her own misgiving, Catherine put a gentle, persuasive hand on his back.

"You never know," she said, "one day you might regret the omission."

Looking down at her, he gave a resigned sigh. "Y' just might be right, monisha.

Only Catherine and Junno accompanied Shadiz as he made his way across to where his grandmother was being supported by Imre. After a slight hesitation, he crouched down, taking Wath's place beside the old woman. For fear of hastening her demise, none of the Romany or Garan had attempted to remove the arrow protruding from her thin chest.

"Thou comest," she managed, weakly.

"Ain't I allus," replied Shadiz, tonelessly.

A death rattle threatened her next forced words. In time she succeed, again in the Romi. "She needed to be...punished. I be wrong. Thee...didst...not."

After those people gathered around the old Romany woman had witness the departure of life, Shadiz rose without comment.

He along with Junno and Catherine stood in silence, watching as Imre Panin and Wath took Mamma Petra away to her tribe. There was an unspoken conviction she would be more readily accepted in death than in life, following the revelations of her heinous deeds.

Catherine noticed Shadiz spared a thoughtful look towards Richard. Helped by Benjamin, he carried his mother out of the main hall. Lady Hellena's weeping women crept behind their dead mistress, having emerged from the dark corner in which they had taken fearful refuge.

Shadiz swayed. He would have staggered into Catherine had not Junno's timely grasp kept him upright. His wounded shoulder was hunched up. Blood was now running down his left arm He was holding it tightly across his chest.

Alarmed Catherine bemoaned the loss of her medicinal herbs and accompanying paraphernalia.

"I brought 'em wi' us," Junno informed her. "Thought they might be needed."

"*There is no virtue like necessity*," quoted Shadiz, thinly.

Nick Condor joined them. He took one look at Shadiz and cursed. "Jesus, 'e don't look good!"

"Y' reckon," retorted Junno.

Catherine's experiences during her time at the Lodge and Shannlarrey when the chateau had been attacked, even at Ijuimden, had taught her the valuable lesson that the longer a wounded is left unattended the worse it can become.

"Where are my supplies."

Junno and Condor exchanged a look.

"In Whitby," admitted Junno.

"Oh, wonderful!" exclaimed Catherine. "I need them here."

"Your wish is my command, sweetheart," said Condor. "I'll send a couple of the lads. I want 'em to check on the ships."

"Bob'll see 'em safe," put in Shadiz, vaguely.

Condor gave him an uneasy look. "Is he going to be alright?"

"Develesko Much!" managed Shadiz through gritted teeth.

"Forgive me! O Great One," responded Condor, with forced humour.

Henry Potter approached them looking worried. Switching from Shadiz to Catherine, he suggested, "Mattie is something of a healer. I'll see what stuff she has. Anyway, she might have some of what the Druid's called for. I won't be long."

"In the meantime," Catherine informed Shadiz, looking pointedly at Junno, "Lets get you to my chamber."

Nick Condor walked away laughing. "Now there's an offer y' can't refuse, brother."

The Irishman bent and unceremoniously hoisted Lynette's limp body onto his shoulder and left the main hall.

Following slowly, Shadiz muttered, "Kore, y've taken away all 'urts."

He failed in his struggle against the oblivion of unconsciousness, and slumped in Junno's faithful arms.

"I just hope I can take away one more, my love," murmured Catherine.

Part Three

The Fifth Season

THE FIFTH SEASON

His Wife and All The World

Two coffins were held aloft behind the sedate, droning preacher.

One was carried by Romany. The other by Gorgio.

Two sons paced behind.

Catherine walked between the half-brothers.

The cortege made steady progress to the private chapel down the avenue of silent witnesses. To the right, closest to Shadiz, were those Romany who were not acting as pall-bears, including Junno. Also, Nick Condor and members of his crew, Bob and Laura Andrew, and several of the Master's men, including Danny Murphy and Bill Todd. To the left, closest to Richard, were Benjamin, Henry Potter and the men of Fylingdales who had been loyal to him in difficult times. Also, Mattie and Fylingdales's senior staff and servants. They were present not so much to pay their last respects to Lady Hellena, more to support her son. Only her black-garbed knot of ladies showed any real sadness at her passing.

After the funeral service, Gianca's disturbed remains were laid to rest to the left of Lord Richard's grave beneath an inscribed marble slab. Lady Hellena was duly placed to his right. Francois Lynette had already been committed to the ground with the minimum of ceremony.

The mourners drifted away from the walled cemetery where generations of Massones were buried. Their markers ranging from simple carved crosses to elaborate statues had been weathered by the moorland climate and the passing of time.

Eventually, only Shadiz, Catherine and Richard remained beside the freshly occupied graves. It had rained quite heavily the day before, leaving the ground sodden and well-trodden by the presence of mourners. More rain seemed to be promised in the leaden sky and within the freshening wind that stirred Catherine's long fair-white hair beneath her mourning bonnet.

Richard surveyed the ancestral graveyard beside the small, grey-stoned chapel. He grimaced. "There has been an awful lot of us," he remarked. He turned to Shadiz. "A lot of us," he emphasised.

His half-brother accepted the significance with a quirk of his hard mouth.

"What is more," pointed out Richard. He endured a bout of coughing, before hoarsely continuing, "You are not alone. There are some buried here who were born on the wrong side of the blanket."

"In other words, I'm not the only bastard," retorted Shadiz, ironically,

"Well, neither of you will be coming here for a long while to come," stated Catherine, firmly.

When Richard glanced at her and then swiftly looked elsewhere, she felt the cold unease of premonition.

His next words directed her attention to the difficult past.

Richard sighed. "I just wish Elizabeth could have been buried here," he murmured, wistfully. There was a certain degree of cautious hope in his gradually shift to Shadiz. "Where does she lie?" he asked. "Are you even…aware?"

Catherine, feeling the weight of Richard's inquiry, looked up at Shadiz. Allowing the pent up response to slowly expel, Shadiz quoted, "*O death, where is thy sting? O grave, where is thy victory?*"

Immediately, Richard conjured up the worst possible fates to have befallen his younger sister. "What the hell is that supposed to mean?" he demanded. The understanding the half-brothers had arrived at through recent events seemed to be slipping.

"*The last enemy that shall be destroyed is death,*" Shadiz added in a whispery tone.

"For the love of God, you bastard!" exclaimed Richard. His increased agitation brought on another bout of coughing.

Catherine caught sight of specks of blood on his kerchief upon him lowering it from his mouth.

Trying to ease the sudden tension between the two men, she placed a persuasive hand on Shadiz's uninjured arm. Though he had refused to wear a sling to support his shoulder, he held his left arm close to his chest. She knew the dagger wound inflicted by Lynette pained him. "My love," she prompted, her heart beating out an anticipatory tattoo.

He stared down at her with a queer intenseness before shifting his enigmatic attention to Richard.

"Elizabeth ain't dead," said Shadiz.

For a stunned moment Richard looked at if he couldn't comprehend what his half-brother was divulging. He cast a searching look at Catherine, and found confirmation of Shadiz's admission in her shocked expression. Turning back to his half-brother, he struggled for words. "I...I don't...understand?"

"I came 'ere t' Fylingdales t' see Tom," began Shadiz, in a neutral tone. "Crew that followed me, I left kickin' their heels in Longdrop Hollow. By time I found out Tom'd gone on some errand t' Whitby an' went back t' Longdrop, I found all 'ell'd broke loose. Them that were wi' me'd surprised Elizabeth's retinue. The escort were mostly dead or dyin'. Women'd been...used...an' killed."

Catherine covered her mouth with a trembling hand, staring up at Shadiz. She realised he was waiting for her to spurn him. Instead, she stepped closer to him and when, after a moment's hesitation he put an arm around her shoulders, she leaned into him.

"My mother said, Keeble saw you kneeling beside Elizabeth," muttered Richard, accusingly. "Bending over her."

"She were only one left 'alf alive," went on Shadiz. "I'd a good idea who she was. I was bendin' over 'er, tryin' t' stop 'er from blowin' 'er brains out wi' pistol she'd managed t' reach for on ground.

"Oh, my God!" said Catherine and Richard in unison.

"When I'd settled 'er down as best I could, she begged me not t' tek 'er back t' Fylingdales 'all, not t' let on t' 'er family what'd 'appened t' 'er. So I took 'er instead t' Garan. When 'e'd got 'er summat like, she asked me t' get 'er out o' England. Best place I reckoned t' tek 'er was Shannlarrey. Not long afore I'd been 'orse master there. I knew Louise an' Philippe'd 'elp, especially after Louise'd become widow, an' were free t' do whatever she wanted."

"She's not there now," stated Catherine, having stayed at his chateau in France.

"Elizabeth was far from well, continued Shadiz. "Mostly in 'er mind. Louise arranged for 'er to be looked after by the nuns in a nearby convent."

"Does she still dwell there?" asked Richard, shakily.

Shadiz nodded. "She's become a nun," he answered, quietly.

Richard's forehead gradually creased into a painfully frown. His thin, pale face took on a tormented expression. "You bastard!" he exclaimed.

"Richard," cautioned Catherine.

"All this time, I thought my sister was dead!" persisted Richard, condemningly. "And you never said a word."

Shadiz appeared self-contained, but close to him, Catherine could feel the tension within his big body. "I gave 'er me oath," he answered, simply.

"Did she know who you are?" asked Richard, in a slightly more constrained manner.

"Aye."

"How did she react?" pressed Richard.

There was a slight pause. Eventually, Shadiz replied, "She calls me brother."

At which point, the lump in Catherine's throat produced unshed tears in her glistening eyes. As for Richard, he appeared completely devastated.

He turned suddenly and walked away a few paces.

Shadiz looked down at Catherine and gave her a haunted smile before brushing her forehead with a light kiss.

Richard turned back to his half-brother. "Am I allowed to visit her?"

After shrugging his shoulders in what was certainly a gesture of relief, even if it proved to be painful for him, Shadiz said, "I've been occasionally. I don't see any reason why y' can't nowadays."

Richard hung his head for a couple of moments. Then, decision made, he walked up to Shadiz.

He met his half-brother's unreadable jet gaze. "Thank you for saving our sister," he said. "Brother."

Shadiz stared at Richard, saying nothing.

Richard cast an uneasy glanced at Catherine.

"My love," she prompted, gently.

Shadiz gave a ragged sigh. For once the cloak of detachment had slipped. He raised his uninjured arm in a manner that made Richard stand unflinching. Shadiz gripped Richard's thin shoulder. He reciprocated by placing his hand over Shadiz's.

A couple of tears slipped down Catherine's cheeks as she viewed the exchange between the two men that needed no words.

Benjamin's haste faltered when he caught sight of the poignant tableau in the impressive graveyard of the Massones.

It was Catherine who sensed his arrested presence. She turned and encouraged him to approach with a smile. Drawing near, he was struck by the rare affinity between Shadiz and Richard, even though they had moved apart.

"Summat up?" demanded Shadiz.

Benjamin gave himself a mental shake. "No, sir. Not really. Not at all, really."

"What are you babbling about?" asked Richard, amused.

Benjamin was about to answer him when Nick Condor appeared at his elbow.

"Hey, brother," he said, grinning at Shadiz. "You've got to come an' see."

"Develesko Mush!" rasped Shadiz, "What the 'ell're y' two on about."

"Just come and see for yoursen," urged Condor, scarcely able to conceal his excitement."

While they were following the Irishman's lead back to the Hall through the extensive grounds, Catherine pulled on Shadiz to detain him. He set his head on one side, frowning down at her. "Kore?" he murmured, signalling for the men to continue.

"I would like to ask you two questions," she said, decisively.

He grinned. "Just two?" he queried.

She grimaced. "Well, the other lot can wait."

"Oh, lucky me," he remarked, stroking her arm. "Go on then."

She took a deep breath. "Did you tell Mamma Petra about Elizabeth."

The expression on his dark features grew serious. "Aye, I did."

Catherine felt, for his sake, she had to be frank. "You do realise, she used that knowledge against you?"

He slowly nodded. "Aye, I do now." He gave her a regretful half-smile that was more of a wry grimace. "Better late than never, I reckon."

Catherine moved into his warm embrace. "You have nothing to be guilty for."

"I only wish it was true."

They stood together for several heartbeats, while she gave him comfort simply by her treasured presence.

"Anyway," Shadiz said, eventually. "'Y' said two questions."

"H'm," murmured Catherine, looking up at him. "Was Richard the reason for you giving a second oath to Elizabeth?" When he failed to answer, she added, "Why he resided at the Lodge? Why, when you were recovering at Bob's cottage at Whitby, you insisted on going to extract him from Lynette's clutches at Saltersgate?"

"I ain't off t' get away wi' owt wi' y', am I?" he growled. Yet his gaze resting upon her was appreciative. And his lingering kiss was infinitely tender.

The previous night, Catherine had finally been able to attend to his shoulder wound in the chamber she had occupied since her arrival at Fylingdales Hall. Mattie had helped her to staunch the bleeding and with the medicinal herbs while Junno had supported Shadiz during the painful procedure. Before unhealthy weakness and pure exhaustion claimed Shadiz, he had managed one last order. That his faithful cousin watch over Catherine. Junno was only to happy to comply. He was still blaming himself for the harrowing loss of Catherine from Formentera, even though she had prevailed upon him to except the blame lay elsewhere. He had settled for the night in the corridor beside the door to Catherine's chamber.

After Junno and Mattie had left Catherine alone with Shadiz, she had changed into her night attire and curled up on the four-poster beside him. She had taken comfort in his steady-breathing nearness, even though he was oblivious to her presence. Come the morning, she was awakened by his gentle caress to be enfold in his loving courtship until both of them were borne away on the freedom of their wedded intimacy.

Shadiz and Catherine caught up with Richard, Benjamin and Nick Condor at the leafy, arched entrance to the Quadrangle. The buzz of numerous voices caused Shadiz to take a step in front of Catherine.

"Oh, there ain't any reason for that," assured Condor, grinning.

The moment they walked into the Quadrangle silence dropped like a stone. To be followed by cheering and clapping.

It was rare, indeed, for Shadiz to be utterly nonplussed. Richard and Catherine shared his shock at the barrage of loud approval that washed over them.

Before Catherine had a chance to recover, Lucinda ran up to her and threw her arms around her. The two young women, who had been parted in difficult circumstances, clung to one another, laughing, slightly tearful. When Peter, not to be excluded in their joyful reunion, tugged hard on Catherine's skirts, both her and his mother lifted him up and included him in their happy embrace.

Meanwhile, Junno and Henry Potter joined the other men where they had paused on the flagged stoned path beside the statues of the Fates.

Henry Potter had to shout to make himself heard above the persistent, noisy approval. "They've arrived from all over the estate, sir," he explained, smiling. "Rest are from the coast and inland. All over the place!"

Bob and Laura Andrew joined them. While Laura moved closer to Catherine and Lucinda, the robust captain used his seagoing bellow to explain, "*Eagle's* sailed a ship full o' folk 'ere from Whitby, Staithes, you name it. Paul Robson's dun same on *Swan*. An' there's them from Mercy Cove, o' course."

"A lot o' ours've turned up," put in Junno, raising his deep, bass voice.

At the same time as nodding to indicate his understanding, Shadiz caught Catherine's eye. She immediately returned to his side. His uninjured arm lightly around her waist, he led the way deeper into the Quadrangle.

Halting close to one of the tall windows set in the moorland grey stone of the Hall, he gave a long whistle.

"Jesus Wept!" objected Condor, rubbing his ears. "You keep that up and we're all going to be as deaf as Old Doley's dog."

Shadiz's piercing, high-pitched command for silence had had the desired affect. The enthusiastic welcome had been replaced by an obedient, expectant silence.

Shadiz turned to Richard. "They're all yours."

Richard was not the only one to be taken by surprise. "What am I supposed to say to them?"

"Develesko Much," muttered Shadiz, "Y' lordship should say summat."

Richard continued to regard Shadiz for a couple more seconds. When he switched to Catherine, she encouraged him with a persuasive nod.

Richard took a deep breath, stifled a bubbling cough and address the people crowded into the Quadrangle.

"Thank you for coming and showing your support for what will be a new regime here at Fylingdales Hall. In the future, there will be only one reason for any kind of military might. To keep everyone safe from the affects of the present troubles throughout England. Hopefully our location in the North East of Yorkshire will prevent any major problems."

Richard took a moment to replenish his breath. "As you no doubt are aware, my uncle, Francois Lynette and my mother are no more. I shall do my utmost to repair the damage inflicted by their arduous ruling of the Hall and the Estate. But I cannot do it alone. I will not seek a wife. My health is not excellent. Furthermore, the woman I would have wed is now my sister, married to my brother. Their children will inherit Fylingdales."

Richard half-turned to where Shadiz was standing with Catherine a few paces away. "Before you all, I asked my brother for his assistance in not only keeping Fylingdales and all it entails safe, but that he will also assist in the running of what is his land, too."

A boisterous cheer of approval rippled around the crowded Quadrangle.

It was followed by a slight pause, in which the two half-brothers exchanged quizzical looks, as if they were unsure how to respond to each other.

Shadiz stepped forward. "I appreciate the thought," he began. He spoke without seeming to raise his voice, yet those people at the rear of his eager audience could clearly hear what he had to say, with underlying command. "Only thing is, if I stayed, I'd make all o' y' prime targets…including my wife."

The men gathered around Catherine noticed how her left foot and right hand against her sombre gown were tapping out her distinct disapproval of Shadiz's words.

Catherine could not help herself. She took several brisk steps towards Shadiz. "I need to have a word with you," she muttered, coming to a purposeful halt.

Shadiz scowled down at her. "What, now?" he demanded.

"Indeed. Right now," retorted Catherine, not in the least bit intimidated by his black glare.

Locked together in motionless speculation, the men watched as Shadiz stepped around Catherine, shielding her from their large, interested audience with his muscular tallness. He then proceeded to walk her backwards into relative isolation.

"You don't have to've eaten y'r gruell to know what Beast's about," commented Nick Condor, shrewdly.

"What y' on about?" demanded Junno.

He scrutinised Condor's significant nod towards where Prince Ardashir was standing with his young servant beneath a rose-smothered archway.

"You must've noticed the chin-wags he had with the Persian on Formentera," said Condor. "Convinced the wily old fox got hissen captured so as to meet the Beast."

"Why'd Persian do owt like that?" demanded Junno, scowling.

"Well, big man," answered the Irishman, looking up at him. "By all accounts, the Persian's brother, the present Shah, is dying. And his son'll inherit the Peacock Throne. Only, the lad's about nine. So, Ardashir is after ruling through his nephew. But what he needs to stave off opposition is good strong backing – by an outlander's force."

"Shadiz!" breathed Benjamin in total shock, having taken close interest in the conversation of the two men.

As Junno switched from Condor to Shadiz, he appeared so worried that Lucinda joined him. She spoke to him in their language. It took a couple of moments for him to realise she was alongside him, and had addressed him.

When he passed on to her the implication of the Irishman's words, his shock infected her. "He surely won't leave Catherine again?" she queried. The alternative was just as distasteful to her. "'e'll take 'er wi' 'im?"

"There's just one person who can persuade him to stay," put in Condor, "an' she's doing it right now. Keep y' fingers and toes crossed."

"What?" growled Shadiz.

"Do not what me!" hissed Catherine, glaring up at him. "I'm young, but not stupid."

"We've 'ad this conversation afore, Kore," pointed out Shadiz.

"I understand what you are about to agree to," she said, accusingly. "You are going to agree to accompany Ardashir to Persia. To act as protector for him and his young nephew."

"It'd get y' away from what's goin' on in England," he retorted. "I've been told Rupert was defeated at Maston Moor, an York's about t' fall t' Crop-Ears."

"*Ye gods and little fishes,*" exclaimed Catherine. "Don't I have a say in the matter." She rushed on. "Besides, if what you say is correct – and I have no doubt your Romany spies are sure of their information – then it seems to me, your presence is needed even more here."

"Y' won't need t' stick a target on me chest afore every bastard from north, east, south an' west is likely t' come try for the prize catch. An' anybody round me'll also be a prime target," he retorted.

Catherine took a calming breath, though her heart was beating almost out of her chest. "How many estates did you tell me you owned when we were on Formentera?"

Shadiz black eyes glittered. "What the 'ell's that got t' do wi' owt?"

"Just," said Catherine, striving for patience. "Humour me."

Looking far from please, nevertheless he informed her. "Like I told y', I bought the deeds for Fylingdales Hall and Estate from Isaac when Lynette put them up as security against a loan he weren't able t' repay. The other two, bordering Fylingdales. Derwent 'all, cos old Sidney Courtney 'as no 'eirs. An' Driffield 'all, cos Sir Neville got into so much debt, 'e was starin' at bein' bankrupt. " His stern darkness melted somewhat upon adding, "An' o' course, I've a claim t' Nafferton Garth through me wife."

Catherine gave a false grimace. "So, all in all, I would imagine there are quite an extensive amount of people on those estates as well as Fylingdales."

"More than y' imagine at Nafferton Garth," he responded, grinning. "I sent Maggie an' Marianne out o' York wi' orphans Maggie collected at Starre Inn."

"Really?" said Catherine. "That's excellent." She gave a triumphant smile. "So that obviously adds more people into the mix."

"Into what bloody mix," he rasped, scowling once again.

"All the people you are about to abandon," she pointed out.

"A wife'll go where 'er 'usband goes," Shadiz stated, ominously.

Catherine shook her head. "Not me," she answered. "Not when she believes him about to make the wrong turn East instead of remaining North-East."

"Kore…what the 'ell. Dammit."

Her response was to smile at him. He had known enough aggression in his life. Indeed, it had become a way of life for him. "You and Richard are both Lord Richard's sons. Richard carries the burden of his title. You possess your father's strength of leadership, whether you like it or not. All these people who have come here today respect Richard's aristocratic inheritance. They are also here to pay their respects to Lord Richard's other son. Not the bastard born on the wrong side of the blanket because of an old woman's malice. Not the mercenary. Not the corsair. But the man they willing accept as their leader. Moreover, I am quite certain today's spontaneous response to you is multiplied throughout all of the other estates you have ownership.

"You are needed *here* to defend North East Yorkshire and Yorkshire people. Not to defend strangers in a distant land. Whatever storms might come our way, all of us will weather them far better with your leadership."

Shadiz continued to meet Catherine's blue soulful gaze. She had shattered him, torn down whatever defensive measures he had attempted to put in place by her heartfelt words. He could do no other than gather her to him, and hold her tight.

"Y' my soul, my heart. I love you, beyond love. Kore. My beautiful, courageous wife," he whispered into her fair-white hair.

Catherine lifted her head and looked up at him, the radiance of her love for him polishing her gaze and shining in her delicate young face. "You are home, Sebastian," she told him, softly.

"Should we cheer now?" wondered Nick Condor.

Richard slowly approached Shadiz and Catherine. Halting a couple of paces away from them, he quietly asked, "You will stay in England?"

Shadiz continued to hold Catherine close. He glanced beyond his half-brother at the expectant people thronging the Quadrangle.

"Y' two bright sparks got any idea 'ow t' *feed the five thousands*?"